DE...
DO US
PART

Stephen Edger has been writing crime thrillers since 2010. An avid reader, Stephen writes what he likes to read: fast-paced crime thrillers with more than a nod to the darker side of the human psyche. In all, he has published over a dozen novels – four trilogies, and the rest standalone psychological thrillers.

The one common location to each of the novels is the city of Southampton, where Stephen has lived since attending the university there. This local knowledge gives each of the stories a unique and edgy realism that few can match.

Stephen was born in the north-east of England, but grew up in London, meaning he is both a northerner and a southerner. By day he works in the financial industry using his insider knowledge to help shape the plots of his books. He also has a law degree, which gives him a good understanding of the inner workings of the UK justice system.

Stephen is married, and has two children and two Westie dogs. He is passionate about reading and writing, and cites Simon Kernick and Tony Parsons as major influences on his writing style.

www.stephenedger.com
: /AuthorStephenEdger
: @StephenEdger

Also by Stephen Edger

The DI Kate Matthews Series
Dead to Me
Dying Day
Cold Heart

The PI Johnson Carmichael Series
Trespass
Fragments
Downfall

Standalones
Snatched
Blackout
Then He Was Gone
Little Girl Gone

STEPHEN EDGER

TILL DEATH DO US PART

KILLER READS

A division of HarperCollins*Publishers*
www.harpercollins.co.uk

KillerReads
an imprint of HarperCollins*Publishers* Ltd
1 London Bridge Street
London SE1 9GF

www.harpercollins.co.uk

This paperback edition 2019

First published in Great Britain in ebook
format by HarperCollins*Publishers* 2019

A catalogue record for this book is available from the British Library

ISBN: 978-0-00-832063-8

Set in Minion by
Palimpsest Book Production Limited, Falkirk, Stirlingshire

Printed and bound in the UK by
CPI Group (UK) Ltd, Croydon CR0 4YY

MIX
Paper from
responsible sources
FSC C007454

This book is produced from independently certified FSC™ paper
to ensure responsible forest management.

For more information visit: www.harpercollins.co.uk/green

For my wife
(for not killing me after all our years together)
xxx

Prologue

She'd learned many years ago that people will do just about anything for money, it was just a question of negotiating the right price. Reaching for the towel, she wiped the remains of the cream from her breasts, before refastening the straps of her bra and shoving the wad of notes into her cleavage. Straightening, she caught a glimpse of her reflection in the crusty mirror on the wall, and ran her fingers through her long blonde hair, before tying it into a ponytail.

There were plenty of other ways she could earn the rent for the flat, but no other job could pay what she earned per hour with these strip gigs. Who was she kidding? She enjoyed dancing to the music and watching as men gawped lustfully, each thinking they could satisfy her, none realizing that the last thing she wanted was to have sex with any of them. There was only one special man in her life, and he was thankfully tucked up at home in bed. Pressing her locket to her lips, she kissed his tiny photograph, reminding herself that he was why she took these gigs. She'd never told him what she did for a living, and if she had her way, she'd never have to.

Zipping up her knee-length boots, she pulled on her miniskirt and leather jacket, and collected the iPod and speaker, dropping them in her bag. The stop for the night bus was a ten minute walk, and she'd already mapped the route in her mind. It was tempting to call a taxi, but it would probably take longer to arrive and drop her home than the walk and bus ride, so what was the point.

Lighting a fresh cigarette, she pushed the fire doors open, and stepped into the cool night air. Despite the lampposts lining the streets, there wasn't a great deal of light on the road as she made her way out to the pavement and turned right. How she wished she'd brought something warmer to change into. That would have meant an extra bag, though, and she hadn't needed the stress earlier.

Condensation billowed from her mouth as she took a fresh drag on the cigarette and wrapped her jacket tighter around her middle. A set of car headlights passed, briefly lighting the path ahead of her before disappearing into the black void. If she could squeeze in some extra gigs, she'd have enough to buy a car – nothing fancy, but a little runabout that could get her to and from these gigs with the minimum of fuss.

A sudden rush of footsteps approaching from behind put her on edge. Reaching into her handbag, she rustled around for her penknife, and, clasping it, she paused and spun on her heel, ready to thrust it at any potential attacker. She gripped it tighter as she recognized his face.

'Help you with something, pal?' she said, trying to keep the fear from her voice.

His shirt flapped in the breeze. She couldn't deny he was attractive, in a goofy kind of way. Not her type by any means, but certainly someone who would receive plenty of female attention.

'I wondered whether you wanted to join me for a drink.'

'Thanks, but I already have plans.'

'Are you sure? I would make it worth your while.'

She dropped the cigarette to the floor while surreptitiously slipping her penknife back into her handbag and made a show of squashing the cigarette with her boot. 'I dance for money, and that's it. I'm not that kind of girl.'

He pulled a large wad of notes from his pocket and began to count them into his hand. 'Are you sure I can't persuade you?'

Her eyes were on the cash. It was tempting, but she'd made a personal vow never to sleep with anyone for money. What she did – albeit a nefarious activity – was professional. There was a line she wasn't prepared to cross, and the glint in this man's eye told her exactly what he was thinking.

'As I said, I'm not like that.'

'There's three grand here, and I have another two back in my car. I'll give you the lot if you come back with me?'

She pictured her son Finn at home in bed, dreaming of knights and dragons, unaware of what his mum was doing to put food on the table. She thought about how that five grand would be more than she needed for a car and a few months of petrol.

She was still staring at the cash. 'I told you: I'm not that kind of girl.'

He refolded the notes and returned them to his pocket, shrugging in disappointment. 'Oh well, it's your loss.' He turned to walk away.

'Wait!' she called out, before she could stop herself. 'Just you, right?'

His grin widened as he turned back to face her. 'Just you and me.'

'What exactly is it you want me to do?'

He moved closer; her hand tightened around the penknife with each step.

'I want to know what it would be like to fuck you.'

Everyone has their price, but she'd never imagined hers would be so low. 'Where's your car?'

'It's back over by the lock-up. Don't worry, it's parked where nobody will see us.'

'I want the money upfront.'

3

He wrapped a gentle arm around her shoulders. 'Of course.'

'Normal sex, yeah? Nothing kinky.'

He rested a hand over his heart. 'Scout's honour. Missionary all the way. I want you underneath me.'

She allowed him to lead her back along the road that led to the lock-up, passing by the fire doors, and continuing for a further two minutes, until they reached the 4x4.

'Nice car,' she commented. 'What do you do for a living?'

'Why do you care? All you need to know is I have your money. Here,' he added, as he passed her the roll of notes from his pocket, which she promptly dropped into her bag.

'Where's the rest?'

'It's in the glove box.'

The car beeped as he unlocked it, and he moved to the passenger door, opening it and reaching in. He handed her the second wad, smaller than the first; she could only guess it was the amount he'd indicated.

'You want a line?' he asked, waving a small packet of white powder at her.

It had been years since she'd last put coke up her nose, and as tempting as it was to feel that hit once more, she resisted. After all, she didn't know this guy from Adam, and couldn't be certain what he was offering or where it had come from.

She waited while he cut a line on the car's bonnet and snorted it, rubbing the remnants into his gums, and then stared at her with lustful anticipation.

She opened the rear door, looking up at the sky and hoping she wouldn't one day be judged for this momentary lack of sound judgement, and that's when her head was yanked backwards. Grabbing hold of her ponytail, the man forced her forwards, pressing her face into the seat cushion, flicking up her skirt in one action.

She tried to yell, to push him away, chiding herself for under-estimating what this low life had in mind. Thrusting her heel up, she felt his flesh as she struck at his groin, and suddenly her hair was released. Relieved she'd demanded the money up front, she grabbed her bag and left him writhing as she tried to move off as quickly as she could.

He wasn't incapacitated for long, though, and she heard him chasing after her as she tottered on the heels.

'You're not going anywhere until I get what I paid for,' he grizzled, wrapping an arm around her neck and heaving her backwards. He was much stronger than she'd given him credit for, and her feet barely made contact with the concrete floor as he dragged her back to the car.

Reaching into her bag once again, she located the penknife and flipped out the blade; but as her hand emerged, he was too quick for her and he grabbed her hand and drove the knife back towards her. She yelped as the cold blade tore into the flesh above her hip, and the fight immediately left her.

He released his hold on her neck, and her body slumped to the ground. Just as she was coming to terms with the fact that she'd been stabbed, and hoping he would call for an ambulance, he lifted her feet and dragged her back to the front of the car. On her back, her breaths coming in swift and shallow bursts, he was suddenly sat astride her, grinning with those white teeth. As he pulled the blade out, the last thing she'd expected was for him to drive it back into her chest.

That was the moment Kerry Valentine realized just how low a price she'd sold her life for.

1

The bubbles in the flute of Prosecco tickled Alice Tandy's nose as she tried to sip from it without spoiling her make-up.

'Relax,' her best friend, Tara, said. 'He'll be here.'

Alice tried to force a smile, but the frown gave away her true feelings. This day had been two years in the making, but in truth she'd been imagining it since her seventh birthday when she'd received Bridal Barbie, and had known that one day it would be her turn to wear the big white dress and celebrate with her closest friends and family.

Tara raised the bottle, offering to top up Alice's glass, but the bride pressed a hand over the top. 'Thanks, but I want to keep a clear head.'

Tara shrugged, before filling her own glass. 'Well, I don't. As your chief bridesmaid, I expect to get trollied, dance until closing, and then end up in the sack with some guy I have no possible future with. Remind me, which of Ben's friends are single?'

'There will be loads of single men coming tonight,' Alice confirmed.

'Oh no, tell me you haven't invited Andrew from work?'

'What's wrong with Andrew?' Alice teased. 'I think you two would make a lovely couple.'

Tara wasn't biting. 'Apart from the fact he's old enough to be my dad, and has no fashion sense, he's in love with you, not me.'

Alice shook her head. 'No he isn't, and don't worry, Andrew wasn't invited. Just pick one of Ben's friends you fancy and make a move on him.'

Tara nearly spat out her Prosecco. 'That's easy for you to say, when you look like *this*. I'm sure if I had platinum blonde hair, a rack you could eat dinner off, and a figure that wouldn't look amiss on a Parisian catwalk, I wouldn't have an issue scoring. Even though I like this dress, I look frumpy, and the concealer on my face is barely covering my latest outbreak of acne. It's just not fair! I'm twenty-six now, and I still suffer with a teenager's worst nightmare!'

'You are beautiful, Tara, and some day some lucky guy is going to come along and sweep you off your feet. You just wait and see!'

Tara looked down at the light blue satin dress she'd had to have altered on no fewer than three occasions since they'd first chosen it. 'I reckon I've got better odds of winning the lottery.'

Alice smiled at her friend's lame efforts to distract her from the fact they'd been sitting in the Rolls Royce outside the church for ten minutes and Ben had still yet to arrive. It was almost ironic that he ran a logistics company and was late for his own wedding.

'I told him he had to be here by twelve,' Alice said for the third time. 'I didn't say ten past, or twenty past, I said twelve on the dot.'

'He'll be here,' Tara reassured. 'If there's one thing I know about your Ben it's that he is absolutely smitten with you.'

Alice put her hand to her mouth, before remembering the nails were acrylic and couldn't be chewed. Tara was right, of course she was. Ben was a good man, and he wouldn't not turn up for his own wedding. She'd read plenty of stories of brides and grooms being stood up at the altar, but Ben wouldn't do that to her. Would he?

'He'll be here,' Tara repeated, as if reading Alice's mind. 'Anyway, your mum and Scott are already inside, and will give the thumbs up when it's time. We're still early, remember.'

Scott's fist hammered against the glass. Dressed in grey tails and a matching cravat, her stepbrother's expression was one of relief. 'They'll be here any minute,' he said, as Tara lowered the window. 'I managed to get them on the phone. Dave and the boys took him for a final pint and they're just stuck in traffic. Ben's spitting feathers too if it's any consolation.'

Alice allowed herself a moment's respite, closing her eyes and focusing on her breathing. Having Scott give her away had seemed the only logical option. She'd lost her father when she was still at school, and the unexpected passing of her stepdad earlier this year had taken its toll. It saddened her deeply that neither of the paternal figures in her life would be there to share the biggest day of her life, but she felt their spirits nearby. The white gold locket around her neck contained a picture of both of them, so they would remain close to her heart all day.

'Can I get back in now?' Scott asked through the window. Scott and Alice's mum had travelled to the church in the car with them, but her mum had complained it was too warm and had headed on in, while Scott had made desperate calls to find out why Ben had yet to arrive.

Tara waved a finger at him. 'Sorry, it's girls only for now. You need to keep a lookout for Ben and make sure he gets in that church without seeing Alice in her dress. It's bad luck for him to see her before she arrives for the ceremony.'

Scott looked ready to argue as the midday sun beat down on him, but Tara's stare was enough to put off even the most confident of men. 'Okay,' he reluctantly said. 'Why don't you have the driver take you for a little drive and I'll make sure everything's ready for when you return.'

Tara wound up the window, filled Alice's glass before she could object and instructed the driver to take them on a detour around

9

the city centre. It really was turning into a beautiful day, the sun shining high in the sky, and barely a cloud to blot the crystal blue sky. It was in stark contrast to the early morning rain that had greeted them when they'd woken at Alice's mum's house four hours earlier.

The rain had felt like an omen.

Every minute of the day had been planned, from the pastries and Prosecco at the house when the hair and make-up ladies arrived, to the 1932 Rolls Royce Phantom II that had arrived to collect them at 11:30 in case heavy traffic threatened to spoil the timetable. Alice was a perfectionist and she was determined that nothing would be left to chance; and yet she'd had a horrible feeling in the pit of her stomach since waking that something she hadn't accounted for would spoil everything.

Ben's late arrival had done little to ease her nerves.

'You know what Ben and Dave are like when they get together,' Tara said, as she sipped from her flute. 'Thick as thieves since school. We should have expected them to find a pub before the ceremony. And in fairness we did arrive early at the church.'

Alice nodded. Ben had been the only variable to the day that she hadn't been able to totally organize. Once they were all at the church, she felt more certain that events would run like clockwork. The ceremony was due to start at half twelve, and be finished by one, at which point they would congregate for confetti and photographs, before Alice and Ben were whisked to the hotel ready to greet their guests upon arrival. The champagne reception would run until two, followed by the professional photographs in the grounds of the hotel, with the wedding breakfast formally commencing at three. Food would be followed by speeches, before a break at five, with everyone returning for the evening party from six. They'd decided to cut the cake prior to the first dance, so that as many of their friends and family would be there to witness it.

'Cheer up, Faye,' Tara said suddenly to the second bridesmaid, who'd been squashed up on the seat next to her in silence. 'You want some more bubbles?'

Faye shook her head and continued to stare out of the window. She'd been another variable Alice had been unable to predict. Faye was married to Johnny, another of Ben's good friends, and the two women had hit it off instantly when Ben had first introduced them four years ago. Faye wasn't the same person now though. Once bubbly and wildly outgoing, she was barely a shell of the woman from years ago, though Alice couldn't put her finger on exactly what had changed or when.

Alice shuffled along her seat, so she was directly across from Faye. 'Hey, you. Is everything okay? You've been so quiet today.'

Faye's eyes were wet as she fixed Alice with a troubled stare. 'I'm fine. I'm sorry, just got one or two things on my mind. I don't want to spoil your big day.'

'You're not spoiling anything, I just don't like to see you looking so down. Is there anything I can do? Is it Isabella?'

Faye's eyes widened at the sound of her daughter's name. 'No, Isabella's fine. I told you, she's with my mum today.'

'What is it then? I'm worried about you.'

Faye plastered a smile across her face. 'I'm okay. Really.'

Alice frowned at her. 'Okay, but the two of us are going to have a proper catch-up when Ben and I get back from the honeymoon. Agreed?'

Faye's smile widened. 'I'd like that. Sorry again.'

'More bubbles is what we all need,' Tara said, filling all of their glasses. 'I think we should also toast the most gorgeous bride and the best looking bridesmaids the world has ever seen.'

'I'll second that,' Alice said, clinking her flute against theirs.

'It really was a smart move if you ask me,' Tara continued. 'Picking two chubby bridesmaids, so we don't show you up in the photos.'

Alice gasped in shock. 'That isn't why I picked the two of you!'

Tara chuckled to show she hadn't meant any offence. 'Don't

worry, I intend to do the same thing if some bloke is ever stupid enough to fall on one knee for me, but in my case the bridesmaids will have to be real heifers so as to make me look like the slim one. That probably rules the two of you out as future bridesmaids, so I'll apologize in advance.'

The Rolls Royce returned to the outside of the church two minutes ahead of deadline. Scott was still waiting on the kerb where they'd left him, and he raised two thumbs to confirm everyone was inside and waiting.

'Are you ready for this?' Tara asked.

Alice took a deep breath, before lowering her veil. 'Ready as I'll ever be.'

As the three women emerged from the car and made their way to the church doors, the feeling of dread continued to bubble just beneath the surface of Alice's skin.

2

'You look amazing,' Ben whispered as he leaned in and kissed her cheek. 'I feel like the luckiest guy alive.'

Alice brushed her hand against his smooth cheek. 'I'm the lucky one. I'm glad you took my advice and had a shave this morning too.'

It was just the two of them, now, in the back of the Rolls Royce, heading away from the church and starting their first journey as husband and wife. Ben's parents, Alice's mum, Scott, and the bridesmaids would follow behind in two further Phantoms hired for the day. Everyone else had directions to the hotel and would make their own way there.

'I was convinced I would fluff my lines,' Ben said, leaning back and interlocking his fingers with hers. 'My throat was so dry up there, and even though the vicar was prompting us with what to say, I was sure I'd say the wrong thing.'

'It went by in a blur, didn't it? I'm so glad we hired someone to film it. My memory of it is already fading, and I want to hear us exchange vows again.'

'We could always do a do-over,' Ben teased. 'We could phone for an annulment and head back there now.'

She pressed her head into his arm. 'Don't think you're going to be able to get away from me that easily. You're mine for keeps now, and it will take someone far stronger than you to break us.'

He kissed the top of her head. 'Nothing will break us, I promise. I have a really great feeling about our future.'

'I worry about Tara though. She's obviously still really down about Jack breaking up with her. She was so sure he was going to pop the question, until he ditched her last week. It must be tough for her seeing how happy we are.'

'She'll be fine. The way I look at it, she's your best mate, and she'll be happy to share in our joy today.'

'She's so self-conscious about her size though. I think she's beautiful, but she doesn't see it. All she focuses on is her larger dress size.' Alice adjusted the front of her own dress as it squeezed her middle.

'You want me to have a word with Dave?'

Alice raised her head with a confused look. 'What do you mean?'

Ben raised his eyebrows. 'I could ask him if he'd . . . you know . . . size doesn't bother him.'

Alice slapped his arm. 'She doesn't need us fixing her up with a sympathy shag, especially with someone like Dave.'

Alice hadn't meant to be so blunt, but could see the hurt look in Ben's eyes.

'What's wrong with Dave? He's sound as a pound.'

Alice wrinkled her nose. 'I know he's your best friend, but he isn't always . . . I just mean, I don't want Tara to settle.'

'He's like a brother to me, and she could do a lot worse than Dave.'

'I know, I know . . . listen, I don't want to fall out over something so silly. I just think they're too different. Tara is passionate about teaching, and she yearns to meet someone who will sweep her off her feet. Even you have to admit, Dave is no romantic lothario, is he?'

Ben shrugged begrudgingly. 'I guess not. Didn't stop you going out with him back in the day though, did it?' He was grinning at her as he spoke, and she playfully slapped his arm again.

'That was a long time ago, and it was a blind date. Besides, if I hadn't met up with him that night, you never would have met me, and we wouldn't be here now.'

'He has a thing for schoolteachers, too, though I doubt he'll ever find one as gorgeous as you.'

'It's not easy for her to meet new guys. If you think about it, the only men we tend to come into contact with are either teachers or parents. Not exactly a plentiful pool.'

'Ha! You think it's easier running a logistics company? Most of my clients are middle-aged men with less hair than Dave!'

She smiled coquettishly. 'Well, you don't need to worry about that any more. God help you if I ever catch your eye wandering, Mr Goodman. As an experienced junior schoolteacher, I'm very handy with a pair of scissors.' She made a point of staring at his crotch as she spoke.

He pressed his hands against her cheeks and pulled her in for a deep and meaningful kiss, sending tremors along her arms and legs.

'I do believe we just had our first argument as husband and wife. Should I ask the chauffeur to pull over so we can have make-up sex?'

Alice couldn't be sure if he was being serious or just teasing her again. His ability to make her laugh was what had first attracted her to him. Conventionally handsome, with dark hair and a brooding look that he could flip to at the drop of a hat, physically Ben was a fine specimen. Dave on the other hand had a large frame, with deep-set eyes and a rapidly decreasing hairline. The two had the ability to wind each other up, but when push came to shove, there was nothing one wouldn't do for the other.

'Make-up sex will have to wait until tonight, I'm afraid,' she said, kissing him back. 'I don't want to do anything to mess up my hair before the photographs.'

He pressed the back of her hand to his lips. 'Fair enough. Hey do you reckon our parents are behaving in the other car?'

Ben's parents were staunch Christians who attended mass without fail every Sunday. Ben had once told her a story about how his mother had strapped a pair of tennis rackets to her feet so she could plough through a foot of snow to make it to the service. Alice's mum on the other hand was far less religious, and rarely hid her opinions on outdated religious practices. It had been stressful having to break the news to her that they'd decided to get married in a church, especially given that neither Ben nor Alice were regular church attendees.

'Hopefully they're sitting in silence and enjoying the view,' Alice said. 'If Scott is with them, I'm sure he'll make sure Mum bites her tongue.'

'Hey, you could always set up Tara with Scott.'

Alice scrunched up her face. 'I love my stepbrother and I love Tara, but I cannot see what they would have in common. Besides, Scott's married to his cycling career. He's never around long enough to maintain a relationship. When he's back in Southampton he seems to spend all of his free time at the gym anyway.'

'Yeah but he probably only does that so he isn't trapped under the same roof as your mum. It amazes me that they still live together after all this time.'

'It's good for her having him around, even if that's less and less these days. For him it offers a roof over his head when he's in the city, and somewhere he can store all his stuff.'

'I'm pretty sure I saw him crying when the vicar asked him to give you away. He definitely wiped something from the corner of his eye.'

'Yeah? I'm pretty sure I saw Dave do the same thing when he realized he was giving you up.'

She chuckled at her own quip, but the joy was short-lived when she remembered they had yet to hear Dave's best man speech. Dave wasn't known for his tact, and although Alice had begged and pleaded with him to show her the final version, he'd refused. She'd insisted though that he keep it clean for the sake of Ben's parents as well as her own feelings.

She accepted that she didn't know everything from Ben's past, and although the two of them had done the thing where they'd shared the names of previous partners, it hadn't been something either had wanted to dwell on. It grated that Dave was privy to so much of Ben's life prior to her arriving on the scene, and she now desperately hoped he wouldn't parade all of the skeletons from Ben's closet in front of her friends and family.

The first road sign for the hotel appeared ahead. Old Mill Lodge, on the edge of Hampshire's New Forest, was a grand-looking building, so named because it was built on the site of a mill that had operated in the late nineteenth century. When the business had failed, an eccentric developer had bought the land with a view to building the finest mansion the area had seen; but a year after completion he had suffered a heart attack and the deeds had passed to his unscrupulous son, who had immediately sold it. Shortly after the Second World War, it had been turned into a fine manor hotel where wedding costs started from thirty thousand upwards.

'You've gone quiet,' Ben observed. 'Are you okay?'

Pushing the fear from her mind, she snuggled into his shoulder contentedly. 'With you by my side, I have everything I'll ever need.'

3

'I promised I'd go easy on him,' Dave said, his large arm brushing against Alice's shoulder as he reached for the bottle of wine on the table between them. His jacket was now slung over the back of the chair, and he looked more like himself.

'Thank you,' Alice replied over the loud music already pumping out of the room next to them, grateful that Dave's ribbing of Ben throughout the best man's speech had been gentle. 'It was a good speech.'

'You should hear the first draft,' he teased, a wide grin breaking across the stubble on his cheeks. 'I should let you read a copy of it, so you get to see the man you've really married.'

She gave him a cursory stare, but found her own lips reflecting his smile. 'I wonder what sort of speech Ben would write about you though, Dave.'

His expression changed to one of mock hurt. 'Moi? Didn't you know? I'm an angel. They broke the mould when they made me. Scout's honour.'

Alice doubted very much that Dave had ever been in the Scouts. No matter how hard she tried to picture him in shorts and a woggle, she just couldn't do it.

Now that the speeches were complete, it felt like a huge weight had been lifted from her shoulders. She'd even caught both of Ben's parents chuckling as Dave had relayed stories of how the two of them had met, how Dave viewed himself as something of a Cupid for helping the happy couple connect, and had avoided all references to previous partners.

Dave's hands had trembled as he'd read out his speech, but Ben had looked even more nervous, sipping his wine every sixty seconds or so, clearly dreading the potential grenades Dave could have dropped.

The hotel staff had kicked them out of the room just after five, as Dave's speech had dragged on a little longer than expected, and Alice had taken the opportunity to change into her evening gown and freshen up. The honeymoon suite was everything she had hoped for. High ceilings, a four-poster bed and a balcony with a view of the lake and luscious green lawn where the photography session had taken place. Picture-perfect didn't come close to describing it, but then she'd left nothing to chance, and had spent the majority of her free time in the last two years planning every minute detail. From the embossed 'Save the Date' cards, to the individual handheld dessert selection that had been served during the speeches, she had overseen every detail.

Today was *her* day, and nothing was going to spoil it.

She hadn't seen Ben since the breakfast, but Dave had found her and promised the rest of the lads were looking after him, which probably meant they were drinking and exchanging banter where they couldn't be overheard. The evening guests were now gathering in the suite ready for the evening disco and buffet, awaiting the newlyweds' arrival and the cutting of the cake.

'Are you having a good day?' Dave asked, leaning closer again.

'The best,' she gushed.

'I'm sorry I was late getting Ben to the church,' he continued sombrely. 'It's absolutely my fault, and you shouldn't blame him. It took us ages to find an open pub. The one I'd planned for us to go to was closed, and we had to drive around until we found one. Ben kept saying we should just forget about it, but I wanted him to have a proper send-off. I hope you can forgive me. The last thing I'd want is to spoil your big day.'

She patted his arm warmly. 'It's okay, Dave. No harm done.'

A sudden crash into the table was followed by a hand resting on Dave's shoulder.

'Hey mate,' the owner of the hand slurred. 'You got a cigarette I can steal?'

Dave looked annoyed at the interruption, but turned to face the man. 'You don't smoke, Abdul.'

'Yeah, but I like one every now and again, when I've been drinking. Go on, don't be tight.'

Dave shuffled the chair back and stood, reaching for the suit jacket draped over the arm. 'Sure, I'll come out and join you.' He paused and turned back to Alice. 'Have you two met? Alice, this is Abdul. Abdul, this is Ben's better half.'

Alice hadn't met Abdul before, but she'd heard Ben and Dave talking about him. From India originally, he had met the other two at university and they'd spent most of their time high as kites, before going their separate ways at graduation.

'Hi,' Alice waved.

'Great day,' Abdul replied. 'Appreciate the invite.'

'I'll see you in a bit.' Dave winked at Alice, before following Abdul away from the table and towards the hotel lobby.

A moment later, Alice's mother plonked down in the chair Dave had vacated.

'You're supposed to be waiting for us in the hall, Mum,' Alice said patiently.

'Your dads would be so proud of you right now,' her mum replied, her eyes welling instantly. 'It's been a lovely day so far.'

It had taken enough planning, but it felt good to have all that effort vindicated by someone who could be so judgemental.

'Thank you, Mum. Are you okay?'

Her mum removed a tissue from the sleeve of her violet

cardigan and dabbed the corner of her eyes. 'I'm hanging in there. I wish both your dads could have been here to see you walk down the aisle. You looked like a princess from one of those stories we used to read to you as a child.'

Alice could feel the sting of tears and took a moment to compose herself. 'Stop it, Mum, you'll set me off.'

Her mum hugged her tightly. 'I'm so proud of all you've achieved, Alice. I wanted you to know that.'

Alice eyed the large glass of wine tentatively poised in her mum's hand; she always became more emotional under the influence.

'Well I'm so glad I have you here to celebrate with,' Alice said, squeezing her back.

She saw Ben stumbling towards the table before she heard him. 'Here are my two favourite ladies,' he said, planting a kiss on Alice's lips.

She could smell the whisky on his breath; he looked happier than she'd ever seen him.

'It's time for us to make a grand entrance,' he slurred. 'You'd better take charge of the cake knife though.'

Alice had enjoyed a couple of glasses of wine, but she'd wanted to keep a clear head so she could commit every second of the day to memory.

'How is my new son-in-law?' her mum asked.

Ben leaned forwards and planted a kiss on his mother-in-law's cheek. 'Does this mean you're happy with me calling you Mum at last?'

It had been a running joke between them since he'd first strolled into her parents' kitchen and called her Mum. They'd only been dating for three months at the time, but he'd later revealed that he'd already known he would marry Alice one day. He was a determined individual, and when he set his sights on a goal, nothing would stop him achieving it. It's why he now headed one of the largest logistics companies on the south coast, and why they lived in a six bedroom house in the affluent area of Chilworth. He wanted to fill the property with the sound of children's laughter and had implied he'd like at least four children; Alice, though, would wait until they'd managed to conceive one before thinking about more.

Smiling and nodding as she moved through the sea of smiling faces in the suite, she tried not to think about how uncomfortable being the centre of attention made her feel.

Ben was holding her hand, as ever her rock, leading her through the crowd to the large table in the corner where the three-tiered cake stood, miniature marzipan figures of Alice and Ben on the top. The smallest layer was fruit cake, the middle a moist choco-late sponge and the bottom a jam and vanilla mix. Something for everyone.

Moving behind the table, Ben took her hand, and together they coiled their fingers around the cold knife handle and held it on the white icing, pausing and smiling at the cameras as the room erupted with bright flashes, startling them both. In her head she counted to ten, before she pushed down together with Ben, cutting through the light sponge as another wave of flashes erupted.

It was as close to perfect as she could have imagined.

The gathered guests applauded the moment, and as Alice posed with Ben, both beaming into the continued flashes of cameras and phones, she wished she could freeze the moment in time forever.

Tara was the first to come over and hug her, swiftly followed by Faye, who looked much happier than she had in the car. 'We've got something for you,' Tara said into her ear, just as a man in a shabby-looking brown suit approached Ben and began to say something into his ear. Alice didn't recognize the man's face; moustachioed, wrinkles bearing the passing of time, she was sure she'd never been introduced to him.

Before she could interrupt the two men though, Faye and Tara whisked her away to the opposite side of the room, and the two men disappeared behind the throng of guests.

'Here you go,' Tara said, handing over a small jewellery box.

Alice craned her neck to see whether she could catch a glimpse of Ben and the stranger, but it was no use.

'Go on, open it,' Faye encouraged. 'We had it specially made.'

Alice unclasped the box and lifted the lid, gasping at the olive-coloured stone hanging from the silver chain.

'It's peridot,' Tara explained, 'the birthstone for the month of August.'

'Peridot brings its wearer success, peace and good luck,' Faye chimed in.

'My birthday is in June, though,' Alice said, confused, as she lifted the stone out, reading the encryption.

'Today is the third of August,' Tara continued, 'and this stone represents the birth of your union with Ben.'

Alice held the gemstone up to the light and marvelled at the luminescent green colour, with just a hint of gold. 'It's beautiful,' she said, returning it to the box and pulling her friends closer.

Suddenly Scott burst through the crowd of guests, skidding across the floor towards them, his face drained of blood. 'Alice, you need to come with me quickly,' he said.

The ball of worry that had been in the pit of her stomach all day suddenly sprang back to life. 'What is it? What's going on?'

Scott opened his mouth to speak, but no words emerged. Grabbing her hand, he pulled her with him, pushing through the guests to where Ben was standing at the cake.

'This must be some kind of joke,' Ben was saying, his cheeks red with anger.

The man in the brown suit said something that Alice couldn't hear as the DJ restarted the disco music.

'What is it?' Alice asked, wrapping her hands around Ben's arm. 'What's going on?'

'There's no need for us to make a scene,' the moustachioed man said to Ben, ignoring Alice's appearance.

'It's my wedding day,' Ben shouted back. 'You don't realize you're making a huge mistake.'

The moustachioed man turned and nodded at two men standing beyond the cake. It was only when they moved closer that Alice saw what they were wearing, and realized who they were.

'Ben, what's going on?' she said, the anxiety reaching her voice.

'Ben Goodman, I am arresting you on suspicion of the murder of Kerry Valentine. You do not have to say anything, but it may harm your defence if you do not mention when questioned something which you later rely on in court. Anything you do say may be given in evidence.'

4

Murder.

The word echoed around Alice's head as she tried to reason what the detective had said.

Ben wasn't a violent man; didn't they realize that? He wasn't capable of such a heinous crime. Not Ben. Not *her* Ben.

Murder?

It had to be somebody's idea of a sick joke. The kind of twisted prank that only Ben's friends would think to play on him on such a big occasion.

'I don't even know who that is,' Ben was pleading, as one of the officers in dark uniform pulled Ben's arms away from Alice and placed cuffs around his wrists.

'Might be best to keep quiet for now, son,' the man in the brown suit – presumably a detective – warned.

'I didn't do this,' Ben protested. 'You've got it all wrong. I'm not who you think I am.'

Ben's face was a mixture of shock and anger, and his head snapped round as he made eye contact with Alice, his eyes begging for her to make the nightmare stop.

She was frozen to the spot, studying his face for any sign as to whether he was in on the joke, and she was the intended victim. She kept expecting Dave and Johnny to appear holding a video camera to capture her shocked reaction. She'd give anything for them to deliver the punchline sooner rather than later.

With the handcuffs secure, the uniformed officer looked to the detective, who nodded, and suddenly they were escorting Ben away from her.

'No, you have to stop,' Alice said, taking hold of Ben's arm again. 'He's not going anywhere. Not now. Not today. This is our wedding day.'

The officer was stronger than she'd anticipated, and no amount of digging her heels into the slippery dance floor would stop him achieving his objective. Alice tried to ignore the shocked faces of their friends and family as the police cut through them with Ben, and herself in tow.

Then suddenly they were marching through the hotel's lobby as other guests gawped at the unfolding scene, Alice scrabbling to keep up with them.

'Get Dave,' Ben called out to her.

Alice paused momentarily. What could Dave do? He wasn't any kind of legal professional. She picked up the pace again, following them out through the revolving doors, down the marble steps and onto the gravel, where a police van and marked car waited.

It was the stuff of nightmares, and she was beginning to question whether the perfect ceremony had all been part of a dream that had suddenly turned sour. The cool breeze blowing at her exposed shoulders, though, suggested she was very much awake. She didn't want to think about all the gossip-mongering now underway within the hotel as the news of Ben's arrest spread like wildfire.

'Please stop,' she said, hurrying after the detective. 'Please, just wait. This is a huge mistake. You've got the wrong man. This is *Ben Goodman*. Can you just call your office and check? They'll tell you that he couldn't possibly have anything to do with what-ever is going on.'

The detective cocked a sceptical eyebrow in her direction. 'I'm sorry about your wedding, but I'm just doing my job.'

Alice took a breath, fighting down her anxiety and frustration. 'Please, just tell me what it is you think he's done. What is he supposed to have done? He's been with me all day.'

The detective sighed, nodding for the two officers to put Ben in the back of the van. 'Your husband has been arrested on suspicion of murdering a young woman called Kerry Valentine last week. That's all I can say at this time.'

Alice tasted vomit in the back of her throat. 'Who is she? We don't know anyone by that name.'

'I'm sorry, but I can't say any more right now.'

'Please,' she reasoned, forcing eye contact. 'There must be some kind of mistake. That man there is Ben Goodman; my *husband*. We have literally just got married. You must have the wrong person.'

The detective frowned at her, as he tried to get past and into the waiting patrol car. 'There's no mistake, we know who he is. Now, please, I need to do my job.'

The van door slammed behind them.

'Where are you taking him?'

'We're taking him to the Southampton police headquarters building. It's in the centre of the city on the Millbrook Road. You know it?'

She knew exactly where he meant – down by the docks where visiting cruise ships dropped and collected passengers. The tall building was an eyesore on one of the busiest routes in and out of the city.

'Well, that's where he'll be,' the detective continued. 'I'd suggest you contact whatever legal representation you have and tell them where he'll be.'

With that, he barged past her and was in the car before she

could ask anything else. Over her shoulder a small crowd had now gathered by the entrance, eager to see why the blue flashing lights were brightening the night sky.

5

Alice's legs gave way and she crumpled to the ground, the small and sharp gravel quickly digging in to her skin. Her world had flipped upside down and she couldn't work out how to move forward.

The sound of quick and heavy footsteps on the gravel behind her was followed by Dave crouching down at her side. 'Are you all right? What happened? Scott said something about police?'

Alice opened her mouth to speak, but the words stuck in her throat, and she soon felt tears dampening her cheeks.

'Come on,' Dave said, pushing his large hands beneath her arms, 'let's get you up and back inside.'

She allowed him to lift her like a ragdoll, but instead of following him back inside, she kept her feet where they were. 'You need to drive me to the police station. I need to make sure Ben is okay and find out what the hell is going on.'

Dave glanced back at the crowd watching them. 'You have a room full of guests who've come to see you,' he said calmly. 'The best thing you can do is go back in and be with them.'

'Not without Ben. I can't just carry on like nothing's happened. They *arrested* him, Dave.'

Dave looked as uncertain as she felt. 'Okay, okay, tell me what they said. Did they say why they were arresting him?'

She stepped towards him so that the people on the hotel steps wouldn't hear. 'They said they suspect he murdered someone called Kerry Valentine; do you recognize that name?'

She thought she saw a flicker of recognition in his eyes, but it could have just been the reflection of the moon.

'Doesn't ring any bells. Are you sure they said murder?'

Alice replayed the detective's words in her mind, nodding. 'They've clearly mixed Ben up with some other Ben Goodman, right?'

Dave nodded, but she could see he was holding back.

'What is it?' Alice pressed. 'What aren't you telling me?'

He looked down at his feet. 'It's just . . . you don't need to hear this.'

'Tell me, Dave. Whatever it is you know about this mess, I need to know. Ben is my husband.'

Dave raised his eyes, narrowing them as he met her gaze. 'In my experience of the police . . . they have to have a pretty strong suspicion that the target is involved before they can initiate an arrest warrant.'

'What are you saying? That Ben did it?'

He shook his head vehemently. 'No, no, no. What I'm saying is, it won't be a case of mistaken identity, at least, not the way you're thinking. There must be dozens of Ben Goodmans across the UK, but they're unlikely to have simply arrested the wrong one. For whatever reason, they suspect that your Ben – *our* Ben – is involved.'

'That's ridiculous! Ben's not a killer.'

'Believe me, I know!' He looked back at the people gathered behind them, each clearly wondering whether to head back inside or come down the steps and offer comfort and support. 'Listen, let me go to the police station and see what I can find out. Okay? You should probably make some kind of announcement to quell the rumours circling inside. Just tell people there's been a mix-up, and Ben has had to temporarily go and fix it. Meanwhile, I'll go down there and keep you posted via the phone.'

It wasn't what she wanted, but she could see the logic in his suggestion. 'You can't drive, you've been drinking.'

'I'll get Scott to give me a lift; he's been on soft drinks all day because of his training. Okay? Will you go inside for me? If you'd prefer, I can make an announcement before I go.'

She rubbed his arm, for once grateful that Ben had chosen him as his best man. 'I'd rather you go down there straight away, and let me know what's going on. I'll make the announcement, or I'll get Tara to do it.'

He nodded. 'Try not to worry. I'm sure you're right, and this is just a huge mistake.'

'Just bring him back to me, Dave,' she said as fresh tears fell. 'Please bring Ben home.'

Tara was waiting for her just inside the swivel doors. 'Here, I got you this for the shock,' she said, handing over a tumbler of something caramel-coloured.

Alice accepted the glass, but one sniff of the brandy had her swiftly passing it back. 'I need to keep a clear head, but thank you.'

Tara led her through the lobby to a small room where the wedding gifts were being stored during the party. Closing the door behind them, Tara wrapped her arms around Alice and gently squeezed.

'I saw what happened. How are you holding up?'

'I just saw my husband arrested on suspicion of murder . . . I'd say I'm somewhere between shocked and outraged.' Alice had seen Ben's face as they'd put him in the back of that van, somewhere between anger and panic. The cool demeanour which was usually his trademark had evaporated before her very eyes. 'You didn't see the fear in his eyes.'

'Fear?' Tara replied. 'Ben? No chance. You know what he's like: could charm the hind legs off a donkey. They'll probably drive him to the station, make him give his name, take his fingerprints and then realize they've got the wrong guy.'

Alice stopped. 'You really think so?'

Tara exaggerated her nod. 'Absolutely. You'll see.'

Alice could only hope she was right. The best outcome now would be for Ben to be back before eight so they could continue their celebration and put this nightmare behind them.

Tara extracted herself from the hug. 'I don't want to add to your stress . . . but I think someone needs to make an announcement. It's better to say something than let rumours spread.'

Alice fixed her with a hopeful look. 'Would you mind doing it? I don't think I could stand everyone staring up at me. Just say that Ben's been called away on urgent business, but will be back later.'

Tara nodded sombrely. 'Of course, of course, that's what I'm here for. We should probably have a quiet word with your mum and Ben's parents first though.'

Alice nodded. 'Can you find them for me, if I wait here?'

Tara agreed, before handing Alice a small bag. 'Might be an idea to fix your mascara as well. We don't want people seeing how upset you are.'

Alice unzipped the bag as Tara slipped out of the room and went in hunt of the parents. Opening the compact mirror, Alice stared at the panda eyes looking back at her. Of all the things that could have gone wrong today – guests not turning up, the caterers messing up the food, Dave making an inappropriate best man's speech – the thought of Ben being hauled away by the police had never entered her mind. If Dave was right, and the police hadn't just mixed up Ben with another Ben Goodman, then what did that mean? She'd known Ben for more than five years, and they'd lived together for the last three, since she'd graduated from university. Surely in all that time she would have picked up on any murdering tendencies?

She shook her head dismissively. Of course she would have. Despite Dave's caution, the police *had* made a mistake, of that she had no doubt.

A knock on the door was followed by Tara smuggling in Alice's mum and Ben's parents. All three looked white as sheets. Ben's parents, Ray and Hermione, were the first to embrace her.

'Are you okay?' Ray asked.

Alice fought back the tears as she nodded. 'Did you see what happened?'

Ray looked at his wife before shaking his head. 'We saw the two of you cut the cake, but then we went to the bar to buy drinks. When we returned, neither of you were in sight, nor was anybody dancing. We didn't know what to think. Then someone mentioned the police and an arrest, and . . .'

Dressed in the jacket he always wore on special occasions – embossed with his many military awards from years in the services – Ray looked ready to cry, and Alice couldn't bear to watch. Pulling him towards her, she hugged him warmly.

'It will be all right,' Alice assured him, hoping to convince herself.

Alice's mum remained by the door, watching the scene unfold. 'What did they arrest him for?'

Alice had hoped that news of the arrest would be enough to pacify them, without going into sordid detail. Admitting that Ben had been arrested on suspicion of murder felt like she was going behind his back and muddying his name. Alice looked to Tara for support, but her friend stared blankly back at her.

'It's all just a big mistake,' Alice said. 'When they realize they've screwed up, he'll be back here with their grovelling apology.'

'Do you think we should cancel the party?' Hermione asked.

All the months of planning that had gone into today, striving to make the day perfect, it would be such a waste to just send the guests home. The last thing Alice wanted to do was plaster on a fake smile and pretend everything was okay, but what choice did she have?

'The guests are here, there's a ton of buffet food waiting to be served, and the DJ is paid until midnight,' Alice said. 'When Ben returns, I want the party in full swing, so he can see how much we all love him and trust him.'

Ben's parents nodded, Ray looking calmer now.

'I'll go make that speech,' Tara said, opening the door and leading the parents back out to the lobby.

Alice remained where she was, reaching for the make-up bag, ready to conceal just how terrified she really felt.

6

Slumped at a table, with only a quiet Tara and her mum for company, Alice's anxiety had only deepened in the two hours since the police had interrupted the celebration. Her only distraction was the disco ball spinning on the desk by the DJ. Cheesy pop song after cheesy pop song blasted out of the large speakers, and those who were already drunk enough to have forgotten the earlier ruckus were making shapes on the dance floor. Alice had handpicked the list of songs the DJ was allowed to play on the night – classic songs from her time at school, university and since she'd known Ben. Songs that she loved to listen to, each stirring happy memories. Yet as she watched the party carrying on without her, the songs brought nothing but sadness.

It should have been her on the dance floor, with friends and her new husband, but the thought of getting out there and pretending everything was okay was making her head spin as fast as the disco ball.

Ben's parents had headed up to bed shortly after Tara's announcement over the speaker system. Ray had said his wife had a headache, but she didn't blame them for wanting to be away from the furtive glances of those who weren't dancing – the ones who were still looking over and gossiping. Sitting at the round tables around the edge of the room, Alice could only imagine what they were whispering to each other.

The music was loud enough that Tara hadn't attempted to offer false platitudes and positive but fruitless statements. Every time a new figure entered the room, Alice would look up in hopeful expectation, desperate to see Ben's smile and kick things back on course. As yet there was no sign of him though, and despite her dozens of calls to Dave's mobile, he had yet to respond, save for a single text message to say he and Scott had arrived at the station.

Picking at one of the pearls embroidered into her dress, Alice leaned towards Tara, practically shouting so she would be heard over the music.

'Where is he? Why haven't they released him yet?'

Tara looked like she didn't know how to answer the question. 'These things take time I guess,' she called back. 'It must be a fifteen to twenty minute drive from here to the police station, right? So multiply that by two – there and back – plus another hour to process him and realize their mistake, and you can see how it would add up.'

'I should have gone there with him. I should have told everyone the party was over and gone to support him. I can't believe I let Dave talk me into staying.'

'Ben wouldn't want you to worry, would he? He knows they've got the wrong man – as we know too – and it will be eating him up inside knowing how hurt you're feeling. It wouldn't surprise me if he wasn't already speaking to his solicitor about how to sue the police for ruining the day.'

Alice fixed her with an affectionate look. 'I don't know what I would have done without you here. You really are a true friend.'

Tara waved away the praise. 'It's like you said, you'll have to return the favour one day, and when it's my wedding day going up in flames, you'll be the one fighting to keep me sane.' Tara suddenly gasped as she realized what she'd said. 'Oh, honey, I'm sorry, I didn't mean that your day was going up in flames. I just meant—'

Alice strained a smile. 'It's okay, Tara, I know what you meant. I just keep thinking about that moment when they burst in. It was like I was watching a film or something, or like it was happening to someone else.'

'I'm sure he'll be back soon enough.'

'Some of our colleagues are out there though, which means the story will get out at school when the summer holidays are over, which means no matter what happens tonight, there'll still be gossiping about me even when all of this is over.'

Tara reached for the tumbler of brandy and took a long sip. 'Only if you let them. The best thing you can do is to go out there, plaster a huge smile on your face, and show them you're stronger than this. Hell, you can even lie to them and say Ben has been released. Make it a non-story. The longer you mope and keep yourself hidden away, the more people will talk. Let's show them. Let's show them that Alice Tandy – sorry, *Goodman* – is not a bitch you mess with!'

Alice suddenly gasped as a new thought hit her. 'The honeymoon! Our tickets to Barbados are non-refundable. We're supposed to be at Gatwick tomorrow night!'

Tara didn't look concerned. 'Worst-case scenario, you have travel insurance. Best-case scenario, Ben will be here shortly, and you'll still make tomorrow's flights. I don't think you should worry about that right now. I know you're looking forward to it, but it might be that you just have to delay the honeymoon until all this has blown over.'

'I'm not sure travel insurance will cover the costs of the flights and hotels because Ben was arrested.'

'No? Let me look into that for you. It's the least I can do. Either way, Ben is loaded, and the cost of the honeymoon was probably a drop in the ocean for him. You'll just have to go in a month or so.'

'I'll be back at school in a month. That's why we booked the wedding and honeymoon during the summer holidays.' Alice blinked back tears. 'I need to know what's going on. I'm not prepared to just sit back and let someone mess all of this up. Can you tell everyone the party is over? Then you and I will get a taxi to the police station, and we won't leave until Ben is released.' Alice sighed in satisfaction, feeling adrenaline coursing through her veins.

Alice's mum seemed oblivious to their conversation, tapping her foot in time with the music, making no effort to console her daughter.

The door to the room opened, and Alice once again looked up in hope. She recognized Dave's large outline immediately, and without a second's thought raced across the room to him. 'What's going on? Where's Ben?' she shouted over the din.

He bent low and spoke into her ear. 'Can we go somewhere for a quiet word?'

'I'm not going anywhere until you tell me where my husband is.'

'Please, Alice, let's go somewhere where we won't be overheard. Please?'

Tara was at her side a moment later, linking arms, and staring questioningly at the best man.

Dave nervously glanced around, feeling the burn of people's eyes on them. Leaning forward once more, he whispered, 'The police have processed him, but won't interview him until the morning. They can keep him in custody for twenty-four hours before they have to release him, and apparently they intend to make full use of the time. He won't be out until tomorrow.'

7

Slumped on the four-poster, Alice tried to flatten the crease in her satin evening dress without success. Dave had insisted they go somewhere quiet to talk, and with no other obvious options, they had headed to the honeymoon suite, Faye and Tara, too.

Dave was crouched down by the minibar, grabbing handfuls of small bottles and dropping them on the floor. He hadn't asked whether he could help himself, but money was the last thing on Alice's mind as she watched him pop open the lid of a box of Pringles and offer her one. She hadn't eaten since the wedding breakfast earlier, despite the large buffet spread downstairs. She shook her head politely though, as her appetite was missing in action.

Tara and Faye were standing on the balcony overlooking the lake, talking quietly. The cool breeze coming from the gap in the doors was welcome. So many questions were peppering Alice's mind that she was struggling to keep up with the pace.

Dave slammed the door to the minibar fridge and reached for one of the bottles, unscrewing the cap and swallowing the contents before tossing the bottle towards the small plastic bin by the desk. She watched him, for the first time seeing what resembled fear in his eyes. He unscrewed a second miniature and held it close.

'What aren't you telling me?' Alice asked.

Their eyes met, before he quickly looked away. 'I don't know what you mean.'

Alice's gaze hadn't left his face. As a teacher, she'd learned to pick up on tells when she was being lied to, and Dave's body language was screaming at her right now.

'Who is Kerry Valentine?' she asked.

Dave's shoulders instantly tensed, as he turned his back to her. 'Who?'

The only thing worse than being lied to was recognizing the deceit.

'The woman they think Ben killed,' Alice continued. 'Who is she?'

'How would I know?' Dave was still facing the wall, but she could see he'd put the miniature to his lips.

She had no doubt he was keeping things from her; he was a terrible liar at the best of times, but the question was *why* was he lying? To protect Ben? To protect himself?

Sliding off the bed, she moved around Dave so she could look into his eyes when she asked the next question. 'What else did the police say to you?'

'Nothing. They wouldn't speak to me.'

She saw a flicker of doubt in his eyes again. Keeping her tone calm but even, she said, 'Please don't lie to me. Ben's my husband, and I deserve to know the truth.' She reached for his hand and held it, surprised by how cold it felt. 'Please, Dave, whatever it is you're keeping from me, it can't be any worse than the paranoid thoughts whizzing through my mind right now. Please?'

The balcony doors opened wider and the two bridesmaids entered the room, Tara making a beeline for the collection of bottles on the floor near the fridge. Picking up two bottles of vodka, she held one out for Alice, who shook her head. Tara shrugged and carried the two miniatures back to the bed.

As Alice turned back she saw Dave had escaped to the balcony and followed him out. The breeze was stronger out here and she felt the hairs on her arms stand on end.

'Whatever the truth is,' she said, 'I will find it out. They won't be able to keep Ben in there forever. The two of you will have to come clean soon enough. Just put me out of my misery. What did the police really say?'

Dave remained where he was, staring out at the full moon peeking out from behind a single cloud in the dark night sky.

'Nothing. I didn't speak to the police. It was the solicitor who told me they were keeping Ben in.'

Alice frowned. 'Solicitor? Since when does Ben have a solicitor?'

'He's a mate of mine. I called him on the way to the police station and asked him to just go and check on Ben.'

Alice didn't want to ask why Dave happened to have a solicitor on standby, but given some of the stories Ben had told her about Dave, she could guess.

'Why would Ben need a solicitor if he hasn't done anything wrong?' She hadn't expected the question to sound so callous, but she couldn't reason how the police could be so certain they had the right man unless there was a lot more she didn't know.

'The police, they . . . they can twist things. I promise you, Ben didn't do what they say, but I need to make sure he doesn't get himself into trouble by saying the wrong thing.'

A tiny voice in the back of her head didn't like the mention of *the wrong thing*, but now wasn't the time to question what Ben could possibly say to implicate himself.

'Will this solicitor look after Ben then?'

Dave's focus remained on the moon, but he nodded.

'Will you tell me one thing?'

He turned and looked straight at her, nodding again.

Alice took a deep breath. 'Who is Kerry Valentine? I know you know more than you're saying. I know you recognize her name. Does Ben know her?'

Alice had been trying to ignore the voice of doubt, but it was now too loud to ignore. She didn't pretend to know all of Ben's friends, but she was certain she'd have remembered him mentioning a name like Kerry Valentine. If he hadn't mentioned her name, was there another reason for keeping her identity a secret? Alice's last two boyfriends had cheated on her, and she was now dreading the possibility that history had repeated itself.

'Please, Dave?' she said when her question was greeted with silence. 'Who is Kerry Valentine?'

Dave buried his face in his hands and growled as he summoned the words. 'She was a stripper I hired for his stag do.'

Alice let the words sink in. 'A stripper?'

Dave lowered his hands and stared apologetically at her. 'I'm sorry. I wanted him to have one last hurrah before he settled down.'

'Wait, his stag do? So this stripper was with you in Malia?'

Dave shook his head. 'No, Malia was two weeks ago. This was last weekend.'

Alice's mind fogged with confusion. 'A week ago? I was in France a week ago. The deal was he went to Malia with his friends, and then I'd go to Paris with mine the week after.'

Regret was plastered all over his face. 'It wasn't Ben's fault. He didn't know anything about it. I just thought it was an opportunity to relive our old uni days. I called together some of the guys who couldn't afford to do Malia with us and suggested we get together and knock back a few shots.'

'I phoned Ben from Paris. You answered and said you were both at our place watching films and getting drunk. You told me Ben was in the toilet.'

The crevices in his forehead sank deeper. 'He was tied up in the back of my car at that point. We kidnapped him and made him come out with us, because we knew he wouldn't want to break his promise to you.

'I drove us to Bournemouth, to a few of the bars we used to hit in our uni days. You should have heard him though; the whole

42

time he kept saying how guilty he felt about not staying home as he'd promised. We all swore a pact that we'd never let slip what we'd done or where we'd been. He was terrified you'd blame him for breaking the promise, but I swear to you, it was all my doing.'

She didn't doubt that Dave was the ringleader, but she couldn't believe Ben had kicked up that much of a fuss. He wouldn't deliberately lie to her, but if there was a chance of booze and clubbing, Ben wouldn't take much persuading. Dave was obviously laying it on thick in an effort to protect his best friend.

Alice walked back into the room and reached for her shawl, spotting Faye on the bed, next to Tara. 'Did you know about this?'

Faye frowned at the question. 'Know about what?'

'Apparently Ben, Dave and the boys went to Bournemouth last weekend when we were in Paris. Did Johnny mention it to you?'

The look of surprise on Faye's face indicated he hadn't. 'Johnny can't have gone. He was looking after Isabella because I was away with you.'

8

Dave had now left the balcony and re-entered the room. 'Johnny left Isabella with his mum for the night and then collected her Sunday morning. I'm sorry. He was sworn into the same pact, and couldn't tell you the truth. There was no reason why any of you should have found out where we were. Nothing of incident happened, and we all returned to Southampton first thing on Sunday.'

Alice felt saliva building at the back of her throat as she asked her next question. 'Did you pay for Kerry to have sex with Ben?'

'Absolutely not! I wouldn't do that to you, Alice. Nor would Ben. He is absolutely smitten with you, and wouldn't look at another woman.'

It was the answer she wanted to hear, even if she wasn't sure whether she could believe a single word out of Dave's mouth.

'So you went to some kind of strip club then?' she pressed.

Dave reached for a bottle of lager from the collection on the carpet and snapped the lid off. 'You remember Abdul from earlier?'

She nodded.

'He had the keys for this old bar. It had gone out of business, but it was quiet and we knew we wouldn't get disturbed. So we went there, buying some booze from a local grocer's, and then someone suggested we get a stripper and pay her to give Ben a private dance.' He suddenly fixed her with a hard stare. 'He knew nothing about it until she arrived. We tied him to a chair and watched as she performed a lap dance for him.'

Alice could feel the vomit rising in her throat again as she pictured Ben on a chair while a beautiful young woman danced provocatively for him. 'Where did you find her?'

Dave whipped out his phone and presented the Internet search history. 'I typed: "private dancers, Bournemouth", and I called one of the first numbers that came up. She rocked up twenty minutes later, with her own music and speaker. Ben emerged from the toilets and we quickly grabbed him and tied his wrists behind the chair with some rope Abdul found behind the bar. She did a dance using some squirty cream and made him lick it off her, and that was it.' Dave swigged from the lager. 'Then she cleaned herself up, I handed over the money and she left. We stayed at the lock-up for another ten or so minutes and then we tied Ben to a pole outside and pulled down his trousers. We left him there while we headed out to buy more booze.'

Her eyes widened. 'You left him tied up in the street? He could have got mugged or killed, or God knows what!'

'It's what you do on a stag do. We were just messing with his mind; we never had any intention of leaving him there all night, we just wanted to see how scared he got. We eventually went back and let him go, drank for a further hour or so before we all passed out. We woke up and headed home, stopping for breakfast on the way.'

'Did you tell the police all this?'

'I tried, but they weren't willing to listen. They told me to come back in the morning and someone would take my statement then.'

'What about Ben?'

'They said because he's been drinking today, they're not allowed to interview him until the morning, but they've said they'll do so first thing. All being well, the solicitor reckons he'll be out by lunchtime.'

The gentle vibrations in the carpet suggested the loud music from the party was still going. If Ben was back by lunch, at least they wouldn't have to cancel the honeymoon, but right now she would happily give up the trip to Barbados to have him here with her.

By ten o'clock, even the happiest of revellers had left the dance floor, and as Alice looked around the room, the only people who remained were those who were staying the night at the hotel. Through the fire exit window, Alice could see what looked like a heated argument between Faye and Johnny. Faye had been furious to learn that Johnny had abandoned their daughter for a night out with his mates, and it didn't look like he was too pleased to be challenged on it.

Alice's stepbrother Scott was chatting to Abdul and a second man that Alice vaguely recognized. She knew he was someone that worked with Ben, but for the life of her she couldn't remember his name. The three of them were sitting at a table on the other side of the hall, so it was impossible to know what they were talking about, though she suspected Ben's arrest wasn't far from any of their minds. Dave had promised to round up the group from Bournemouth and have them go with him to make statements at the police station in the morning.

Alice's mum had headed up to bed shortly after Alice had returned to the party, and Tara looked as though she might fall asleep at the table at any minute.

'You should go up to bed,' Alice suggested.

Tara suddenly gave a jolt as she realized she was being addressed. Reaching for her glass of wine, she knocked it back. 'I'm not going anywhere without you.'

Alice was touched by her friend's loyalty, but it wasn't fair to be keeping her up unnecessarily. 'I'm probably going to head up too. The sooner this day ends the better.'

Tara pulled a sympathetic pout. 'Do you want me to stay in the room with you? I'll be lousy company, but I don't think it's a good idea for you to be alone tonight.'

Alice choked back the emotion building in her throat. 'You don't need to do that. I'll probably be asleep as soon as my head hits the pillow.'

Tara crossed her arms. 'I'm not taking no for an answer.'

Alice leaned across and hugged her. 'Thank you.'

The two women stood and Alice took a final cursory glance around the room to check she hadn't missed anyone she should thank for attending. Faye and Johnny had disappeared from the window, presumably to return to their room, and Alice waved goodnight to Scott and the other two before peeling out of the room and heading up to the honeymoon suite. Tara said she would collect her things from her room and return.

Once inside, Alice changed into her negligee and dived under the covers. Next door it sounded like Johnny and Faye's argument had resulted in the noisiest make-up sex Alice had ever heard. Tara knocked on the door moments later and climbed into bed too.

'Do you want me to stay awake until you're asleep?' Tara yawned, the alcohol in her system making her drowsy.

'No, I just want to sleep,' Alice replied, switching off the bedside lamp.

Barely two minutes had passed before Tara began snoring. It was the cue Alice had been waiting for. Reaching over to the bedside table, she switched on her phone and opened an Internet search window, typing in the name 'Kerry Valentine'. It had been a long and stressful day, but Alice's mind wouldn't allow her to rest until she knew as much as she could about this mystery woman.

9

Sunlight was already streaming through the open balcony door, and the cool morning breeze was enough to raise goosebumps on Alice's arms as she stirred. Rising from the bed, she moved across to the door and gently closed it, pulling the curtain back across, casting the room in a dim shadow.

When sleep had come, it had been interspersed with memories of the cuffs being snapped around Ben's wrists and the sound of the van door being slammed. So vivid were the visions in her dreams that she'd woken believing the whole experience had just been a nightmare brought on by the stress of planning the wedding. Then she had turned to look at the other side of the bed and, seeing Tara's face where Ben's should have been, she'd realized how true the visions were.

Unlike Alice, Ben was a positive soul; rather than looking for worst-case scenarios, he always sought to find the green grass in every situation. If he were here now, he wouldn't be worrying about the arrest or what others would say. Instead, he'd be telling her what a great anecdote it would make.

'Remember that time I was arrested on our wedding day?' he would laugh.

He would probably be back in her arms by lunchtime, and

hopefully the whole sordid mess could be put behind them, yet her old self-doubt continued to niggle away: *they wouldn't have arrested him if they weren't sure he was guilty; you always thought he was too good to be true; mud sticks.*

Alice headed into the en suite bathroom, closed the door and switched on the shower, cranking up the heat before stepping in and feeling the hot and forgiving waters wash away the pain of yesterday. Emerging from the bathroom through a thick cloud of steam, she felt like a contestant on *Stars in their Eyes.*

Tara was still fast asleep, bless her. Her face looked like a child had come in and tried to fix her make-up: black smears running down both cheeks, her lipstick spread up at awkward angles.

Hours spent searching for details about Kerry Valentine online had proved fruitless. News of her death had yet to be picked up by any news agencies, and Alice had learned there were six Kerry Valentines listed in the Bournemouth and Poole areas alone, and there was no guarantee any of them was the victim.

Alice had even searched for her on Facebook, but with no idea what Kerry looked like, it had been impossible to work out which profile – if any – belonged to the victim. The profile images ranged wildly, from a woman in her early twenties with jet black hair, to an octogenarian with a purple rinse. For all Alice knew, Kerry Valentine may not have been active on social media or from Dorset. Alice had eventually given up her search shortly before three.

Her phone beeped on the duvet cover to indicate she'd received a message. Opening it, she saw it was from Dave. A simple:

How are you feeling? Can I do anything for you?

The only thing she wanted was for the clock to be reset so that she could relive yesterday without the interruption of the police, but nobody could provide her with that.

Tara pushed herself off the pillow and, bleary-eyed, stared at Alice. 'Morning,' she croaked.

Alice smiled warmly. 'How did you sleep?'

Tara blinked several times and yawned. 'Fine, I guess. What time is it?'

'Just gone seven,' Alice said, a small towel now wrapped around her head to dry her hair. 'We should probably think about breakfast.'

Tara gasped at the time. 'What are you doing up so early, you evil woman?'

Tara wasn't a morning person, and Alice could forgive her reluctance to be awake so early on a Sunday morning.

'I couldn't sleep,' Alice said apologetically. 'You can go back to sleep if you want?'

Tara's expression changed as the reality of last night filtered through the hangover fog in her head. 'What kind of friend would that make me?' She slid her legs off the edge of the bed, heading into the bathroom and closing the door. A scream a moment later meant Tara had seen her reflection in the mirror. The door to the en suite flew open and Tara's face appeared around it.

'I should probably shower and dress before breakfast. Can you give me twenty minutes to freshen up?'

Alice nodded and moved across to put on the room's kettle, dropping teabags into two mugs before dressing in the summer dress she'd brought for the trip to the airport later. Their bags were all packed at home, waiting for collection, but if the police didn't release Ben until this afternoon, it would be a rush to get to the airport for check-in.

The shower thundered to life, the sound reverberating off the connecting wall. The thought of seeing the guests who'd stayed at the hotel filled her with dread. Without Ben at her side, she felt so vulnerable.

A knock at the bedroom door startled her.

Dave's hulking figure was leaning against the woodwork. 'Morning,' he offered.

'Hi,' she replied, surprised to see him looking as fresh as he did.

'I sent you a message,' he explained, 'and then I thought that was pretty callous when you're just down the hall. Did you manage to get any sleep?'

'Some,' she said. 'You?'

'I never sleep well in a different bed. So what I did do was jot down details of the stag night in as much detail as I could remember. That way, when I go to the police station, I can make it clear that Ben couldn't have had anything to do with what happened to that poor girl, because he was with us all night.'

'Thank you.'

He shuffled from one foot to the other. 'Listen, Alice, there's . . .' he paused as if trying to find the right words. 'I . . . what I mean to say is . . . I'm sorry about all of this. It was my idea to drag Ben to Bournemouth, and it was my idea for none of us to mention where we'd been or why, and I was the one who hired the girl to strip, and . . .'

She was surprised to see his eyes welling, and felt obliged to put her hand on his arm reassuringly. 'It's okay, Dave, you couldn't have known any of this would happen.'

She had met Dave at the first school she worked after graduating as a teacher. He was the son of one of the older members of staff, and he'd pestered her for months to go on a date with him. At the time she had been trying to focus on settling into her new career, but eventually she had reluctantly agreed. Rather than going for a drink or some food, he'd taken her to a party – a birthday party – for one of his friends. Suddenly thrust into a crowd of strangers who all seemed to know each other, she'd never felt so awkward, and had been trying to think of excuses to take off when Ben had walked into the room.

They talk about thunderbolts, and there was no other way to describe the instant attraction she'd felt to the handsome man in the Hawaiian-style shirt, his brown hair styled to within an inch of its life, his physique firm but not overly toned. She was sure her mouth had hit the floor. As he had approached, her hands had become clammy, her heart rate had increased rapidly, and by the time he was greeting Dave she was putty in his hands.

He'd respected the boundary, waited for Dave to introduce them, and had then asked questions of her. She could still feel the burn in her cheeks as her mind had gone blank, and she'd barely managed to string together two words. Despite her own awkwardness, Ben had discreetly slipped her his number before he'd been dragged away by one of the other partygoers.

She'd texted him her number as soon as Dave had dropped her home, and although Dave had leaned in for a kiss, she hadn't reciprocated. Dave just wasn't her type, with a shaved head and thick dark beard, his outer image was that of a bouncer at a nightclub. She preferred men in softer focus, more naturally handsome. Ben had ticked all of the boxes, and even some she hadn't realized she wanted ticking.

She'd felt guilty when they'd started texting each other. It turned out Ben was quite the charmer and hugely flirtatious. Alice had insisted he speak to Dave before they went on their first official date, and he was happy to do so. It wasn't like she and Dave had been an item, so her developing relationship with Ben wasn't wrong. Within four weeks, she'd totally forgotten about Dave's interest in her.

For the first six months of their relationship Ben had called and spoken to her every day. Sometimes the calls would last no more than two minutes, on other occasions they spoke for nearly an hour. Whenever he picked her up for a date, he was a gentleman from the first minute to the last. The sex, when she did finally succumb, had been everything she had imagined it would be. When he'd proposed two years ago, she'd known she was marrying her best friend and soulmate.

When Dave had first taken her to that party, she never would have guessed that this was how things would end up.

'I will get him back to you,' Dave said, wiping his eyes with the back of his hand, clearly ashamed at having allowed his mask to slip. 'I'll speak to the other boys in a bit and we'll all go and make statements. We were with him all night, and I'm sure all of this will blow over when we give him an alibi.'

Alice thanked him and watched him walk back along the corridor before closing the door behind her. Something Dave had said was itching at the back of her mind, but she couldn't place what or why.

The bathroom door opened a moment later and Tara stumbled out, a towel around her middle and one around her short auburn hair. 'Who was at the door?'

'Just Dave,' Alice replied.

'Oh yeah?' Tara smirked.

'What?' Alice frowned.

'Oh come on, you must know he's carried a torch for you for years?'

Alice's frown deepened. 'No, don't be silly. He's Ben's best friend, and he's just as worried as I am.'

'If you say so.'

Alice didn't like the implication. 'It isn't like that, Tara. Dave might have his flaws, but I don't think he'd try and do the dirty on Ben.'

'No, of course not,' Tara said matter-of-factly, as she dried herself and dressed. 'I'm sure you're right. Forget I said anything.'

Alice didn't need the stress of worrying about Dave's feelings, and pushed it from her mind. It was time to face the music, and thank those who'd made the effort to come and celebrate with them. She just had to hope she'd stay composed enough not to cry.

10

The sun was now shining brightly through the glass of the honey-moon suite, and although they'd opened the window for fresh air, only warm air was blowing in as they packed the wedding dress away in its protective liner. Breakfast had thankfully passed without incident. They'd been too early for most of the guests who'd stayed. Alice's mum had joined their table just as they were leaving and had asked for any updates, but Alice hadn't been able to tell her anything new.

'Where d'you want me to put the shoes?' Tara asked, lifting the ivory-coloured heels.

'There's a box for them somewhere,' Alice replied, without looking up. She'd been staring at the stack of prettily wrapped gifts for at least ten minutes, still trying to work out the quickest way to get them downstairs without Ben's help.

Tara suddenly appeared behind her and wrapped an arm around Alice's waist. 'It'll be okay. You'll see.'

Alice allowed her head to tip back and rest on Tara's shoulder. 'Try telling my mother that. When we left her at breakfast, she was practically in tears.'

'Do you want me to have a word?'

Alice patted Tara's hand on her waist, but shook her head. 'I appreciate the offer, but I think she just needs space. You know what she's like: this whole catastrophe casts a shadow over the family, and in her eyes the rest of her social circle will never allow her to forget it. She doesn't seem to realize that given their age, most of her friends will have forgotten anything by this time next year.'

Tara snorted and released her arm, returning to the open drawer in the dresser. 'How much underwear did you bring?' she enquired, looking into the drawer.

Alice shrugged. 'Better to be safe than sorry. Just drop them in the case with the rest and I'll sort it all out when I get home.'

They both jumped at a heavy knock at the door. Tara looked over to Alice before moving across to the door and opening it. Alice had to crane her neck to see, but her heart still skipped a beat when she saw Ben's tall figure framed in the doorway. His tie was gone, his shirt untucked and his hair in need of a wash and comb.

'I'll make myself scarce,' Tara offered, reaching for her handbag and ducking beneath Ben's arm as he came into the room.

'Are you a sight for sore eyes,' he said, with no trace of a smile. 'I wasn't sure you'd still be here.'

It was like a huge weight had been lifted from her shoulders, and suddenly she was free to run. Rushing across to him, she threw her arms around his neck and kissed him hard.

'I am so sorry,' he whispered, pressing his forehead against hers, his eyes shining with the sun's reflection.

The skin beneath her eyes moistened. 'Just tell me it's all over, that they know they had the wrong man.'

Ben pulled away but held onto her hands. 'They released me on bail; not enough evidence to charge or something, the solicitor said. I've told them everything I know, and as far as I'm aware, Dave and the others are doing the same now. It's just a case of being in the wrong place at the wrong time.'

'On bail? What does that mean? Have they cleared you or not?'

'They will once the others have confirmed my story. The solicitor feels pretty confident that they'll move on soon enough.'

It wasn't quite as positive as she'd hoped, and he must have noticed the disappointment in her face, as he quickly raised her chin to look into her eyes.

'I am so sorry I didn't tell you about that stupid trip to Bournemouth. I swear I didn't know what Dave had planned, but it all went without incident, and I thought it would only upset you if I told you where we'd been and what they'd arranged. You had enough stress on your plate with the wedding.'

She could understand that; she'd tried not to let him see the strain the preparations had been having in the final weeks, but she'd clearly failed to keep it secret.

'I wish you had told me,' she said sadly.

'I knew you'd be angry at Dave, and I didn't want your day to be spoiled because of that. He meant well – at least in his eyes he did – and I know how devastated he is about what happened yesterday. He blames himself for what happened.'

'What was it like? At the police station I mean?'

Ben lowered his eyes. 'It wasn't as bad as it could have been. They were very talkative, and treated me well. After they'd taken my prints and things, they gave me some food and a cup of tea and then this morning they started the interview just after seven. I'd told them how keen I was to get back to you, and I think they were trying to be accommodating.'

'Did they say why they arrested you?'

He nodded grimly. 'Apparently Kerry – the victim – never returned home after she'd been at our party, and because her appointment had been booked in my name . . . it's an easy enough conclusion for them to jump to.'

Alice was trying to keep her emotions in check but she couldn't ignore the paranoia taking control. Pulling her hands away from him and widening the gap, she said, 'Did you fancy her?'

Ben grimaced at the question. 'I'm not saying she wasn't pretty, but I just felt really awkward, especially having all my friends huddled round, watching. It was creepy more than anything else.'

'What did she look like?'

'Does it matter?'

She didn't answer, but glared at him as her vision fogged with tears.

'She had long blonde hair,' he said, avoiding looking at Alice's own platinum-blonde locks. 'Probably in her early twenties, slim, pretty, as I said, but not the sort of girl I'd look at now. There's only one woman for me, and you *know* that.'

'Did you sleep with her?' The words were out before Alice could stop herself.

He looked into her eyes and rested a hand on his heart. 'No I did not. I know I let you down, and I will do whatever it takes to win your trust back, but I . . .' His voice cracked under the strain. 'I-I-I need you by my side through this. I don't know why they want to try and pin this poor girl's murder on me, but they have the wrong man. I didn't do it.'

It hurt not to go over and embrace him, but Alice remained still. 'Tell me it's over and done with. Tell me they're not going to come back for you again.'

He lowered his eyes. 'They've asked me to surrender my passport while they continue their investigation.'

Alice gasped. 'That means –'

'I know,' he interrupted. 'It means we can't go on our honeymoon tonight. I'm going to phone the travel company and see what they can do for us. I'm so sorry, Alice.'

Alice furrowed her brow as another question pushed to the forefront of her mind. 'The police aren't in the habit of arresting suspects without good reason. What aren't you telling me?'

He glanced away for just the briefest of moments, but she spotted it.

'Nothing.'

His denial set her blood boiling. 'Don't lie to me, Ben. Not again. Our marriage needs to be built on trust. I don't buy that they would arrest you just because your name was the last one in her appointments book. There must be more to it than that.'

Ben clamped his eyes shut and bowed his head. 'They said they found traces of my DNA on her clothing or something. That's all. I explained to them how she'd been dancing and how it must have transferred over.'

Alice was struggling to believe anything he was saying, and then a new question leapt forward that sickened her to the stomach. 'How did they know it was your DNA?'

He kept his eyes closed. 'They took a swab inside my mouth. Standard practice apparently.'

Alice wasn't buying it. 'They wouldn't arrest you on a hunch and then hope to prove it when they'd got you to the station. If they found traces of your DNA on her clothes, they must have known that before they came here yesterday. I swear to God, Ben, you'd better start telling me the truth or I'll—'

'Okay, okay,' he sighed. 'They already had my DNA on their database. There's something I've never told you before that I'm hugely ashamed of.' Staring straight into her eyes, he said, 'Yesterday wasn't the first time I've been arrested.'

11

Alice took slow and steady breaths, as her wobbly legs threatened to spill her to the carpet of the honeymoon suite. Could this be real? Or was she still in the throes of a hideous nightmare?

'It was a long time ago,' Ben said, taking her silence as a cue to continue. 'Before I knew you. It was a wrongful arrest back then, just as it is now. I never told you because . . . because that's not who I am, and I'm deeply ashamed to have ever spent any time under suspicion of the police.'

Alice braced herself for yet another revelation. 'Why were you arrested before?'

Ben screwed up his face, clearly unsure how to spin this chapter in his life. 'I was accused of something I didn't do by a malicious woman I'd been seeing. She saw me as an opportunity to make some quick money and when I wanted to leave her she started firing all sorts of accusations at me. She went to the police and told them a pack of lies, and before I realized what was happening, they'd brought me in for questioning. The solicitor they provided told me to keep my mouth shut until he knew what evidence they thought they had against me, and he was as surprised as I was when they charged me.'

Alice reached out for the edge of the desk as her left leg buckled, and she just about managed to stay upright. 'How could you keep something like that from me?'

Ben quickly moved across and took her arm to support her. 'I know none of this can be easy to hear, and if I'd had my way you never would have found out.'

Her mouth dropped. 'Do the vows we exchanged mean nothing to you? I've not kept any secrets from you. I'm an open book, and now I'm beginning to question everything I know about you.'

'I'm still the same man you fell in love with. I swear I'm not keeping anything else from you. That period of my life isn't something I'm comfortable thinking about, let alone discussing openly.'

'Who else knows about your previous arrest? Does Dave know?'

Initially, Ben looked like he might deny it, but clearly thought better of it, and nodded. 'He was there for me, and he knew it was all a pack of lies, as this nonsense is. I swear to you, Alice, I'm the man you've always known, and my feelings for you are stronger than ever. You asked about our vows. I meant every declaration I made at that altar. I will live up to every one of those promises, for better or worse, in sickness and in health; till death do us part.'

Something niggled at the back of Alice's mind. 'If you weren't convicted of anything, why do they still have your DNA sample on record? I thought the police were only allowed to retain DNA samples when suspects were convicted.'

'So did I, but my solicitor told me this morning that because the last case reached court, they are allowed to retain the sample. I'm going to get my solicitor to fight for my sample to be destroyed. They shouldn't be allowed to ruin people's lives like this.'

She continued to watch him, feeling an invisible wall growing between them. It was like she was no longer looking at the man she'd exchanged rings with. He was a shadow of his former self. Like in some trashy soap opera when the protagonist's evil twin brother turns up and tricks the rest of the cast into thinking he's the other brother. It looked and sounded like Ben, but the Ben she knew and loved wouldn't have deceived her like this.

'About our honeymoon. I think you should still go. It seems silly for us both to miss out on the trip. My solicitor should get this all sorted in a day or so and then I'll book the next flight to join you.'

Her eyes widened. 'I'm not going on our honeymoon on my own!'

Ben took her hands in his. 'I know it isn't ideal – God knows it isn't ideal – but I know how much you were looking forward to going to Barbados. If we cancel I don't think the travel insurance company will pay out. I don't give a stuff about the money, but it would be silly to cancel the trip and then I get my passport back a couple of days later. You could fly out tonight and get the lay of the land, and then I'll join you for the last ten or so days. We can still have our honeymoon, I'll just be late to the party.'

She looked into his eyes, his beautiful brown eyes, matching his hair colour so perfectly, and so full of love. 'That's just it, Ben: it's supposed to be *our* honeymoon. Going there without you won't feel right.'

'What if I paid for Tara to go with you until I'm able to join? We can speak to each other every day until I can get a flight out, and when I arrive Tara can head home. I don't want you to miss out. You start back at school in a couple of weeks, and if you don't go on this break, it could be months until we get another chance.'

It was typical of Ben to think that throwing money at the problem would fix it, but as much as she wanted to enjoy their honeymoon in the Caribbean, it now felt tainted, along with the rest of their wedding.

He must have sensed her reticence. 'If I can't convince you to go, then we'll cancel the trip and rebook somewhere for Christmas.

You get a couple of weeks off. We can do New York, or Vegas, or even Barbados again. Wherever you want. Money is no object. We will have our honeymoon, it'll just be a bit delayed. It's up to you. I'll agree with whichever choice you make.'

Staring into those beautiful brown eyes, she felt the frost in her heart slowly start to thaw. Resting her hand on his cheek, she pulled his face into hers and kissed him, stopping only when there was a knock at the door.

'I'll send whoever it is away,' he said, pulling away and moving to the door. As he opened it, though, his parents pushed into the room, and Alice knew he wouldn't have the heart to dismiss them.

Ben's mum hugged him tightly. 'Dave said you were back. Are you okay? Did they hurt you? Is it all over?'

His cheeks reddened. 'I'm fine, Mum. Are you two okay? You don't know how sorry I am about what happened yesterday.' Ben's eyes met Alice's. 'They ruined the day.'

Ben's dad, Ray, strode across the room, still dressed for the wedding, and hugged Alice. 'How are you holding up, love?'

It was all she could to blink away the sudden onrush of emotion. 'I'm okay,' she whispered.

Ben and his mum moved away from the door and joined them by the desk.

'I can't believe they've messed everything up again,' Hermione said. 'They can't just go around pointing fingers willy-nilly. Someone should have a word. They almost messed up your chance of going to university last time, and now this on your wedding day. It isn't right!'

So that meant Ben's parents had known about his previous arrest, and hadn't thought to mention it to her on any of the occasions she'd seen them. It shouldn't have surprised her that they would know, but that didn't make it hurt any less that she had been excluded from the big family secret.

'You ought to sue them,' Hermione continued. 'That would make them think twice about trying to frame you for things you haven't done. Although actually, it wouldn't surprise me if *that woman* was somehow behind all of this.'

'Now now,' Ray soothed, putting his arm around his wife's waist. 'I'm sure yesterday had nothing to do with all that.' His eyes flickered with doubt, and he looked to Ben for reassurance. 'It isn't anything to do with all that, is it?'

Ben shook his head. 'No, no, this was something different. Apparently, me and my friends were the last people to see the girl before she was murdered, and so they put two and two together and ended up with me as the answer.'

'Whatever happened to innocent until proven guilty?' Hermione retorted.

'Can we do anything?' Ray asked. 'Do you need anything? A lift to the airport?'

Ben wrinkled his nose in distaste. 'Looks like we're going to have to postpone the honeymoon for now. The police have my passport and want me to stick around in case I can provide any further help with their enquiries. I've told them everything I remember about that night, but they were the grounds on which they released me,' he added with a disappointed sigh.

Alice remained in silence, watching the three of them speak dismissively of the police and their involvement in ruining the big day. What they failed to acknowledge through all of their anger was that ultimately an innocent woman had lost her life. Yes it was frustrating that the police had chosen such an inopportune moment to locate Ben, but their intention wasn't to spoil the wedding; they'd been charged with getting a murderer off the streets. For all she and Ben knew, this Kerry Valentine had family who were grieving her loss, and the frustrations of yesterday evening paled into insignificance against that.

'I need some air,' Alice suddenly said, cutting off Ben mid-sentence.

'Of course, of course,' Ray said, shuffling his wife towards the door. 'I'm sure the two of you have a lot to talk about. We should make ourselves scarce, but if there's anything you need – either of you – don't hesitate to phone.' He directed his attention to Alice. 'Remember, you're family now, and nothing is too much to ask. Okay?'

Alice forced herself to smile in acknowledgement and went out on to the balcony, sucking in deep breaths as Ben showed his parents to the door.

She heard the door close, followed by Ben dropping to the bed. 'You know the worst part of all this is the effect it's had on you. I mean, spending the night in that cell was horrible – really sobering – and then being quizzed for three straight hours this morning, but all I keep reliving is that look on your face when they put the cuffs on my wrists. It kills me that they ruined our big day, a day you'd spent so long organizing.'

Alice looked over at the beautiful green lawn and lake, a view she had fallen in love with when they'd picked this venue, but which now just served as a reminder of what could have been.

'Can we get out of here?' she asked. 'I just want to put all of this behind us as quickly as possible.'

'Sure,' Ben said. 'Let's pack our stuff and check out. Then I will spend the rest of the day proving to you how important you are to me.'

She turned to face him. 'Just promise me one thing: no more secrets.'

He immediately agreed, but she couldn't ignore the feeling that her nightmare was only just beginning.

12

The main reception desk in the grand lobby of Old Mill Lodge had the look and feel of living history; the thick varnish and ornate carvings were clearly made a time long ago. As Alice patiently waited in line for the checkout queue to process, she couldn't help but wonder about the range of people who had passed through the hotel over the years, each with their own story and reason for staying in the grand building. How many of the brides and grooms who'd celebrated their nuptials in the same room as she and Ben were still happily married? She'd bet none had had their ceremony interrupted in quite the same way.

Ben had acquired a luggage trolley from somewhere and was busy transporting their luggage and stack of gifts down to the large taxi he had ordered. Although it had taken months of visiting different venues before she'd chosen this one, she wouldn't now care if she never laid eyes on the hotel again.

The elderly couple ahead of Alice moved to the front of the queue and began to explain their enquiry to the young lady behind the desk. Olive-skinned and with jet black hair, the receptionist spoke with an accent Alice couldn't place, but her grasp of English was as strong as any native.

'It's so inherently British, isn't it?' the man behind her commented.

Alice turned and looked at the man in the tan suit and red tie, smiling in her direction. He was alone with a small blue holdall at his feet.

'Excuse me?' Alice asked.

'Queuing,' he confirmed. 'There's nothing us Brits like quite as much as a queue, is there? I mean, on a day as glorious as this, when we should be embracing nature at her finest, we choose to stand in a stuffy room in an orderly manner.' He smiled warmly. 'I'm sorry, it always makes me laugh. This sort of thing just doesn't happen in other countries.'

Alice politely smiled back. 'No, I suppose you're right. At least we're nearly at the front.'

'Are you checking in or out?'

'Out,' she said, smiling again.

'Ah, well, did you happen to dine in the hotel's restaurant last night? I'm looking for recommendations of where I can get a nice piece of sirloin for my supper.'

Alice forced a thin smile. 'We didn't eat here last night, I'm afraid.'

'Not to worry,' he continued, a mischievous look on his face. 'Here, you weren't at the wedding where the groom was arrested, were you?'

Shock went through her. 'How did you hear about that?'

'I overheard one of the staff talking about it. Were you there then?'

She nodded, and subconsciously covered her wedding ring with her right hand.

'Oh, how awful,' he continued. 'The poor bride. Probably the last thing she expected to happen. Can you imagine how awful that would be? Just tied the knot and then learning that your husband is a murderer?'

Alice had to bite her tongue to keep quiet, and took a second glance towards the elderly couple in front who were still chatting away to the woman behind the counter.

'I wonder if maybe she already knew,' the man mused. 'I mean, that's what they say, isn't it? Spouses always know deep down when their partner is up to no good. They might claim innocence, but it's like a sixth sense, isn't it? Are you friends of the couple, then?' His cheeks suddenly reddened. 'Heavens, have I spoken out of turn? You're not related to one of them, are you?'

'Sort of, but I won't take offence.'

His cheeks were now glowing. 'You'll have to forgive me, I'm always putting my foot in it. Please accept my apologies.'

'It's fine,' she said as casually as her bubbling anger would allow.

If the hotel staff were gossiping about the incident, it was possible the story could leak to the press, and the last thing she and Ben needed was their privacy to be trampled on, particularly as the police still hadn't officially ruled Ben out of their inquiry.

'Are you related to the bride or groom?' the stranger pressed.

'Bride,' she said, still not prepared to tell him it was her horrid nightmare he'd just described.

'How's she coping? Have they said if or when the husband will be released from prison?'

'I'm sorry,' she said abruptly, 'but I'd rather not talk about it. I think they should just be left to their privacy.'

'Of course, of course, and far be it for me to be a spreader of idle gossip. Have you known them long?'

The couple in front moved on and the woman behind the counter thanked Alice for her patience and asked how she could help.

'I'd like to check out please,' Alice said absently, sliding the key across the desk.

'You are checking out of the honeymoon suite?' the receptionist asked.

Alice's cheeks burned as she nodded, refusing to meet the eye of the suited man who could overhear the entire conversation.

'How was the wedding? Did everything go as well as you hoped?'

Alice wasn't ready to even try and answer that question, and simply nodded. 'It's a lovely venue.'

'Was the catering and organization up to scratch?'

Clearly the receptionist hadn't been working yesterday, and had yet to hear the gossip. Either that or she was doing an incredible job of playing dumb.

'It was all fine. I'm sorry, can we hurry this up? My husband is waiting for me.'

'Certainly, madam,' the receptionist said, standing. 'I'll just go and get your receipt and you should be good to go.' With that she disappeared into the small office behind her.

Alice could see the man straining to make eye contact with her, but she refused to acknowledge him.

He slid a business card across the desk towards her. 'If you'd like to tell your side of the story, I'm sure we can make it worth your while. Right now, you'll probably want to throw the offer back in my face, but think about it over the next day or so.'

She looked down at the card for 'Liam O'Neill, Freelance Journalist', and felt bile building in the back of her throat. So that's why he was so interested in the details of the big day. Alice left the card where it was.

'People will want to hear your story, Alice. I'm sorry if I misled you to begin with. You should know that I'm on your side with this. I don't really think you knew what your husband was capable of, but to learn about what he'd done on your wedding day, it beggars belief.' He paused, allowing her to process. 'The story will get out, as these things do. It's up to you whether people hear your side of it, or an amalgamation of other eye witness accounts and suppositions. Think about it.'

'Here's your receipt,' the receptionist said, offering the sheet of paper to Alice.

'All checked out?' Ben's voice suddenly said over her shoulder.

Turning, Alice was relieved to see him, and reached for his hand, pulling him closer.

'Is everything okay?' he asked. 'You look like you've just seen a ghost.'

She turned back to point out the grubby little journalist, but saw that he had scarpered.

'It's nothing,' she said. 'Is the car all packed?'

'Yep, and I even stopped by to speak to your mum, just to reassure her that I'm sorting everything. She wasn't happy, but she listened to what I had to say. I suggested she come round tonight, unless you've changed your mind about the flights.'

The thought of escaping people like Liam O'Neill suddenly sounded very appealing, but then how would it look if she left Ben to face the music alone?

'Let's just go home, I've got a pounding headache. I feel like everyone is watching us, and I'd rather be somewhere alone.'

He wrapped his arm around her shoulders and led her outside to where the taxi was waiting. Dave, Scott and Abdul were the only guests gathered to wish the bride and groom on their way.

Taking one final look at the venue that had promised so much joy and happiness, Alice wondered whether they had seen the last of Liam O'Neill, or whether he would just be the first in a long line of people wanting a piece of their lives.

13

Silence descended on the car journey through the New Forest, passing wild ponies, donkeys, and tourists making the most of the luscious summer heat. Families sat on picnic blankets, enjoying good food and conversation, while children hunted for frogs and fairies in the undergrowth. The scene was picture-perfect, and Alice couldn't help but imagine the day when she and Ben would load the car with their own children and head out into the wilds of the countryside.

Despite patches of heavy traffic, they made it back to the village of Chilworth, a stone's throw from the end of the M3 motorway, inside thirty minutes. A blue saloon car parked in front of the gates to the property greeted them as they turned onto their road. It had no formal markings, but even Alice could tell what profession its driver had.

'Let's just keep driving,' Alice suggested. 'Let's not let them ruin another day.' She meant every word. They could drive past the house and head to her mother's or one of their friends' houses – anywhere to keep the wolves at bay for a while longer.

Ben shook his head. 'We can't run forever.' With that he pressed the remote control to open the automatic gates, instructing the taxi driver to go past the blue saloon and continue up the driveway.

To their right, the large house stood in all its glory, the view from the road blocked by the high fence and bushes, looking magnificent and modern as the sun reflected off the large windows. Despite the proximity to the motorway, only the slightest hum of traffic carried on the wind. To the left of the main building stood the brick enclosure housing the near-Olympic-size swimming pool and hot tub; to the right, the double garage containing her Audi and his Mercedes. Their bedroom was the largest in the centre of the first floor, with two smaller rooms each side; a sixth bedroom was downstairs towards the rear of the property.

Ben and the driver were first out of the car, and as the bags were removed from the boot, the blue saloon pulled up alongside them. Ben paid the driver and thanked him, waiting until the taxi was through the gates before closing them once more with the remote control.

He turned to Alice and whispered, 'Why don't you head inside, and leave me to deal with whoever this is?'

Alice pulled her handbag over her shoulder like a sash. 'We'll do this together. We'll show them we're united.'

The two plainclothes detectives exited the blue car, lifting their identification into the air.

The woman spoke first. 'Ben Goodman? I'm DC Vanessa Hazelton, and this is my colleague, DC Wayne McTeal.'

'What do you want?' Ben asked defiantly. 'I told you lot everything I know. I didn't kill that poor girl.'

'We're not here to arrest you, Mr Goodman,' Hazelton replied. 'I believe DI Vernon would have informed you we need to collect the clothes you were wearing on Saturday night? That's what we're here to do.'

Hazelton had a quiet voice, but there was a determination in the tone that suggested she was used to getting what she wanted. A pretty face, her brown hair was cut short, giving her an androgynous look. If it weren't for the two bulges in her pink blouse, it would be easy to mistake her for a teenager.

Alice followed Ben and the detectives through the front door. The high ceiling in the grand hall kept the room light and airy, but as they moved through to the kitchen, the sun's rays on the large bifold doors meant the room was obnoxiously warm and stuffy. It had been three days since Alice was here last. Stepping to the panel on the wall, she adjusted the temperature on the thermostat and welcomed the cool rush of air as the ceiling fans kicked in.

Hazelton had followed Alice into the kitchen while Ben had taken McTeal upstairs.

'Once we have the clothes bagged up, we'll leave you to enjoy the rest of your weekend,' Hazelton offered with an empathetic smile. 'I assume Ben has told you why we took him to the station yesterday?'

'Of course. We don't keep secrets.'

Hazelton's face remained passive.

'He didn't do it, you know,' Alice suddenly blurted. 'He told me he didn't and I believe him.'

'I'm in no position to disagree, Mrs Goodman.'

The comment threw Alice. 'You don't think he did it either?'

'I'm not paid to have an opinion. I just follow the evidence. With all due respect, Mrs Goodman, a young woman has been brutally murdered. Whomever was responsible is still out there, somewhere on the streets evading justice. He – or *she* – needs to be brought to justice, and before they do it again. Our only priority is finding this individual. Imagine if she was your best friend: wouldn't you want us to do everything in our power to find her killer?'

Alice sipped her water but remained quiet.

Hazelton moved across to the bifold doors, staring out. 'You have a beautiful garden. How far back does it stretch? Sixty feet?'

'Something like that,' Alice sighed.

'Is this your own work or do you have a gardener?' Hazelton continued, pointing at the raised flowerbed that ran the length of the lawn on the left side.

'A gardener tends to it once a week. I'm not green-fingered.'

'Nor me,' Hazelton smiled. 'I live in a third-storey flat, and whenever my mum brings over a houseplant, it never lasts more than a month. Sometimes I don't know why she bothers.'

'Are you from Southampton?'

'No, I'm based in Bournemouth, but the inquiry is being led by the Major Crimes Team here in Southampton, so a small group of us are here supporting.' She paused. 'It isn't my place to say, but I'm sorry that the arrest was so public. Ordinarily, someone would have had a quiet word and been more discreet; I don't know why DI Vernon made such a big fuss.'

Ben appeared in the kitchen, McTeal following behind, holding a large sealed bag and wearing blue protective gloves.

'Did you get it?' Hazelton asked him.

McTeal lifted the bag and nodded.

'You won't find anything on the clothes as they've been cleaned,' Ben warned. 'If I'd known I would need to prove my innocence, I would have left them unwashed.'

Hazelton approached him, meeting his stare. 'That's all right, Mr Goodman, you'd be surprised at how difficult it is to remove the telltale signs of blood. We'll have our forensic specialists review the clothing and let you know the results. Of course, these could be key to ruling you out of our investigation. Let's hope so, hey?'

'They will,' Ben replied curtly, before following them back to the front door and showing them out.

14

A long soak in the bathtub was exactly what Alice needed. Something DC Hazelton had said had stuck with her: what if it was her best friend who'd been brutally murdered? Wouldn't she give anything to see the killer caught and punished? Would she really care how many innocent people were arrested along the way?

Ben had said he would phone the holiday and travel insurance companies and explain the situation, to see if anything could be done to reclaim any of the payment they'd made, but he hadn't sounded hopeful as he'd reached for the phone.

As the temperature of the water cooled, Alice climbed out of the tub and returned to the bedroom, drying herself with a towel before dressing. Their bedroom faced out to the garden, but she'd closed the curtains when the bath had been filling. Heading to their shared wardrobe, she pulled out a fresh summer dress to wear, thinking they would just order takeaway from the local Chinese restaurant for dinner. They should have been at the airport getting ready to check-in now, and she wasn't sure what food was in the house. Spotting Ben outside on the decking with a bottle of beer in his hand, she saw Dave nursing a bottle in a chair to his right.

'Dave's just come from the police station,' Ben explained, as Alice joined them outside in the warmth. 'Tell her what you told me.'

Dave put the bottle to his lips and took a long swig, wiping his mouth with the back of his hand. 'The solicitor reckons they're clutching at straws. They pulled Ben in on account of the DNA, but had it not been there they'd be clueless. They've put some hotshot detective inspector in charge; he's the one who made the arrest. I overheard one of them say he's made some promise to his boss that he'll nail the killer within forty-eight hours, but they're nowhere near.'

Alice still wasn't happy that Ben's DNA had been so readily available to the detective in charge, and she still didn't really know what he'd been charged with the first time around. It wasn't fair to put Dave in the awkward position of hearing her ask Ben now, but she would demand the truth as soon as Dave was gone.

'I told them where the bar was, and how Abdul had arranged for us to be there,' Dave continued. 'Gave them the names of all those who were there and a detailed timeline of what we did and when. They're planning to scour the area for signs of blood or a struggle or something. They're hoping the incident might have been captured on CCTV, but I told them I don't remember seeing much in the way of cameras where we were.'

'I don't understand why they can't return Ben's passport,' Alice said.

'I guess they have to rule him out completely before they can give it back. I only stopped by to see if there's anything the two of you need,' Dave said. 'You know I'm there for you – both of you – and if there's anything you want or need, please just let me know.'

'Cheers, man,' Ben said, shaking his hand. 'Appreciate it. Can you send me over the copies of the pictures from that weekend? You know, the ones you shared with the police? I'll forward them onto the solicitor.'

Dave pulled out his phone and began to tap at the screen.

'Pictures?' Alice asked. 'Can I have a look?'

Dave fired a nervous glance at Ben.

'It's all right,' Ben confirmed. 'I've told Alice exactly what happened. She knows everything.'

Shrugging, Dave handed over the phone, opened on the photos app. Alice stared at the screen, an image of Ben and Dave looking worse for wear in the back of a taxi. The next three images were of the group of men laughing and messing about, empty shot glasses in the background. Then a picture of a woman in a miniskirt and black leather jacket appeared on the screen, and Alice nearly dropped the phone.

'Is this her? Is this Kerry Valentine?' Alice asked.

Dave nodded grimly. 'It's hard to imagine that only hours after this picture was taken, she was dead.'

Alice studied the photograph. Kerry Valentine was exactly as Ben had described: a petite blonde who looked like she should still be in college, though her face also bore the strain of someone who had suffered more than her fair share of knocks over the years. Alice was certain she hadn't seen the face among those she'd searched for online last night, but the image on Dave's phone was grainy.

Alice frowned as a thought stirred. 'How do you know she died only *hours* after the photograph?'

Dave's eyes narrowed. 'That's what one of the detectives said. Reckoned they knew for certain that she'd been dead for several days, though they didn't confirm if she died on Saturday night or Sunday. The victim was still wearing the clothes she had on in that picture apparently.'

Alice continued to scroll through the photos of Kerry in various stages of undress; and the ones of Ben licking the cream from her body made Alice want to gag as the images seared on her memory. The next picture had been captured outside; Ben's trousers were down around his ankles and his shirt was unfastened, his arms draped around a lamppost. This was followed by a shot of the rest of the group, laughing at Ben's predicament. Then there was a second shot of Ben at the lamppost, but this time he was sitting on the floor, his head bent low, like he was sleeping.

'That's the one I took when we got back from the off-licence,' Dave explained, pointing at the screen. 'That was the only time we weren't together all night. Which is what I told the police.'

Ben stood, his bottle now empty. 'You want another?'

Dave shook his head. 'I'd better not, I'm driving. Also, I'd better check on Abdul, his boss is probably gonna give him shit about letting us use the venue. Besides, I should probably get out of your hair. The last thing you two need is me hanging around as some third wheel.'

'Wait, don't go yet,' Ben said, retaking his seat. 'There was something else I wanted to run past you. The detective who interviewed me at the station wanted to know if anyone might have it in for me. Asked if I have any enemies, or whether anyone had made any threats.'

Dave frowned. 'Yeah they asked me the same thing. I said I didn't know, that nothing sprang to mind. What did you say?'

'The same thing, but it got me wondering whether anyone could be trying to set me up to take the fall for this. I do business with several multimillion pound companies, and my competitors can be pretty ruthless. What if one of them followed us to Bournemouth and attacked Kerry, knowing the police would tie us lot back to it?'

'You want me to ask around?' Dave asked gruffly.

'Please. I'm probably just being paranoid, but I'd like to know for sure. Kick over some stones and see what you find out.'

Dave nodded and handed Ben the empty bottle as the two of them proceeded through the house, leaving Alice alone in the garden.

Her phone started ringing and, seeing Faye's profile picture on the screen, she quickly answered. 'Hi, sweetie.'

Alice hadn't anticipated hearing Faye sobbing. 'I'm . . . I'm . . . I'm . . . sorry,' she moaned, her breathing erratic. 'I . . . didn't . . . know . . , who . . . else . . . to . . . call.'

A ball of worry developed rapidly in the pit of Alice's stomach. 'Faye, what's going on?'

'It's . . . it's . . . Johnny . . . He's . . . left . . . me.'

15

Five minutes later, Alice closed the patio door and joined Ben in the living room. 'You're not going to believe this! Johnny just walked out on Faye. Packed his bag and took the car. She's distraught!'

Ben's mouth dropped in astonishment. 'I knew they'd been having some problems, but I never expected—'

Alice's brow furrowed. 'You knew they were having problems? How long for? Why didn't you tell me?'

'I assumed Faye would have told you. I'm sorry.'

Alice wasn't sure what hurt most: that Ben had known and didn't tell her, or that her good friend had kept her troubles from her.

'They've been seeing a marriage guidance counsellor for a few months,' Ben continued. 'I honestly thought you knew. I thought that was why you'd asked her to be a bridesmaid, as an act of solidarity.'

Alice scoured the kitchen worktops for her handbag. 'I need to go over there. She needs a friend.'

Ben reached for her hand in a calming gesture. 'We shouldn't get involved. Okay? I don't mean to be cruel, but what Johnny and Faye get up to in their own time is none of our business.'

'She made it my business when she called,' Alice said firmly. 'I'm not going over there to interfere, I just want to support her.'

He sighed loudly. 'Just remember that things between them probably aren't as rosy as they looked yesterday. Sure, on the surface they're a lovely couple who can't do enough for others, but behind closed doors their relationship hits highs and lows.'

She could tell Ben was holding out on her. Standing in silence, she allowed his discomfort to grow until he felt compelled to break the silence.

'All right, all right,' he said. 'She gets jealous, that's what he says. She hates that he works in a large office where there are lots of attractive women. He tells me she checks his phone constantly. He's got one of those fingerprint readers, but she knows his PIN and unlocks the screen when she thinks he's not looking; checking emails; text messages; private messages. She's obsessed with who he speaks to. Of course they end up having fights about it, and when we were in Bournemouth he told me he's not sure how much more of it he can take. I assume you saw what happened at the airport before you flew out to Paris?'

Alice remembered that Faye had been late checking in and had almost missed the flight, but had caught up with the rest of the group at the boarding gate. She'd looked upset, but had blamed it on traffic and Johnny being late home to drive her. Before Alice had been able to get Faye alone, the group were all seated and the champagne was flowing. In hindsight, Faye hadn't been her usual bubbly self on the trip, but Alice had put that down to her missing her daughter back home.

'What happened at the airport?' Alice questioned.

'You mean she didn't tell you? From what Johnny said, she almost cried off going to Paris altogether. They were late arriving, right? *That's* why! She was all packed and ready to go, but then she started to get paranoid about leaving Johnny at home. She doesn't trust him, but he's never given her any reason not to. He's never cheated on her – at least, not that I know about – and I think her paranoia stems from some ex who did the dirty. She's got serious psychological issues and needs her head examining.' He stopped himself when he remembered who he was talking to. 'I'm sorry, I know she's your friend, but I'm just relaying how crazy she's making him. All *this* – the phone call to you – it's probably Faye making a mountain out of a molehill. They've probably just had a barney and he's left to cool down and clear his head.'

Alice picked up her bag, uncertain whether or not to go. 'Was she really going to cry off coming to Paris? Even though the tickets and hotel were all booked?'

'He had to drag her to the airport, telling her how disappointed you all would be if she missed the trip. Even as they pulled up at the drop-off point, she was threatening to phone you and make up an excuse about their daughter being unwell. He had to march her through the security barrier out of fear that she would leave the airport as soon as he'd gone. Did she really not tell you any of this?'

Alice's guilt was on overload. Had she been so caught up in organizing hers and Ben's big day that she'd missed her friend's unhappiness? It would be typical of Faye to bottle up her own troubles, to avoid spoiling the wedding. Now that it was over, did Faye feel it was the time to come clean?

'I'll phone Johnny for you if you want,' Ben offered. 'Check that everything's okay and find out what's really going on.'

Alice thought back to last night. Her own world had seemingly fallen apart when Ben had been dragged off by the police and had it not been for Tara's support, God only knew what state she'd have been in now.

'No,' Alice said, pulling her handbag over her shoulder. 'Faye's my friend and she needs my help.'

16

The late afternoon traffic was light and Alice reached Johnny and Faye's semi-detached home within fifteen minutes. The house was part of a newly built estate, the orange brickwork not yet faded by decades of harsh sunlight. Each surrounding property had the same rectangle of lawn at the front, a driveway barely wide enough for the average modern car, and the same art deco style of front doors. It looked a warm and friendly place to live, but then the average house price was ten per cent higher than the houses on the older estate that led to this one.

There was no sign of Johnny's car on the driveway as Alice made her way up to the front door, pressing the doorbell. Faye opened it a moment later, eyes red, cheeks puffy. As soon as she saw Alice, fresh tears welled.

Wrapping her arms around Alice's shoulders, Faye pulled her into the house. 'I can't believe you came. I'm so sorry, I know you should be enjoying your honeymoon, but I didn't know who else to turn to.'

Alice closed the door behind them. 'That's what friends are for. I had no idea things were so bad. I wish you'd told me sooner.'

Faye broke the embrace and nodded, heading to the kitchen. Alice followed slowly behind, leaving her handbag by the front door. Faye was already filling a second glass with wine and passed it to Alice, who had little choice but to accept it. The two empty bottles next to the dustbin told Alice everything she needed to know about Faye's current state of mind.

'Let's go and sit down,' Alice suggested, as Faye tottered unsteadily.

Leading them to the adjoining lounge, Alice made sure Faye was seated before resting a box of tissues on the table next to her and dropping into the closest armchair.

The large flat-screen television on the main wall dominated the room, and made it feel like they were in a tiny cinema. Surround speakers stood in each corner of the room. Johnny had always been into his gadgets, and this monolith was just the latest addition.

'What's been going on?' Alice asked, keen not to mention Ben's earlier revelations. 'Have you heard from Johnny since you phoned me?'

Faye reached for one of the tissues and dabbed her eyes. 'No.'

Alice chose her words carefully. 'Does this have something to do with what happened at the airport last weekend? I knew something wasn't right when you reached the boarding gate. You looked like you'd been crying, but you didn't seem to want to say anything. I'm sorry if I made you feel you couldn't be honest with me.'

Faye grimaced as she wiped her nose. 'You didn't need to be dealing with all my shit with everything you had on. Now I feel even worse for reaching out considering what you and Ben must be dealing with after last night.'

'It's okay,' Alice said quickly. 'It was all just a misunderstanding. Ben's back at home now.'

Faye nodded. 'I never doubted it. He's a good one, your Ben. You chose well. Unlike me.'

The sound of a child's laughter upstairs revealed where Faye's daughter, Isabella, had been squirrelled away.

'Is Isabella here? I'd love to say hi,' Alice asked, glancing back at Faye's wine glass.

'She's watching a movie in my room. I didn't want her to see me crying, though she must have heard Johnny shouting before he left. It's all such a mess.'

Alice quickly placed her hand on Faye's. 'None of this is your fault.'

'We've been going to marriage counselling,' Faye suddenly blurted. 'Not that I think it's helping. Especially after today.'

Alice hadn't wanted to mention it herself, and was relieved Faye had brought it up. 'Things haven't been good for a while then?'

Faye shook her head. 'Nobody ever warns you about the fights. On the surface, married couples always seem so happy, but things have been strained between the two of us for nearly a year now. We put a brave face on it when out in public, but it's hard, you know?'

Alice heard her phone beep and excused herself to fetch her handbag. Opening it, she saw a message from Ben asking whether she'd arrived safely, and confirming Dave was going to drop some groceries around later on. She quickly messaged back to say she'd arrived and that there was no sign of Johnny at the house. As she carried the phone back into the room, she froze when she saw a small hand towel on the floor, stained with patches of blood. Picking it up, she marched back to Faye, her mind connecting the dots.

She'd thought Faye's cheeks had looked puffy from crying, but now as she looked closer, she noticed the unmistakeable shade of purple starting to peek through the yellowing of the skin around Faye's eyes.

'Did Johnny do this?' Alice asked.

Faye looked up, and gently nodded as her eyes fell on the towel.

'How many times has he hit you?'

Faye's eyes watered. 'I know he doesn't mean to do it. He just gets stressed out, with me, with Isabella, with work. If things aren't right when he gets home, we argue and then he lashes out. He's always so sorry afterwards and promises it won't happen again, but then something else will trigger it.'

'It's never okay for him to strike you. You know that, right? If Ben ever . . .' her words trailed off. 'I wouldn't give him a second chance to repeat the mistake.'

'It was my fault today. I knew that challenging him would end in him lashing out, but I needed to know.'

'Know what?'

'I wanted to know the truth about that weekend in Bournemouth.' Faye dabbed her nose again, the flakes of blood inside her nostrils now so apparent. 'I overheard Johnny and Dave chatting this morning. Dave was telling him he needed to go to the police station and make a statement about the weekend they'd organized for Ben. I asked what they were talking about and they refused to say before the two of them left for the police station together. So when Johnny got home I was determined to find out what he'd been keeping from me. He eventually admitted where they'd been and how they'd hired that poor girl to strip for them. I was fuming – understandably so – and that's when he punched me. Usually it's just a slap or a blow to the midriff, but today he punched me hard in the face, twice. My nose wouldn't stop bleeding for ages, but he just didn't seem to care. He stormed out and drove away.'

Ben had made out that the marriage counselling was because of Faye's crazy jealousy, but now Alice could see the real reason, and her heart ached for her broken friend on the sofa.

'You need to speak to the police,' Alice encouraged. 'Johnny has no right to treat you this way. You need help. If you want to come and stay with us while you sort out a divorce, then that's fine.'

Faye's head shot up. 'I'm not divorcing him.'

'What? Why not?'

'Because I love him. I know he doesn't deserve to have me stick by him, but he wasn't always this way. If he gets some help to deal with his stress and anger, I know I can find the man I first fell in love with – the man who treated me like a princess and would do anything for me. He's still in there.'

Alice dropped to her knees, near Faye's feet. 'Sweetie, I'm only telling you this because I'm your friend and I don't want to see you hurt, but you are lying to yourself if you think things are going to get better. I don't doubt that you love him, but you can't allow yourself to suffer at his hands. What if he strikes out at Isabella? You'd never forgive yourself.'

Faye's face fell. 'He wouldn't.'

'How can you be so sure? I bet you never thought he'd hit you until the first time it happened. For both of your sakes you need to kick him out of the house, at least until he's sorted himself out. From what you've said, his violence is escalating – what if next time he goes further?'

As she said the words, Alice couldn't help but wonder whether it was already too late. What if the police were right to be looking at the members of the stag party but had arrested the wrong man?

'I can't leave you here,' she continued. 'I want you to pack up some things for you and Isabella and come home with me tonight.'

Faye reached for her glass and took a long gulp, draining half of the contents. 'No. It's bad enough that I've interrupted the first day of your honeymoon, you don't need me getting in the way.'

'We cancelled our trip away because the police took Ben's passport. If anything, I could do with the company.'

'I can't drag Isabella from her home. It would be too difficult to explain.'

'Okay, well go to your mum's instead. She'll understand.'

Faye shook her head. 'I can't tell her. I know I sound crazy, but Johnny will get better. This was a real turning point. I made a vow all those years ago to stick with him in sickness and in health. How would it look if I abandoned our marriage at the first hurdle?'

Alice wanted to understand, but couldn't accept leaving her friend in danger. 'What happens when he flies off the handle again, and does more permanent damage? You need to report him, Faye. Even if you decide to give him a second chance, I don't think the two of you should stay under the same roof for the moment.'

Faye wasn't listening, instead stumbling back to the kitchen to top up her glass once more, leaving Alice to wonder how much Ben really knew about Johnny's behaviour.

17

The sun hung low in the sky as Alice drove back through the electric gates. She had left the house only when Faye's mum had arrived to take over. Faye had reluctantly agreed that Alice could call her, if for no other reason than to watch over four-year-old Isabella. There'd been no sign of Johnny returning, and Alice hoped he had crashed on someone's sofa and was in the process of sobering up.

Closing her front door, Alice was surprised to hear voices coming from the living room at the rear of the house, and as she pushed the door open with her foot she immediately recognized Dave's raucous laugh as Ben cracked a lame joke.

'Finally!' Ben said, turning and spotting her. 'We bought Chinese. I got you your usual, but you might want to reheat it in the microwave. I thought you'd have been back ages ago. How was everything with Faye?'

'I'll tell you later,' Alice said, nodding in Dave's direction.

Dave had a can of beer in his hand, and from the empty cans scattered over the coffee table in the centre of the room it looked like they'd both had a few. Some wildlife documentary was playing out on the big screen, but the volume was low.

'The food's in the kitchen,' Ben added.

'Great, thanks,' Alice replied. 'Can I get either of you anything?'

'We're fine,' Ben said, opening a fresh can.

The kitchen was in a worse state than the living room. Empty white carrier bags, open foil pots containing the remains of whatever the boys had ordered, spoons with grains of rice stuck to them, and then two foil pots stacked on top of a plate, presumably her dinner. Moving across, she spotted three bags of groceries on the floor near the fridge. As she looked inside them, she saw the frozen goods slowly thawing.

'Hey, babe,' Ben called from the other room. 'Can you bring some more beers in when you come back? Should be a six-pack in the fridge.'

She shouldn't have been so surprised. The two of them had been inseparable for as long as she'd known them. That's what came from two men who'd known each other since school, and had survived the perilous challenge of falling for the same woman. It was nice that they had such a strong friendship, particularly given neither had any siblings, but it did irk her when they were in one of these moods, where it was like she didn't even exist.

Carrying the cans through, she placed them on the table nearest Ben, but neither he nor Dave looked up to acknowledge or thank her. Returning to the kitchen she reheated her food and carried it upstairs to the bedroom.

Half an hour later, and with nothing exciting on the television, she ventured back downstairs. The television volume was much louder now, and as she carried her plate through to the kitchen she was sure they hadn't even noticed she hadn't joined them in the living room. They'd made no effort to clean up the mess in the kitchen and she was almost certain they'd yet to leave their pit in the other room. It was now after nine and the sky was darkening as she stared out at the back garden. The thought of filling the sink with hot soapy water and attacking the greasy plates wasn't tempting, and as she lowered the kitchen blind she couldn't prevent a yawn escaping her mouth.

All in all it had been a stressful few days. Firstly worrying about whether everything would go to plan for the big day and if people would enjoy themselves, then the arrest. She had hardly slept last night, and now it was catching up with her.

Ready to tell Ben she was heading to bed, she was about to push the lounge door open when she heard him and Dave talking animatedly.

'Yeah, but don't forget what happened in Malia,' Dave said, interrupting Ben mid-sentence.

Alice pushed her ear closer to the door, careful not to knock it as she strained to overhear what they were saying.

'Don't get me started on Malia,' Ben countered. 'I knew we'd have trouble before we went out that night. That's just how he is.'

'We never should have brought him along with us.'

'We couldn't leave him at home. How would it have looked, all the lads invited apart from *him*? We had no choice.'

'Yeah but we should've had a word with him, told him to keep his dick in his trousers for once.'

Ben snorted. 'You can talk. He wasn't the only one who pulled in Malia from what I remember.'

'Yeah, but I didn't get off with the missus of some hard nut looking for trouble. It's amazing we didn't get arrested by the local cops after the mess we left at that bar.'

'That wasn't technically our fault. They threw the first punch. We had no choice but to defend him, did we?'

Alice rested her hands on the door frame and leaned her ear closer to the gap.

'I was as nervous as anything when we made it to the airport,' Dave admitted. 'I was sure the Malia police would be waiting at passport control, but I guess we got lucky.'

'I could've killed him for that.'

'You and me both, bruv, but now I can't stop thinking that maybe he had something to do with what happened to that girl in Bournemouth. Did you see the look on his face when she was squirting that cream on her tits?'

'Yeah, but he wouldn't do anything like that,' Ben said, the doubt in his voice obvious. 'Would he?'

'Hey, the last thing I want to think is that one of our mates could have gone after her and killed her, but you can't say the thought hasn't crossed your mind too.'

'Listen, we'd better shut up about this for now, yeah? I'd better go and check on Alice, let her know you're gonna stay over. You want another beer while I'm up?'

Alice didn't wait for Dave's answer, peeling away from the door and racing up the stairs on tiptoes, hoping Ben was too drunk to hear her padding on the carpet.

18

The trouble with falling asleep before ten p.m. was that Alice's body woke her at six, fully rested and raring to go. As she lay in bed, the sunlight creeping beneath the line of the curtains, she tried hard to drift back to sleep. After ten minutes of trying to get comfortable, she gave up, pushing the blanket back and stretching her arms up and over her head.

Ben hadn't come up to bed, and she didn't need more than one guess to figure out where she'd find him: exactly where she'd left him and Dave.

The memory of what she'd heard from outside the lounge door flashed through her mind: *now I can't stop thinking that maybe he had something to do with what happened to that girl.*

The question was who was the *he* they were referring to? Dave hadn't confirmed exactly who had gone to Bournemouth with them, though she knew Johnny was there, as was that Abdul who had the keys to the abandoned bar they'd ended up in. But who else? Dave had described it as a night out for those who hadn't made it to Malia the week before, but from what she'd overheard, whoever *he* was had been at both stag parties.

And, what was that they'd said about a fight in Malia? Ben hadn't mentioned a fight, but now that she thought about it, she had noticed some bruising on his torso after the trip. He'd dismissed it as a drunken stumble, which she'd initially accepted, knowing how clumsy he could be even when sober. Thinking back to the bruising, she tried to remember whether it had resembled fist marks, but came up blank.

Showering and dressing, Alice tried to think things through. She didn't know whether the police had confirmed the victim's exact time of death – Ben certainly hadn't mentioned it – so had he and Dave only been speculating about one of their group being involved? Whatever the answer though, clearly they knew more than they'd been letting on until now.

Reaching for her phone, she opened Facebook and loaded up Ben's profile. He'd been tagged in a few pictures from the trip to Malia, and she located the group shot she'd been searching for and used her fingers to zoom in.

Studying the faces from left to right, she spotted Ben and Dave, Johnny, Scott, Pete, James, and two others she'd met but whose names she couldn't recall. Eight of them in total. Could one of this group have been responsible for killing Kerry?

She shuddered at the thought. She'd met all of these men. Could one of them really be a killer?

What she needed now was an image of the group from Bournemouth, but given the secrecy of the event, she doubted Ben would have been careless enough to take any photographs. Even if he had, he wouldn't have uploaded them. Dave had mentioned some pictures he'd shared with the police though – maybe if she could get hold of them, she might be able to identify which of the eight were in both Malia and Bournemouth. She wouldn't want to betray a friend, but if passing the list of names to the police cleared Ben's name once and for all, it would be worth it.

Heading downstairs, she could hear heavy snoring echoing from the lounge. Gently pushing the door open, she surveyed the mess. Half-crushed cans of beer were scattered across the low table, and an empty bottle of vodka was precariously resting upside down in an empty tube of crisps. A rancid smell – a cocktail of sweat, BO, and stale lager – hung like a cloud just below the ceiling.

It was no wonder Ben hadn't attempted to come up to bed. When he started on the vodka he was a noisy and restless sleeper. He probably hadn't wanted to disturb her. Either that or he'd passed out on the sofa before he'd had chance to think about it.

She spotted a pile of matchsticks on the table top, and some playing cards. They'd probably been playing poker. Tentatively stepping over Ben's outstretched legs, she carefully avoided the empty cans on the floor until she made it to the long curtains at the back of the room. Ducking behind them, she opened the small window at the top before re-emerging. At least that would help dispel some of the pong.

Treading carefully back through the carnage, she fetched a bin liner from the kitchen and slowly made her way around the lounge, dropping cans into the sack. Both men continued to snore loudly but almost harmoniously. As she reached for the tube of crisps, the bottle fell onto the floor, striking the edge of the table as it went. Alice held her breath, waiting for them to wake.

Neither man stirred, oblivious to her presence in the room.

There was no sign of Ben's phone – it was probably still in his pocket – but she did spot Dave's near the pile of playing cards. Leaning over, she discreetly picked it up, careful not to bump into him.

Stooping, she tried to work out how deep a sleep he was in. If she could just get his thumbprint on the sensor, the screen would unlock and she could send any images on it to her own phone. If he woke while she had hold of his hand though, he would demand to know exactly what she was doing and then she'd have to come clean.

It felt like a risk worth taking, if only to see who had been in Bournemouth that night. Dave was left-handed, so it was a reasonable assumption that she'd need his left thumb. Calmly sinking to her knees, she held the phone in her left hand and carefully pressed her thumb and index finger around his wrist, lifting it ever so slightly. His snoring didn't miss a beat. Twisting the arm so his palm pointed up, she carefully selected his thumb, but as she did his rhythm suddenly altered and the snoring stopped.

Alice froze.

She was staring straight at him, willing his eyes to remain closed as she continued to grip his thumb. A single bead of sweat travelled the length of her spine, but she remained rooted to the spot.

'Alice,' he mumbled, and her breath caught in her throat.

His eyes remained closed.

'Alice,' he groaned again, before his face dropped to the side and the snoring returned.

She exhaled slowly through her mouth, manoeuvred the phone so the sensor was just below his thumb, then brought the two together. The first attempt failed, but suddenly the screen unlocked. Clicking on the gallery icon, she swiped until she found the images from Bournemouth, stopping momentarily when Kerry Valentine's face filled the screen.

Alice hadn't realized just how pretty Kerry had been. The outfit she was in left little to the imagination, but beneath the hard stare and make-up, Alice was sure she could see regret in those eyes.

There were half a dozen images of the group laughing and drinking and Alice quickly forwarded them to herself before deleting the message from his phone's records. Lowering the phone back to the table, she was about to stand when she spotted a piece of paper underneath the pile of playing cards. She hadn't noticed it earlier, but now it was hard to see how she'd missed it.

Sliding it out, a fog of confusion descended as she read the contents. It was scrawled in Ben's terrible handwriting and a pen rested nearby. At the top of the page the word 'Suspects' had been double underlined, and below it was a list of names she recognized.

Had Ben and Dave been doing their own sleuthing during the night? Pulling out her own phone she snapped an image of the list before dropping the bit of paper back to the table.

She left the half-full sack of rubbish on the floor where it was and headed out of the living room. Her heart was racing as she pulled the door shut and pocketed her phone. She needed some space now, and she'd never get that if she stayed here. Grabbing her car keys, she thought of the one place she wouldn't be disturbed.

19

The grounds of St Michael's School were a ten minute drive from Alice's home in Chilworth, and as she pulled up at the gates, she was relieved to find the onsite caretaker had already opened the entrance to the staff car park. Although many people seemed to believe teachers only took up the vocation for the extended summer holidays, this failed to acknowledge the level of planning activity undertaken in the months when the children were away.

Alice had already spent the three previous weeks prepping syllabus activities, so that when she returned from honeymoon she wouldn't have to rush to have things ready. Now, it was the perfect place to skulk at a desk, away from the prying eyes of Ben and Dave. As far as any of the other teachers would be concerned, she was simply preparing work for the start of September.

As she parked the car in her usual space and made her way towards the front doors, she clutched her mobile close to her chest. If Ben and Dave suspected one of their friends could be somehow involved in Kerry Valentine's murder, Alice wanted to know who and why. For one reason, the victim's family deserved to know, but also it had the potential to clear Ben's name once and for all.

The door creaked as she waved her pass next to the lock and

pulled it open. For safety precautions, all the doors into the school were controlled by security passes, to prevent unwanted strangers wandering in off the street. Making sure the door was closed behind her, Alice moved across to the reception office and signed her name in the visitors' book – another core requirement of teachers working during the holidays. The official line was it enabled the caretaker to understand who was in the building in the event of a fire, but there was a rumour among the teachers that it was the head's way of monitoring who had spent the most time preparing for the new school term. Tara often joked that she added extra hours on to keep him off her back.

Seeing the list was empty so far, she was relieved nobody would come knocking at her classroom door asking inane questions about how the wedding had gone.

Making her way along the corridor, Alice stopped when she reached the modern languages department, which was a corridor of four empty classrooms and a small office at the far end where the three modern languages teachers had to share two desks between them. It was primarily used as a port to vent frustrations following a lesson in one of the adjoining classrooms. Scanning her pass against the door, the usual cloud of musty books, stale sweat and dust hung in the air.

Alice had always had a natural ear for languages and had excelled in French and Spanish at school, so when it had come to choosing a specialist area of study during her PGCE, it had been an easy decision. As with any subject, there were students who excelled, students who made a sincere effort, and students who simply didn't give a toss about conjugating the past participle of *être*. Alice remained passionate about her areas of study though and every once in a while a student would engage and all the dull and challenging lessons would drop away for the satisfaction of seeing just one pupil fly.

Allowing the door to close, she opened the double windows, though there was little breeze waiting to come in. That was the problem with how this part of the building was positioned – even on the windiest of days, hardly any fresh air made it in. Which was why a can of air freshener remained a permanent fixture on the window ledge. Pinching her nose, Alice sprayed the can liberally in the air, the whoosh of fragrance slowly dropping like tiny rain drops and landing on the two old wooden desks.

Pulling out a chair, she dropped behind one of the desks and immediately unlocked her phone, opening the list of names and doing her best to interpret Ben's handwriting. She recognized Johnny's name at the top, followed by her stepbrother Scott, then Abdul, James, and Pete. These were the names she recognized from the Malia photograph, though she didn't know much about Abdul, James or Pete. She didn't recognize the remaining three names on the list: Gary, Duke, and Michael. Had Ben mentioned them before? She didn't think any of them had been invited to the wedding, but given the hall's capacity and their extensive families, they hadn't been able to invite everyone.

There were no surnames and no indication of why Ben and Dave had chosen to flag these individuals as suspects. Was it enough to pass to DC Hazelton? Surely she would already have spoken to everyone who was present at the stag do, so the police would be aware of the names. Would a phone call and chat be seen as a lame attempt to interfere with the investigation? Would she be better off speaking to Ben privately and ask what the list meant?

She was about to reach for one of the office laptops and open a search engine when there was a gentle knock at the door. Alice glanced at her watch. Still not yet seven, she'd be surprised if one of the other teachers had made it in so early. Slipping her phone into the pocket of her jeans, she opened the door and was startled to see the face of Andrew Hook.

'I thought I saw your name in the visitors' book,' he said, smiling broadly and screwing up his face as he blinked rapidly, the way he always seemed to when he was near her.

'Andrew,' she said, trying to sound as welcoming as she could but desperate to get back to her thoughts. 'How are you?'

He used a grubby finger to push his large square glasses back up his nose, but they began to fall back down almost immediately. 'All the better for seeing you. Are you bàck from your honeymoon already? Seems like only yesterday we were doing that collection for you.'

Dressed in a short-sleeve buttoned golf shirt, his maroon coloured shorts were far too short for a man of his age and waist size. She tried to ignore the thick grey socks pulled up over his shins and the brown leather sandals strapped to his feet. His face, weathered by time and too many ales, was friendly but covered in small red blotches, and the dark grey bonnet of hair swept over his head had small specks of white powder, some of which had already fallen onto the shoulders of his shirt.

'We've had to postpone the honeymoon,' she replied cautiously. She didn't want to share the reason why she wasn't currently stretched out on a sun lounger, but the fact that she wasn't abroad would soon be common knowledge, so there was no point in lying to him.

'How's your new husband? Bob or Bill, I can never remember.'

Alice had told him on more occasions than she could remember what Ben's name was, but he always seemed to get it wrong, to the point where she now suspected he was doing it deliberately.

'*Ben* is well,' she corrected, smiling to show she hadn't taken any offence.

He pushed his glasses back up again. 'How was the big day then? I bet you looked like a princess in your dress.'

Alice remembered that Tara was convinced Andrew had a crush on her.

'I'll have to bring in photos when they're ready,' Alice pacified.

'I'd like that,' he said. 'We should catch-up over lunch some time. Or dinner if you'd prefer?'

They'd never shared a meal together. He had to be at least

twenty years her senior, and although he'd never been anything but kind and sweet to her, he could be overbearing, and she considered him more an acquaintance than a friend. His offer of dinner was out of the blue and, as he rocked from one foot to the other, she could see he was feeling just as awkward as she was.

The key was to let him down gently, and not offer any encouragement. 'I'll try and stop by the staffroom for a coffee before term restarts,' she offered, cringing as an excited smile broke out on his face.

She made a show of looking at her watch, but he didn't seem to take the hint.

'I took your advice, by the way,' he continued, still hopping from one foot to the other.

She frowned, unaware of any advice she'd ever offered him.

'I joined a club,' he said, when he saw her look of confusion.

Her frown deepened, she definitely didn't recall *ever* discussing hobbies with him. Their conversations until now had remained strictly professional, she'd made sure of that.

'Right,' she said, nervously. 'How's that going?'

'Oh it's wonderful. Birdwatching can be such a cathartic experience,' he said proudly. 'I've made some new friends as well, and even met someone I knew way back when. She isn't looking for anything romantic, but I'm hoping it could lead to something one day. Never say never in my book.'

'Well, I'm pleased you've found something to be passionate about.'

'Do you like nature, Alice?'

Alice wrinkled her nose. 'I like walking in nature, if that's what you mean?'

'There's nothing quite like it,' he suddenly said, his gaze wandering to some point on the window behind her. 'Birds and insects; I tell you, we can learn a lot from them.' His eyes brightened with excitement as a fresh idea presented itself. 'You ought to come along to one of the birdwatching sessions. The next meet-up is this Saturday. We're meeting in Lyndhurst, and then heading further into the New Forest.'

'That's sweet of you, Andrew, but I don't think birdwatching is really my thing.'

'You know what, I wouldn't have thought it was mine either. Now though, I can't get enough of it. All the fresh air and beautiful surroundings; we're so lucky to live in such a nice part of the country.'

'Thanks again for the offer, Andrew, but I must get back to what I was doing. I'm sure you have a million things to do yourself.'

'I do indeed,' he beamed, finally looking as if he was about to take the hint. 'Students don't understand how much preparation goes into teaching chemistry. Our future doctors and scientists would be nothing without their chemistry teachers.'

Alice shuddered at the thought of her own chemistry teacher, but she smiled in Andrew's direction before closing the door and exhaling in relief. He really was a sweet man and she didn't doubt his good intentions, but the sooner he accepted she was now happily married the better.

Slipping back behind the desk, she once again reached for the image of the list.

20

An hour had passed, and Alice's efforts to learn more about the list of names and how any of the men could be involved in the death of Kerry Valentine had proved fruitless. She couldn't understand how private investigators managed to glean so much information about potential targets, as all her search efforts had failed miserably.

She had started by looking at Ben's friends on social media, focusing on the names that matched those on the list, but it turned out Ben was friends with four men called James, none of whom resembled anyone in the photographs taken in Bournemouth. She'd had just as much luck looking for someone called Duke, as none of his friends had that listed as a name. Could it be a nickname? There was a woman listed as an old school friend called Brenda Dukovsky, so could she have a husband or brother Ben knew who wasn't on social media? It was anybody's guess.

The sun's rays were beating down on the open window, and although the air freshener had cloaked the stale smell, the room was feeling stuffy and she longed for fresh air. Locking the laptop, she reached for her handbag and headed back along the corridor, out through the school's front door and back out through the gates. There was a parade of shops ten minutes' walk away, and it was here she headed, hoping the newsagents would be open so she could buy a cold drink and a snack, only now realizing she hadn't eaten before leaving home.

Ben would probably be awake by now and would have gone looking for her to apologize for the mess and for not coming to bed. He would be sure to phone or message her when he found she wasn't there. Looking at her phone she could see he hadn't made contact, though, and she felt disappointed that he wasn't missing her yet.

The walk to the shop ended sooner than she'd anticipated, and as she stepped in through the door, she realized she now felt even warmer than when she'd left the school. The man behind the counter looked up from the newspaper he was reading, smiled and waved in her direction. She smiled back, skimming the labels in the tall drinks fridge and looking for something refreshing. She didn't want a fizzy drink, but her energy was waning and her blood glucose could do with a boost, so she reached for a bottle of juice, pressing it against her forehead, savouring the cool relief.

'It's a hot one today,' the man behind the counter commented, although he was dressed in a thick yellow woollen cardigan and donned a flat cap.

'Yes,' she acknowledged, quickly reaching for a cereal bar and placing both items on the counter.

'A beautiful day for a beautiful lady,' the newsagent said, chuckling to himself bashfully.

Alice paid and put her change in the charity box on the edge of the counter. Placing the bottle of juice against the back of her neck as she left, she held it there for the duration of the walk back to the school. A tiny breeze took the edge off the heat, but the cloudless sky was a sign that today was going to be a scorcher.

The staff car park was fuller now, and as she headed back to the modern language centre she was relieved not to run into anyone else who might casually enquire how the wedding had gone and why she wasn't on her honeymoon. A knock on the door five minutes later was followed by Tara's enthusiastic face poking around it.

'So it's true,' Tara commented as she slumped into the spare chair.

'What is?' Alice asked, opening the bottle of juice.

'That the great Alice Tandy – sorry, *Goodman* – has returned to our humble establishment.'

Alice cocked a curious eyebrow.

Tara grinned mischievously. 'Andrew's been in the staffroom telling anyone who'll listen that you're back and how beautiful you looked on Saturday.'

Alice's cheeks flushed. 'Is he really? Oh that's so awkward. He stopped by a while ago and I didn't have the heart to ignore him. I don't understand how he knows what I looked like on Saturday though; he wasn't invited to the wedding.'

'He was probably watching from across the street with a pair of binoculars like some peeping Tom.'

Alice thought back to what he'd said about birdwatching.

Tara shrugged and lifted the cereal bar, reading the ingredients. 'I assumed you'd showed him a picture or something. When I walked in, he was busy telling Sheila Retnor from Modern History how resplendent you'd looked. "Like a princess at a fairy-tale wedding," was my favourite quote.'

'I swear I didn't show him any pictures! He called by earlier and asked how the day went, but I obviously didn't tell him the whole story.'

Tara lowered the cereal bar back to the desk. 'You shouldn't lead him on. You're married to Ben now, it isn't fair to encourage Andrew to hold a torch for you.' Tara erupted into a fit of giggles as Alice scowled at her. 'Anyway, I had to see it for myself,' Tara continued. 'I mean, *this* is commitment! Married less than five minutes and already back at the grindstone. You put the rest of us to shame, Alice Goodman, you really do!'

Alice laughed and took a sip of juice.

'I take it the police haven't returned Ben's passport yet?' Tara said when she'd composed herself.

'Not yet, but it shouldn't be long. The rest of the stag party have made statements corroborating Ben's version of events and explaining why his DNA was on her body.'

'Were you able to rearrange the trip to Barbados?'

Alice shook her head. 'Ben is sorting that side of things today. He's hopeful we might be able to claim something back from somewhere, and then we'll book to go away later in the year.'

'Ah, I am sorry you didn't get to go to Barbados. I mean, I *was* insanely jealous that your gorgeous new husband was sweeping you away to a tropical paradise, but you don't deserve this.'

'Thanks.'

'So why are you really here? At the wedding you told me you were all prepped for the first term – don't tell me the two of you have fallen out already?'

Alice fixed her friend with a look before deciding to come clean. 'I think Ben suspects one of his friends could have been involved in that girl's death. I found a list of names he and Dave drew up last night and I was trying to work out who they are.'

Tara frowned. 'You're serious? You've turned amateur detective overnight. Should I refer to you as Jessica Fletcher from now on?'

Alice gave her a withering look and handed over her phone. 'Do you recognize any of the names at the end of the list? I'm curious about Michael, Duke and Gary primarily as I have no idea who they are.'

Tara studied the list. 'Ben could have been a doctor with this handwriting; it's terrible!'

'Do any of the names mean anything to you?'

'I went on a date with a Michael a couple of years ago. Do you know what *this* Michael's surname is?'

Alice shook her head. 'How did you meet him?'

'Faye and Johnny set us up on a blind date, with *blind* being the operative word. I don't think they'd described me to him nor had he seen a picture. I've never seen such a disappointed look on a man's face in all my life. I found him at the table and as he looked up from the menu it was like I'd come in and stolen his Xbox or something. He was pleasant enough, but having walked me home, he made no effort to kiss me goodnight, and when I asked Faye if he wanted to see me again she tried to let me down gently. Shame really. He was cute.'

Alice chewed on her fingernail. 'Well if he knows Faye and Johnny then it's possible it's the same person. Can you describe him to me?'

Tara considered the question. 'Tall, six foot maybe, short, cropped blond hair, no sign of facial hair. Clearly someone who loved spending every spare minute at the gym. I really don't see why we weren't compatible.' She laughed again.

'Swipe the screen left,' Alice suggested. 'Do you see him in any of the next few pictures?'

Tara studied the screen. 'Mm, this could be him, but the image is a bit grainy. I can't say for sure.'

'What was his surname?'

'Mayhew, or something like that. I only remember as I thought it was odd that his first name and surname began with the same letter, like that serial killer, Michael Myers.'

Alice's eyes widened.

'That's a fictional character, Alice,' Tara chided. 'Doesn't mean this Michael wears a hockey mask and haunts women on Halloween. Don't let your imagination get the better of you.'

'Did you hear the latest about Faye and Johnny?'

Tara nodded slowly. 'She phoned me this morning and asked whether you'd spoken to me about it. She said you went over?'

'She was in a bad way. He'd punched her at least twice from what I could see, but she was adamant she didn't want to tell the police. I told her she must be mad to put up with that kind of behaviour, but she didn't want to listen.'

Tara looked away for a moment. 'Do you blame her? She loves him, and nothing either one of us can say will change that. Think about how you'd react if I told you Ben was a killer. You wouldn't believe me.'

'That's because he isn't,' Alice scolded, not enjoying the microscope being so suddenly pointed at her own marriage.

'I know he isn't, but even if he was and I presented you with irrefutable proof, would you believe me? You'd probably tell me I was way off and that you wouldn't believe it unless you heard the words from him. I mean, just look at this Jessica Fletcher thing you've got going on here, all to help clear his name with the police.'

'Yeah, but Faye's situation is different – she was there when he hit her. If Ben tried to kill me, then I'd be more convinced of his bad nature.'

'I know, I know, it was a shit analogy, but my point is valid. She loves Johnny and she will cling to the possibility that he might change for as long as she can. All we can do is support her and encourage her to continue with the counselling sessions.'

Alice stared at her in amazement. 'They ought to give you your own radio show. I reckon you could give Oprah a run for her money.'

Tara smiled. 'I know, I'm actually thinking of charging for my relationship advice; I'll drop an invoice off for you later on, okay?'

Alice smiled. 'It does raise a few questions about Johnny's presence in Bournemouth last Saturday. After all, if he can do that to his wife, what's he capable of doing to a stranger?'

The question hung in the air like a bad smell, with neither of them able to overlook it.

21

Another hour of fruitless searching later, the office phone on the corner of the desk rang, snapping Alice's mind back to the present. Stretching, she lifted the handset.

'Hello?'

'Alice? Hi, it's Tina in the administrators' office. I have a young man here holding a large bunch of flowers hoping you'll come out to meet him.'

Alice glanced at the screen of her mobile and saw she'd missed a call from Ben.

'Tell him I'll be right out,' Alice said, before hanging up and checking her hair in the small compact mirror from her bag.

She'd made virtually no progress with tracking down the remaining names on the list and had now decided to just bite the bullet and come clean to Ben. She would tell him she'd stumbled upon the list and ask him why he'd jotted the names down. The Kerry Valentine murder was like an irritating itch that just wouldn't go away. Even though Alice had never met the poor girl, and knew virtually nothing about her, she couldn't help but feel involved. Every time she tried to think about something else, her mind always went back to the woman who had indirectly threatened to spoil not only Alice's wedding, but her marriage too.

Alice now sensed she would never get any rest until the police formally announced they'd captured whomever was responsible for the crime.

Turning off the laptop and checking she hadn't left anything in the office, she closed the door and made her way back along the musty corridor, waving at Tara as she passed the Drama block. Tara mimed a phone with her hand, and Alice nodded enthusiastically to confirm she'd call her later.

Ben was busy talking to Tina in the administrators' office, his back to Alice, as she approached. Hearing her footfalls, he turned, both arms full of flowers.

'The florist was having a closing down sale,' he joked. 'It was buy one, get ten free. You know how I hate to pass on a bargain.'

Alice couldn't help but grin back at him. Moving closer, she leaned in and kissed his cheek, breathing in the sweet scent of the lilies; her favourite.

'I'm just disappointed there's no chocolates too,' she joked.

Before she'd finished speaking, he passed her an arm's worth of bouquets, reached into his jacket, and pulled out a cellophane-wrapped box of Belgian chocolates. 'You didn't give me a chance to finish.'

Alice accepted the box, studying the label, and salivating at the thought of the sweet chocolate on her tongue. She hadn't realized how ravenous she was, and it was all she could do to stop herself tearing the box open and devouring the contents in one go.

The clock on the wall said it was nearly midday, and she had no idea where the time had gone. It didn't feel like she'd been in the school that long; she certainly didn't have five hours of work to show for it.

'I tried to call,' Ben continued, 'but you didn't answer, so I decided to come straight here instead. You don't mind, do you?'

The woman behind the office window was smiling absent-mindedly as she watched the two of them, like someone reminiscing at an old movie they remembered. Not wishing to be the object of someone else's attention, Alice dragged Ben away to the main door.

'You didn't need to buy me flowers.'

'Are you kidding? It's the first thing I should have done the second they let me out yesterday. These are just a token gift to try and show you how sorry I am for my part in what happened on Saturday. I cannot begin to tell you just how sorry I am.'

She pulled him closer and kissed him hard. 'You already apologized, and I know it wasn't your fault. You really didn't have to buy up an entire florist's display window.'

He examined the flowers, only now realizing just how absurd the gesture had been. 'In fairness, she really did do me a deal because I was buying so many. I didn't quite buy the whole shop, but I think she's now planning on finishing early for the day.'

'How did you know I was here?'

He looked away, staring out at where his car was parked, before fixing her with a long stare. 'When I woke up and found the half-filled rubbish sack in the living room, I figured you'd come down, seen the state of the room and gone for a breather. Listen, I know Dave can get a bit much, and I'm sorry I didn't speak to you before telling him he could stay last night. I felt a bit guilty because he'd done all that shopping for us. He looked sad, and so I said he could crash on the sofa. I swear, I never intended to pass out on the sofa with him. Can you forgive me?'

He was making his puppy dog eyes at her. 'It's okay,' she caved. 'I know he's your best mate; I just wish you'd warned me before I got home. I might have stayed out longer.'

'Well, the good news is he's gone now and I've told him he's not allowed back until I call him. I plan to spend the rest of this week showing you just how sorry I am for that trip to Bournemouth and everything that's followed. Money is no object. So, what do you want to do?'

Her stomach grumbled in response to the question. 'Can we go and get a bite to eat? I'm happy with a sandwich, but I need some sustenance.'

'Absolutely! I could eat a horse as well. Are you done here? Or are you planning to come back after lunch?'

There really wasn't any point in trawling through his list of friends, trying to work out who was who, how they could be involved, or why. She was no detective, and could spend the rest of the week trying to uncover a pile of secrets that might not even exist. She decided not to mention the list to Ben. For all she knew, Kerry Valentine returned home after her show with the boys and was killed for some reason that had absolutely nothing to do with any of them. She would just need to try and ignore the itch and hope it eventually faded.

'No, I think I'm done here,' she said. 'What do you fancy for lunch?'

He pushed himself closer so his lips were practically touching her ear. 'Well, now that you mention it, I do have a few ideas in mind. Maybe after lunch we should get home and spend the rest of the afternoon in bed.'

Alice felt her cheeks flush, and desperately hoped the woman behind the window was no longer paying them any attention.

Alice whispered back coquettishly, 'I should warn you my husband will be home at some point, so you'll need to make yourself scarce when he shows up.'

She could feel his lips curl into a smile. 'Is that right? I bet he's a scary guy, right?'

Alice turned her head to face him. 'Oh yeah, he'd skin you alive just for looking at me.'

'Well we'd better get out of here then,' he said, his grin widening.

She pushed him away playfully. 'Lunch first. I think I'm going to pass out if I don't get something to eat soon.'

He nodded. 'Very well, we shall eat, and then I'm taking you home and won't let you out until you're fully satisfied. I know where we should go and eat too. I won't tell you where, but they do the best garlic dough balls.'

Her stomach rumbled, knowing exactly what he had in mind.

22

Alice's stomach growled in dissatisfaction as the car stopped at another set of traffic lights. Ben had piled the flowers into the back seat, and anyone passing by would think they were heading to a wedding or funeral as the blooms pressed against the windows. It was lucky she didn't suffer from hay fever because the pollen count in the car had to be through the roof.

'We're nearly there,' he muttered, reaching for her hand and tenderly kissing the back of it.

She knew exactly where he was taking her. On their third date he'd tried to impress her, taking her to a very fancy restaurant he'd never been to before and ordering champagne the moment they'd arrived.

The owner had shown them to a small table in the window where a single candle flickered, showing off the delicate alcoves in the old building. It was a beautiful setting, and it had impressed her. As they'd sat at the table though, both excited by the prospect of getting to know each other better, they had felt so out of place, Alice because she wasn't used to such finery, and Ben because, in his words, he'd never imagined falling for someone as beautiful as her.

Although Ben had told her to ignore the exorbitant prices and choose what she wanted, she'd made an effort to pick one of the cheapest things on the menu. After all, she'd barely known him at that point and hadn't wanted him to think she was a freeloader. She'd studied the menu, unable to find anything she wanted to eat.

Ben had looked none the wiser as he'd studied the items, and had asked her to recommend something to him, eventually admitting he'd never been there and didn't know what duck confit even was. She'd then come clean and told him she was happy to stay if he wanted, but would be just as happy to leave. He'd then suggested they scarper before the waiter came to take their order. Dropping some money on the table for their drinks, Ben had grabbed her hand and the two of them had charged out, erupting into a fit of giggles as they'd made it onto the street. To this day, they'd never stepped back inside that particular restaurant.

He'd then driven her to an Italian restaurant near to where he was living at the time. When she'd suggested they go for pizza instead, she hadn't expected him to take her to a proper restaurant, but the second they'd stepped inside, Alice had immediately felt more comfortable. The hostess had clearly recognized Ben and had put them at a small table away from the other diners, where they could talk undisturbed. After the hilarity of their earlier experience, the conversation was no longer stilted. That had been the first moment she'd allowed herself to imagine a future with him.

Now, Ben indicated as he pulled the 4x4 into the restaurant's small car park and killed the engine.

'It looks busy inside,' Alice commented, as they exited the car and headed for the door.

'I'm sure they'll make space for us.' He winked.

Alice hadn't known back then, but Mariella – the owner of the restaurant and effervescent hostess – had once been Ben's babysitter before she'd gone on to open her own restaurant with her cook husband. As far as Mariella was concerned, Ben was always welcome. Even if the restaurant was packed to the rafters, she would find them a space to eat, and the garlic dough balls really were to die for.

Mariella clapped her hands in delight as she saw them walk in through the door. She kissed them both on the cheeks. 'I am so glad to see my favourite couple,' she cooed in her Italian accent. 'It has been too long since you have eaten with us.'

A small television screen was on behind the bar, not that anyone appeared to be watching it, too busy with their own conversations. Ben gave Mariella a hug and asked if she could squeeze them in.

She looked around the packed restaurant. 'I have a special table for my two favourites. Follow me.' She picked up two menus and led them towards the back of the restaurant, where a small table was already set up with two candles and a rose in a flute-like vase. A bottle of champagne stood in a metal ice bucket to the side of the table, and on one of the plates was a small jewellery box.

Alice gave Mariella a curious look, but the hostess simply looked over to Ben.

'Wait,' Alice said, as she connected the dots, 'did you arrange this?'

Ben couldn't stop himself laughing as his latest surprise was revealed. 'I phoned ahead before I came to the school,' he confessed. 'I asked if they could keep our original table free for when we stopped by.'

'How did you know . . .' but her words trailed off as he gave her a knowing smile.

'I didn't know, but I hoped you'd want food. I thought we should come back to where it all started. I still remember that first night I brought you here.'

Mariella waited for them to sit before handing them menus and telling them she would return in a few minutes.

116

'You only remember that night because you seduced me when we got back to your place,' Alice whispered affectionately.

'That's not the only reason I remember it,' he smiled back. 'Why don't you open the box,' he said, nodding at the gift on her plate.

'You didn't need to buy me anything else,' she said.

'I didn't,' he promised. 'Just open it.'

She sighed, knowing there was no point arguing with him. His guilt must have been in overdrive for him to have gone to such effort, and she did hope he would stop spoiling her soon. Lifting the box carefully, she snapped open the lid and gasped as she saw the beautiful jewel-encrusted ring inside.

'This must have cost a fortune,' she admonished, studying the finish.

'A small fortune once upon a time, maybe, but it didn't cost me a penny. It was my grandmother's. She bequeathed it to me on the understanding that one day I give it to someone deserving of its splendour. I had it cleaned up and adjusted so it will fit the index finger of your right hand. I had planned to give it to you on our first day in Barbados, but with that messed up, I had to come up with a plan B. Do you like it?'

She felt happy tears welling in her eyes. 'Are you kidding? I *love* it!'

'Phew,' he said, exhaling loudly. 'My grandfather was given it by *his* grandmother who managed to take special care of it throughout the Second World War. That ring has survived the Blitz, and it's an antique. I can't think of anyone more worthy to wear it. My grandmother would have loved you, and I know she'll be looking down and smiling from ear to ear right now.'

One of the tears escaped down Alice's cheek, and she quickly wiped it away with the back of her hand. Carefully lifting the ring from the small cushion inside the box, she held it for a moment. 'Are you sure you want *me* to have it?'

He took the ring from her and slipped it over her finger. 'A ring this beautiful requires the wearer to be just as beautiful, if not more so. I can't think of a single woman in all the world better suited to wear it.'

The ring slid over her knuckle, and felt so natural that she couldn't imagine ever taking it off. Pushing herself across the table she kissed him. 'I don't know what to say. Thank you.'

'You're more than welcome.'

She pushed her chair back. 'Would you excuse me for a moment? I'd better go and fix my face before Mariella returns.'

In the bathroom, she couldn't stop looking at the ring, and as she washed her hands ever so carefully, she dabbed a tissue against her eyes and took several breaths to compose herself.

Then, stepping out of the bathroom, Alice froze as she saw Kerry Valentine's face filling the screen of the television behind the bar.

23

The camera zoomed out, and Alice could now see the image of Kerry Valentine was one of two posters on a pale blue wall, in front of which were sitting DC Hazelton and two other detectives. A scroll of text at the bottom of the screen advised the press conference was live.

Next to Hazelton was the older man who'd cuffed Ben at the wedding: DI Vernon. His shirt and tie looked just as dishevelled as it had done on Saturday night, and the dark bags beneath his eyes looked like they'd been there most of his life. He was clearly thinning on the crown of his head, but he'd made no effort with the rest of his hair, as the granite-coloured strands sprouted out in all directions. He was anything but the poster boy for modern law enforcement. He bowed his head, silently rereading the page of typed notes that had probably been prepared for him, as a flurry of camera flashes lit up the screen.

He coughed. *'Right ladies and gentleman, if I can have your attention, please?'*

His voice wasn't what Alice had expected. She didn't remember the Yorkshire twang when he'd briefly spoken to her outside the hotel, but with everything else that had been going on that was hardly surprising.

He scratched a dry finger over his cheek and looked up, his eyes meeting Alice's through the glare of the screen. '*We are here today to share details of a horrific crime perpetrated around ten days ago in the Bournemouth area. The victim – whom you can see on the screens behind me – is Kerry Valentine, 22 and local to the Boscombe area. She was last seen in the town centre around half past eleven on the night of Saturday, the 27th of July, just over a week ago. We are today appealing for witnesses who may have seen her after this time, or may have any information about what happened to her.*'

Alice's eyes hadn't left the screen since he'd started speaking. The image of Kerry over his left shoulder made her look even younger and more vulnerable than she had appeared in the pictures on Dave's phone.

The detectives were alone at the desk, there was no sign of upset parents or a boyfriend, and Alice could only assume they were gone or couldn't bring themselves to share their grief on camera for the world to see. Even so, it didn't seem right that there was nobody there to reflect this poor girl's humanity.

The images of Kerry disappeared, replaced by a road map with a large green line at the centre.

'*We know this is the route she would have taken home,*' DI Vernon continued, his accent even more noticeable now. '*She was last seen at this abandoned building, the former Merry Berry bar, where she was performing a dance routine for a group of men. She exited the premises at approximately eleven thirty, leaving through the bar's fire escape, which would have brought her out onto this road.*' He paused, stood and pointed at the map. '*Bennett Road. We have no record of what happened to her after this time. There is no CCTV in that area, so we are asking any drivers who happened to be in the area at that time to come forward.*'

Vernon retook his seat and glanced down at his notes before staring into the camera again. '*The forensic pathologist has confirmed time of death as between eleven thirty and one a.m. that*

Saturday night, so it is vital we speak with anyone who may have seen Kerry during this time, or who may have spotted someone acting suspiciously.'

Alice's pulse quickened.

Kerry *had* died in the immediate aftermath of her dance with Ben.

'Kerry's body was pulled from the River Stour on Friday morning, which means whoever killed her held onto the body for at least a couple of days before disposing of it.' He paused and exhaled deeply. 'Somebody out there knows what happened to this poor girl, and we urge that individual to get in touch as quickly as possible. It is also an offence to harbour a criminal, and if you know who was responsible and keep quiet, you too will be subject to the full force of the law.'

The camera panned out so the three detectives and two images of Kerry filled the screen again.

'We have taken statements from the witnesses who saw her leave the bar,' Vernon continued, 'and they have confirmed that Kerry was dressed in a miniskirt, lace top and petite leather jacket. Do you remember seeing anyone matching that description near Bennett Road on Saturday night or early Sunday morning? Did you hear a woman screaming for help anywhere in that vicinity? While we don't wish to share the exact cause of death at this time, her slaying was brutal and deliberate.'

DC Hazelton had yet to stare into the camera, keeping her head gently bowed, her eyes fixed on a single point on the table before her. Dressed in a black T-shirt, she clearly wasn't one who revelled in the media's spotlight, and Alice would bet it hadn't been her idea to be sitting behind that table.

'The number for the enquiries line is on the screen now,' Vernon continued. 'You don't have to give your name, but any information that leads to the capture of the person responsible will be gratefully received. My team and I will be on standby waiting for your call.'

Alice jumped as Ben appeared behind her and wrapped an arm around her waist.

'I was beginning to worry,' he said, pressing his lips against the side of her neck. 'I was about to send out a search party. What are you watch . . .?' His words trailed off as his eyes landed on the screen and he saw the image of Kerry.

'The police are appealing for witnesses,' Alice said, turning to face him. 'They've confirmed she died in the hours following her booking with you guys.'

The blood drained from his face. 'Oh God, it's all our fault.'

Alice stepped back, and for the first time saw just what an impact all this stress was having on Ben. Until now, she hadn't considered what all this must be doing to him. He'd gone out of his way to apologize to her for messing up the wedding, and she didn't doubt his sincerity. She hadn't considered how much it had to be eating him up inside, knowing that he and his friends were an indirect cause of Kerry's death.

'If they hadn't hired her, she wouldn't have been in that area that night,' he said, swallowing slowly. 'We're responsible.'

Alice's heart sank. 'No, Ben, you can't blame yourself for what happened. You weren't to know that hiring her to strip would result in someone killing her.'

'One of us should have offered to walk her home or ordered her a taxi.' He collapsed into her as his legs turned to jelly, and it was all she could do to get him onto one of the stools beside the bar.

'Can we have a whisky?' Alice asked, as the barman returned.

The barman nodded and poured a measure. Pressing the glass into Ben's hand, Alice told him to take a sip.

'It will help with the shock,' she advised. 'I can drive us home afterwards.'

She'd never seen him look so upset, and it seemed as though he was carrying the weight of the world on his shoulders.

'I can't help it,' he said, lowering the glass. 'Every time I close my eyes I see her dancing in front of me. I should have done more to help her. We could have ordered her a taxi, or offered to give her a lift home. We just left her. We should have done more.'

Although Alice's stomach grumbled again, her appetite was gone. 'Let's get out of here. We can pick up some chips on the way home.'

He didn't disagree and climbed down from the stool, leaving the remains of the whisky in the glass. Alice escorted him out to the car before returning to explain to Mariella that Ben wasn't feeling very well, and apologizing for rushing off. Mariella insisted they return again when Ben was feeling better, but from the look of him, Alice wasn't sure if he'd ever feel better again.

24

Ben had insisted on driving, and Alice couldn't determine if that was because he was worried about her driving his expensive car, or if he wanted something to distract him from the overwhelming guilt. If it was the latter, his silence was doing nothing to distract him. Several times Alice looked over to him, trying to think of something to break the tension, but every thought seemed petty in comparison to the heavy weight of what he was bearing.

It wouldn't matter how many times she repeated that he shouldn't blame himself; he'd always been obstinate about his feelings, and she knew better than to poke a bear.

She sat silently, staring out of the window at the wild vegetation and animals roaming the countryside of Hampshire's New Forest. There would be an occasional break in the heavy undergrowth and she would spot a pony or a donkey chewing on the tall grass without a care in the world. In that moment, she would stare at the animal and yearn for such an uncomplicated life.

The vibrant green countryside didn't last forever, and almost as soon as they'd entered, they were back out on the grey and dreary motorway, leaving peace and serenity in the distance. Alice was about to try and engage Ben again when the Bluetooth system announced Ben had an incoming call. He answered it without a second's hesitation.

'Ben Goodman,' he announced to the car.

'Ben? It's James Tomlinson, did I catch you at a bad time?'

James was the Operations Manager at Ben's logistics company, and one of the party to have been at both stag weekends. A quiet man, he only tended to speak when spoken to – at least in Alice's experience. She'd briefly met James at the company's Christmas party, an event Ben always asked her to attend. She used to tease him that he only wanted her there to keep the other women in the office at arm's length – an accusation he had yet to deny. James was certainly not the kind of person she would ever have expected Ben to hire, but maybe that was why their working relationship was so strong: they were polar opposites.

Ben glanced at Alice. 'No, I'm just driving Alice home. What is it?'

'I'm guessing you haven't heard the news then? Major RTC on the M3 near Basingstoke. Four cars involved, and two HGVs, one of which is ours.'

Alice had overheard enough of Ben's work conversations to know an RTC was a road traffic collision, and if it involved another lorry and four cars, it was a major headache that he didn't need.

'Shit!' Ben sighed.

'Sorry, boss,' James continued. 'I know we're not supposed to disturb you because you're officially on holiday, but I thought I should let you know.'

Ben looked over to Alice again as if trying to choose the words to ask her a question, but then he turned back to face the road. 'I'll just drop Alice home and then I'll come to the office. Do we know if anyone's hurt?'

'News is still coming in, I'll keep you updated. I've sent a team down there to assess the situation, but we're going to need to have the solicitors on standby until fault is determined. I've already put a call into the insurance company. Should I wait here for you before heading down there?'

'Yeah, hang tight. I shouldn't be too long. Who was the driver?'

'Yann.'

'Shit!' Ben exclaimed again, and Alice suddenly noticed how much he was sweating, despite the high-powered air conditioning.

'As I said, I've spoken to the solicitors and they're waiting for your call.'

'Thanks, James. I'll be there in twenty minutes,' Ben said, disconnecting the call. 'I'm sorry, do you mind? I'll be back in time for us to go out together later.'

Alice reached for his hand and squeezed reassuringly. 'No, I understand. I just hope nobody's hurt.'

He raised her hand to his lips and gently kissed the back of it. 'That makes two of us. Yann isn't exactly working for us legally. That's to say, he's allowed in the country and he had a working visa, but it expired a few weeks ago and he's still waiting for the renewal to be approved.'

Suddenly Ben's anxiety became clearer. The fact that Yann had been involved in the accident would throw a huge spotlight on their operation, but if he was also the cause of the accident then the civil litigation alone could be enough to sink the business.

'I can't believe you're still giving him work to do knowing his visa had expired,' she exclaimed.

'The renewal process is just a tick-box exercise. He's had visas renewed before and it was only a matter of time until this one was renewed. Yann is . . .Yann works in the UK because he gets paid well and can send money home to his wife and children in Macedonia. A few weeks of unemployment would have a huge impact on his family. I thought we were doing the right thing for him as a person. The visa process is just a load of bureaucratic red tape.'

There was no point arguing with him. He'd been running the

logistics business a long time before he met her, and although she benefited from its successes, it was *his* business, not something they shared.

Pulling up at the gate, she kissed him on the cheek and climbed out of the car, standing at the kerbside as he pulled away and sped off in the direction of the office. The gates creaked and groaned as they slid open, and she didn't wait for them to close before heading up the driveway. As she got closer to the house, she was surprised to find Dave's car still parked where it had been this morning. Ben had assured her that Dave was gone and would be out of their hair for a few days, so why was he still parked here? Unless, of course, he'd caught a taxi home, but it wouldn't make sense for him to leave his car here. Even if he was still over the limit from their drinking last night, she knew it wouldn't stop him driving.

She was tempted to phone Ben and tell him, but he had enough on his plate already. So, heading up to the front door, she opened it and was about to call out Dave's name to find out where he was when she heard his voice booming from the living room. He didn't sound happy.

Leaving the front door open, she slipped off her shoes and crept closer, curious to know what had got him so animated. The door was ajar and it soon became clear that the conversation was one-sided – he was on the phone.

'Don't be fucking ridiculous!' he admonished gruffly. 'I told you I'd get you the fucking money, I just need some more time.' A pause. 'Don't threaten me! Don't forget, you're the one who got us into this mess to begin with ... I don't care what you bloody tell him, but threatening me isn't going to get him what he wants any sooner.'

She'd always known Dave moved in different circles to her. In all the years she'd known him, she'd never seen him do a traditional nine-to-five type of job. He was someone who seemed to dabble in a number of different fields, but always had cash on the hip to spare. He owned his own house as far as she knew, but long-term planning had never been his thing.

A breeze blew at her feet as she pressed her hands into the door frame so she could hear him better.

'No listen, the last thing either of us needs is the heat on us, not with this Bournemouth thing hanging over our heads.'

Alice froze, straining to hear more.

'No, I think that should all blow over, and they bought our version of events. The others are too shit scared to go against what we told them . . . *yes*, I'm sure. We all stuck to the same story, so they've no reason to doubt what we said. Don't worry, I made sure everyone knew the timeline of activity.'

Her eyes widened. Whoever Dave was speaking to, they'd been together the night Kerry was murdered, and they'd lied to the police. Part of her wanted to tear out of the house and pretend she hadn't heard, but she needed to know who Dave was speaking to, and why they'd lied.

The breeze whipped into a gust and the front door slammed shut. Alice sensed Dave just the other side of the door. She'd never have enough time to get away from the door before he opened it, so she did the only thing she could. Releasing her grip on the door frame, she pushed the lounge door open, as if Dave wasn't even there, and then made a show of surprise when she came face-to-face with him.

'What are you doing here?' she asked, unable to remove the trace of anxiety from her voice.

'I'll have to call you back,' he muttered into the phone, before disconnecting it and putting it in his pocket. 'I was just making a business call before I left,' he said to Alice.

His face was as clear as a book – he was trying to suss out how much of the conversation she could have overheard.

'Ben just dropped me off,' she said, ignoring Dave's inquisitive stare and hoping he wouldn't see through her lie. 'He's been called to work because of an accident.'

She moved to the French doors, letting out a small breath of relief where he wouldn't see. Staring into the garden, she willed him to go.

'You need me to do anything before I leave?' he asked, pulling on his leather jacket.

She spun on her heel and forced a grateful smile. 'No. Thanks, but I'm just going to have a swim and chill out. Don't let me keep you.'

He moved across and kissed her cheek, the booze and tobacco still heavy on his breath and the stubble grazing her cheek. She didn't reciprocate.

Watching him head out of the room, she held her breath until she heard the front door closing once more, and then she dropped to her knees, fighting against the sting in her eyes. There was only one reason she could think of for Dave to have lied to the police about what had happened in Bournemouth, but what frightened her more was the prospect that Ben also knew more than he was telling her.

25

Alice's arms tore through the water as her mind battled with the prospect that Dave wasn't the only one keeping secrets about what had really happened in Bournemouth.

Her arms ached and her lungs burned as she reached the pool's edge, but rather than stopping and resting, she flipped over and pushed herself back towards the other side. What had Dave meant when he'd said they had bought their story? Presumably the 'they' he was referring to were the detectives who had interviewed the group after the wedding, but why had they needed to manufacture a story, rather than detailing exactly what had happened? As much as she tried to find a rational answer, her mind could only reach a single conclusion: at least one of them had killed Kerry Valentine.

Bursting out of the water, she grabbed at the tiled edge of the pool, clinging on as she sucked in lungfuls of air. Snapping off her goggles, she threw them at the wall in frustration, as the oxygen-filled blood penetrated her tired muscles. There had to be another reason for what Dave had said on the phone. Who the hell was he talking to anyway?

Stretching out her arms, she pulled herself up onto the ledge and continued to take deep breaths. Her towel was resting on the small plastic chair by the wall, and she picked it up and wrapped it around her middle, snuggling into its warm Egyptian cotton comfort. The swim cap was pinching at her head, and she squashed her finger in at the edge nearest her neck and felt an instant relief as she peeled it off.

It had been Ben's idea to buy a house with a pool. not that either of them made full use of it. It was a nice addition to the property, but what with work and social engagements, it was rare that either of them got to spend much time in it, let alone together. The maintenance cost of keeping it heated and clean didn't bear thinking about, but she'd never been more grateful to have it than she was today.

Slipping the dressing gown from the back of the chair to her shoulders and shimmying out of the towel, she stepped into her flip-flops and exited the enclosed area, skirting across the driveway to the main house. Immediately she noticed her mum's car at the gates.

Alice waved and stepped into the house, pressing the switch on the side of the wall to let her mother in. Alice's face lit up when she saw her stepbrother Scott step out of the car.

'So this is how the other half live,' he commented, leaning in and giving her a squeeze. 'There was no need to get dressed up on our account.'

She rolled her eyes and blew her damp fringe from her forehead. 'Well, Scott, if you'd phoned ahead I'd have had the servants lay out the red carpet for you and had the brass band play the national anthem.'

He chuckled. 'How are you, sis?'

'Surviving. You?'

He nodded. 'Your mum asked me to drive her over, she's been worried,' he said with a whisper, as the lady in question appeared at the door.

Alice directed the two of them through to the dining room while she went off to make tea. Carrying the tray through, with a plate of biscuits to snack on, she found her mother sitting at the large dining table, with Scott staring out of the window.

'Where's your husband today?' her mother asked as Alice poured tea into three cups.

'An emergency at work. Was there a reason the two of you stopped by, or were you just coming to check on me?'

Alice saw the two of them exchange looks, and slumped down into the chair closest to her mum. It certainly wasn't Scott's style to turn up unannounced.

'What's the latest on Ben's situation with the police, dear?' her mother asked. Alice knew her mother wasn't asking because she was concerned about her only daughter. She was old-fashioned and still worried about intangible matters like reputation and social standing.

'Nothing's changed since I messaged you last night. The police released him while they continue their enquiries. I don't know what else to tell you.'

'There was a press conference earlier. Did you see that?'

Alice nodded. 'Some of it.'

'So was your Ben the last person to see her alive?'

Alice didn't like what her mother was implying. 'I think the killer was probably the last person to see her alive.'

'Don't be obtuse, Alice. You know what I mean. How is Ben taking the news?'

'He's actually pretty cut up about it all. I know you two haven't always seen eye-to-eye, but the police do occasionally get it wrong, you know.'

It wasn't that Alice didn't love her mother, but their relationship had been strained since Alice's father had passed away when she was only seven. Although Scott's father had been a decent stand-in, Alice had never really forgiven her mum for marrying less than a year after her father was cremated. As an only child, it had taken a lot of adjustment to suddenly have an older brother, but Scott had made an effort to welcome her into the family, and she couldn't have hoped for a better stepbrother. Relations with her mum had never returned to what they'd once been, though, and that was partly why Alice resented her mum's attitude towards Ben.

'I forgot the sugar,' Alice said, standing and heading for the kitchen so she could compose herself.

Scott followed her out. 'Hey, are you sure everything's okay? You don't seem yourself.'

'I'm fine,' Alice sighed, suddenly remembering seeing Scott's name on Ben's list. 'What happened in Malia?'

He frowned in confusion. 'What? I don't understand.'

'I know there was a fight or something and I want to know what happened.'

He narrowed his eyes. 'How do you know about that? Did Ben tell you?'

She murmured noncommittally.

'How much did he tell you?' Scott demanded.

'Just that there'd been a fight and you lot had been lucky you hadn't had your collars felt.'

Scott pushed the kitchen door closed. 'Listen, before I say anything, you can't tell your mum, yeah? Promise me. She doesn't need to know and you know how she worries.'

Alice nodded.

Scott ran a hand through his blond locks. At six foot three, he towered over her petite five foot frame. 'Did Ben tell you there was a girl?'

'He said one of the group slept with the girlfriend of some other group and that all hell broke loose.'

'Well you should know that when I came on to her, I had no idea she was already spoken for, let alone that her boyfriend was as big as he was and was in the same resort.'

Alice's mouth dropped. 'You're the one that caused the fight?'

'Yeah, I thought you said Ben had told you.'

'I thought he meant someone else from the group, not you!'

'It isn't something I'm proud of, okay? But it wasn't me who went looking for trouble. We were out at the bar, it was late and we'd been drinking all day, and one of the lads said this girl was giving me the eye, so I went over to talk to her. I could see she was upset and I offered to buy her a drink. Then, before I knew what was happening, she had her tongue down my throat and was dragging me back to her room. It was only when her boyfriend rocked up the following morning that I worked out why she'd been so keen to get me into bed. I managed to scarper before he could catch me, but then we ran into him and his friends that night and that's when he broke a bottle and threatened to run me through with it. If it hadn't been for Dave and Ben, God knows what would have happened.'

Alice could see the genuine relief in his eyes as he spoke, and maybe for once brawn had won out over brain. 'Sounds like you were lucky they had your back.'

Scott nodded, looking eager to change the conversation. 'How is Ben doing after . . . well, with everything that's going on?'

'He's surviving,' Alice smiled. 'It's stressful though, for both of us.'

'Is there anything I can do to help?'

Alice considered the offer. 'You were in Bournemouth with them last weekend, right? What can you remember about Kerry Valentine leaving? Did anyone go out after her? Did she look worried, or concerned?'

'I was there when she arrived, but I left before the end of her show because I had to get back home for an early start the next day. I drove that night, and I wasn't drinking like the rest of them. I must have taken off about ten minutes before she finished, I think.'

'Did you tell the police that?' Alice pressed.

'Of course. I went with Dave and the others yesterday and made a statement. I told them what I saw and when I left.'

'Did you see anyone hanging about outside who might have been waiting for her?'

'No, but to be honest I wasn't really concentrating. I headed out and walked back to where I'd parked my car, and then I drove home. That was it.'

'Are you sure that's all that happened?'

'Absolutely. Why, what do you think happened?'

'I overheard Dave talking on the phone today, suggesting that he and the rest of you had lied to the police about what really happened that night. Listen, I won't be angry with you, but I just want to know what Ben's mixed up in. I'm going crazy with worry, panicking that the police will come back and arrest him again.'

'Okay, well I don't know what Dave's referring to. He didn't ask me to lie to the police.'

She wanted desperately to believe him.

Scott's eyes narrowed. 'I may be many things, but I'm not a killer. I don't think Ben is either. When Kerry was performing, I've never seen someone look as uncomfortable as Ben. He wasn't enjoying it – probably paranoid that you'd find out. He loves you.'

She let him hug her, grateful for his words, but she still felt there was more he was holding back. Before she had chance to challenge him, her mum called out to them from the lounge.

26

It was after five before Alice's mum and Scott left. There was still no word from Ben, which had to mean he was still busy dealing with the fallout from the motorway accident. Not for the first time she hoped that he was okay. He'd been white as a sheet at the restaurant when he'd caught a glimpse of the press conference, and she hadn't wanted him haring off to another crisis, but perhaps there was some truth in the idea that nothing cured stress like the distraction of more worry.

She was tempted to phone him and let him know she was thinking of him, but if he was in the middle of work, her call would be unwelcome. He'd said he'd be back for them to go out, and if that wasn't going to be possible, he'd message her and let her know. So in the meantime, she had just as well get ready to go out.

Heading up the winding staircase, she entered the main bedroom, flicking on the television as she passed through to the en suite. Her eyes looked tired in the mirror, with the skin slightly sagging. Nothing that a bit of concealer wouldn't fix. The highlights in her hair still shone from the appointment she'd had the day before the wedding, but the stress of the last few days was beginning to take its toll.

As she headed back into the bedroom and pulled off her T-shirt, the sound of the television distracted her. On the screen was a picture of Kerry Valentine. A reporter's voice confirmed the victim's name and summarized what the police had said in the earlier press conference. The screen then cut to DI Vernon in his withered shirt and tie, the Yorkshire accent as thick as it had been earlier.

'The victim – whom you can see on the screens behind me – is Kerry Valentine, 22 and local to the Boscombe area. She was last seen in the town centre around half past eleven on the night of Saturday, the 27th of July, just over a week ago. We are today appealing for witnesses who may have seen her after this time, or may have any information about what happened to her.'

The screen filled with Kerry's face – one of the images that had been on the screen during the press conference.

'Kerry had a difficult upbringing: in and out of foster homes after her single mum died, she spent time in a young offenders' institute for drug-related crimes. She had cleaned up her act in recent years, holding down a part-time job at a local supermarket and earning money through her late-night dance routines.'

An image of a road now appeared on the screen with cars passing by, before the camera panned around to a small block of flats, graffiti covering several of the nearby walls, and an abandoned washing machine propped up near a rusting shopping trolley. A scroll at the bottom of the screen identified the area as Boscombe.

'We visited Boscombe earlier this afternoon,' the reporter's voice continued, *'and spoke to some of Kerry's neighbours. They had this to say.'*

A woman's large face appeared, her cheeks puffy, eyes thick with liner, and lipstick that looked like it had been put on in a dark room.

'Yeah, I knew Kerry,' the woman said, glancing from the reporter to the camera like she was trying to work an angle to make some

137

extra cash. *'She was a good girl, not like the cops made out. Yeah she danced for money but she didn't turn tricks or nothing like that. That boy of hers, she doted on him. Poor blighter.'*

Alice slumped to the bed.

Suddenly the camera was inside a warm-looking living room, an elderly woman with grey hair perched in a tall armchair. It was obvious she'd been crying.

'I was looking after the little lad that night,' she said. *'I knew something was wrong when she didn't call me. She should have been back by midnight, and when I tried phoning her, the phone was off. I called the police as I was so worried.'*

She then went on to explain how Kerry had fallen pregnant at seventeen and how that had been her wake-up call to turn her life around. She got herself clean, found a place to live and relied on community support to watch over her son while she worked.

'She was an only child and had no other family, but she was determined to give her boy the life she never had,' the older woman continued. *'He was her entire world; everything she did was for him. Now he'll never know just how much he was loved.'*

The scene cut back to the reporter at the bar as he concluded his brief report into the life of Kerry Valentine. *'There has been a lot of activity just a few yards from where we're now standing, with Scene of Crime vans blocking the view off to our left. We'll bring you more as soon as we have it.'*

Alice muted the television as she blinked away the sting of tears. Kerry had a son. Whomever killed her had made that poor boy an orphan.

Ben and Alice had talked about starting a family, and both accepted it was the next obvious step in their relationship. They would give children a good life, but was that now fair when they had indirectly ruined the life of an innocent child? Would Kerry's son now spend his formative years in social care, wondering why his mum had been taken from him?

In that moment, Alice made a vow to find out more about Kerry's son, and to do everything in her power to support him, whether that be financially or in some other manner. It was the very least she could do for Kerry.

27

'Is everything okay?' Ben asked down the line. 'You sound upset.'

Alice dabbed her eye with a corner of tissue, not wanting to add to his guilt by mentioning Kerry's orphaned son. 'I'm fine. How are you? Is everything sorted?'

'I wish!' Ben sighed. 'That's why I'm calling – I'm sorry, but I'm going to have to cancel our plans for tonight. I'm up to my eyeballs in insurance contracts and dealing with the police investigators. You'd better go ahead and eat without me, I don't know what time I'll be able to get away from here.'

'Is it that bad?'

'One of the car drivers was crushed beneath the other lorry,' he said glumly. 'They had to cut her out, and she died before they could get her to hospital.'

'Oh, Ben, I'm sorry.'

'It was difficult to watch. Thankfully, Yann is fit and well and wasn't at fault for the accident, but because of his visa issue, it's not as straightforward as it could have been. According to the other drivers, Yann was in the inside lane when the other HGV driver pulled out to overtake, but didn't see one of the cars also moving into the lane. They collided and hit into the back of Yann's vehicle, and the other cars couldn't brake in time to stop the collision. It's a real mess. They've had to shut the M3 north-bound and they've only just cleared the backlog of cars that were stuck behind the pile-up. They've put diversions up, but it'll be several hours before they've cleared the roadway. Doesn't help that the other lorry was carrying some kind of hazardous material.'

She couldn't bring herself to tell him about the news report on Kerry, he had enough on his plate.

'I'm sorry to let you down,' he continued. 'I hate leaving you at home alone; is there anyone you can call to come over, or who you could go out and see? What about Tara?'

'I'll be fine, don't worry about me. Just get yourself home as quickly as you can. I really need a hug, and by the sounds of it, so do you.'

'I'll message when I'm on my way back, but I don't know when that will be yet. Did Dave leave the place tidy?'

She thought back to the phone conversation she'd overheard. 'Yeah, the place was fine when I got back here. Mum and Scott came over this afternoon and passed on their best wishes.'

'Hey, babe, I'd better go, I've got an incoming call. Love you.'

'Love you, too,' she replied as the line disconnected.

Returning the phone to its cradle, she looked around the silent house and knew staying inside would slowly drive her crazy.

One of the benefits of their home's location was the presence of a family friendly pub two minutes' walk away. Making her way down the road on foot, the sound of laughter and chat emanated from the beer garden at the rear of the large charcoal-coloured building, and the lights inside were welcoming. Reaching the main entrance though, she couldn't shake the feeling of being watched. Turning quickly, she scanned the horizon, but there was nobody in sight. Pulling open the door, she entered the bar and headed straight for the dining area before being escorted by a waiter to a small table, where a tealight flickered playfully in the slight breeze from the nearby kitchen.

The dining area was large enough to feed a small army, and the same charcoal-coloured paint covered the brickwork of the various pillars and walls. The carpet was maroon with yellow chequered patterns, though she couldn't tell exactly what the shapes were meant to represent. The high ceiling gave the place an airy feel, even though the tables were quite close to one another, but at the moment the dining area was only half full.

Her chair faced the rustic bar area while, over her shoulder, the large expanse of green lawn and picnic benches stretched out to the wooded perimeter. She switched chairs so she could watch the groups gathered at the picnic benches, hoping their revelry would distract her from the gloom of her own thoughts.

The waiter took her drink order – a large glass of dry white wine. She didn't usually drink during the week, but she had a terrible fear that she would struggle to get to sleep tonight, and anything that would help was more than welcome.

Reading the menu, she settled on the barbecue chicken with a portion of skinny fries and a salad. The waiter asked if anyone would be joining her, and although she initially took this as a judgemental question, he quickly explained that he just wanted to know whether to leave the spare cutlery in place. Blushing, she told him she would be dining alone tonight.

Out in the garden she spotted a young boy with a shaved head, his face pressed up against the glass like he was looking for someone. Their eyes met and he smiled sheepishly before waving. Alice instinctively waved back, but then another woman suddenly brushed past her and approached the glass, wagging her finger at the boy and telling him to come back inside as it was time for them to leave. As Alice glanced behind her, she saw the vacant chair from where the woman had emerged, and realized the boy hadn't been waving at her at all.

Reaching for her glass, Alice took a sip of wine and avoided looking at the harried mother as she returned to her seat and gathered her possessions.

'Is this seat taken?' a man's voice said, startling Alice.

Looking up, she instantly recognized Liam O'Neill, the journalist who had approached her in the hotel on Sunday morning.

'I have nothing to say,' she said, taking another sip.

Dropping into the other seat, he reached for the menu, turning his nose up as he scanned the prices. 'No Ben tonight?'

He was trying to bait her, and the best thing she could do was to keep her mouth closed and ignore him until he left.

'What's he up to tonight? Do you know what your husband does when you're not around?'

The anger rose in her throat before she could stop it. 'He'll be here in a minute actually, so you should get out before I set him on you!'

O'Neill made no attempt to move. 'It's only a matter of time before the police pull him back in for further questioning. You know that, right? They released him on bail so they can get their house in order before they present their case to the CPS and charge him accordingly. His was the only DNA found on the victim's body according to my source.'

'He's explained how that got there,' she flashed, angry that she was allowing him to get under her skin so easily.

'He always was good at formulating believable lies.'

'Who are you? Really, I mean. What's your interest in this story? Why are you so keen to spread lies and rumours about my husband?'

He opened his mouth to respond, before rethinking and closing it again. 'An innocent woman was brutally murdered and your husband was one of the last people to see her. His DNA was found on her body and for a period of time on Saturday night, around the same time that she was killed, he was left unattended by his friends. Plenty of time for him to get free, kill Kerry, and then return to where they'd left him.'

She snorted with derision. 'He was pissed and cuffed to a lamppost. He's not Houdini.'

'I think you'd be surprised about the situations your husband has escaped from in the past.'

O'Neill appeared confident in what he was saying, but there was something darker behind his eyes; he wasn't just here to gloat.

'What have you got against Ben?' Alice fired back, desperately hoping her food would arrive so she could ask the waiter to escort O'Neill away from the table.

'Tell me something, Alice. Have you always been so naive?'

'Don't pretend to know anything about me.'

'I know you're a teacher at St Michael's School, you teach French and Spanish and you graduated with honours from Southampton University.' He paused, fixing her with a quizzical look, trying to read her reactions. 'Does the name Mary mean anything to you?'

She shook her head as a fog of confusion took hold.

Standing, he said, 'Find out what you can about Mary, but watch your back – Ben won't like it if he finds out you're digging into his past. And we both know what he's capable of when he's not happy.'

With that, he spun on his heel and headed back to the bar area, leaving Alice alone to contemplate his warning.

28

It was only Alice's lack of a proper meal all day that ensured she finished the barbecue chicken dish. She hadn't realized how ravenous she was, but it had done little to satisfy her appetite.

Who the hell did Liam O'Neill think he was to be harassing her at odd times and places, making accusations against Ben but not following them up with anything resembling proof? It was like he'd mixed up her Ben with some other Ben Goodman. Ultimately, if he was as bad as Liam made out, why wasn't he still in police custody?

He was trying to drive her insane; that was the only reasonable conclusion she could draw. Clearly, there was bad blood between Liam and Ben, though she couldn't even begin to fathom what that might be. She wanted to phone Ben and ask him why Liam O'Neill was making such accusations, but something was holding her back.

Watch your back – Ben won't like it if he finds out you're digging into his past. And we both know what he's capable of when he's not happy.

Had Liam meant it to sound so sinister? In Alice's experience, when Ben wasn't happy about something he tended to vent his anger verbally, usually with a side order of Scotch. He'd never been violent, certainly not towards her, and Liam's warning felt like just another feeble attempt to push a divide between them.

The question was why.

Checking her phone, she was disappointed to see Ben had yet to message her again, which meant he still wasn't on his way home. Dropping cash on the table, she picked up her handbag and left the dining area, heading back through the bar and out into the warm night air. Although the sky was still quite bright, the treeline at the edge of the road was much darker now, and it would probably be less than half an hour until sunset.

The car park had more spaces as she made her way past it in the direction of home, but once again she couldn't escape the unease of someone watching her. Circling around, she returned to the doorway of the pub, looking left and right, searching for anyone who looked out of place or was paying her undue attention, but the street was empty.

The lamppost across the street flickered to life, brightening the treeline, but there was nobody there. She was being paranoid, that's all it was. It had to be a result of the stress she was under. She closed her eyes, took two sharp breaths and forged forwards, determined not to allow her paranoia to get the better of her.

The gates of her home came into view, and with them momentary relief. As she neared the gates though, she immediately noticed a small packet crudely stuck to the locking mechanism. Hurrying towards it, she saw it was a yellow envelope with her name scrawled on it. The envelope came away from the gate with a tug, having been taped in place. Looking around for any sign of who may have left it there, she suddenly felt vulnerable.

If it was a late wedding card, why hadn't they put it in the letterbox at the side of the gate? Why use tape to attach it to the gate directly?

A twig snapped from somewhere in the trees across the road, and suddenly she desperately wanted to be in the safety of the house. Using her remote, she opened and closed the gate before sprinting up the driveway, not daring to look back in case some stranger was following her. As she crashed into the front door, panting, she finally dared to turn around.

The driveway was empty.

Once inside, she locked the front door just to be safe, leaving her key in the lock. Heading through to the kitchen, she flicked on the light and tore at the envelope. Inside she found an A5 piece of paper with Ben's face on it. It was a crude photocopied image of a much younger looking Ben. His hair was longer, his cheeks lacked the designer stubble he now wore, and there was a hardness to the eyes she'd not seen before, even at his most angry. Next to the front-facing image was a sideways profile, showing his hair hanging over most of his ear.

A police profile picture of Ben – a mugshot – but it had to be at least a decade old. Turning the image over, she gasped as her eyes fell on the typed message on the back.

Dear Alice,
Roses are red,
Violets are blue,
Your husband's a killer,
And you haven't got a clue.

The message wasn't signed, and because it was typed there was no way to be certain of who had sent it. Given the run-in she'd had with Liam O'Neill at the pub though, she assumed it must have been left by him, to toy with her emotions even more.

She still couldn't understand what was motivating him. Also, why would he leave the note on the gate when he knew she was in the pub? He could have just as easily handed her the mugshot. It wasn't exactly news; Ben had told her he'd had trouble with the police before and had admitted to her there was a reason they had his DNA profile on record. So what did Liam hope to achieve by sending her this picture?

There was an alternative conclusion that she was desperately trying to ignore: what if someone else had left the envelope?

A shiver rippled down her back as she pictured a faceless character in the shadows, watching as she'd left the house, making his move and then creeping back to wait and watch.

Panic flowed through her at a second thought: if he had been watching her out there, did that mean he was still nearby? Before she could begin to dismiss the panic rising in her throat, a loud thumping echoed off the front door.

29

Boom, boom, boom.

The front door was practically shaking beneath the force of whoever was trying to break through. Alice was frozen to the spot in the kitchen, only the hallway separating them.

Boom, boom, boom.

The noise snapped her mind into action. Diving across the kitchen she reached for the large chef's knife in the block, coiled her fingers around the handle and held it firm, slid it free of the block, and thrust it forward in an upwards trajectory.

Hopefully, just the threat of the blade would be enough to keep her safe.

Boom, boom, boom.

She shuddered with each bang against the thick wooden door, the noise echoing off the walls in the hallway. Tiptoeing towards the door, the blade primed in her right hand, her mind raced with how to proceed.

Should she open the door and confront the intruder, or was calling the police the better option? What if they arrived too late?

Boom, boom, boom.

'I have a knife,' she called out, her voice cracking under the strain. She cleared her throat and tried again. 'The police are on their way.'

'Baby? Baby?' Ben's familiar voice came from the other side of the door. 'It's me. Thank God you're there! Didn't you hear me banging?'

The breath left her body and she crumpled to the floor, her legs unable to support her frame.

'My key won't open the door. Have you locked it or something? What's going on?'

The adrenaline settled, allowing her to drag herself the rest of the way to the doormat. Dropping the knife into the umbrella stand, where Ben wouldn't see it, she pulled herself up and unlocked the door with the key she'd left in the lock.

'Jeez, you look white as a sheet,' Ben said as the door swung open and she fell into his arms. 'Babe? What's going on? Why was the door locked? I kept trying to put my key in the lock, but it wouldn't fit. Were your keys the other side? Babe?'

She nuzzled her forehead into the crook of his shoulder, her arms wound tightly around his neck. She didn't ever want to let go.

'I thought maybe you'd gone to bed,' he soothed. 'That's why I was making such a rumpus, I was worried you wouldn't hear me and I'd be stuck outside all night.' Ben held her tightly, gently running a hand across her back. 'I'm pleased to see you, too, but we should probably shut the door,' he said, manoeuvring her out of the doorway and kicking the door closed with his heel. Gently easing her off him, Ben lowered his head so he could look into her eyes. 'What's going on, Alice?' he asked. 'I'm worried.'

She didn't know how to begin to tell him. A tear rolled down her cheek, and rather than speaking she simply took his hand in hers and led him through to the kitchen, where the photocopied mugshot and typed message remained on the counter. She handed it to him without speaking.

'What's this?' he asked evenly.

'It was stuck to the gate when I got home. Addressed to me. Someone left it.'

'Who?' he said in frustration.

'I don't know.'

'When was this?'

'It must have been in the last hour to ninety minutes. After you phoned to say you wouldn't be home till later I went down the road to the pub, and it was stuck to the gate when I got back.'

'No name? Nobody suspicious hanging around?'

She wanted to mention the confrontation with Liam O'Neill, but O'Neill's warning was still holding her back.

'No,' she said, with a shake of the head. 'Nobody.'

Ben reread the note.

Dear Alice,
Roses are red,
Violets are blue,
Your husband's a killer,
And you haven't got a clue.

'This is sick,' he said in disgust. 'Who the hell would . . .?' His words trailed off as a new idea rose. 'You said last sixty to ninety minutes, right, and it was stuck to the gates?'

She nodded uncertainly.

Ben slammed the message down on the worktop and peeled away, taking the stairs two at a time. He returned a moment later, clutching a laptop which he now rested on the counter next to Alice, his fingers dancing across the keyboard as he opened an app.

'CCTV,' he said proudly. 'I knew it would come in useful one day.'

A live image of the house filled the top left quarter of the screen, with smaller images of the property from different angles in smaller boxes filling the rest.

151

'Now,' he said, to nobody in particular, 'if we just scroll the time back . . .'

'There I am.' Alice suddenly pointed at one of the smaller images.

Ben stopped the app's activity and clicked on the smaller image, which immediately appeared in the larger frame in the top left corner.

'So this is you going out,' he said as the gates closed behind the figure that was clearly Alice. 'What time did you get back?'

'Just before you,' she said. 'A few minutes ago. I found the letter, came inside and opened it and then you started banging on the door.'

The tip of his tongue poked out as he slowly moved the footage on, looking for any movement at the gate. 'There,' he blurted as a figure approached the closed gate and pressed the envelope into place.

Alice studied the screen. 'Where's his face?'

The figure was dressed in a large, beige Macintosh, a wide-brimmed rain hat pulled down over his head.

'Let me see if we have a better angle,' Ben said, flicking through the remaining images. The one at the gate was the only angle you could see the figure from.

'Shit!' he declared, as he returned to the original shot. 'The guy must have known the camera was there.'

Alice considered the bulk beneath the large jacket, certain she'd seen it somewhere before. It could have been O'Neill, but he hadn't been wearing that jacket or hat when he'd confronted her. A disguise maybe?

Ben caught her eyeing the mugshot poking out from beneath the typed note. 'I can't believe they've left this; like they didn't think I'd already told you that I was stitched up for something years ago. I was accused of something I didn't do and was arrested. Clearly whoever is trying to get back at me now must have managed to get access to the original image.'

'Someone getting back at you?' Alice said cautiously. 'Is that what you think this is about?'

'Well, what else could it be?' he asked, the anger in his voice growing.

'Did you read the note, Ben? This is more than someone just trying to get back at you.'

He looked at the typed note dismissively. 'It's probably just some rival I pissed off who saw my name in the paper and is trying to make life unpleasant by driving a wedge between us. Logistics is a cut-throat business, and you'd be shocked by some of the antics people get up to when there's a big contract up for grabs.'

'Is there a big contract up for grabs now?'

'Isn't there always? Listen to me, Alice. I will find out whoever left this here and I will make them pay for freaking you out. Don't waste any more time worrying about it. Okay?'

'What if he's still out there now, Ben? Watching us.'

He considered her, before reaching for his phone.

'Who are you phoning?'

He didn't respond, as the line connected. 'DC Vanessa Hazelton, please.'

He was phoning the police. Not an unreasonable response to a threat, she supposed.

Watch your back – Ben won't like it if he finds out you're digging into his past.

He still hadn't told her exactly what the mugshot related to, but she sensed now wasn't the time to ask. If she wanted answers, she would have to go to the source. In the morning, she'd call Liam O'Neill directly.

30

Alice stirred as the title music of the breakfast show blared out of the television. The smell of fresh coffee filled the air and as she rolled over, refusing to open her eyes, she could hear the faint hum and splash of the shower.

Propping the pillows, she sat up and looked over at the mug of coffee on the nightstand. A handwritten Post-it was stuck to the edge, which simply read 'Sorry x'. She peeled off the note and allowed it to drop to the floor, putting the mug to her lips and savouring that first shot of caffeine.

DC Hazelton had finally phoned Ben back, and despite his demands for a unit to be stationed at the property for protection, the most they'd agreed to was sending a patrol car to check the immediate area. Ben hadn't been happy and had told the young detective where she could stick the patrol car.

The door to the en suite opened and Ben appeared, a cloud of steam billowing around him, a thin cotton towel tied around his waist, his carefully sculpted abs in full view. If he'd been trying to present himself in an Adonis pose, he'd succeeded. His hair was damp but pushed back over his head, and it took him a moment to work out that she was awake.

'Thanks for the coffee,' she said.

'Sorry, I didn't mean for the shower to wake you.'

'I can think of worse ways to wake up,' she said, nodding at him. 'The view's not bad either.'

He moved quietly to the bed before plonking himself near her feet, his head bowed. 'I'm sorry about . . . last night. I still don't know what—'

'Forget about it,' she soothed as reassuringly as she could manage. 'These things happen. You're not the first, and I'm sure you won't be the last.'

He looked up at her. 'I swear that's *never* happened before. I don't understand why it didn't want to work.'

He'd already spent half an hour apologizing during the night. It had been a disappointing end to a pretty awful day, and not how she'd anticipated things going when he'd playfully run his hand up the length of her leg.

'It's probably just the stress of everything that's been going on,' she offered. 'Plus you went for that run before bed too, which can't have helped.'

'You know it had nothing to do with you, right? It was all me. I mean, you're gorgeous, and I fancy the pants off you. I can't explain why it didn't . . .'

She quickly shuffled across to him and took his face in her hands. 'You don't have to keep apologizing. I understand.'

He kissed one of her palms. 'I promised you we'd start a family as soon as we were married, and that's still very much something I want to do. You feel the same, right?'

'Absolutely,' she said, without hesitation. 'That was the plan, and nothing's changed.'

'So you haven't had second thoughts now that I've been wrongfully arrested, and because you now know I've been in trouble with the law before.'

She rested her forehead against his. 'Everyone has a past. Yes, I wish you'd told me about it sooner, but that's done now. I'd still like to know exactly what happened back then, but I can wait for you to be ready to tell me. As for my feelings for you, I *love* you, Ben. I always have and I always will. I cannot think of a single person I'd rather make babies with.'

She raised his face and pressed her lips against his.

He got the message. His hands were around her back pulling up her nightdress a moment later. As his lips kissed that spot on her neck that always drove her wild, the television presenter's voice broke through the mood.

'Police have now identified the primary scene where 22-year-old Kerry Valentine was murdered just over a week ago.'

Alice's eyes snapped open and she stared at the screen, as Ben ran his hands over her breasts.

'There are signs that someone attempted to clean the area, but traces of Kerry's blood were discovered not far from the Merry Berry bar, where she was last seen at half past eleven on the night of Saturday, 27th July. There were faint tyre tracks the police are hoping might lead them to Kerry's killer.'

Alice peeled Ben away from her. 'I'm sorry,' she said with a shrug and nod at the television. 'It kind of killed the mood.'

He turned and saw the now-familiar picture of Kerry Valentine on the screen. The bulge beneath the towel disappeared almost as quickly as it had emerged.

'I feel like she's beginning to haunt us,' he muttered in frustration. 'Everywhere I look I see her face, and it brings the guilt flooding back. I wish Scott had never contacted her.'

Alice turned to face him. 'What do you mean? I thought Dave arranged it?'

'Well, Dave, or Scott, or whoever it was. I can't even remember. It was one of them.'

She let the statement go, but she was almost certain he'd said it had been Dave before, and Scott certainly hadn't mentioned his involvement.

'I'd better get dressed,' he said, standing and turning away from the television screen. 'I need to go into the office to check all the paperwork is in hand following yesterday's crash. Is that okay with you?'

She nodded, without really listening, her eyes and ears on the reporter on the screen. The screen cut to the image of the old neighbour, a recycled clip from yesterday's broadcast, and finished with DI Vernon's speech from the press conference.

'*Kerry's body was pulled from the River Stour on Friday morning, which means whoever killed her held onto the body for at least a couple of days before disposing of it.*'

Alice felt saliva building at the back of her throat. Although she'd seen this clip before, only now did she really consider what Vernon had said. Whoever killed Kerry *held onto her body* – what kind of sicko would do that? Post-death her body would have begun to decompose, and the smell alone would have been awful.

That statement was enough to prove to her that Ben couldn't have killed Kerry. Where would he have stashed a body while tied to a lamppost? As she thought it through, she considered that in all likelihood, whoever was responsible knew somewhere in Bournemouth where nobody would notice the putrid smell of a decaying body for a few days. Didn't Abdul live in Bournemouth? An image of Abdul dragging a body-shaped bin liner from the back of a car filled her mind.

Ben leaned in and kissed Alice's cheek, and a whiff of his cologne brought her mind back to the room. He was now dressed in shirt and trousers, the sleeves rolled up and the top button unfastened. Ben had never been one for ties. For him, formal attire meant matching blazer and trousers.

'What have you got planned for this morning?' he asked as he tied his shoelaces.

She had no plans, and simply shrugged.

'Let me know if you want me to pick up anything for dinner,' he said, smiling. 'Or maybe we should go out like we'd planned last night.'

The image of Abdul with the body-shaped bin liner was still at the forefront of her mind. 'Um, yeah, maybe.'

'You should stop watching this crap,' he said. 'The sooner they stop showing it, the sooner we can move on with our lives. Let's just hope they catch whoever's responsible sooner rather than later.'

She was frozen in bed, transfixed by the picture of Kerry as the two anchors continued to discuss the murder.

Ben kissed her cheek again. 'When I get home, we'll pick up where we left off. I will impregnate you, Mrs Goodman, if it's the last thing I do.'

The remains of Alice's toast clung to the plate as she slouched at the small table in the kitchen. She'd done her best to eat, but had spent more time picking at the toast than actually eating it. She usually had such a voracious appetite, but at the moment food was little more than a distraction. She'd spent the last half an hour trying to convince herself that nobody on the stag do was involved in Kerry's death. As possible as it was that one of the group had followed Kerry from the bar – unnoticed by the others – it was more likely that someone unconnected had seen her leave and made their move. According to the news, the area where they'd found traces of Kerry's blood was less than two minutes' walk from the bar.

If the police had any reason to believe one of the stag party was involved, wouldn't they have made an arrest by now? They were quick to pull in Ben, but as far as she knew nobody else had been arrested.

Yet, just as she'd almost convinced herself, the memory of Dave on the phone yesterday returned: I think that should all blow over, and they bought our version of events. The others are too shit scared to go against what we told them.

What other reason would there be for lying to the police, and who were *they*? Dave undoubtedly knew more than he'd shared, but who had he been speaking to? She couldn't just ask him outright. She'd never witnessed him being violent, but if he was backed into a corner she couldn't be certain of his reaction.

Reaching for her MacBook, Alice lifted the screen and typed her password before opening a fresh Internet search engine. Dave had said he'd searched for 'private dancers, Bournemouth' and he'd found Kerry's site from there. Alice performed the same search and was surprised by just how many hits came back. The first five she clicked on made no mention of the dancers' names, just described the girls and what they would charge.

Narrowing down the search to images rather than sites, she found what she was looking for on the second page. She had no doubt that the girl dancing provocatively with the pole was Kerry. Clicking on the image, she was taken to one of the first five sites she'd visited. A telephone number listed at the bottom had a Bournemouth dialling code, and Alice reached for her mobile and punched in the number.

The line rang and rang, but nobody answered and no answerphone cut in. Frustrated, Alice hung up and tried again. The ringing went on and on, but just as she was about to hang up, the line was answered.

The woman's voice sounded dry and gruff, like she'd been gargling with nails. 'Yeah?'

'Is that Danse Privée?'

'Yeah, who are you?'

'I'm phoning about Kerry Valentine, I wondered if she was one of your—'

Before Alice could finish the sentence, the woman cut her off with a violent hacking cough. 'What is it with you fucking reporters? How many times do I have to tell you she didn't work for me? Okay? Can you get that through your fucking heads?'

'I'm sorry, no, I'm not a—' Alice began.

'She was nothing to do with me! I didn't fucking send her to that gig. Right? Now leave me the fuck alone!'

Alice pulled the phone from her ear as the other end was slammed down. She lowered the computer's screen and carried her plate to the sink, dropping the remains of the toast in the pedal bin. Her hands were trembling. Clearly the woman on the line had been hounded by journalists trying to tie her site – her business – to the murder. She'd obviously done her best to remove all traces of Kerry from the site, but had missed that one image. That's the problem with the Internet, once your secrets are out there, there's always a trace.

Returning to the MacBook, Alice jotted down the business address from the bottom of the homepage. If the woman wasn't prepared to speak to her on the phone, maybe she'd be more willing in person.

31

The air conditioning kicked in as the car's climate threatened to exceed nineteen degrees. It was almost nine o'clock and traffic remained heavy as they passed by Ringwood. The radio had been playing on low volume since Alice had called at Tara's and begged her to come along for moral support.

'I still think this idea is crazy,' Tara said, for the third time since they'd left the motorway. 'What exactly are you hoping to learn?'

'I just need to know,' Alice said, and in all honesty that was the only answer she could give. It was like some invisible force was dragging her towards the life of Kerry Valentine, and the more she tried to fight against the impulse, the stronger it grew.

'If she wouldn't speak to you on the phone, what makes you think this woman will be more willing if you turn up in person?'

Again, Alice couldn't answer, but that hadn't stopped her punching the address of Danse Privée into the satnav. The remaining twenty minutes of the journey were completed in virtual silence: Alice's mind focusing on different members of the stag party and ruling them in or out of her suspect pool, Tara watching on, hoping her best friend wasn't losing her mind.

'*You have reached your destination,*' the robotic voice declared as they pulled up on a residential street with no sign of any local businesses.

'Are you sure you put the correct address in?' Tara questioned. 'I once put in the postcode of a hotel, but it took me to the opposite end of the postcode and it took me the best part of half an hour to find the bloody hotel. In the end I had to phone them for directions.'

'No, it's the full address. According to the website, the head office is here, *somewhere.*'

The road resembled a typical residential street, packed with ex-council terraced houses, but in among the uniform concrete structures there were several brightly flowered gardens and expensive-looking cars. There was no obvious clue of what they were looking for.

'What number is it supposed to be?' Tara asked. 'I can see number 21, and 25 on this side. Have you got even numbers your side?'

Alice studied the satnav screen. 'Should be 24, so I guess that's my side.'

Tara leaned across the handbrake, scanning the houses outside of Alice's window. 'Well that one is 22, so I guess that one on the end is 24?'

Alice unfastened her belt, killed the engine and climbed out of the Audi. Tara joined her on the pavement a moment later.

'Maybe they relocated to a different address and forgot to update the website?' Tara offered.

'This makes more sense though,' Alice countered. 'Think about it. If you were running a cash-in-hand business with questionable morals, would you paint a bright neon sign over your door?' She shook her head. 'Far better to keep your business where the authorities would never come looking.'

Tara wasn't convinced, but the two women edged nearer to the door. On the side wall, the view obstructed from the street, was an A4-sized plastic sign with the large pink initials 'DP'.

'It's the same font as the one on the website,' Alice confirmed. 'This *has* to be the place.'

'It isn't too late to turn back.'

'We've come too far to turn back now,' Alice said, her finger trembling as she jabbed it against the doorbell. The sound echoed through the two-storey property and she strained to hear any movement from inside.

'We should just go,' Tara said, looking anxiously back towards the road.

'Calm down, Tara, we're not doing anything wrong.'

Pressing the doorbell again, Alice lifted the letterbox hatch and peered into the gloom. A door at the end of the hallway was closed, as was the door to the left which led through to the front room. A staircase was just visible to the right, and at the top, a pair of fluffy purple slippers appeared.

Alice quickly lowered the hatch and straightened. 'I think she's coming.'

A moment later the front door opened.

'Yes?' the woman in the slippers said, a freshly lit cigarette in one hand, a pair of dark glasses in the other. She was wearing a lilac-coloured kimono which did little to hide the thick green veins protruding from her otherwise pale legs. Her hair was as dark as coal, but as Alice looked closer, she spotted it was a wig.

'Hi,' Alice began nervously. 'I called earlier, hoping you might be willing to speak to us about one of your dancers?'

The woman took a long drag on the cigarette and exhaled the smoke in their faces, causing Tara to cough. 'Don't know what you're talking about, luv,' she said hoarsely.

Alice pointed at the 'DP' initials near the bell. 'Danse Privée? This is the registered address for the site.'

Another drag on the cigarette. 'You a reporter?'

'No,' Alice coughed.

'Police?'

'No.'

163

Deep lines appeared on the woman's forehead, the crow's feet at her eyes widening. 'What do you fucking want then?'

'It's going to sound crazy. I wanted to speak to you about Kerry Valentine.'

The woman flicked the cigarette out of the door, narrowly missing Alice's nose, and then the door was closing.

'She's her sister!' Tara suddenly yelled, and the door halted.

'Kerry didn't have a sister.'

'Foster sister,' Tara added. 'Please? They grew up together. I swear we're not police or journalists, we just want to learn more about Kerry's final few months. Please?'

The woman looked from Tara to Alice, before nodding and stepping away from the door so they could enter.

Alice and Tara followed the woman through the hallway and into the large living room at the back of the property. It led out to a garden, but apart from a couple of dead pot plants, there was no other vegetation. Instead, a two-tiered patio stretched ten feet, fully enclosed by rotting fences along the perimeter.

The woman slumped into an armchair that faced the television and flicked it on, the volume muted, before pulling a fresh cigarette from a packet on the table and sparking up. There was one other single armchair, which Tara sat in. Alice perched on the arm.

'You've got five minutes to ask your questions and then I want you out of here,' the woman said, pushing the dark glasses over her eyes.

'Kerry Valentine did work for Danse Privée then?' Alice asked.

A single eyebrow poked up over the edge of the glasses. 'You recording this?'

Alice held her hands up to show no hidden recording devices. 'Absolutely not.'

'Put your phones on the table,' the woman said, nodding towards the coffee table nearest to her where the ashtray was overflowing with cigarette butts.

Alice pulled the phone from her pocket and waited for Tara to pass hers before resting them on the table.

'We don't want to cause you any trouble,' Alice said, when she was perched again. 'Had you known Kerry long?'

'Must be going on three years, on and off. We met at a police station of all places.'

'Have the police spoken to you about her yet?'

The woman eyed her suspiciously, but shook her head. 'No, but if you found me, it won't be long until they come knocking too. I should emigrate.' She coughed, the sound long and scratchy, and Alice could only begin to guess how many cigarettes had already been smoked this morning.

'Would you like a glass of water?' Alice offered.

'I'm sick,' the woman replied. 'Cancer. It's spreading, so I suppose even if they do come for me, I'll probably be dead before they get me close to any kind of trial. Waste of bloody taxpayers' money, if you ask me.'

'Can you explain how it worked? The business, I mean. Kerry's last dance on Saturday night, can you remember how she ended up at that bar?'

'Some bloke phoned, looking for someone young and blonde – that's what he asked for – and so I asked Kerry whether she wanted to earn some cash. She said yes, so I sent her along. She never made it back.'

'Can you remember the name or number who called you?' Alice asked, keen to find out if it was Dave or Scott who'd been in touch.

The woman paused mid-exhale. 'My customers rely on my discretion. Even if I had the number, I wouldn't give it to you.'

'Did Kerry have any regular clients, do you know?'

'What does it matter?'

'The police said they were looking into the possibility that she was killed by someone she knew, that's all. I just wondered whether you might remember someone who was . . . a bit *too* keen on her.'

The woman gave it some thought before shaking her head. 'She was pretty and young – how most men like them – so she was always a popular girl. Usually got some pretty big tips as well. I can't remember any client ordering her more than once, though.'

'How did the money structure work? Did the customers pay you? Or pay Kerry?'

'You sure you're not police?'

'I swear we're not police,' Alice confirmed.

'The punters agreed the fee with me on the phone and paid the girls after they'd finished. Then they'd bring the money back and we'd split it. They always get to keep their tips though.'

'Did Kerry ever have sex for money?'

The woman squashed the cigarette into the overflowing ashtray and immediately lit a fresh one. 'We're not that kind of service. It was just dancing and stripping. I have a strict code as that goes.'

'She had a son, didn't she?' Alice asked.

'That's right. Finn. Poor kid.'

'Do you know what's happened to him? Is he with the police?'

Tara fired a concerned look at her friend.

'Probably in social services care by now. She really doted on him. That's why she used to do these gigs, at least that's what she told me. Although I think she also enjoyed the power her dances had over the men who paid her. She liked to flaunt her shit and have them begging, but leave them unsatisfied.'

'Did you ever meet her son? I'd really like to see him.'

Alice had pushed things too far. The woman suddenly lurched forward. 'What did you say your name was? I want some identification *now*!'

Alice quickly stood, backing away towards the door. Tara quickly followed, grabbing the phones. The woman faltered as a fresh bout of extreme coughing took hold, and Alice took it as her cue to leave.

32

Tara's heavy breathing and crimson cheeks told Alice everything she needed to know about Tara's mood as they got back in the car. 'What was with all the questions about Kerry's kid?'

Alice remained quiet, focusing on the road, looking for something familiar to help her get her bearings.

'Stop ignoring me, Alice Rose Goodman.'

Alice's head slowly craned around. 'You full-named me. Why do I feel like a naughty school child?' She couldn't help but grin.

Tara's face remained stern for a moment longer, before a smile slowly broke through. 'Seriously though, I thought you just wanted to find out if there was anyone else who could have attacked Kerry.'

'I did. I do. You heard what she said: Kerry didn't have any regular clients.'

'You're just going to take her word for it?'

Alice had been asking herself the same question. What other choice did they have but to believe her, though? And besides, why would she lie?

'I don't want to believe that one of our friends could have been involved in her death,' Alice said.

'Then don't!' Tara fired back. 'The police aren't looking at any of them, so what makes you suspect they could be?'

'Because of the lies! Dave, Scott and Ben have all lied to me about what really happened that night, I'm sure of it. But I don't understand why. If the three of them are lying to the police then there has to be an ulterior motive; either they're covering for one of the group, or they're covering for each other. I know these people, it frightens me to think that one of them could be capable of . . . *that*.'

Tara stared out of the window, biting her nail as she considered the predicament. 'Okay, go through the list of who was there again that night. Who are our suspects?'

Alice took a deep breath and pictured the photos from Dave's phone. 'Ben, Dave, Scott, Abdul, Johnny, James, and Pete. Plus I think Abdul brought three friends along that Ben and Dave had known at uni, but I don't know much about them other than their names: Gary, Duke and Michael.'

Tara counted on her fingers. 'So, that's ten altogether?'

'Yeah, but Scott left the party early, and I didn't see Gary, Duke or Michael in any of the later photos so I'm guessing they didn't hang around at the Merry Berry bar for too long.'

'Have the police interviewed them all?'

'Apparently so, that's what Dave said.'

'There must be CCTV in and around the bar. I can't believe there's no image of Kerry being attacked,' Tara mused.

Alice had been thinking the same thing, but the police hadn't confirmed what – if any – security footage they had identified from the night.

'Wait,' Tara suddenly blurted. 'You should have gone right at that last roundabout. Home is right.'

'We're not going home,' Alice replied absently.

Spotting the road she was looking for, Alice took a sharp left, narrowly avoiding the kerb.

'West Cliff?' Tara enquired quietly. 'We going to the beach?'

Alice gritted her teeth but didn't respond, her eyes darting left and right as she searched for the road she'd seen on the news.

Turning right, she spotted the police tape lining the small space at the rear of the brick building, the dilapidated 'Merry Berry' sign hanging above it.

Tara gasped. 'Tell me you didn't just bring us to the crime scene. Are you crazy?'

Alice did a U-turn and found a space near a parking meter before killing the engine. The bar and police tape were a hundred yards up the road from them.

'We're not doing anything wrong by being here,' Alice said nervously, her effort to reassure her friend missing the mark. 'I wanted to see where it happened for myself. We'll just walk around, that's all. I promise.'

Alice exited the car, leaving Tara rooted to her seat until the fear of being found alone in the car got the better of her and she hurried after her friend.

'If you start trying to break in somewhere, like some amateur detective from the telly, I'm out of here,' Tara warned.

Alice had no intention of doing anything to draw unwanted attention to their presence in the area.

The Merry Berry bar looked like somewhere time had forgotten. She hadn't noticed all the graffiti surrounding the abandoned building when she'd seen it on the news, and hadn't realized just how rundown an area they were now in. This part of the town had once been a central nightspot, but as more rival bars and clubs had opened closer to the town centre, this area had become too much effort for socialites to get to. Alice could still remember Ben dragging her around the town on a pub crawl three years ago as he'd tried to recreate his university days for her. He'd pointed out plenty of places that had either now closed or been rebranded since his student days.

There was the usual supply of fast food wrappers, cardboard coffee cups and crisp packets lining the street. Alice scanned the road as they moved closer to the bar, looking for any sign of the off-licence Dave had mentioned, but it was only when they doubled back, passing the car and returning to the main road, that she spotted anything. The neon white sign would have glowed brightly against a night sky, and the stickers in the window promoted 'Beers, Wines, and Spirits'. It had to be where they'd gone.

It wasn't obvious which lamppost they'd tied Ben to, or whether or not he would have been able to see any of them from where they'd left him. Pulling out her phone, she looked at the image of Ben and the lamppost that she'd sent herself from Dave's phone. Apart from a dark coloured wall several feet behind him, the picture could have been taken next to any lamppost on any street in the world.

'Mrs Goodman? Alice?' a familiar-sounding voice called from across the street.

Turning, Alice desperately hoped the voice didn't belong to who she thought it did. She cursed under her breath as she spotted DC Vanessa Hazelton waving her over.

'Who's that?' Tara asked.

'Just keep quiet and let me handle this,' Alice muttered between clenched teeth as they crossed the road towards the puzzled detective.

'I thought that was you,' Hazelton began, pleasantly enough. 'Were you looking for something in particular? I saw you park up, are you lost?'

There was no point trying to come up with a plausible excuse.

'Just passing through,' Alice said.

'Who's this?' Hazelton asked, nodding at Tara.

Tara's cheeks reddened, but she kept her mouth shut.

'She's a colleague,' Alice explained. 'We're both teachers.'

Hazelton's eyes burned a hole in Tara. 'Are you from Bournemouth?'

Tara glanced nervously at Alice before shaking her head. The trouble was, Tara had been raised by a father who had served in the police until he was killed in the line of duty. Whenever trouble reared its head she tended to race off in the opposite direction, hoping the stench of the trouble didn't follow. She'd been the same at university.

Hazelton's glare returned to Alice. 'I hope you're not interfering in my investigation, Mrs Goodman. You can see how this looks, right? The wife of one of our potential suspects shows up in the vicinity of the crime scene while we're still searching for clues. It looks suspicious.'

'I just wanted to find out a little more about Kerry Valentine,' Alice admitted, feeling her cheeks on fire.

Hazelton sighed. 'That's not your job, Alice. Ben hasn't been totally ruled out of our investigation yet, and your presence here does nothing to help his cause. Do you understand? Don't come back to Bournemouth until the investigation is complete or you're going to force my hand and we'll have to have a more formal conversation about your interest in Kerry Valentine. Am I making myself clear?'

Alice nodded. 'I just wanted to know if there's anything I can do to help her poor son.'

Hazelton narrowed her eyes. 'You need to stay away from him too, Mrs Goodman. For your own sake.'

Hazelton escorted them back to Alice's Audi and remained on the street until Alice had pulled away.

'I hope you're happy now!' Tara chastised. 'Can we go home before she changes her mind and fetches the shackles?'

Alice ignored the question. Despite the warning, she'd come too far to turn back now.

33

The 'Welcome to Boscombe' sign loomed large ahead of them as the stop-start traffic moved along the road. It had taken an age to get this far as the British public made the most of the fine weather and headed for the beach. The Audi's air conditioning was operating at full blast, but was doing little to cure the clamminess of Alice's hands as she gripped the steering wheel.

She didn't need to tell Tara why they had come.

As the traffic lights turned red, Alice scanned the roadway ahead, looking for any kind of clue as to which road Kerry had lived on. She knew she'd recognize it from the news reports she'd seen yesterday, but so far nothing looked familiar. Tara was gazing out of the window, deep in thought, probably pissed off that she'd agreed to come on this wild goose chase at all.

'I really do appreciate you being here,' Alice said quietly, the words almost sticking in her throat.

Tara looked at her. 'Just tell me one thing. Why are you so keen to go digging into something that has nothing to do with you? What is it about this girl?'

Alice put the car into gear as the lights turned green. 'She didn't have to die. That's what irritates me the most. She was hired to do a job, did it and should have been on her way home to her child. Instead, some monster snatched that away from her and orphaned her son. That poor lad will never understand how much he was loved or why it happened. I just . . . I feel compelled to find out the truth for him.'

'Why, Alice? Why you?'

'Because he doesn't have anyone else. I know what it's like to lose two parents. Both my dad and stepdad were taken from me too soon, and although I'm coming to terms with my grief, I still miss them every day. How are you supposed to explain to a five-year-old boy why his mummy never made it home?'

Tara didn't respond.

The parade of shops was made up of a pizza delivery store, a local supermarket, a barber's, and a fish and chip shop. As she turned into the road, and the one after that, she did recognize the street the reporter had been standing on. One of the properties had been cordoned off – Kerry's house – and a single officer in shirt and tie was melting in the sweltering heat just outside of it.

'There you go,' Tara said. 'That was her house according to what I saw on the news. Has that satisfied your need?'

It hadn't. Alice had felt compelled to drive to the street, to get an inside knowledge of the journey Kerry was due to make that night before she'd been attacked, but it hadn't brought her any kind of answer.

That's when it hit her: the real reason she was so fascinated by this girl.

As she imagined Kerry leaving the Merry Berry and walking into the darkness of the street, she could see a dark figure chasing up behind her. The man in her head was Ben. Even though she knew he couldn't be guilty, that he was tied to the lamppost, she couldn't escape the nagging voice that had her wanting to believe he was the one responsible. As she pulled the car into a space across the street from the police cordon, she felt her eyes welling up.

Tara immediately wrapped a protective arm around her friend's shoulders. 'Oh, sweetie, what's the matter?'

'She . . . could . . . have . . . been . . . me,' Alice stuttered between sobs.

Tara looked confused and waited for her to elaborate.

'At university . . . I used to pose for men.' She took a deep breath and wiped her eyes with the back of a hand. 'I posed nude for local artists.' A beat. 'I would see the way some of them would look at me – men old enough to be my father – and I knew what they wanted, the things their sick minds were contemplating. Every time, one of them would offer me a lift home, but I never accepted; I was too scared to be alone with any of them. But I needed the money and posing was easy. All those times I walked home alone . . . I could have ended up like Kerry. Had she not been out *that* night, she could have become *me*. I *was* that girl.'

Tara pulled her in closer. 'You never told me you did anything like that at university.'

'I was too embarrassed! You worked at the student bar a couple of nights a week for cash, but I earned double what you did for just one gig. I thought if I told anyone what I was doing, they – *you'd* – get the wrong idea and think I was pimping myself out, which I wasn't. All I had to do was strip and sit still for two hours. Now Kerry's life has been snuffed out, leaving that terrified boy with a broken heart. I feel . . . I feel it is *my* responsibility to help him, but to do that I need to find him.'

Tara frowned empathetically. 'How can you help him?'

'I don't know, Tara, but I have this overriding voice in my head telling me to track him down. Maybe we could set up a trust fund for him, or, I don't know, *adopt* him.'

Tara's eyes widened. 'You're getting way ahead of yourself, Alice. Adoption? You've never even met this kid, and as sweet as he might be, you don't know who else is in his life who might be able to look after him. For all you know, Kerry might have had a long-lost brother or sister, or an uncle or aunt, or I don't know what.' Tara bit her bottom lip. 'I wouldn't say this if we weren't friends, but you're starting to sound obsessed.'

Alice was staring at Tara when she spotted an elderly woman pushing a shopping trolley towards the property they were parked in front of. Without a second's thought, she was out of the car, approaching the woman.

'You're Kerry Valentine's neighbour, aren't you?' Alice began. 'You were the one who was looking after her son on the night when she . . . well, when she went missing.'

The older woman was panting slightly, deep sorrow filling her eyes. 'Yes, dear, are you another journalist?'

'No,' Alice said, stepping closer so the police officer across the road wouldn't hear her speaking. 'I was an old friend of Kerry's.'

The woman's brow furrowed for a moment, and then she squinted. 'What's your name?'

'It's Alice.'

The older woman's frown deepened. 'I don't recall her mentioning you.'

Alice ground her teeth against the shame of misleading this poor woman. 'To be honest, I hadn't seen her in years. Can I help you with your shopping?' Alice suddenly asked, keen to change the subject. 'From what I hear, you were very good to Kerry before the end, so it's the least I can do.'

The woman smiled welcomingly and fished in her bag for a set of house keys. She handed them to Alice, who promptly lifted the trolley towards the door and then inside.

'Would you like to stay for a cup of tea?' the woman asked as she removed her thin anorak and hung it on a hook by the wall.

Alice glanced back at the car where Tara was mouthing questions with a shocked look on her face.

'Tea would be lovely,' Alice said, closing the door. 'You sit down, and I'll make it.'

34

Seated at the small dining table which faced the tiny green over-grown lawn at the back of the mid-terraced property, Alice sipped her tea and remained quiet while the woman – Mrs Jones – spoke warmly about the Kerry she had known and watched thrive in recent years.

'I hadn't realized what it was she was doing at night,' Mrs Jones said sorrowfully. 'She must have thought I'd judge her and not agree to watch over little Finn. That poor lamb. The police came and took him from here on the Sunday morning when she didn't return. I was so worried that my calling them would get Kerry into trouble again, but she wasn't answering her phone and I was concerned.' She paused and looked out of the window for a moment. 'If I'd known what was going to happen I would have insisted she not go out. I would have refused to watch Finn for her. I would have . . . I would have . . .' Her words faded as the loose skin beneath her eyes moistened.

The room they were in was open plan, with two armchairs, both with flattened cushions. The faint smell of urine hung in the air. It reminded Alice of when she'd been to visit her grand-mother at the nursing home shortly before she'd passed away. Alice didn't want to imagine what her life would look like in sixty-plus years. Hopefully, she and Ben would have had a life full of fun and joy, with a family for them to cherish memories of. She wondered whether Mrs Jones had had such lofty hopes when she was younger.

'You can't blame yourself,' Alice said, reaching for her hand. The skin was cold and hung loosely. 'How well did you know Kerry? Had you been neighbours for long?'

Mrs Jones squeezed Alice's hand. 'I don't want you to think badly of me for speaking ill of your friend, but I first met her when she broke into my house and tried to steal some of my jewellery.'

Alice gently nodded to show she'd taken no offence.

'She was only a kid herself then,' Mrs Jones continued. 'Must have been three or four years ago. I remember hearing noises late one night, and when I came down to see if it was one of the cats I found her in this room, going through one of my drawers. Well, I was terrified, let me tell you. I didn't know if she had a weapon or what she might do, and my legs turned to jelly and I fell from the bottom step, bashing my hip on the way down. She came over to me and I feared for my life, but rather than hurting me, she helped me to sit up and called an ambulance. She could have taken off and left me there so she could get away, but she didn't. She stayed by my side, saying she couldn't leave until she knew I was okay. She apologized for breaking in and handed back the few trinkets she'd stuffed into her pockets.'

A white and ginger cat brushed past Alice's legs, startling her.

Mrs Jones continued to stare out of the window. 'I was taken into hospital and was kept in for a couple of nights while my heart settled back down, and Kerry came to visit me both days. I could see she was in a bad way. Her clothes were filthy, and she was little more than skin and bone. I told the doctors I'd fallen and called out for help, and that she'd been passing and stopped to help me. I never reported the burglary to the police – I thought Kerry deserved a second chance.

177

'She told me about her upbringing: in and out of various foster homes – some abusive – and she also told me about her little lad, Finn. Her face would light up when she spoke about him, and I could see how much he meant to her. He was the apple of her eye, and she would do absolutely anything for him.'

A few photo frames on a nearby unit showed a much younger Mrs Jones with a tall, handsome man. In others she spotted images of Kerry, one of which she had already seen in the press. Then Alice spotted a frame with Kerry and a little blonde-haired boy. He couldn't have been much older than four in the photo, and was pulling a grumpy face. He was the spitting image of his mother, and Alice recognized the look of adoration in Kerry's eyes.

'She was only seventeen when he was born,' Mrs Jones said, spotting Alice staring at the photo and handing it over. 'Not even a toddler when we first met. She never told me who the father was, and I'm not altogether sure *she* knew to be honest. I got the impression she'd been badly treated by a few men. She'd had a number of run-ins with the police: shoplifting, antisocial behaviour, and the like, but after that night we met, something changed in her. I don't know what it was – I'd like to think I had an influence – but she got her act together. She temporarily moved in here with me. I didn't charge her rent so she did various chores – cooking, cleaning, that sort of thing – and in return she had a roof over their heads. She managed to get a job a few hours every other night, enabling her to save money to start renting the place across the road. It took time, but she got clean of whatever she was on, and I was proud of the woman she was becoming. I didn't mind Finn sleeping here when she went to work – he was never any bother. Then she'd collect him while he was having his breakfast.'

'It sounds like she was lucky to find you,' Alice said sadly, certain Mrs Jones had probably added more years to young Kerry's life.

'I feel like I was the lucky one. You wouldn't understand yet, but it gets lonely when you reach my age. I do what I can to get out and about and to speak to the people that I meet, but in this day and age, most of you younger people – and I don't mean you any offence – walk along the street with things shoved in your ears, or staring at tiny screens, or both! People don't seem to want to talk like they once did. There was a time when I knew everyone's name in the street and who to turn to if I needed help or support, but not now. I try, but it's a struggle.'

'Do you know where they took Finn to? I'd really like to meet him.'

Mrs Jones wiped the corner of her eye with a mottled tissue. 'I wish I knew, dear. They took him and said he'd be safer in their care. That's one of the worst parts of what's happened. I miss him. His little face would brighten the room when he came in. He always had one of the biscuits out of my tin. They were nothing fancy, but I got the impression Kerry didn't let him have cakes and biscuits at home. She was determined to give him a better upbringing than she'd had and swore by fruit and vegetables as snacks. I certainly haven't eaten as well since she moved out, but she was young and needed her own space. I understood that, but I used to cherish the days when I knew she was coming around with Finn. Even if she only dropped him off, it was a joy to see how well she was doing. A real angel died that night.'

Alice stayed with Mrs Jones for half an hour, listening to her stories about when Kerry had taken Finn to the zoo for the first time, and how Kerry went over the top with gifts and food every year on Finn's birthday, even though it was only ever the three of them there to eat it all. Alice's guilt was on overload as she relayed what she'd learned to Tara.

'It's a real tragedy,' Alice concluded. 'It's silly but the more I hear about her, the more I can see myself in her struggles. If I had lost both parents so young, how might I have ended up? It just makes you think how lucky you are. You know?'

'Too true!' Tara agreed. 'I appreciate how this situation is making you feel, but there's nothing you can do to fix it. I don't think you'll be truly happy unless you manage to invent a time machine, go back and stop her being killed that night. Speaking as your friend, I think you need to work out a way to deal with your guilt. It wasn't your fault, Alice. You didn't send those boys to Bournemouth. Don't forget, as far as we knew Ben was at home while we were in Paris. You weren't the one who hired Kerry to come and strip, nor are you responsible for whoever attacked her as she walked home. I don't want to sound callous, but I think it's time for you to realize that Kerry herself should have known she was putting herself at risk.'

Tara was right, as much as Alice didn't want to listen, but that didn't ease the tension in her neck and shoulders.

'I think I need to go and speak to DC Hazelton,' Alice said after a minute. 'I think she deserves to know what I heard Dave saying on the phone.'

Tara looked shocked. 'You have no idea what that conversation was about. Plus how's it going to look: throwing Ben's best mate under the bus?'

'If he had nothing to do with Kerry's death then he'll be just fine. I also want to tell her about Johnny. You didn't see Faye's face the other night. She looked like she'd gone several rounds with a heavyweight boxer. If he's capable of that kind of behaviour with his wife, what's he capable of with a stranger?'

Tara sighed loudly. 'What happens when it turns out neither of them had anything to do with it? How will you explain to Faye what you did? What she told you about Johnny was said in strictest confidence. If she's not willing to go to the police about his abuse, she won't thank you for going behind her back. Give the police some credit and space to carry out their investigation. I got the impression from DC Hazelton that she won't rest until she has the correct suspect in custody anyway.'

Alice pulled up outside the gates of St Michael's School. 'Maybe you're right. Are you sure this is where you want me to drop you?'

Tara looked at the large brick building. 'Yeah. Unlike some, I'm nowhere near prepared for the new school term. What I'd give for your organizing skills and energy! It's a struggle for me to get out of bed most days.'

'Do you want any help? I'm a dab hand at stapling pictures to walls and notice boards, you know.'

Tara pecked her on the cheek. 'I appreciate the offer, but you should get yourself home to that gorgeous husband of yours.'

Alice suddenly looked at the time. Nearly two, but her phone was in the boot and she had no idea whether Ben had called or messaged to say he was done at the office.

'Shit! I didn't realize it was so late. You're right, I'd better get home. Thank you for today. I know I stopped you getting work done but I really appreciate you being there.'

Tara hugged her tightly. 'Promise me you won't go speaking to the police without discussing it with Ben first. Try to do something to take your mind off this murder business. Remember, there's nothing you can do to help that girl or her son now.'

Tara opened the Audi's door and climbed out, waving as she closed it. Alice was about to pull away when a sudden tapping on the window startled her. Looking up she saw Andrew's big smiling face staring back at her through the closed window, a filled baguette in his hand.

'I thought I recognized your car,' he said, as she lowered the glass. 'Are you coming or going?'

'Going,' Alice said. 'I was just dropping off Tara.'

'That's too bad,' Andrew said, resting his arm on the window frame, the smell of tobacco now permeating the interior of the car. 'I was going to offer to split my sandwich with you. Have you eaten?'

'It's kind of you to offer,' she said politely, 'but I'm meeting Ben for lunch.'

'Of course you are,' he said, unable to keep the disappointment from his voice. 'Have you got five minutes though? Do you remember that old friend I mentioned to you? The one I bumped into at bird watching? Well, the thing is . . . I asked her if she'd like to go out for something to eat with me, and . . . I haven't heard back from her. It's been a couple of days, and I'm sure she will have heard my message by now, and I'm worried I might have overstepped the mark.'

Alice applied the handbrake but left the engine running. 'Andrew, you're too hard on yourself. You're a lovely person, very kind and affectionate, and she'll probably be back in touch before you know it.'

Alice glanced at the clock again, hoping Ben wasn't already home and wondering where she'd been all morning.

Andrew pushed his glasses back up the bridge of his nose. 'Do you think?'

Alice nodded encouragingly. 'I really do. I'm sure she'll be happy to reignite your friendship, and from the way you spoke about how things have been going, I'm certain it will all work out for the best.'

He was grinning like a Cheshire cat, revealing the yellow nicotine stains on his teeth. 'I hope you're right. She's a couple of years younger than me, but she said she was looking for someone a bit older, as she's had younger boyfriends before and despises immaturity. Would you say I'm mature?'

'Very mature, Andrew. Listen, I'm sorry to be abrupt, but I really do need to get home. I'm sure she'll message you back and agree to meet. Mark my words.'

She put the car into gear and he straightened up, allowing her to raise the window and pull out of the space. She continued to watch him in the rear-view mirror as she headed for home. He was still standing on the pavement watching the Audi when Alice turned into the next road. The smell of the garlic sausage in his baguette and his tobacco breath lingered and she flipped the air conditioning switch to maximum.

35

Ben's car wasn't parked outside the house as she pulled in through the gates, which meant he'd yet to return from the office and so wouldn't know she'd been out. Alice didn't know how he'd react if she told him where she'd been or what she'd been doing, but sometimes it was just better to let sleeping dogs lie.

Pulling her phone from her bag in the boot, she saw he'd messaged her twice to say he was running late. She fired him a quick response telling him she'd see him soon. There was also a voicemail from a withheld number.

'Alice? It's Ray,' Ben's dad's voice crackled. 'We called by the house to see how you're coping, but nobody was home. Can you give us a call when you're back? Just want to check that you're both well, and to see if there's anything you need or . . . sorry . . . I'm sure you probably just want some space and to put this whole mess behind you. Hermione asked me to leave the message. Just send a text if everything's okay, and we'll say no more. Okay? Oh, and don't let that son of mine think he can get away with not taking you on honeymoon. Okay, okay, that will do. Hope to speak with you both soon. Bye.'

Alice clutched the phone to her chest, straining to stop her eyes from watering. Ray and Hermione had seemed standoffish when she'd first encountered them, but now they'd become like a second set of parents, particularly Ray. Alice didn't doubt that Hermione had told him to phone and leave the message. Of course, if they let slip to Ben that they'd called round and found the house empty, it might raise suspicion; she would have to think of a reason why she wasn't home.

The large house blocked out the sun, and she took a moment to savour the cool freshness the shadow brought. Pulling her handbag over her head and shoulder, she marched into the house.

Dropping her bag to the countertop in the kitchen, she meandered to the fridge, pulling it open and looking for something to snack on. Closing the fridge door, she reached for a banana, peeled the skin and devoured it in four mouthfuls. It was the boost of energy she needed. Spotting the now very dry laundry hanging on the clothes airer, she scooped up the items, folded them neatly into a pile and carried them upstairs. She'd always enjoyed the smell of fresh laundry, and was tempted to change into fresh clothes there and then. The car journey to and from Bournemouth had been hot and sticky, despite the air conditioning.

Heading into the main bedroom, she was disappointed to find the bed still unmade. She'd been the last one in there, and was usually very good at folding back the thin duvet and straightening the sheet, but apparently she'd left it in a crumpled mess this morning. Lowering the pile of laundry to the bedside table on Ben's side of the room, she shook the king-size duvet before flattening it on the bed and pulling it back in half, grabbing handfuls of sheet and pulling and tucking as she completed a circuit of the mattress.

Letting out a sigh of satisfaction, she returned to the pile of clothes. Sorting them into a pile for her – bras, knickers, and tops – and a pile for Ben – socks, pants, work shirts, and trousers – she carried her pile to the chest of drawers on her side of the large room. Opening the top drawer, she remembered how desperately she needed to sort through her clothes and get rid of the things that looked tired or would never be worn again. Anything still usable she would bag up and donate to charity, and the rest would be dropped in the bin. Rifling through some of the tops, she decided she wasn't in the right frame of mind to do it now. Ben needed to go through his clothes too, and it would be much better if they did it together, particularly as she didn't trust him to do his at all without her there supervising.

Closing her drawers, she was just going to leave Ben's pile on the bed, when she figured it would be kinder to put them away for him. Moving to his wardrobe, she opened both doors. The large space was filled with various tailored suits to the left, neatly hung and not squashed, followed by his work shirts, and then his more casual trousers and jeans. Beneath this were two stacks of drawers, into which she deposited the socks and pants. Finding the vacant hangers, she carefully hung the shirts, flattening any creases with her hands, and then moved onto the trousers. The final item left in the pile was a towel he used when he went to the gym and kept on the shelf above the hangers. He was taller than she was and could easily reach up there, but even on tiptoes, she struggled to grip the shelf edge. As she strained to reach, her efforts to swing her other arm and essentially launch the towel onto the shelf were thwarted by a battered old shoebox she'd never noticed before. It was pushed into the wardrobe wall, but jutted out slightly. The towel landed in its space, but as it did, her trailing hand caught the corner of the shoebox and before she could react to stop it, it tumbled forwards out of her grasp and onto to the floor, spilling its contents.

Alice tutted in frustration as she dropped to her knees and began to scoop up the contents, but as she turned the box the right way up, she realized she'd never seen any of the photographs before. She immediately recognized a younger looking Ben. There were images of him under ten, playing sports, sitting in tall grass, posing in school uniform. Then there were pictures of him as an adolescent, and the youth by his side in most of them had to be

Dave, albeit with none of the tattoos and with a full head of hair. She found herself giggling as she took the time to look at each one, wondering why Ben had never shown these to her before.

She remembered asking to see older photographs of him once, but he'd said something about his parents not being very snap-happy when he'd grown up. She'd seen a couple of him as a grumpy-looking baby, but these were priceless. The next one she turned over showed both Ben and Dave, maybe fifteen years old with bright bleached hair. Both were striking hard-faced poses, trying to look much older and failing miserably.

In the next image, she saw Ben looking more like the Ben she'd first met all those years ago. On his arm was a woman with a shock of auburn hair, gelled up and pointy. Resembling something of a punk, she had a pretty face and an engaging smile, but looked older than Ben. In the next one, she was sandwiched between Ben and Dave, the three of them crying with laughter at some-thing.

She knew Ben had dated before, as she had dated plenty of men before him. They didn't keep their previous relationships a secret, but nor did they waste countless hours discussing their exes. At first, she couldn't be sure if this woman was Ben's girl-friend or Dave's as she seemed close to both of them. Then she froze as her eyes fell on a photo of Ben stooped on one knee before the woman, her hand in his and her other hand at her mouth. The next picture was of Ben holding the woman's hand out for the camera, his grandmother's beautiful jewel encrusted ring on her finger.

She bequeathed it to me on the understanding that one day I give it to someone deserving of its splendour.

Alice raised her hand and compared the ring on her finger to the one in the image. She had no doubt that it was the same. Her heart aching with sadness, she flipped through the next set of images. Ben and this woman holding hands; Ben and her linking arms; Ben and her kissing; Ben and her drinking champagne.

He'd never told her he'd been engaged before, and although in the grand scheme of things it wasn't that important, seeing the evidence still felt like a betrayal.

Then she spotted the woman's necklace. The name 'Mary' was written in joined-up handwriting, clasped between the two ends of the chain.

Liam O'Neill's words in the pub echoed around the room: *Does the name Mary mean anything to you?*

It hadn't, and still didn't, but could it be that the person Liam was referring to was the same red-headed punk as in these pictures?

Find out what you can about Mary, but watch your back – Ben won't like it if he finds out you're digging into his past.

She'd thought he'd only said it to get a rise out of her, but what if there *was* something she needed to know about this woman?

The front door slammed downstairs, and Ben's voice called out. 'Babe? You home?'

Alice felt a jolt of panic go through her. He'd be up the stairs in a shot, and if he spotted her on the floor with his box of hidden photographs, he'd think she'd been snooping. She'd be within her rights to demand an explanation about why he'd kept this part of his life a secret for so long, but Liam's warning still resounded loud: *we both know what he's capable of when he's not happy*.

Grabbing the remaining images from the floor, she pushed them into the shoebox as quickly as she could, no longer caring about trying to get them back in the correct order. She could hear Ben on the staircase and leapt to her feet, wrestling to get the shoebox lid back on, stretching up on the tips of her toes to try and get it back into its dusty space in the cupboard.

'Babe?' Ben called out from the top of the stairs.

She had one corner on the shelf and pushed with all her might. Closing the wardrobe, she had just turned to face the bed when the bedroom door was pushed open. Ben approached her and kissed her cheek. Alice held her breath, hoping he couldn't hear the rapid thumping of her heart.

'Everything okay?' he asked her with a concerned look.

'Just putting away the laundry,' she quickly fired back, nodding at the drawers. 'All finished now, though.' She took a deep breath. 'How's everything at the office?'

'Ongoing,' he replied in a disappointed tone. 'The lawyers are still on the case and hopefully we can avoid a lawsuit. Even though Yann didn't cause the accident, he shouldn't have been on the road. We either need to fess up and take the inevitable fines and reputational hit, or keep quiet and hope nobody finds out. I feel like I'm stuck between a rock and a hard place.' He forced a smile. 'Don't let any of that worry *you* though. I'm sorting it. You eaten yet?'

She thought about the banana she had wolfed down, and shook her head.

'Good, then let's go out to lunch. It's about time you and I remembered we're supposed to be on our honeymoon. I want to go out and forget about everything else that's going on. I also have a surprise for you, but I don't want to say until we're away from here. Sound okay?'

She was just desperate to get out of the room before he opened the wardrobe and noticed his box had moved.

36

'A toast,' Ben said, raising the thin flute, 'to a happy marriage.'

Alice clinked her glass against his. The bubbles tickled her upper lip as she sipped the champagne. 'A girl could get used to this,' she said, playing along, even though the image of her ring on another woman's finger continued to taunt her.

'I can think of no place I'd rather be,' Ben replied, 'than with my stunning wife on such a beautiful day. If I had my way, we'd both quit our jobs and dine like this every day.'

Alice casually glanced around the fine décor of the small French restaurant he'd brought her to. They were the only couple in there now, and had only been given a table on the promise that they wouldn't have starters or puddings and would eat quickly. Despite the watchful eye of the maître d', it was a welcoming environment, and gentle harmonies played on surround speakers.

'I don't think we'd survive for long if neither of us had a job,' Alice cautioned.

'I don't know,' he mused, 'I could sell the business. That ought to be enough to keep us dining for a few years at least.'

He wasn't being serious, which is why she didn't bother to point out that she actually enjoyed being a teacher, and so giving it up wasn't an option, at least, not yet.

'I brought you here for two reasons,' Ben continued, lowering his glass and reaching out for her hand. 'Are you ready for some great news?'

She nodded.

'Well, I heard from that DC Hazelton today. Do you remember her? The woman who collected my clothes on Sunday?'

Alice's pulse quickened. Had Hazelton told him that she'd seen Alice in Bournemouth this morning?

'Well, the great news is, they found none of that girl's DNA on my clothes. I'm in the clear! I mean, I always knew I would be, but it's nice to hear the police finally confirm it.'

Alice was relieved to hear the news; a small victory for common sense over her cynical imagination.

'That's wonderful, Ben! What does that mean for us in terms of their constant intrusions?'

He frowned. 'My solicitor is handling all of that. She said I've now been shelved as a person of interest in the inquiry, that they would hold onto my clothes for the time being, but that they would be returned in due course. She also said I'll be getting my passport back. I was buzzing when she called.'

Alice allowed herself a moment to process the news. If they'd ruled Ben out of the investigation then that had to mean he couldn't have killed Kerry. But that didn't necessarily rule out any of the others.

'Did she mention if they have any other leads?' Alice asked as casually as she could manage.

'She didn't say, and to be honest, I couldn't care less. I know that sounds like a terrible thing to say, but I've been doing a lot of hard thinking since yesterday, and you were right. I shouldn't be blaming myself for what happened. I didn't make some jerk attack her, and it wasn't even my idea to have her at the bar, so it's about time I gave myself a break. Right?'

Alice nodded, even though she wasn't sure the entire group could be let off so easily.

'Who do you think killed her then?' she asked.

Ben frowned. 'How would I know?'

Her mind returned to the list of suspects she'd found scrawled yesterday. 'So you don't think it was someone else from the stag party?'

His expression changed to one of surprised anger. 'No! Why would I?'

Alice bit her lip. 'I found the list you and Dave drew up on Sunday night.'

'List? What list . . .?' His face changed as the memory returned. 'That? We were drunk and just spitballing ideas. It's nonsense. When did you see it?'

'I came into the living room first thing yesterday to tidy up and saw it then.'

His face softened. 'Is that what's been bothering you the last couple of days? I knew something wasn't quite right. You've been . . . I don't know, distant? I couldn't figure out exactly what it was, but now I know. Forget about that list. We ripped it up when we woke up. We both realized how ridiculous it was to think that one of our friends could have snuck away and gone after her with nobody noticing.'

'I overheard the two of you talking, too, on Sunday night. You were talking about Scott and some trouble he got you into in Malia.'

Ben was smirking now. 'So you leapt to the conclusion that he – or one of the rest of us – could be responsible for killing that girl? Babe, seriously, do you realize how crazy that sounds?'

She didn't like that he was laughing at her. 'What do you expect when you keep secrets from me?' she scowled.

'Secrets? What secrets?' he fired back evenly.

'The fight in Greece, the trip to Bournemouth, the striptease Kerry gave you, the fact that the police had your DNA on record . . . need I go on?'

He looked at her quizzically. 'Just then you referred to the victim by her first name.'

'And?'

'*And*, it's just a weird thing to do.'

'Don't change the subject, Ben. And there's another secret we haven't talked about – how long did you know Johnny had been beating Faye?'

The look of guilt in his eyes told her everything she needed to know.

'He told me he lashed out at her a few months ago. He was in shock when he told me. Said he'd never dreamed he'd ever be the type of guy to strike his wife and felt horrible afterwards. That's why he suggested they go and see a marriage counsellor. It only happened that one time, as far as I know.'

'Honestly? Because she told me it's happened several times, and that he did it again on Sunday. Can you, hand on heart, say that he was with you guys all night in Bournemouth?'

'You think Johnny killed that girl?' He snorted with derision. 'No way! I've known him for years.'

'If you'd seen Faye's face on Sunday, I don't think you'd be saying that.'

'I'm not condoning his behaviour. Abuse in a relationship is unacceptable, but the victim wasn't beaten to death – she was stabbed. Multiple times from what I was told at interview. Besides, Johnny *was* with us all night.'

'How can you be sure? What if he snuck off while you were tied to that lamppost?'

'Dave told me he was with him all night.'

The maître d' was looking over at their raised voices, but made no effort to interfere.

Alice leaned closer and whispered loudly. 'I heard Dave on the phone telling someone he'd cajoled the rest of the group into telling the police a different version of events.'

Ben snorted again. 'What? Now I know you're winding me up.'

'I'm *serious*, Ben. When you dropped me home after lunch yesterday he was still at our place, and he was acting suspiciously. He definitely said they'd lied to the police.'

He squeezed her hand tighter. 'Babe, I know *I* didn't lie to the police. Are you sure you know what you heard? Who was he talking to?'

'I don't know.'

'So how do you know it was anything to do with what happened in Bournemouth?'

She couldn't remember the exact words she'd overheard, but she was sure he'd mentioned Bournemouth. Hadn't he? Or had she put words in his mouth based on her own assumptions?

She wanted to reply, to convince him she wasn't putting two and two together and getting three, but the words wouldn't form coherently in her mind.

'Listen,' Ben continued. 'I realize you've been under a huge amount of stress. What with the wedding and all this other shit that's come up since. I really think the two of us should go and book somewhere last minute and just fly out of here, put all this behind us.'

'What about your passport?'

'I told you, that'll be back with me soon enough. My solicitor said she just had to complete the paperwork and then they'd drop it round. I think we should go to a travel agents as soon as we've finished our lunch. We'll find somewhere tropical, all-inclusive, and then just *relax*. I know it won't be Barbados, but that doesn't mean we can't still have a great time. You can choose the destination, and a swanky hotel. We could be sipping cocktails on a beach this time tomorrow. What do you say? I think it's what we both need.'

She frowned at him. It sounded wonderful, and there was probably some truth in the idea that they should do whatever was necessary to put this nightmare behind them, but she couldn't help feeling she'd be somehow abandoning Kerry and Finn.

'Did you manage to get a refund from the insurance company?' she asked.

He shook his head in disappointment. 'They said that wrongful arrest isn't covered within the terms and conditions of the policy. I told them that was bullshit as it wasn't our fault we couldn't fly on Sunday night, but they said even if the police wrote to them and explained that they'd made a mistake, it wouldn't be enough. My solicitor reckons our best chance is petitioning the police to pay compensation to cover what we lost. There are no guarantees, but we'll see.'

'So how do you propose we pay for a last-minute break?'

'We have savings, let's just use them. We can save more in the future, but right now I want to take you away from all of this. I can see the stress and worry is affecting you and that needs to stop. Okay?'

She was about to reply when she spotted a pair of familiar eyes staring at them from the main door to the restaurant.

37

'Babe?' Ben repeated, as Alice continued to stare at the door over his shoulder. 'Are we agreed then? We use our savings for the holiday?'

She looked to Ben and then back at Liam O'Neill, who was now opening the door and entering the small dining area. The maître d' was nowhere in sight, enabling O'Neill to head straight for their table.

What was he doing here? Why now? She wasn't worried about how Ben would react when O'Neill accused him of killing Kerry – he'd laugh it off – but she couldn't be as convinced of his reaction to learning that Alice had met O'Neill twice before and not told him.

'Ben? Ben Goodman?' O'Neill said, loudly enough for Ben to turn and stare at him. 'It *is* you,' O'Neill continued enthusiastically. 'You know, I thought it was. I saw through the window and I said to myself, I swear that person looks just like Ben Goodman.'

Ben's cheeks flushed slightly as he tried to work out who O'Neill was. Alice hid her face behind a napkin, willing O'Neill to leave, but her efforts appeared to be in vain as he pulled over a chair from another table and promptly joined them.

'How've you been?' O'Neill continued, his voice filled with

excited enthusiasm at this false reunion. 'I bet you don't remember me,' he added, helping himself to one of the breadsticks in the middle of the table and taking a bite, crunching it loudly between his teeth, a huge grin plastered across his face.

What the hell kind of game was he playing? If he was just looking to get under Ben's skin, then he was doing a great job of it.

Ben glanced at Alice and she was sure he could read her mind, but he didn't react to the fear and anxiety in her eyes.

'I'm sorry,' Ben offered. 'I'm pretty lousy at remembering faces. Where do we know each other from?'

O'Neill feigned embarrassment, also making eye contact with Alice. 'Well this just got awkward!' he erupted into laughter, playfully slapping Ben's arm in the process.

Ben didn't react, but Alice saw his fists instinctively clench.

'Liam O'Neill,' he said, showing no sign of any offence at Ben's apparent lack of memory. 'We went to school together. We were in Mr Ewing's class.'

The statement was made so plainly that Alice couldn't help but believe the words, but then, O'Neill had tricked her when they'd first met, pretending to be just another guest at the hotel. Something stirred in Ben's eyes. A moment of recognition perhaps?

'I think you've got me confused with someone else,' Ben said apologetically.

'No, I'm sure it's you. Cattle Hill Secondary School, right? Come on, you must remember Mr Ewing? He had an out-of-control beard that resembled a bird's nest. Remember? He wore socks and sandals and we used to refer to them as his Nike Air Jerusalems on account of his deep Catholic faith. He taught us Geography and Religious Studies.'

Alice knew that Ben had attended Cattle Hill Secondary School – he had told her as much. Was that sort of information public knowledge? It must have been for O'Neill to be using it now.

'Come on, Ben,' he continued. 'You *must* remember! I was a lot smaller back then, skinny too. I had thick glasses and suffered with dandruff. You used to call me Snow Shoulders. Remember now?'

The flutter of recognition grew across Ben's face. 'That was you?'

'A lot can change in twenty-five years,' O'Neill acknowledged. 'I wear contacts now; I discovered antidandruff shampoo at college, and two divorces later, my midriff has inflated. Otherwise it's the same old me. You've hardly changed at all. Still got a thick head of hair – the fringe has probably receded a bit, but not as much as mine. You're in pretty good shape too. And if that car of yours parked outside is anything to go by, you must be doing all right for yourself.'

'I remember you now,' Ben admitted. 'I can't believe you recognized me after all these years.'

O'Neill suddenly turned and stared at Alice. 'And who's this beautiful lady?'

'This is my wife, Alice,' Ben replied, as O'Neill held out his hand for Alice to shake.

Her cheeks were on fire as she reluctantly shook his hand.

'Lovely to meet you, Alice,' he said innocently. 'What do you do for a living?'

She couldn't believe he was maintaining this pretence. What was the point? He'd spoken so freely when they'd met at the pub yesterday, but maybe he didn't have the bottle to repeat his accusations with Ben in earshot. What choice did she have but to play along? If she admitted she knew why he was really here, she'd be admitting to Ben that she'd kept the first encounters a secret.

'I'm a teacher,' she said between gritted teeth, hoping the maître d' would return with their food imminently.

'A teacher?' O'Neill cooed. 'Now *that's* a profession to be proud of. The finest people in the world, teachers are,' he said, patting Ben's upper arm with the back of his hand. 'Don't you reckon, Ben? I mean where would any of us be without great teachers?'

Alice could tell Ben's patience was wearing thin.

'Here, Ben, do you remember that girl who joined our class for that one year? It must have been when we were fifteen or so. She was from France. Oh, what was her name . . .? Patricia? Paula? No, wait, it was Penny. That was it, wasn't it, Ben?'

Ben nodded at the memory. 'Penny Duncan. I dated her for a bit.'

O'Neill was staring into the distance, as if the memory was being projected onto the window. 'That's right. Oh I *remember* her. She was the most beautiful girl I'd ever seen. I genuinely think I fell in love with her the first time she walked into class. I couldn't believe it when I won the lead role opposite her in theatre class.' He patted Ben's arm again. 'Here, do you remember what you did to me the night of the first show?'

Ben lowered his eyes. Was that shame? 'That was years ago. We were just stupid kids.'

O'Neill was laughing hard at the memory, staring at Alice. 'Ben, the little prankster, thought it would be hilarious to dose my milkshake with laxatives so when I went out on stage for my big scene with Penny I would shit my pants, and I almost did!' He was laughing still, but there was anguish in the sound too. 'The pain became so unbearable that I had to run from the stage. I only just made it to the toilet before my bowels erupted. The show continued with my surprise understudy stepping in at the last minute. It was lucky you knew all the words of my part, Ben, or I think they'd have had to cancel the show altogether. God knows how much you put in that milkshake, but I had to stay in hospital for three days until things were sorted. I missed the whole week of shows.'

Ben's head was bowed even lower. 'Yeah, well, I'm sorry about that.'

O'Neill waved away the apology. 'Hey, don't worry about it.

We were just stupid kids, like you said. It's all water under the bridge as far as I'm concerned. I've always wondered what it would have been like to kiss Penny, though. To be honest – and I can admit it now, because we're all much older – the only reason I auditioned for the school play was because I knew the male and female leads would kiss. I came so close to my dream, only to then have it snatched away.'

'If I'd known—'

'If you'd known you'd have still done it,' O'Neill interrupted, the laughter gone. 'I don't bear you any ill will. The thing is, Penny had that effect on us boys. She was so beautiful that we'd have done anything to be with her.' He fixed Alice with a stare. 'Some women just have that dynamic magnetism; we can't be blamed for our actions.'

The maître d' appeared at the table, carrying two plates of steaming food. He raised a confused eyebrow in O'Neill's direction.

'I'm so sorry,' the reporter said, standing suddenly. 'I'm interrupting your lunch, and that's incredibly rude of me. I didn't even ask if I could join you. Forgive my interruption.'

The maître d' lowered the plates to the table.

'I'll be on my way,' O'Neill said, patting Ben's shoulder. 'This was fun. We should arrange to meet and catch-up on old times sometime. There's nothing more stimulating than a trip down memory lane. Wouldn't you agree, Alice?'

She started at the mention of her name, and as she looked up from her food she saw that both men were staring at her, reading her reaction. 'Sometimes, but some things are better left buried in the past.'

O'Neill fixed her with a knowing look, mouthing the words, 'Call me,' before turning on his heel and heading out of the door.

'Sorry about that,' Ben said, as he reached for the salt and pepper and ground them liberally over his venison.

'It's a small world,' Alice replied nonchalantly, eager to move the conversation on.

'You're probably not surprised to hear I was a bit of a shit back at school,' Ben admitted, tearing into the meat. 'I wasn't the brightest student and I think on some subconscious level I was jealous of boys like Liam, for whom subjects seemed to come so easy. I worked damned hard to get my B and C grades at GCSE, whereas someone like him swept the board with A grades. I think I did things out of spite – things I'm not proud of.'

'Like putting laxatives in a milkshake?'

He chuckled at the memory. 'You should have seen his face when he wandered out onto the stage. He looked in agony and was desperate to carry on with the scene, but then he doubled over and raced away. I was already in costume, and took his place. For years he was referred to as the kid who shat himself on stage. The thing is, nobody knew what had really happened; I think the teachers assumed he got struck with stage fright. It was a stupid thing to do, and looking back on it, I wish I hadn't done it. You do believe me, don't you?'

She'd never seen him look so ashamed about anything. The fact that O'Neill had revealed this mischief from Ben's past left her with only one thought – the real reason O'Neill had been trying to drive a wedge between her and Ben was out of revenge for childhood trauma.

'You called him Snow Shoulders?'

'That was just banter. Liam was one of those Goody-Two-Shoes characters. You know? The ones who suck up to all the teachers.'

Alice knew only too well. 'I was one of those students, Ben. I worked so hard at school, and dreaded the prospect of getting into trouble. I knew lots of kids like you: people who called me names, and put me down out of jealousy. There were nights I would cry myself to sleep because of something someone else had said. It wasn't easy being good all the time, and it was really tough when others made fun of me because of it.'

Her eyes stung at the memories.

Ben reached for her hand and squeezed it affectionately. 'Then on behalf of all the bullies, I would like to formally apologize to you. If I'd known the impact of my actions, I would have revised my attitude.'

She knew in that moment that he meant every word.

38

Alice noticed the envelope first.

As they approached the front gate, Ben's view was obstructed by the overhanging hedge, but she knew he'd seen it as soon as the car slowed.

'You've got to me fricking kidding me,' he growled as he slowed to a stop, applied the handbrake and leapt from the car, tearing the white envelope from the gate's locking mechanism.

He stared at it for several moments, as if trying to read the contents without opening it. Slowly his eyes rose, first looking left, and then right, hoping to catch a glimpse of the person who had deposited it there. The road was empty, save for two cars going in opposite directions.

'Take this,' Ben scowled, throwing the envelope onto her lap as he returned to the car.

He pressed the remote and the gates slowly slid open – Alice noticed remains of the tape strands clinging to the gate's iron bars as they drove onwards.

Ben parked up outside the garage and snatched the envelope from her lap as he pushed open his door and headed for the house, leaving Alice scanning the property's perimeter for the pair of eyes she instinctively felt watching her.

Whoever it was, they were hidden from view and wouldn't emerge until long after she'd gone inside. She wanted to yell and scream, to tell him to leave them alone. They'd done nothing wrong, they didn't deserve this kind of harassment.

'You coming in?' Ben asked.

Overhead, thick grey clouds were blocking out the sun's rays, but they were doing nothing to fight the thick humidity as the high pressure once again threatened a storm. Alice couldn't help but think that a downpour was exactly what was needed right now: fresh rain to rejuvenate the brown, dry lawns; lower pressure to cool everyone's temperatures.

Ben was already tearing at the envelope as she reached the kitchen. He probably should have left it for the police to search for prints and DNA, and his impatience was causing one of the pages' corners to tear slightly. She watched as he read the note, his face darkening with every word, and when he looked up to meet her gaze his eyes were shining.

'What is it?' she asked. 'What does it say?'

He was speechless as the page fell from his fingers and floated silently to the floor. Screwing up the sticky envelope, he slammed it into the bin and stomped from the room.

Fearing the worst, Alice scooped up the page, holding it carefully by the edges, and read the typed words.

Dear Alice,
Why do you love Ben?
He's killed before,
And he'll kill again.

She shuddered at the message, now seeing why Ben had been so angry. It had to have come from Liam O'Neill. It was no coincidence that he'd turned up at the pub yesterday when she was there alone, nor was it an accident that he had happened to appear at the door of the French restaurant when they'd been there. It would have been easy for him to leave them there with their meals, knowing he had plenty of time to get back here and leave the note before they'd even finished their food.

Was this intimidation really the result of childhood bullying? What did he hope to achieve? To drive a wedge between them? If anything, these notes were only forcing Ben and Alice together more.

Ben marched back into the kitchen, holding the laptop with the security camera feeds. 'I'll find out who you are, you bastard,' he muttered under his breath as he began to fiddle with the cursor.

'I'll make us some tea,' Alice suggested, reaching for the kettle and carrying it to the stainless steel sink. If her mother had taught her anything, it was that a strong cup of tea could put even the most troublesome of issues into perspective. She filled the kettle before carrying it back to its stand and turning it on.

She studied the note again, recognizing the same font and size as the first. Again, there was no name left on the note, making it all the more sinister.

He's killed before, and he'll kill again.

As angry as Ben was to read the words, he had yet to deny them, and her mind couldn't help wandering back to those images of the older woman he'd been engaged to.

Find out what you can about Mary, but watch your back.

Was O'Neill suggesting that Ben had killed this Mary woman and got away with it?

'Son of a bitch!' Ben yelled from behind the laptop. 'The bastard smashed one of the cameras. Have a look.'

He swivelled the laptop's screen as she approached and replayed the clip. It was from the camera on the wall above the gate. At first there was nobody in sight, and then just as suddenly a large figure in a wide-brimmed hat came into view in the bottom right corner of the screen. He only appeared for a moment, though, as in the next shot he swung up the end of a cane and the screen smashed, before the camera's signal was lost to grey fuzz.

'The son of a bitch smashed the camera!' Ben exclaimed. 'Not only is he invading our privacy, he's now done criminal damage. When I find out who's behind this, I'll . . . I'll . . .' He allowed the threat to hang in the air, either unwilling or unable to complete the sentence.

'We should phone the police again,' Alice said as the kettle reached boiling point. 'Maybe they can still recover a DNA trace from the envelope or the tape, or maybe the cane left a trace on the camera. Either way, we should report it.'

'You report it!' he said, pushing the laptop away from him. It teetered on the edge of the counter, but thankfully gravity didn't take it over. 'I'm done with the police, they've brought us nothing but trouble so far. It's time we take care of things ourselves.'

'What's that supposed to mean?'

He was silent for a moment before fixing her with an understanding look. 'Your safety is my paramount concern, and the only way either of us will be safe is with our own private army patrolling the grounds. I dare this prick to come within ten yards of this place when I have a crew tooled up inside the boundary.'

'Don't do anything illegal, Ben. The last thing we need is to give the police any more reason to hound you down.'

'Who said anything about acting illegally? I intend to hire a private security firm to bring guard dogs and patrol the outer edge of the property 24/7. Whoever's behind this won't stand a chance if he comes back. Once he's caught, and I've had my time to interrogate him, we'll turn him over to your friends in blue.'

He came over to her and delicately placed his hands either side of her waist. 'I just want you to be safe, which is why I think it's even more important we get away from here for a few days. Okay? Give me a couple of hours to get some security sorted and then we'll go online and pick a last-minute deal. Money is no object. Okay?'

She allowed him to kiss her, though did little to reciprocate the gesture, and watched as he moved away, grabbed the phone from the side, and put it to his ear.

'Dave? I need a favour.'

Alice remained in the kitchen filling two cups with water from the kettle and swishing the teabags around. Ben might not have any faith left in the police, but she still did, and something deep inside told her it would be for the best to report the latest threatening letter. At the very least, she wanted someone to realize the pressure they were being put under by Liam O'Neill, or whomever else was behind the letters. It was the latter prospect that sent a shiver down her spine: what if someone else was behind the threats?

Reaching for her mobile, she dialled Hazelton's number.

39

It was as if her life were being played out on a big screen before her eyes: she was powerless to interrupt as Ben and DC Hazelton went back and forth. Neither acknowledged Alice in the room, and neither seemed aware that she was even sitting there while they argued.

Ben had only just finished his phone call with Dave when Hazelton had arrived. She'd been about to finish for the day, she'd told Alice on the phone, but had agreed to make a detour on her return to Bournemouth.

Ben had glared at Alice as he'd opened the door to the detective; it had felt wrong to go against his instructions, but he'd left Alice with little choice.

'It's not bloody good enough. I told you yesterday we were in danger,' Ben moaned, pacing the floor in front of the French doors that led out to the garden. 'That's two threatening letters left for us to find in less than twenty-four hours, and now the shit has destroyed one of my cameras. Who's going to pay for the repairs? Hmm? It'll be muggins here who has to foot the bill! In the same way as you lot buggering up my honeymoon, leaving me with the financial headache. It's not cheap, flying to Barbados, you know! One of those once-in-a-lifetime holidays, and that got flushed down the toilet because your overzealous DI pinched me with no evidence of wrongdoing.'

Hazelton was struggling to keep her cool this time. In fairness she'd been under attack for the best part of ten minutes, and now some of Ben's remarks were clearly starting to cut at the fibre of what she believed in.

'As I've already explained, Mr Goodman, we had valid grounds to arrest you initially as your DNA profile was the only one identified on Kerry Valentine's body. Given the nature of how she was killed, and us learning that you – our only suspect – were about to fly abroad for two weeks, we had no choice but to pull you in. I am personally sorry that your honeymoon had to be cancelled, but given the circumstances, it seems a small price to pay.'

'Small price to pay? You have a spare six grand you can give back to me, do you?'

Alice remained where she was, watching them parry and joust, Ben with blatant insults, Hazelton's more reserved, but equally cutting.

'Perhaps we should concentrate on who might have sent the letter,' Hazelton said, keen to switch direction. 'Do you have any enemies who might want to interfere with your recent nuptials? Anyone who would be keen for you to be distracted with personal matters instead of business ones? Perhaps a rival firm, or someone you double-crossed in business?'

Something in Ben's demeanour changed, as if she'd read his mind. 'I'm already exploring those avenues myself, thank you very much. If I leave it up to you lot, I'll still be waiting to hear at Christmas. I told you on Saturday that someone was trying to set me up, but what have you done to explore who that might be?'

Hazelton was silent for a moment. 'What about you, Mrs Goodman?' she said, turning to face Alice, but her voice somehow wasn't coming through clearly. 'Is there anyone you can think of who would send you these letters? After all, they are addressed to you.'

'It's nothing to do with her,' Ben challenged. 'She's just a pawn in this madman's twisted game. Leave Alice out of it.'

Alice could see Hazelton biting her tongue, could see that steely determination to remain professional to the end. 'Okay then, if you have no idea about the perpetrator, how about the content, Mr Goodman? Both notes make reference to you being guilty of killing in some way – any idea what that's about?'

He looked from Hazelton to Alice and then back again, exasperation tightening every muscle in his face. 'Isn't it obvious? Whoever's trying to screw me over is trying to convince Alice that I'm guilty of killing that girl, even though you've already cleared me as a suspect.'

Hazelton made no effort to face Alice again. 'The letters make no reference to Kerry Valentine, Mr Goodman. Is it possible they're referring to something else?'

The two exchanged a knowing glance, but Alice had spotted it too.

'This is nothing to do with *that*,' Ben insisted. 'I'd prefer it if you didn't go dragging up the past. Your lot were wrong back then, and you're wrong again now. Why do you seem to think it's okay to pin other shit on me, just because the lead investigator screwed up last time?'

Alice kept her head low, holding her breath, waiting for the answers she'd been craving for days.

Hazelton rested her palms on the counter across from Alice, leaning into it and letting out a deep sigh. 'Is there anybody who was around at that time who could be looking to take advantage now? Someone who knew what happened before and is keen to use it against you now? Anybody? You run a very successful business, don't you? Is it not possible that somebody within your organization sees this as a chance to oust you and take control?'

'Absolutely not! They're family.'

Hazelton had seen the momentary hesitation. 'Tell me, Mr Goodman, is there maybe one person who was with you in the early days, who witnessed what you went through and is seeking to rectify matters? Maybe someone you've trusted down the years with your secrets?'

A cough caused all three of them to look suddenly towards the kitchen entrance.

Dave glanced at each of them in turn, trying to work out what he'd stumbled into. 'I've sorted the security,' he said, nodding at Ben. 'They'll be here inside half an hour. I thought I'd take up guard until then.'

Ben cut across the room, wrapping an arm around Dave's shoulders and leading him away so that Hazelton wouldn't overhear what he had to say. There was little point though, as Alice could hear every word.

'Did you get it sorted like I asked?'

'Yeah, no problem, all sorted.'

'Thank you, mate, I owe you for this. You know what to do if they catch him. Alice and I are going to be away for a few days, but I want you to phone as soon as you have him. Then you can keep him on ice until I get back.'

Dave looked up and smiled at Alice, a pained look in his eyes that she didn't quite understand. It was gone in an instant though as Ben shook his hand, and he headed back out towards the front door.

'Anything I should be worried about?' Hazelton asked, raising her eyebrows sceptically.

'I hired some private security to keep an eye on the place,' Ben said nonchalantly. 'Alice and I are planning to go away for a few days. Which reminds me, I'm going to need that passport back pretty sharpish. Did you bring it with you?'

She shook her head.

'I don't understand why you're still hanging onto it.'

'As I tried to explain earlier, we have procedures in place for a reason. As soon as the paperwork is complete, it will be released. For all I know, it could be ready now. I'm happy to drive you down there if you want to see if it's ready.'

'How about you stop dicking me around and phone someone instead?'

'With respect, Mr Goodman,' Hazelton began, but Alice wasn't prepared to sit and listen to yet another argument.

The room was spinning and her heart was racing, her whole upper chest burning with pain. She had to get out. She couldn't cope with anyone else trying to control her life.

Leaping from the bar stool she'd been perched on she tore at the door, pushing Hazelton and Ben apart, offering no apology in her wake. Then she was out of the door, running towards the gate, grateful to find it was still open from where Dave had just exited. As he turned to see her running he reached out to stop her, but she ducked beneath his outstretched arms and darted to the right.

Fat raindrops splashed against her thighs as she pumped her arms, and the faster she moved the heavier the drops seemed to get as they streaked against her face. In the distance she could hear Dave calling after her but she pushed the sound of his voice from her mind, just needing to get free, just needing to breathe. As she made it to the end of the pavement, a car suddenly pulled out ahead of her, causing her to stumble as she tried to avoid crashing into it. Skidding to the floor, she lowered her arms to brace for impact, cursing as the sodden floor scraped her legs.

Straining to see who had caused her fall, her heart skipped a beat as she instantly recognized the face staring back at her through the misted window.

40

Liam O'Neill wasn't smiling. A mask of concern descended as quickly as the passenger window of the battered Honda.

'Jesus!' he exclaimed. 'Are you all right? I didn't mean to startle you.'

Alice remained where she was on the ground, one leg stretched out ahead of her, the other tucked beneath her bottom, bearing her weight. The rain continued to fall around her, but it was too late to worry about being wet and dirty; the fall had already seen to that.

O'Neill climbed out of his side of the car and hurried around, extending a hand and helping her back to her feet. Her thin cotton dress was soaked through and red scuff marks were already glowing on one knee and the other shin. Opening the passenger door, he helped her into the seat before hurrying back around to his side and slamming the door against the rain.

Alice kept her door open for now. She wasn't in the habit of getting into cars with strange men, and the need to run wasn't far from her mind, not that she was sure her legs would be up to much yet. Every other raindrop seemed to splash against the wet material of her dress.

'What are you doing here?' Alice began, though she already suspected the answer.

'I was driving to your house, as it happens,' he said.

'Driving *to*, or driving *away*?'

He pulled a face. 'Away? I only just got here.'

Alice picked some grit out of the gash on her knee, dropping it out of the side of the car. There was now bright red sticky blood just beneath her kneecap, but the sting was worse than the pain.

'Don't pretend it wasn't you who left those letters stuck to our gates,' Alice challenged.

She regretted rushing from the house without her phone and handbag. If he wanted to drive away with her locked in the car she'd be powerless to stop him, and nobody would know where she was or what had happened to her.

'What letters?' he asked, his face contorting in confusion.

She looked at him scornfully. 'I know it was you who sent them. What is it you want from us? Turning up at the hotel on Sunday, following me to the pub, then appearing at the restaurant today: what do you want?'

He reached into the panel in his door, pulled out a packet of tissues and passed them to her. 'Have you found out anything about Mary yet? Have you asked Ben about her?'

Alice took the tissues, tearing open the packet and pressing one to her knee, wincing at the further sting. She thought about the photographs from the secret shoebox; the older woman wearing the necklace and her ring.

'Who is she? What does she have to do with Ben?'

Liam fixed her with a cautious look. 'Are you sure you want to know?'

Part of the tissue remained attached to her knee as she tried to pull it free. At least it would stem the blood for now. She could worry about cleaning it up later.

'I found some photographs,' she admitted, allowing curiosity to get the better of her. 'Mary – she was older than Ben?'

'A good fifteen years older than him. Are you sure you want to hear what I'm about to tell you? This is your red and blue pill moment, Alice. If you'd rather keep your head buried in the sand, you can get out of the car and head home. You'd be back inside within five minutes, none the wiser about the man you married.' He paused, and looked away for a moment. 'Or, you can close the car door and allow me to take you to meet someone who will tell you everything you need to know about Ben but were afraid to ask. You won't like what we have to say – in fact, you'll probably refuse to believe it – but I promise we won't lie to you.' He turned to face her again. 'What's it to be?'

She stared out of her door. The rain was still falling, the ground sodden, but the clouds overhead were lightening, suggesting the downpour wouldn't be around for too much longer.

Reaching out, she coiled her fingers around the door handle and pulled it inwards. 'I prefer to know all the facts before I make any decisions. I'll listen to what you have to say, but if I get any sense that you're trying to trick me, I'll be gone in a shot. Do you understand? Now, where's this friend of yours?'

He smiled as he started the engine. 'Buckle up.'

They'd travelled for five minutes before he switched off the car's stereo. 'How are your legs?' he asked.

She glanced down and was satisfied the healing process had started – the skin around the gashes was starting to yellow. 'I'll live. How far do we have to travel?'

He sighed. 'I'd say you should make yourself comfortable. We've got at least another half an hour, depending on traffic.'

'Swear you didn't send the letters.'

He stared into her eyes. 'On my life. What do these letters say?'

She couldn't recall the exact words of the two letters, and without her phone, she couldn't show him an image either. 'Basically, they're addressed to me, stating Ben is a killer and that he will kill again.'

O'Neill's shoulders tensed. 'What does Ben say about them?'

'He says they've been sent by someone looking to set him up for something he hasn't done. You know the police have cleared him of any involvement in the murder of Kerry Valentine, right?'

O'Neill looked surprised by the news. 'I didn't know that. They examined his clothes?'

'Apparently so. From what the others said, they stripped him of his clothes before Kerry started dancing, so the only way her DNA would be on his clothes is if he'd seen her again afterwards. Their tests confirm that didn't happen.'

'I won't say I'm not surprised.'

She looked down at the wedding band Ben had placed so delicately on her finger only three days earlier, and thought about the vows they'd exchanged. Was she betraying those vows by hearing what O'Neill had to say? Her fingertips brushed Ben's grandmother's ring.

'I saw an image of Mary wearing this ring as well. What can you tell me about her? Were they in love?'

'Mary was thirty-three when she first met Ben. He was eighteen, but she was absolutely captivated by him. I don't know if you've seen images of him at that age, but he looked older than he was. I remember, back in school he was one of those kids who managed to buy beer and cheap spirits when he was only fifteen, whereas I was still being asked for ID when I was in my twenties. I don't think she realized just how young he was at first. They met at a music festival and she fell hard for him. Being that bit older, she was ready to settle down, get married and start a family. While he told her he wanted those things too, as their romance blossomed she always sensed he was stringing her along, waiting for something better.'

O'Neill lowered his window and lit a cigarette, keeping one hand on the steering wheel. 'It was a whirlwind romance. Three months after they met, he moved in with her and they were talking about getting engaged. That ring you're wearing there, she had that at one point. He gave it to her as a symbol of his love. He said it had been his grandmother's and he wanted her to have it as a sign of his feelings. She kidded herself that her doubts were just paranoia.

'He would come home at all hours – going out with his mates, he said – but his clothes would smell of other girls' perfume. It soon became clear he was using her. He was having a gap year from university, but made no effort to get a job or travel abroad. He lived at her place, borrowed money he never repaid, and used her place as a doss house.

'One night, she confronted him about it, and she saw a darkness emerge that she'd never witnessed before. He wasn't violent with her, but he threw several pieces of crockery at the walls, and tore her flat to shreds. Hundreds of pounds' worth of damage. She was terrified, but like most victims of domestic abuse, she forgave him as soon as he apologized and promised it wouldn't happen again. She was naive.'

41

The Honda pulled off the road onto a narrow farm track. The rain and clouds had cleared in this part of Hampshire's New Forest, and a fading rainbow was now evident on the horizon. Alice felt far from relaxed. The smell of farm animals had been present in the air for the past ten minutes, and although she had a vague idea of where they were, she wasn't certain she'd be able to find her way back to the main road unaided.

O'Neill had spent the remainder of the trip telling her about the passionate and extreme relationship Mary and Ben had shared, but every time she asked questions about Ben being guilty of murder, O'Neill quickly changed the subject, or assured her that she'd get all the answers she needed soon enough.

'We're here,' he commented, killing the engine.

Through the windscreen she could see a large barn filled with stacks of hay, and beyond that large green hills populated by sheep, cows and ponies. Alice was a city girl through and through, and couldn't ever imagine herself in the cut and thrust of an agricultural lifestyle. The grazing hills were surrounded by lines of dense forest separating the land from the neighbouring farms. There was no sound of cars or people, and only the occasional moo disturbed the silence: it was too quiet for her liking.

'It's this way,' O'Neill muttered under his breath, leading them away from the car and barn.

It was then that Alice clocked the medium-sized detached farmhouse. Made of stone and slate, the thatched roof looked dry and aged.

As soon as they stepped through the rickety old door, Alice realized exactly who they'd come to see. Although much older than she'd appeared in the photographs, the necklace still hung around the woman's neck.

O'Neill kissed Mary's cheek before turning and introducing Alice.

'She knows who you are,' he told Mary, 'but not what you know.'

Mary had to be in her early fifties. The skin beneath her eyes was tired and there were splashes of grey in her once auburn hair, but she still had a slight frame. She was wearing a yellow floral dress with sleeves that stopped at her elbows. There was a fresh pot of tea on the table, along with three cups and saucers and a plate of chocolate biscuits.

'Please sit,' Mary said, her voice thick with an Irish accent Alice hadn't expected.

The wooden table was big enough for four, and had that well-used look – scratches in the paintwork where plates and cutlery had been scraped and deposited. Alice pulled out one of the tall varnished chairs and sat delicately, sending a small cloud of dust into the air.

'Would you like a cup of tea?' Mary asked, lifting the pot.

'Thank you,' Alice said, her throat suddenly feeling dry.

'Help yourself to a bickie too,' Mary added as she filled one of the cups. 'There's milk in the urn.'

Alice reached for the cup and saucer before pouring a shot of milk from the silver jug. Mary was at the opposite end of the table with O'Neill sitting between them. He reached for one of the biscuits and offered the plate to Alice, who politely declined. Her appetite was yet to return.

Mary finished filling the cups and then took a sip of her black tea. 'You're just his type, you know. Pretty and petite; it's how he likes them.' She smiled to show she wasn't passing judgement. 'I suppose you're wondering why Liam brought you all this way.'

Alice nodded.

'I take it you know Ben and I were once—'

'Engaged?' Alice interrupted.

Mary smiled at some memory. 'A little more than that, actually. We were married for a time.'

Alice's heart sank.

How could Ben have been married before and never told her? Neither of them had wanted a church wedding, because neither of them had religious inclinations, but surely he would have had to confirm to the registrar if he'd been married before, wouldn't he? She had no recollection of any such conversation, and he had certainly never told her that their marriage was his second. All of a sudden it felt like he wasn't quite hers any more. She'd thought their marriage was a new experience for them both, and although it didn't ultimately matter, she couldn't ignore the pain in her heart knowing all those new experiences weren't new to him.

'He was young and impetuous,' Mary continued, again smiling, 'and I was smitten enough to believe I could change him. I can see from the paleness of your face that he never told you he was married before. I'm sorry if what I have to say causes you any pain; you're a victim in all of this, just as I was.'

Alice sipped her tea. 'I want you to tell me why I'm here.'

Mary looked over at O'Neill, who gave a reassuring nod while reaching for a second biscuit.

'Ben was . . .' she began, before thinking better of it. 'Ben and I were in love, at least I was in love with him. Looking back on it, I think he was too young to know what love was, not *really*. He cared for me, I have no doubt of that, but I think maybe I expected too much of him. When I remember the good times we shared, my heart still skips a beat, but when I remember the pain and anguish he brought, I hate myself for ever allowing him through my door. You must understand that my motive for sharing this with you is not to ruin what you have but to help you understand the man you fell in love with – the *real* Ben.'

Alice looked around the small kitchen. There was an Aga in one corner, a stone sink and a tall refrigerator tucked behind the door to the rest of the house. It was comfortable for one, but any more would cause strain.

'Are you the reason the police had Ben's DNA?' Alice asked abruptly. 'He told me there was a misunderstanding with an ex; was that you? Was he violent?'

Mary considered the question. 'His temper could be scary, but no he was never violent towards me. If he had been, maybe the police would have taken me more seriously.'

'Please just tell me whatever it is you have to say. I've been out for forty minutes already and Ben will be worrying about me.'

'You can phone and let him know you're safe,' Mary offered, nodding at the antique spin-dial phone hanging on the kitchen wall. 'I don't mind if you want to tell him where you are.'

Alice eyed the phone, but shook her head. How could she explain she'd driven off with O'Neill after the earlier exchange? How could she tell him she was having a tête-à-tête with his ex-wife?

'Very well,' Mary continued, adding milk to her tea and stirring it. 'Eighteen years ago I walked into a police station and I reported that Ben had murdered my mother.'

Alice blinked several times.

'The police officer gave me the same look,' Mary said. 'He thought I was just reacting to my grief following her recent passing, but there was more to it than that. Yes, she was frail and in her late seventies, but she didn't die of natural causes. The coroner recorded an open death because he couldn't conclusively say whether she'd suffered a heart attack before she fell down the stairs or as a result of it. And I knew what Ben stood to gain from her death.'

Alice could feel bile bubbling at the back of her throat and choked it down.

'One month before my mother's unexpected death, your husband arranged for a new life assurance policy to be prepared in her name. She underwent various medical tests before the company would agree to insure her, but all her test results came back with flying colours. She was fitter than most women her age. There was no sign of any potential coronary issues. Yet, as soon as the ink was dry on the policy, she suddenly takes a tumble and was dead before she reached the hospital.'

Alice frowned. 'What are you saying? You think Ben pushed your mother down the stairs?'

Mary's face remained expressionless, but she nodded. 'That's precisely what I'm saying. He knew what he was doing. He wanted to go to university and pay off his debts, and having married me he would be legally entitled to half of anything my mother left in her will, including the hundred thousand pound life assurance claim.'

'I'm surprised she found an insurance company willing to cover someone of that age,' O'Neill added, 'but I've seen the policy documents. The original application is in Ben's handwriting; we had an expert look at it. The only parts not in his writing are the signatures, but it would have been easy enough for him to trick her into signing something she didn't understand.'

'Ben always had the gift of the gab,' Mary confirmed. 'He could charm the hind legs off a donkey, so he could.'

Alice couldn't disagree that Ben was a confident and charming speaker, and knew how to get what he wanted, but she couldn't picture him deliberately taking advantage of an older person and then killing them for quick cash. He was many things, but not that.

'I don't blame you for not believing me,' Mary continued. 'I can see how much you love him, and I don't blame you for wanting to defend him. I used to feel the exact same way, but now I know it's all just a mask. I'm not sure anyone knows the real Ben. Apart from Dave of course. I take it they're still thick as thieves?'

Alice recalled how close Dave and Mary had looked in some of the photographs in Ben's box. 'How do you know Dave?'

Mary fired a look at O'Neill. 'You didn't tell her about that?'

He shrugged apologetically. 'I promised no spoilers.'

Mary topped up their drinks. 'Towards the end, when Ben was off with his floozies, I found it hard to live with. I'd come to accept that what we'd had was infatuation rather than love, and that he'd been too young to get married. I selfishly wanted to get revenge on him for cheating on me. So I hatched a plan out of spite to seduce his best friend. Only things didn't quite work out like that, and Dave soon became my confidant. My first impression of Dave was that he was a little rough around the edges, but as I got to know him, I realized he's just a sheep in wolf's clothing. He loves Ben, and I know it killed him to do the dirty, but the more time we spent together, the closer Dave and I became. Until one night, Ben returned early, having been in a fight. Although Dave and I weren't in bed when Ben turned up, it didn't take him long to realize what had been going on.

'I was more than happy to come clean, to wipe the smirk from his face, but do you know what he did? He laughed at the both of us and ribbed Dave about going after his *sloppy seconds*. That's how he described the woman he'd married. He walked out of my flat and didn't return until he filed divorce papers. That wasn't until after he'd wormed his way into my mother's home and bumped her off.'

Alice didn't want to listen to any more, but she found it impossible to stand and walk away. If Mary's version of events was true, then how could Ben's and Dave's relationship have survived that kind of betrayal? She'd seen them together so many times and neither had ever mentioned anything like that.

'I reached out to Dave when I realized what Ben had been up to, but he refused to return my calls. Despite everything, the two of them remained close friends, and I was painted as the jealous and desperate wife. It broke my heart seeing how wrong I'd been about the two of them. In hindsight I now wonder whether they were in it together from the start, and that Dave only slept with me to keep me off Ben's back about the late nights.'

It was like Mary was describing someone else. Ben had always been a character, but surely he wasn't capable of something so vicious and manipulative.

'What happened with the life assurance money?' Alice asked quietly, not sure she wanted to hear the answer.

'The insurance company paid out,' Mary continued. 'Some of it was used to pay solicitor's fees and funeral costs, and the rest was deposited in my account. In his divorce request, Ben cited my affair with Dave as grounds for divorce, and when Dave made a formal statement to confirm what had happened between us, there was little I could do to dispute it. He walked away from our marriage with thirty-five thousand pounds, and headed to university a few months later. I was devastated and never wanted to see him again, and apart from the occasional search of his name online, I've stuck to that promise.'

Mary reached for a tissue and dabbed the corner of her eyes. 'When I heard he'd been arrested in connection with a young woman's death though, I knew it was time to break my silence. That's when I contacted the newspaper. As soon as I spoke to Liam, I knew I'd made the right choice.'

The lines on Alice's forehead deepened. 'I don't understand. Your mother's death has no connection to what happened to Kerry Valentine. He didn't know her before that night.'

'Maybe not, but I bet you assume he's innocent because he couldn't be a killer. Well, I'm telling you not only is he capable of it, he's done it before and got away with it. The police pressed charges, but a jury of his peers found him not guilty. I know what really happened though and so does he. Your husband is not the innocent man he pretends to be. Don't let yourself be his next victim.'

42

Alice was still reeling as O'Neill meandered the Honda back along the road. They'd be back in Chilworth soon, but Alice's mind was spinning as her world crumbled before her eyes.

Ben a killer?

It was impossible, wasn't it?

The Ben she'd met and fallen for was sweet and kind, someone who tried to make her every day better than the one before. The man Mary had described was cold, manipulative and calculating. If it hadn't been for the photographs she'd discovered, she would have argued they were talking about someone else.

What made it worse was that Alice had no doubt that Mary and O'Neill believed every word they'd told her. Alice had spent half an hour questioning Mary, phrasing questions in different ways in an effort to trigger different responses, but the older woman had stuck to her story, and hadn't swayed once from the script.

If Ben had displayed any of the traits they had described in front of Alice, she never would have married him. Was it not possible they had misinterpreted his youthful actions and shaped those memories with the bitterness both felt towards the man who had chewed up and spat them out?

How could Alice trust the words of a woman who felt she'd

been used and cheated on? Or a man whose formative years had been negatively impacted by name-calling and sparring? Both Mary and O'Neill had motives for wanting to paint Ben in a bad light, and neither could deny the pleasure they would get from seeing Ben exposed to karma.

Neither had any hard proof that Ben had done anything wrong. It was certainly suspicious that his handwriting was discovered on the life assurance application form, but that didn't mean he had tricked Mary's mother into signing something she didn't want to sign.

Mary had gone on to explain how Ben had been in possession of one of two spare keys to her mother's property, with the other held by Mary.

'He had the opportunity,' she'd told her.

Mary's mother was discovered by a community nurse who had called round to drop off a prescription. She'd been dead at the bottom of the stairs for at least fifteen hours when she was found, according to the forensic pathologist who had examined her body. There were no signs of a struggle, and a patch of bruising around her ankle was consistent with a twist, which could have led to a fall. It could just as easily have occurred as a result of the fall though, and so an open verdict had been recorded.

Mary had pestered the police until they'd agreed to open an investigation and look into her accusations against her soon-to-be ex-husband. When they learned about the insurance documents they confirmed he had means, motive and opportunity. The fact that his car had been seen at the address by an eagle-eyed neighbour a few hours before the alleged fall was a fact that the police had heavily relied on in court.

Despite all the circumstantial evidence, Ben didn't once change his story. O'Neill and Mary hadn't gone into too much detail about what had happened at court, other than Ben had pled not guilty and been found as such by a unanimous verdict.

* * *

'Are you sure you want to go home?' O'Neill asked as they passed the 'Welcome to Chilworth' sign. 'I could drop you at a friend's for the night while you make a decision about your next steps.'

She glared at him. 'Why wouldn't I want to go home to the man I love?'

O'Neill didn't reply, but the contempt was written all over his face.

'You'd better drop me at the pub; I don't want Ben to see us together.'

'Very well,' he said, indicating as the pub appeared around the bend. 'But if you change your mind, or if you decide you need to get away in a hurry, I want you to call me. Okay? I know you don't want to believe what we told you, but at some point you'll see that we're right. When that happens, I want you to call. Day or night – anytime.'

She still had his business card in her purse, not that she intended to use it.

He pulled into the car park at the rear of the pub and Alice climbed out, slamming the door as she did. Once he'd pulled away, she made her way slowly back along the road towards the house.

As she drew closer, she was surprised to see the shaved head of a man in a skintight black top and combat trousers staring back at her from the other side of the gates.

'What's your business here?' he demanded.

His eyes were cold and dark and his tone sent an instant shiver down her spine.

'I-I-I live here,' she stuttered.

'Name?'

'Alice Goodman. Where's Ben? Where's my husband?'

He held up a finger and whispered into the compact radio hanging from a clip just below his shoulder. He waited for a response before nodding and using the remote to open the electrified gate.

'Sorry, ma'am,' he offered with little sincerity or emotion. 'Can't be too careful. Mr Goodman is waiting for you up at the property. Mind how you go.'

It was like a small army had invaded. More men, more shaved heads, and more skintight black tops occupied the inner perimeter of the property, some bearing large German Shepherd dogs.

'Ben, what the hell is going on?' she asked, as the front door opened.

He didn't reply immediately, instead rushing forward and wrapping two warm arms around her shoulders. 'Oh thank God, I've been worried sick. Where have you been?'

She was about to respond when one of the patrolling guards came near them.

'How about we go inside and talk?' she suggested, and Ben led the way, closing and locking the door behind them.

Alice hadn't noticed Ben's parents' car in the driveway, but she instantly recognized the smell of his mum's perfume and Ray's embossed jacket hanging on the back of the door. It was no surprise that Ray had come running when Ben had phoned. He poked his head around the door of the living room and nodded in Alice's direction before scampering back to update his wife that Alice was back.

'I didn't know what to do,' Ben said. 'You just vanished. I tried calling you, but you left your phone here. I was so worried. Dad and I were about to drive around and search for you.' He paused as his eyes fell on the fresh scabs on her legs. 'What happened?'

'I fell,' she said, waving away his concern. 'I'm fine now, but I was running, and it was wet, and . . . silly really.'

'You raced out of here more than two hours ago, Alice. I've been worried sick. I was terrified the person leaving the notes had abducted you or something. I've even had that DC Hazelton on the phone to report you missing.'

Alice blushed. 'What did she say?'

'She told me you wouldn't be considered a missing person

until you'd been gone for more than twenty-four hours, but agreed to pass your description to the uniform patrol. I'd better let her know you're back. Where did you go? Where have you been?'

Alice moved past him and into the living room. The hushed conversation between Ben's parents stopped instantly. She wouldn't have chosen to confront Ben in front of his parents, but he'd be less likely to lie with them there, and she needed answers.

Dropping onto the sofa, she took a deep breath. 'I was putting your clothes away earlier,' she began, 'and I accidentally knocked an old shoebox to the floor. It contained a ton of old photographs.'

Ben didn't look bothered by her admission. 'And?'

'I wondered why you've never shown them to me before.'

Ben pulled a face. 'They're just old photos. I don't know why I've never shown them to you. There's no reason really. What's this all about?'

Alice looked from her in-laws to Ben. 'The photographs all appear to be from before the two of us met. It just struck me as odd that you hadn't shown them to me, and that you kept them hidden away in a dusty old shoebox.'

'I told you: there's no reason. They're just some stupid photographs from a time in my life I'd prefer to forget, that's all. I'm sure I haven't seen every photograph you've ever been in.' He considered her for a moment, before his eyes lit up with realization. 'This is about *her*, isn't it? You looked at the photos, I take it?'

She nodded.

Ben's cheeks reddened for the first time. 'Please tell me you're not jealous of some woman I dated long before you were ever on the scene. We both had other partners before we hooked up, and I thought we were both happy to leave those things in the past.'

'I was. I mean, *I am*, but you never told me you'd been married before. I find it odd that you would hide something like that from me.' She glanced over to Ben's parents and saw his mum look away.

Ben's eyes narrowed. 'Who said we were married?'

Alice froze. Had there been a photograph of Ben and Mary from their wedding day, or was it because Mary had told her they'd been married?

Ben was now looking closer at her, the lines on his face forming into a suspicious frown. 'What's going on here, Alice? There's something you're not telling me. Where have you really been?'

There was no point in keeping the truth to herself any more. He deserved to know what Mary and O'Neill had said, and she needed to give him a chance to share his side of the story.

'We're going to need a drink.'

43

Lowering the dusty shoebox to the dining table, Ben lifted the lid on the past he'd so desperately tried to bury. Alice slid a tumbler of vodka across the table to him, the ice cubes clinking. Ray and Hermione had hurriedly left, telling them they needed space and promising to call round in the morning.

'I always wondered if she'd come out of the woodwork again one day,' he said, lifting out the picture of Mary wearing the necklace. 'Part of me wanted to keep tabs on her after what happened, but I guess as the years rolled by I thought less and less about her and the nightmare she forced me to endure. Did she look well?'

When Alice had told him about meeting Mary and O'Neill, she'd expected anger, but his reaction had surprised her. He'd looked crestfallen, like she'd uncovered some deep, dark secret he was too ashamed to admit. While she'd poured the drinks, he'd told her he would tell her everything.

'I wouldn't say the years have been kind,' Alice said, recalling the heavy bags beneath Mary's pale eyes.

'You know, I thought it was odd when Liam O'Neill suddenly appeared at our table at lunchtime. It was such a bizarre encounter that it just didn't sit well with me. My guess is he's the one who left the letters stuck to our gates. It wouldn't surprise me if he had something to do with the police interrupting the wedding too – vindictive bastard!'

'He didn't admit to it, but I suspect the same,' she agreed, feeling numb.

'Will you tell me what she said?' he asked, taking a seat and resting his hands on the table.

Alice thought back to Mary's account. 'She said you met at a music festival, had a fling and married soon after. She thinks you only married her to get at her inheritance.'

'I presume she told you that I murdered her mother too?' he ground out sarcastically.

Alice nodded. 'She said many things.'

'And I presume it was all *my* fault when things didn't work out, right?'

Alice remained silent, waiting for him to elaborate.

'Did she also mention she seduced Dave to get back at me?'

'She did.'

He looked surprised. 'It's easier to fool someone into believing your lies when you feed them a little truth, I suppose. Anyway, where would you like me to start?'

'How about at the beginning?'

He stared down at his hands. 'I met Mary when I was barely eighteen. Dave and I were determined to have a summer to remember. We were young and naive back then, and we knew we'd have to do some major growing up if we were to make it through university. We planned this summer of gigs, drinks and girls – a summer we would remember forever as our last blow-out before embarking on our adult lives. I knew I hadn't performed as well in my exams as I could have done and that my grades probably wouldn't be good enough to get into my first or second choice universities. So I applied late for a gap year, figuring I could take a year to get my head straight, work out what I wanted to do with my life or find a job and bin off uni.

'Dave wasn't the sharpest tool in the box, and had no intention of going to university. Even back then he was dipping his fingers into many pies and making deals left, right and centre. He was a proper little entrepreneur even then. That's how he managed to score us entry to so many gigs and festivals over that period.

'It was on our second night at Glastonbury that I first laid eyes on Mary. She was pretty wasted, and from what I could see she was on her own. Dave and I had been sharing a tiny tent, so when she asked if I wanted to spend the night with her, it seemed like a great idea. I knew she was older then, though I had no idea just how big the age gap was until weeks later.

'She came across as someone desperately trying to hang onto what little youth she had remaining – not exactly counting the days until death, but certainly not able to ignore the ticking clock. I don't remember a whole lot about that first night, but I remember her catching me trying to sneak out of her tent in the early hours of the morning. She was insatiable, and she dragged me back to bed. When I next awoke it was daylight and Dave was looking for me. Mary and I agreed to swap numbers and then she packed up and left. I thought that would be the end of it, but to my amazement she tracked me down in Southampton and begged me to hook up again. I know that sounds big-headed but she was really into me. Bear in mind this was back before social media, and when mobile phones were still a luxury rather than an accessory.

'What can I say, we had fun. She had a great sense of humour and was so generous that I allowed myself to become a bit of a kept man.'

Alice turned up her nose in disgust.

'I know it sounds crass,' Ben explained, 'but put yourself in my shoes: eighteen, no responsibilities and an attractive woman offering to put a roof over your head and food on the table. I think we both kind of got swept up in the relationship. She loved having someone young in her life to cling to, and I liked being able to enjoy myself without having to find a job.

'Did she mention that she was the one who proposed to me? I bet she left that salient detail out too, didn't she? She was burying her head in the sand to think that things would remain the same between us.'

He paused and took a long sip of vodka. 'I wanted someone to take care of me and she was offering what I thought I needed. My only valuable possession in the world was that ring of my grandmother's and I didn't want to sell it. Naively, I thought I was in love with Mary and giving it to her as an engagement ring seemed like the right way to pay her back for all her generosity. If I'd realized what a manipulative bitch she was, I'd have slept in a box on the street, rather than stay with her.

'We married at the registry office less than a fortnight after she proposed. I wore an old school shirt and trousers, and she wore some dress she'd got in a sale. We must have looked a right pair!'

Hearing him confirm what Mary had said about marriage cut Alice deep, but she swallowed down the pain and put her glass to her lips, savouring the cool relief of the ice-cold liquid.

'So this was now early September. My grades were slightly better than I'd expected, and with no idea what I wanted to do as a career, I submitted my application for a business course at the University of Bournemouth for the following year. Mary thought it was a great idea and even helped me fill out my application form and apply for a student loan, but once we were married, her attitude to things changed. Suddenly it made her angry when I wanted to go out and see my friends. If I invited Dave round to watch football on the television, she'd kick off at me in front of him. It was embarrassing, and so Dave and I would end up going to the pub to watch matches instead. She was on my case all the time, and by the end of October I realized what a huge mistake I'd made. Shamefully, I stopped caring about how my actions would make her feel.'

He looked down as if trying to come to terms with his poor behaviour. 'I was a shit to her. I started sleeping around with other girls, closer to my own age. I'd come home at stupid times and when she shouted at me that would only make me do worse things. The marriage was spiralling out of control, and it was around about this time that her mother reached out to me. I'd only met her three times: when we got engaged; at the wedding; and once when we'd invited her round for dinner. I think she must have been quite old when she'd had Mary as she was so much older than us. So, anyway, she phoned me up out of the blue and asked me to come to see her, but swore me to secrecy.

'When I got there she told me she'd found some lumps and that she didn't think she had a lot of time left. The strangest thing was, she wasn't upset by the revelation. She'd had a full life and was ready to go, but she didn't want to leave Mary empty-handed or saddled with debt. She asked me to help her set up some life cover so that when the cancer took her, she'd be able to leave Mary with a small windfall. I thought it was a good thing for her to do, and of course I agreed. Looking back on it though, I should have told Mary. Maybe if I had she wouldn't have gone so ballistic when her mum died.

'I was smart enough to know that nobody would insure Mary's mother if they knew about the cancer, so when we filled in the application we lied about her current health. She hadn't been officially diagnosed, so as far as her doctor knew she was perfectly fit and healthy. I knew my actions were fraudulent, but her motives were so pure I figured I could live with the guilt. She was so happy when her policy was confirmed.

'Of course, Mary knew nothing about it and accused me of seeing other women every time I'd been at her mum's. That's when she decided to screw Dave to spite me. She had this perverse look on her face when I found out – like she enjoyed stabbing me in the back. Dave was cut up about it, but he told me what had happened before she had and I appreciated his honesty.

Besides, we've been through so much together that I don't think he could ever do anything that would stop me loving him. He's more than a friend; he's my brother. You know?'

Alice continued to watch him as he spoke. There was no sign of deceit in anything he was telling her. She couldn't help but pity him for the situation he'd unwittingly found himself in. She could understand how he would have allowed Mary to take control of their relationship.

'Her mum's sudden death was a shock to all of us,' Ben continued, draining his drink. 'After that I knew it was time to end things and get my life back on track. Dave even helped me secure a solicitor to instigate divorce proceedings. I had no idea I would be entitled to any of the life assurance until my solicitor sent the paperwork over. I didn't want any of it initially, but after she went to the police and had them arrest me, I decided it was the least I was entitled to. Can you believe she actually said I pushed her mum down the stairs? Hand on heart, her mum knew exactly what she was doing when she signed those application forms. She might have been frail, but her mind was as sharp as a tack.

'It was terrifying standing in that dock, not knowing how a dozen strangers would view our differing accounts, but thankfully they saw through Mary's lies and insinuations. There was no evidence that I'd had anything to do with her mum's tragic fall, but that doesn't mean the relief wasn't palpable. I'd almost convinced myself the jury would believe Mary, and my life was over. It gave me the impetus to stop messing about and craft the life I wanted to lead.'

'I believe you,' Alice eventually sighed.

Ben reached across the table and took her hands in his. 'I really hope you do, baby. I never meant to keep secrets from you, but how could I tell you that a crazy ex had accused me of murdering her mother and that it had gone to trial? You would have run a mile. I knew very early on that you were the woman I was destined to marry and I didn't want to do anything that could jeopardize that.'

Alice chose her next words carefully. 'Would you ever have told me about her or what happened if I hadn't found out?'

Ben's eyes shone in the fading light coming through the dining room window. 'In all honesty, I don't think I would have. I'm sorry if that hurts your feelings, but as far as I'm concerned all that is in the past. It was a lifetime ago. I haven't thought about any of it, of *her*, in years. It was only when that detective dragged me away from you on Saturday night that it all came flooding back. I remembered how utterly terrified I'd been waiting to learn the outcome of the jury's verdict. If they'd found me guilty I would have been sent to prison for life for something I didn't do. I was on my own, staring into the abyss, but fate or God or something else pulled me back from the precipice and allowed me to walk out of that court and make a fresh start. I rebuilt my life: went to university, graduated, set up my own business, and then met you. Every day since you and I got together I've worked my arse off to make you proud of me, to put distance between that old me and the man I want to be. You've been my inspiration and I'm now terrified that everything we've built together is about to disappear because that vindictive bitch has dragged you into all this. Please tell me I'm not losing you.'

A single tear broke free and rolled down his cheek. She'd never seen him looking so scared and so desolate, and her heart reached out to him. She moved quickly around the table and leaned forwards, wrapping her arms around him.

'You could never lose me,' she whispered into his ear. 'Til death do us part, remember?'

She kissed him, hard and fast, slipping her tongue between his lips and showing him exactly what she wanted him to do.

44

Alice collapsed back onto the mattress, breathless, her heart close to bursting. Ben pushed the duvet back, his breaths as short and sharp as hers. A line of their discarded clothes led back from the bed towards the landing like a trail of breadcrumbs to show the journey their passion had taken.

Ben suddenly turned to face her, squashing his elbow into his pillow to prop up his head. 'Mrs Goodman, I reckon some of what you just demanded is illegal in some counties.' He laughed raucously like the huge weight that he'd been carrying for so long had finally been lifted.

She didn't respond immediately, focusing instead on breathing and returning her pulse to a more steady rhythm. She wanted to shower, to clean up, but the mattress was warm and comfortable, and the en suite looked so far away as fatigue took hold.

'Do you know what I fancy right now?' Ben asked.

She looked over to him, amazed at how quickly he'd composed himself. 'You'll have to give me a few minutes,' she cautioned.

'No, not that,' he chuckled. 'I meant I feel like I could eat a horse right now. Let's get an Indian takeaway. I really fancy vindaloo, lashings of poppadum and a cool, crisp beer.'

She hadn't felt hungry since lunch, but suddenly her appetite raised a guilty hand at the suggestion of food.

'I could eat a curry, but you'll have to go and collect it.'

He punched the air in satisfaction with both fists as his head plumped back into the pillow. 'I might need to shower first, but I don't mind picking it up. You grab a menu and phone while I clean up.' He paused. 'You never know, we might have just started our family.'

Instinctively, Alice's hands gently rubbed her belly, small delicate circles where her womb waited to be employed. It was certainly possible, but only time would tell.

Ben leaned over and kissed her. 'I love you so much, Alice. You know that, don't you?'

She smiled. 'Of course I do. I can finally see traces of light at the end of this dark tunnel.'

'Me too,' he said, kissing her again before rolling over and off the bed, practically skipping to the bathroom and closing the door.

Swinging her legs over the bed, she stretched her arms high above her head and allowed a much-needed yawn to escape. It had been a long day, and although sunset was still a couple of hours away, she had no doubt that if she fell asleep now, she wouldn't wake until morning.

Collecting her bra and pants from the carpet, she followed the trail of clothes back to the top of the stairs, finding her mobile off to the side where it had fallen mid-passion. The phone's LED was flashing to indicate a notification, and as she unlocked the screen she was surprised to find she'd missed half a dozen calls from Faye.

Sitting on the top step, she redialled the number and waited for it to connect. 'Faye? Is everything okay?'

'No,' Faye sniffed, her voice tempered with sadness. 'I'm at the hospital. Can you come and see me? I didn't know who else to call . . .' her words faded into a high-pitched whisper as she began to cry.

'What is it, sweetie? What's happened?'

'It's Johnny . . . he's . . . he's dead.'

After a car journey where Alice was sure Ben had consistently been over the speed limit, they finally skidded into the hospital car park.

Thoughts of their lovemaking and the prospect of takeaway were now far from Alice's mind. Faye had been unable to say much on the phone, other than repeating that she needed Alice to come to the hospital. She'd messaged to say Alice should come straight to the Accident and Emergency department, and as Ben pulled up as close to the entrance as he could, Alice's mind was racing with possibilities.

Ben kissed her cheek. 'I'll park up and then I'll come and find you.'

Alice heard without really listening. Pushing her door open, she felt frozen to the core despite the warm breeze clawing at her cheeks. She was nauseous as the bright lights of the waiting room zoomed into focus, but hurried in through the automatic doors and joined a queue of people waiting to check in at reception.

After giving Faye's name to the man behind the desk, Alice was escorted through the secured doors and into the treatment area, where two uniformed police officers stood guard outside a closed door. The nurse identified Alice to them, and they stepped aside to allow her into the room. Faye was sitting up in bed wearing a hospital gown. Her face was swollen, and a single bloody scratch mark scaled the length of her cheek and neck, disappearing beneath the gown.

Alice's hands shot up to her face in shock. The wounds were fresh, clearly not a result of the beating on Sunday, and suddenly the implication became crystal clear. Johnny was dead and Faye was once again banged up, but this time the police were here and that could only mean one thing.

'Oh God, Faye, what's happened?'

Faye's face screwed into an inflated ball the second Alice spoke, and she started sobbing hysterically.

It was as if the dark cloud that had followed Ben and Alice for three days was suddenly back in the room, but this time it was Faye it hovered above like Damocles' sword.

Placing one unsteady foot in front of the other, Alice tottered forwards, moving to the right side of the bed, away from Faye's right arm which was suspended in a sling. A machine bleeped somewhere to the left, but Alice's eyes stayed on the terrified creature struggling in the bed, praying to wake from the nightmare.

Alice pressed a cold hand against Faye's forehead and gently brushed the fringe from her friend's eyes. 'It's okay, sweetie, I'm here. Whatever you need, I'm here.'

Faye's swollen cheeks were wet with tears, and now that she was closer, Alice could see yellow and purple bruising beneath Faye's chin. She had no doubt that whatever had happened between them, Johnny's death had come at a painful price for his wife.

'Can you tell me what happened?' Alice asked nervously, not even sure she wanted to know the full horror, but realizing she had to. After all, if she didn't understand the truth, how could she possibly help?

Faye dried her eyes on the thin sheet covering her legs and abdomen, taking deep, broken breaths as she tried to control her sobs. 'He-he-he had been gone since Sunday.' A breath. 'He came home drunk.' Another breath. 'Turns out he'd been at his mum's.' Another breath, this one the deepest and most settling. 'He hadn't called and I'd been fearing the worst. When I challenged him about it . . . he pushed me away. I told him I wanted a divorce. I couldn't live with his violence any more, and he punched me. I don't know what happened, but something snapped in my head: I fought back. I slapped and scratched his face – I was desperate to make him see what he was doing – but that only made him angrier. He knocked me to the floor and grabbed my neck.' She mimed the action with her own hands. 'He squeezed and I thought I would pass out, but then a second wind came, and I managed to knock him off me.'

She reached for the small oxygen mask near her left hand and pressed it against her face, taking several short breaths before lowering it again, her voice steadier.

'I wasn't going to let him kill me, so I ran towards the front door, but he got there first and blocked my exit. Then I raced upstairs, looking for anything I could use to defend myself. I went into the bathroom and locked the door, but he kicked it in. There was this fury in his eyes – like nothing I'd ever seen, and as I held up a pair of nail scissors he slapped them out of my hand and forced me over the side of the bath. He had his hand on the back of my head and kept pushing my head further into the tub. It was all I could do to keep grip of the side of the bath to stop myself falling in.' She paused again, willing herself to say the words. 'He pulled up my dress from behind, and scratched my legs as he yanked down my pants . . .'

The mask was back over her lips and mouth, her sad eyes staring up at Alice, and a lump rose rapidly in Alice's throat.

'As he tugged at his belt, I managed to wriggle free enough to drive my heel into his groin. He stumbled backwards, and it took all my strength to push myself up and around. I knew he wouldn't be incapacitated for long, and I was desperate to get out. I tried to half-leap and push past him, but as I was about to land, he grabbed my ankle and pulled me back down. I lashed out. I kicked with both legs like a stubborn mule and I must have connected with his face, because the next minute he'd disappeared from view. As I scrambled free, I looked down and saw him lying slumped against the toilet bowl, his eyes wide open but not blinking. Then this patch of blood started to pool on the carpet. He must have cracked his head as he fell or something. I don't know. It all happened so fast.

'At first I thought he was just faking and that he'd suddenly wake and come for me again, but he didn't. I must have been in shock because I froze to the spot. I couldn't move. I must have sat there for an hour or so before I managed to get up and find a phone to call for an ambulance. I killed him, Alice, and now I don't know what I'm going to do.'

45

The cigarette between Alice's lips wobbled as the nurse cupped her hands and lit the tip for her. Alice nodded gratefully before coughing and spluttering as the smoke attacked her virgin lungs.

The sun hung low in the sky in the distance, but the sky directly above the hospital had already turned a much darker shade of blue. Patients with a variety of ailments came and went in a blur as Alice remained perched on the wooden bench, holding the cigarette that she didn't really want but unable to think of any way to calm the nervous tension bubbling through her veins.

Almost an hour had passed since she'd first found Faye in that tiny room, but her friend's confession still stung her ears.

I killed him, Alice, and now I don't know what I'm going to do.

The doctors had set Faye's wrist in plaster after confirming the fracture by X-ray. They had treated her kindly, seeing through the cloud of suspicion now surrounding the badly beaten woman, and focusing on the vulnerable patient who was struggling to grasp the enormity of what had unfolded over the course of a few hours.

Ben had remained in the A&E waiting room initially and had then agreed to go with one of the officers to make a formal

245

identification of Johnny's body. He had yet to return, and Alice was grateful for a moment alone.

It wasn't what Faye had done that most upset her, nor what Johnny would have potentially done had he not been stopped. The guilt of not being there when her friend needed her most was overwhelming and was threatening to swallow Alice whole.

It was bad enough that she'd been too wrapped up in her own wedding day to realize her friend's marriage was under strain, but even when Faye had come clean on Sunday, what support had Alice really provided? A shoulder to cry on maybe, but she'd done little else than send a message yesterday to ask if Faye was okay.

Her friend had reached out and Alice had allowed herself to become distracted by Kerry Valentine's murder and Ben's historical run-in with the law. The more she now thought about it, the more she realized she should have insisted Faye and Isabella join them at their house until things with Johnny were properly resolved. Why hadn't she foreseen that this outcome was always a possibility, given what Faye had experienced on Sunday?

Alice inhaled again, the smoke making her cough once more, but the burn in her throat lessened.

If Faye and Isabella had been with her instead of at home, Johnny would have returned to an empty house and could have slept off the alcohol. He would still be alive today.

Now he was gone, and Isabella would never be able to hug her dad again or hear him say how much he loved her.

The tears broke free – tears for her friend and for Isabella. Three lives ruined when simple action, rather than inaction, could have made a difference.

It wasn't her fault, of course it wasn't, but her guilt was on overload, and nobody would convince her differently, at least, not tonight.

This was where her inactivity would stop. Faye needed a friend, and support, and that was precisely what Alice would provide.

Pulling out her phone, she dialled the only person she knew who would understand what was required.

The knock on the room's door was followed by Hazelton's head popping around it.

'Is it okay if I come in?' she asked.

Alice nodded and moved away from the bed to greet her.

'She's the victim in all this,' Alice whispered, determined to make that part clear. 'Johnny attacked her and what she did was done in self-defence.'

Hazelton looked over to the now-sedated Faye, asleep on the bed. 'Okay, I will do what I can for your friend but I haven't been assigned to this case, and I doubt I will be as I'm only in Southampton to support the Kerry Valentine inquiry. I'll speak to the SIO and make sure he understands their history.'

Alice allowed a small sigh of relief to escape. 'I really appreciate you coming out here. What must you think of me and my friends? We're really not a bad lot.' She instantly regretted her attempt to lighten the tone. It wasn't the time or place for light-hearted quips.

'You said on the phone this wasn't the first time Johnny attacked Faye?' Hazelton said as she pulled out a smartphone and began to record the conversation. 'Don't worry about this,' she said. 'It's only for my purposes. I'll type up notes later.'

Alice tried to ignore the phone. 'She called me round on Sunday and her face didn't look dissimilar to how it does now, though there was no scratch on her cheek. Her eyes and cheeks were puffy and there was blood beneath her nose. She told me Johnny had beaten her and stormed out.'

'Did she report the incident to the police?'

Alice shook her head. 'I told her she should, and now I regret not phoning them myself, but she didn't want the police involved.'

'She doesn't have any choice now,' Hazelton sighed. 'Are you aware of any other altercations between them?'

Alice tried to remember what Faye had told her on Sunday. 'There was an incident the weekend before last when he was dropping her at the airport for my hen do in Paris. They argued then I think.'

Hazelton frowned. 'Are we talking about the Saturday before last? The same night Kerry Valentine was murdered?'

Alice nodded, acknowledging the inference.

'Do you know if he was violent towards Faye then?'

Alice screwed up her face. 'I really don't know. I don't think so, at least she didn't tell me he had, but then I also think she kept it well hidden for a long time. I get the impression this violence has been a regular occurrence for some time.'

'Johnny was at Ben's stag do in Bournemouth, wasn't he? I remember watching the recording of his interview on Sunday morning.'

Alice nodded again, the taste of the cigarette tar clinging to her tongue like mould.

'And on the occasions when you and I have met since Faye came clean on Sunday, you didn't think to mention Johnny's violent streak to me?'

Alice could only shrug. 'I wanted to, but I didn't know if you would think I was jumping to conclusions and throwing my friends under the bus to help Ben. I didn't have any real evidence, and I knew Faye wouldn't back up my story if I told you.'

'Even so, if we'd been made aware of his violent streak sooner, it might have helped steer our investigation.'

'So you think he killed Kerry?'

Hazelton ground her teeth uncertainly. 'I don't know. Maybe. Maybe not. It's possible Johnny could have been responsible for Kerry's death, but if that's the case then one or more of the stag party has lied to us, and there will be repercussions for that.'

Alice recalled Dave's conversation with the mystery caller: *We all stuck to the same story, so they've no reason to doubt what we said. Don't worry, I made sure everyone knew the timeline of activity.*

Alice's eyes fell back on Faye. 'What will happen to Faye? Will they arrest her?'

'As soon as the doctor clears her to go home, we will have to arrest her. It's standard protocol when a domestic disturbance results in a dead body. We need to know what happened in Faye's own words. The important thing for her to remember is the truth.'

'Then what happens? Johnny's dead, but she didn't mean to kill him; she's not that sort of person. I swear on my life!'

Hazelton's thin smile did little to reassure her. 'What happens then is dependent on what she tells us and what the pathologist discovers in the post mortem. If your friend's version correlates with the pathologist's findings, then it's possible no charges will be brought, but it's far too early to speculate at this point. The important thing right now is that Faye isn't in any more danger. We have a duty of care to all – regardless of the crimes they're accused of committing. We just want to make sure she's okay and then the process will begin.'

Alice still felt like she might be sick, but having eaten nothing since lunch, there would be little to come up.

'It looks like she's out for the night,' Hazelton added, keeping her voice low. 'I'll go and speak to the SIO for her case before I return to Bournemouth. Can I give you a lift home?'

'Thanks, but Ben's here. He'll drive me.'

Hazelton nodded and departed the room, whispering something to the two officers still stationed outside the private room. Inevitably, Faye would be moved out of the Emergency Department at some point, but Alice was determined to stay by her side wherever they moved her to. She wouldn't sit back idly any longer.

46

Alice's eyes shot open as the arm that had been propping up her head slipped off the armrest and jolted her awake. The room was still dark, the slat blinds doing a good job of blocking out the morning light. It took her a moment to realize where she was, and why the room looked so unfamiliar. Faye stirred in the hospital bed ahead of her.

'Alice? Is that you?'

Alice stood and stretched, unable to supress a huge yawn. 'Morning.'

'What time is it?'

Alice reached for her phone and checked the display. 'Nearly eight. How are you feeling?'

There was no response, but Alice heard her whimpering a moment later.

'Shall I see if I can find us a cup of tea?' Alice asked, but Faye didn't reply.

Opening the door, Alice stepped out into the brightly lit ward. Faye had been moved up here sometime after midnight – still sedated, which had probably been for the best. Had she seen the two uniformed officers who'd insisted on escorting her up she would have been even more fearful of her future.

There was only one officer stationed in the chair outside the room now. He shuddered as her attempts to remain quiet awoke him.

'Sorry,' she whispered with a nervous smile. 'I was just going to get us a tea. Do you want anything?'

She regretted the question instantly. Who did she think she was speaking to? She didn't even know this man's name, yet she was offering him a drink like he was an old family friend. Thankfully, he didn't seem to notice, smiling back and shaking his head as he stifled a yawn. He didn't look like either of the two who'd been here when they'd come up, but their faces were a bit of a memory blur now. Maybe he was one of them, or maybe he looked nothing like them. She had no idea.

Excusing herself, Alice made her way along the corridor, hunting left and right for anything resembling a drinks machine. There was a great deal of chatter as nurses dispensed medication and breakfast, moving from room to room efficiently.

'Tea?' Alice asked when one looked at her suspiciously.

'You have to go down to the main entrance. There are a couple of coffee shops there or the hospital restaurant is one level below ground.'

'Sorry,' Alice interrupted as the nurse was about to return to her duties, 'do you know what time the doctor will be doing the rounds? I'm just wondering when my friend will be released.'

The nurse sighed, clearly torn between wanting to finish her task and being helpful. 'Who's your friend?'

'Faye Baxter? She's the one with the police officer outside the door.'

The nurse's eyes widened – she clearly knew who Alice was talking about.

'The morning rounds should start at nine, but it all depends which ward the duty doctor visits first. Rounds are finished by eleven, so sometime between then.'

Alice thanked her and made her way out to the lifts, but decided to use the stairs down to the ground level instead. The chair had done little to aid restful sleep, and a burst of exercise was what she needed to kick-start her brain and energy levels.

Alice drained the last of her tea as the nurse finished checking Faye's readings: blood pressure, pulse, vision.

'Do you still feel off balance?' the nurse asked.

Faye shook her head.

'Good, then the concussion is probably passing. How many fingers am I holding up?'

'Three.'

The nurse checked the plaster wasn't too tight before jotting her notes on Faye's record documents and leaving the room.

'Would you help me get dressed?' Faye asked Alice when they were alone.

Ben had agreed to collect some clothing for Faye when he'd left the hospital, and had dropped it back before heading home. He'd offered to spend the night at the hospital with Alice, but the room wasn't big enough for them and Faye. He hadn't complained when she'd told him she wanted to stay the night, and he'd told her to phone as soon as she needed collecting.

Alice untied the hospital gown and helped Faye slip it down and over the plaster cast, then pulled the bra strap over in its place and fastened it at the back. As she then reached for the carrier bag of clothes, Faye grabbed her hand and squeezed it.

'I don't know what I would do if you weren't here.' Her eyes watered. 'Anyone else would have run for the hills when they found out what I did to Johnny. I really appreciate you staying with me overnight.'

Alice choked down her own emotion and scraped as big a reassuring smile as she could muster. 'Everything will be okay. I spoke to DC Hazelton and she understands what has happened and that you're just as much a victim in this – if not more so

– than Johnny, and she was going to try and speak to the lead detective on your behalf. I'm sure once you explain what he was like, they'll see you had no choice but to defend yourself.'

Faye suddenly pulled Alice in to an embrace, wrapping her arms around her neck. 'How do I tell Isabella that I killed her dad? She'll never forgive me.'

In that moment Alice suddenly realized why Faye had been so upset since she'd arrived. Yes, some of those tears were for a man she'd once loved, but the majority were for a daughter who had lost her hero.

Alice broke free of her grip, the skin beneath her eyes wet, fixing her stare on Faye. 'You listen to me, Faye Baxter. You are one of the strongest women I know. You are a role model to Isabella and she will learn that you are not responsible for what happened to her dad. You cannot blame yourself for his drunken and abusive behaviour. Right now, she doesn't need to know *how* he died. There will be time for that when she's older. Right now you need to remain strong for her. You're two parents now, and I will not allow you to jeopardize that.'

The women embraced again, both giving in to their emotions, and both realizing that once the moment was gone, their public displays of emotion would be no more.

DC Hazelton arrived at half past ten and led in the young male officer who Alice had spoken with earlier.

'The doctor has cleared you to leave,' Hazelton said calmly, her glance flitting between Faye and Alice. 'As I explained earlier, we need to bring you in to discuss what happened yesterday and matters leading up to that event. Okay? The SIO has agreed to me sitting in on the interview with you. Okay? The best thing you can do is to be honest.'

'Am I all right to come in with her?' Alice asked, but Faye reached for her arm.

'I don't want you to come in with me,' she said quietly.

Alice frowned in confusion. 'It's okay, Faye. I really don't mind. I want to be there for you.'

Faye forced a smile, but kept her tears in check. 'I know you do, but I'll be okay. There's something more important I need you to do for me. My mum is watching Isabella, but she'll need help. Can you look after Isabella for me until all this is . . . resolved?'

'Of course I can, but I don't think you should be at the police station unaccompanied.'

'I have nothing to hide. That little girl is my whole world, and she'll be confused about what's happening. I want to be the one to tell her about her dad, but she needs a familiar face to tell her it will all be okay. Can you do that for me, Alice? You're her godmother, and I'd feel a lot happier knowing that she's with you.'

Faye didn't wait for a response, giving Alice's arm a final squeeze before heading over to Hazelton and holding her wrists forward.

'I don't think there's any need for cuffs,' Hazelton said. 'It looks like your wrist is in enough trouble without us adding to it.'

Alice watched them leave. As soon as the door closed, she dropped to her knees and let the emotion flow through her.

47

Alice picked at the pastry of the croissant on her plate, not really wanting it, but knowing she should eat something. She checked her phone's display again. Ben wouldn't be much longer. Once she'd composed herself after Faye's arrest, she'd called and asked him to collect her.

Last night's events had certainly put things in perspective. She'd never wanted to see and hold Ben as much as she did right now. She just wanted to put her hands on his cheeks and kiss him like it was the last time. Too often, couples take one another for granted. We all have an end, but when you're in a relationship it's easy to ignore that ticking clock.

Alice vowed she'd never allow herself to take Ben for granted again. Their marriage had got off to a rocky start, but they'd survived it, and it would make them stronger as a result.

A couple were arguing at the next table over. The man was wearing button-up pyjamas and must have been roasting given the warm climate inside the café, and presumably the woman was his wife or sister, who'd stopped by to visit him. He was emptying a fourth sachet of sugar into his mug, and she was slapping his free hand away from reaching for a fifth.

'It's this much sugar that's made you diabetic to begin with,' the woman chastised.

Alice was pretty sure that was an inaccurate statement, but the woman's aggressive neck tattoo dissuaded Alice from confronting her on it.

The man looked older, his hair a shade of mid-grey, uncombed, and hanging down over his ears. The skin hung from his face but the paunch beneath his pyjamas suggested he had been over-weight for some considerable time. He stirred the sugar around the mug and grimaced as he sipped from it.

Alice's phone vibrated on the table. Dropping the croissant, she answered it when she saw her mum's profile picture.

'Morning, Mum. How are you? Did Scott get off to the airport okay?'

There was a huff on the other end. 'You haven't heard then?'

Alice's eyebrows dipped. 'Heard what?'

'It's all over the news; have you had your head buried in the sand today?'

Alice didn't know how to begin to explain where she was or why. 'I've been busy. What's going on?'

'Scott's been arrested. At the airport of all places. Why on earth didn't you tell me he had a drug problem?'

Alice's eyes fluttered, certain she hadn't heard right. 'What? Is this some kind of joke?'

'Do I sound like I'm joking?' her mum said shrilly.

'I'll call you back,' Alice said quickly, hanging up the phone and opening the Internet.

Sure enough, typing in Scott's name, the first half dozen results alluded to an arrest at the airport. She skimmed the first two articles. Apparently, his bag had caused the dogs at Geneva airport to go crazy and after he'd been escorted to a back room, a block of cocaine had been discovered in his hand luggage. The article didn't say where he was being held or what actions the Swiss authorities were planning to take, but the news was barely two hours old.

Scott had told her he was flying out to prepare for his race, but she hadn't realized he'd meant so soon. And he'd certainly given her no reason to suspect he was taking drugs to enhance his performance.

He just wasn't the type. He'd worked so hard to recover his fitness after the accident which had almost ended his career prematurely. That had been three years ago and he had done everything the doctors had told him: physiotherapy, muscle strengthening exercises, a carefully controlled high-protein diet. She'd seen the work he'd put in and it had looked like all his effort would be worth it, with a crack at the Tour de France a very realistic possibility.

All that would be wasted now.

Alice called her mum back. 'I swear I had no idea.'

Her mum huffed again. 'It's bad enough having a son-in-law arrested and questioned by the police, but now a stepson too! What is happening to this family?'

Alice couldn't miss the accusatory tone in her mother's voice. Although she wouldn't utter the words, Alice knew exactly what her mother was thinking.

'You're the one he was living with,' Alice wanted to say. 'If anyone's to blame, it's you for all the pressure you put on him.' She bit her tongue instead. Now was not the time for blame and recrimination.

'Have you spoken to him yet?' Alice asked, after a moment.

'No, he hasn't called,' she sighed. 'Do you think I should try and phone them? What if they're speaking to him in French? You know he wasn't good at foreign languages in school.' Her mother paused. 'You need to go out there. *Today.* I'll pay for your flight if necessary. He needs someone who can speak to the locals. You're a French teacher, you'd be perfect.'

Her mother was being as impractical as ever.

257

'I'm sure they'll provide a translator if necessary,' Alice replied quietly. 'Besides, I can't just up and fly to Switzerland. We don't know where they're holding him, or even *if* they're holding him. They might have extradited him back to the UK for all we know.'

'He'll be terrified. You know what he's like when he's on his own. He needs family around him at a time like this. Someone who can help him through.'

The fact that her mum was more concerned about Scott than her hadn't been lost on Alice. Scott had been the golden boy since the remarriage. Her mother apparently didn't want to acknowledge that Scott was responsible for his current predicament. After all, it was he who had packed the cocaine in his luggage.

'I think we need to sit tight for now,' Alice said calmly. '*When* Scott makes contact we'll deal with the situation, but in the meantime I have more important things on my plate.'

'What could possibly be more important than your brother?' Her mother's tone cut Alice to the core. She hung up the call without a second's thought, dropping the phone to the table. The clatter caused those closest to turn and stare.

Alice shoved what remained of the croissant into her mouth and fumed silently. It was true what they said: you could pick friends, but family you got lumbered with.

The woman at the other table had gone back to the counter to buy a cake, and Alice watched as the older man emptied another sachet of sugar into his mug. He caught her watching him and put a finger to his lips cheekily.

Maybe it was human nature for people to lie to those closest to them. She wasn't surprised that Scott had kept his drug use a secret, nor that Ben had tried to keep his marriage to Mary from her. Had she found herself in Faye's situation, would she have been brave enough to tell her friends that her husband was abusing her? She couldn't say for certain that she would have.

Yet each of these secrets had led to irreparable damage. She had forgiven Ben for omitting Mary from his life, but it would always hang in the air between them; forgiven but not forgotten.

Then there was Kerry Valentine's secret double life. She was a mum to Finn by day, but at night she became an exotic figure of lust. Her secret had borne the ultimate cost.

So many secrets, was it possible that one could ever *really* know another person fully? It was with this thought in her head that she pressed redial and decided to console her mother, rather than judge.

48

'You sure you don't want me to come in?' Ben asked, keeping the engine on so the air conditioning continued to shut out the stifling heat.

Alice looked over to him and smiled, feeling exhausted after last night's uncomfortable sleep in the hospital armchair. 'It's probably best if I go in and bring Isabella out. It's going to be weird for her as it is, without us making it more overwhelming.'

Ben reached for her hand and put it to his lips. 'How did I get so lucky as to land someone as caring as you? I don't deserve you.'

She moved her hand to his face and gently rubbed his cheek with her thumb.

They were parked on the pavement outside a three-storey block of flats. The brickwork was yet to be faded by the extremities of weather and time; it couldn't be much older than Alice herself. The block was one of three situated around a communal square, but nobody was using the park benches in the area, each stained with graffiti and bird muck. It seemed such a shame. Once upon a time a developer would have envisioned this small community coming together to share food and drink on a day as beautiful as this. They'd have had such high hopes, but the problem with optimism is that human nature is the biggest obstacle to it.

Alice pushed the door of the 4x4 open and stepped down onto the road surface, the wave of heat hitting her like a hard slap to the face. Crossing the road and entering the courtyard, she couldn't help but wonder how Faye was coping. Would they have interviewed her yet? She could only hope DC Hazelton was remaining true to her word and taking care of Faye. It was more than one woman's life on the line; Isabella's would be permanently affected by whatever outcome the police reached. Their duty was to assess what had happened, why and whether the law had been broken. A man was dead, but that didn't mean anyone else had to suffer.

Pressing the button next to number two, Alice waited for the communal door to buzz, before heading inside. It was just as warm, if not a fraction warmer, inside the building, where the sun's rays had been magnified by the large glass panels either side of the door.

Faye's mum was waiting patiently just inside her door, and although her face initially bore no sign of emotion, the moment their eyes met her face screwed into a ball and her arms reached out as though she might fall if not propped up. Alice sprinted the remaining steps and caught the woman, and for five minutes they just stood there, supporting each other and allowing the pain to course through them.

'Have you seen her? Is she okay?' the older woman asked once they were inside.

'I stayed with her last night,' Alice said, 'and I was there when they took her to the police station this morning. I never realized just how bad things were between her and Johnny.'

Although Alice had met Faye's mum at Faye and Johnny's wedding and at Isabella's christening and birthdays, they had never really been formally introduced. The woman's name was Dorothy, but everyone called her Dotty, even Faye. Born in

Senegal, she was proud of her African heritage, and although her thick hair was now the colour of a raincloud, the skin beneath the hair remained as dark as ever. Dotty had moved to the UK with Faye's dad, a British-born sergeant in the army, and they had lived together happily until he had been killed in service on the eve of Faye's sixth birthday. So if anyone understood the pain and grief Isabella was yet to face, it was her mum.

Dotty dabbed the corner of her eye with a fresh tissue from the box on the kitchen table between them. 'I should have known. She claimed she was just clumsy. I saw her less and less this last year, but now that I look back on it, I don't remember the last time I didn't see her with a bruise or bandage of some kind. I should have asked – no, I should have *demanded* – to know what was going on, but she never liked to talk about her personal life, only ever about Isabella and school.'

Alice's phone vibrated loudly on the table, but she didn't recognize the number. She was going to ignore it, let the messaging service take it, when Dotty stood and headed over to the kettle.

'I'll make us some tea,' she said. 'Isabella is playing in the garden, but she'll be needing some lunch soon.'

Alice put the phone to her ear. 'Alice Goodman speaking.'

'Is now a good time for you to talk? Is Ben in the room?'

She recognized Liam O'Neill's voice and a shiver ran the course of her spine. 'What do *you* want?' she said, leaving the kitchen so Dotty wouldn't overhear the spite in her voice.

'I wanted to check you were okay?' O'Neill replied. 'After what we told you yesterday, I hoped you'd have had time to think about Mary's warning and would be ready to help us.'

It was all Alice could do to stop herself shouting. '*Help* you? Help you with what exactly? Framing my husband for something he didn't do? Why do you have such a vendetta against Ben?'

His voice sounded uncertain. 'It's not a vendetta, and you're not safe if you stay with him. You heard what we had to say: Ben killed Mary's mother. He got her to take out a huge life assurance policy and then pushed her down the stairs.'

'How dare you!' she shouted. 'How dare you wage this war against me and my husband? I told Ben *everything* you had to say, and I told him how you've been stalking me since Sunday. He paints a very different picture of his doomed relationship with Mary; how *she* took advantage of *him*—'

'Of course he'd say that,' O'Neill interrupted, 'but I have it on good authority that he was the one who chased after her.'

'Whose authority? Mary's? Right now it's her word against his, and I for one know whom I'd rather believe.'

'You're not safe, Alice.'

'Why? Because Ben's bitter ex-wife and some kid he used to bully say so? Ben's admitted he was a shit when he was younger, but that doesn't give you the right to hound him – *and me* – now!'

'If the police didn't think he pushed Mary's mum, the case never would have made it to trial.'

'If he was guilty the jury would have found him so.'

'What about the fact that his was the only DNA found on Kerry Valentine's body?'

'He's explained all that and I think you should get your facts straight before you go accusing him of anything else. The police now think they know who killed her, and the perpetrator is dead.'

O'Neill didn't respond, and Alice suddenly became aware of just how loud her voice was.

'Do you know what?' she continued in a loud whisper. 'If you continue to pester us, I'll have no choice but to tell the police and your editor what a vindictive little man you truly are.'

She disconnected the phone and blocked the number before he'd had chance to respond. Taking several deep breaths, she tried to lower her pulse to a steadier beat before returning to the kitchen, ready to apologize for her outburst. Dotty seemed oblivious that Alice had even left and returned to the room. She was standing by the back door out to the patio, watching Isabella happily playing on the swing apparatus.

Alice wrapped a gentle arm around Dotty's shoulders, but didn't say anything as she too watched the little girl lost in her own world of daydreams and adventures, unaware of the pain and grief before her.

'I'll make that tea,' Dotty said eventually, turning away from the door and filling the two cups.

Alice retook her seat at the kitchen table. 'Did you pack a few things in a bag for Isabella? I don't know how long the police will keep Faye in, but hopefully she'll be back out with Isabella soon enough.'

'I left a bag by the front door,' Dotty said as she lowered the cups to the table. 'Do you think they *will* let her out?'

Alice's heart ached at the possibility that the next time she saw Faye it could be within the confines of a prison. She could see the look of longing in Dotty's eyes, begging for anyone to tell her everything would be okay, but Alice couldn't offer any such reassurance.

'The police don't lock up innocent people,' Alice said through the pain.

Thankfully that seemed enough as the first flicker of a smile appeared on Dotty's lips. 'I know you'll take good care of Isabella. You have a kind face and a warm heart. I just wish there was more I could do, but with my arthritis and the medication I take for the pain in my hip . . . I just wouldn't be able to guarantee her safety.'

Alice squeezed Dotty's hands and made a silent promise to anyone who would listen: she would protect Isabella until the end of her days.

49

It was hard to know what was going on in the little girl's head. Alice used the vanity mirror in the sun visor to watch as Isabella stared out of the window, not speaking, in awe of her surroundings.

'She'll be fine,' Ben muttered, just loud enough for Alice to hear.

Alice looked over at him and tried to smile, but she could see it wasn't convincing. When Dotty had told Isabella that she was going to stay with Alice and Ben for a few days, the little girl had nodded without speaking, somehow sensing that something like this was going to happen, yet unable to understand why. She didn't make a fuss or ask why her grandmother wouldn't be watching her any longer.

Dotty had tried to give Alice some money, but she had refused to accept it. 'There's really no need.'

Dotty had given her a stern look – she was a proud woman who had never accepted charity and wouldn't allow any living relative of hers to accept it either. Alice had eventually agreed to put the notes in her handbag, but made a promise to herself that she would try and get the money back to Faye somehow.

The radio was playing pop songs in the background, but Alice wasn't really listening to them as she continued to try and read Isabella's look and actions. If the little girl was scared, she was giving no sign of it.

'What do you fancy for your dinner?' Alice tried, turning around in her seat to speak to Isabella, but a gentle shrug was the only response she received.

'What's your favourite food?' Alice tried again, certain Faye had mentioned it before, but unable to recall exactly what she'd said.

This time Isabella made eye contact, but the shrugged outcome was the same.

'Well, you don't have to decide now,' Alice said reassuringly. 'Have a think about it and you can let me know later.'

She turned back to face the front as Isabella's stare returned to the window.

There was still no word from Faye, and that couldn't be good. Nearly three hours had passed since Hazelton had come to collect her from the hospital. Surely that was enough time to establish the facts and release her. There was no doubt in Alice's mind that Faye's actions were done in self-defence. Had she not kicked out, God only knew what Johnny would have done. Would Faye have ended up just another lifeless victim in some river?

The gated entrance and men clad in black came into view ahead of them, and Alice suddenly wished she'd thought to ask Ben to give the guards a break for their return. As it was, she thought the place looked like a compound – what would Isabella think? If her first impression of this new home was muscly men with vicious dogs, would she feel safe or terrified? Had they made a mistake bringing her back here when goodness knew who was out there watching and leaving those letters.

Ben opened the gates and pulled up alongside one of the men, who confirmed nobody had been seen in the vicinity since he'd left. Alice hadn't asked how much this private army was costing, and in truth she didn't want to know. It made her feel safer having them there, and she just hoped their presence wouldn't be needed indefinitely. Hopefully once the police formally announced Johnny as Kerry's killer, the Goodman name would simply fade from the spotlight.

Ben parked the car outside the garage and fished Isabella's small satchels from the boot – one containing clothes, and the other some toys Dotty had found lying about her small flat. Hopefully Isabella's stay with them would be short-lived and she wouldn't need anything else.

That still left a question of where Faye and Isabella would end up if Faye was released, though. She would be unlikely to want to return to the house where Johnny had died, and Dotty certainly didn't have room to put them up, so maybe Isabella's stay in Chilworth would be longer than originally intended.

Dave was sitting in his car near the entrance waiting for their return. As soon as he saw them leave Ben's car, he immediately jumped out and walked over.

'I need to speak to you, Ben' he said in a stern voice. '*Alone.*'

Ben gave him a look that Alice couldn't quite read, but Dave nodded quickly, and that was enough to make Ben lean closer to Alice and whisper, 'I need to sort this out. Why don't you take Isabella down to the pool for a swim?' He looked down at Isabella and smiled. 'You'd like that wouldn't you, Isabella? If Auntie Alice took you for a swim in our pool. It's nice and warm and we've got some balls and toys down there you can play with.'

Isabella smiled for the first time since Alice had collected her, and as the young girl bounced excitedly, Alice had little choice but to take her by the hand and lead her inside. From upstairs, Alice heard Ben and Dave talking quietly as they closed the front door and headed for the living room, closing that door behind them too.

Alice did her best to keep her paranoia in check. What was so urgent that Dave had waited for them to return, and now needed to discuss with Ben alone? Was it to do with Johnny and the fact that the police would soon realize the stag party had misled them? Had Ben and Dave known all along that Johnny was responsible and had done what they could to cover it up?

Ben couldn't have known, she reasoned silently, as she searched through Isabella's bag for anything resembling a swimming costume. He'd shown no concern or worry when Faye had called them into the hospital – upset, yes, but not concerned. Nor had he expressed any worry or anxiety when he'd arrived to collect her this morning. He was a smart guy; he'd have known their alibis would be in danger now that Johnny's true nature had been revealed.

Unless that wasn't the reason Dave had come over.

'Is this your room?' Isabella asked absently, as she sat peacefully on the king-size mattress and watched Alice pulling clothes out of the satchel.

It was enough to snap Alice's attention back. 'What's that, sweetie?'

'Is this your room?'

Alice stopped what she was doing, unable to find a bathing costume, and sat down next to Isabella. 'That's right. This is where me and your Uncle Ben sleep.'

'Will I sleep in here too?'

Alice plastered on the widest smile she could manage. 'No, you won't sleep in here. Believe me, you'd never be able to sleep with Uncle Ben's snoring. Would you like to see the room you'll be in?'

Isabella nodded eagerly.

Alice led the way out of the room. 'You have a choice of three rooms to be honest. Why don't we look at all three and then you can choose the one you'd prefer to stay in.'

They entered the room directly across from the master bedroom first, and Isabella rushed over to the window which overlooked the gates and guards below. The room had a double bed – they all did – a television hung from the wall, a built-in wardrobe and a chest of drawers. It was more than big enough for two to live comfortably for several weeks, with enough floor space to allow for an inflatable mattress either side of the main bed.

'I like this room,' Isabella declared. 'Is it okay if I sleep in here?'

'Sure, but don't you want to see the other two rooms first?'

Alice shook her head. 'It's close to your room in case I get scared, and I can watch and wait for Mummy and Daddy from this window.'

Isabella's words were like a cold dagger to the heart, and it took all of Alice's restraint to hold it together. 'Then it's settled. You can sleep in here. If you do get scared during the night, we're a short walk away, but I'm sure there'll be no reason for you to get scared.'

Isabella moved back to the front window and raised the net curtain. 'Do you know when Mummy will get here?'

Alice crouched at Isabella's feet. 'Hopefully not too long, sweetie, but if you need anything in the meantime, you only have to ask. Okay? Anything you want or need, just tell me or Uncle Ben and we'll do what we can.'

Isabella looked her straight in the eye. 'Is Mummy okay?'

Alice desperately wanted to break eye contact, but forced herself not to look away. 'Why do you say that?'

Isabella's face contorted into confusion and suddenly Alice could see the anxiety she'd kept so well hidden from her, from Dotty and from Ben. 'Something bad has happened, hasn't it? That's why she isn't here.'

Alice didn't want to lie, but she'd promised Faye she wouldn't break the news about Johnny, and in that moment she was grateful Faye would bear that burden.

'She's sick, isn't she?' Isabella said, when Alice's answer wasn't forthcoming.

'No, she's not sick, poppet,' Alice battled to say. 'She just has to help someone with something. She's doing really important work, and that's why she needed your grandma and now us to look after you. She loves you more than anything. You know that, don't you?'

Isabella nodded, but the worry remained etched into her face.

'Hopefully she'll finish her work soon and then she'll be able to come and be with you again.' Alice wiped a tear from the edge of her eye. 'She asked if you would teach Ben and I how to be good parents. We're hoping to start a family of our own, and your mum said you'd done such a good job of teaching her how to be a good mum that you'd be an expert in teaching me and Ben. Can you do that for me?'

Isabella's face brightened a fraction, and she nodded before putting both arms around Alice's neck and pulling her closer.

Alice exhaled a small sigh of relief. 'I don't think your grandma packed a bathing suit for you, but that's okay. You can swim in your pants and then we'll put some clean ones on after, and I can wash the wet ones. How does that sound?'

Isabella sniffed, but her head bobbed in agreement.

'Good. Then let's head down to the pool now and we can get changed down there.'

Isabella broke free of the embrace and rushed back into the master bedroom, snatching the teddy bear from the bed. 'Can Mr Squiggles come too?'

Alice nodded. 'He can't get in the water, but he's welcome to sit in one of the chairs at the side if you like?'

Isabella grabbed Alice's hand and the two headed down the spiral staircase. Reaching the bottom step, Alice could hear Ben's and Dave's muffled voices behind the living room door, and gave in to curiosity. Miming for Isabella to stay put by the front door, Alice tiptoed back towards the living room and listened.

'For fuck's sake, Dave!' Ben's muffled voice yelled. 'You screwed up big time!'

'I know, and I'm sorry,' Dave mumbled back, further away from the door.

'Have you spoken to Abdul yet? Is everything still in place?'

'I can't get hold of him.'

'What's that supposed to mean?'

'He's not answering his phone, and I don't want to leave a message. I'm using a burner phone so they can't trace it back to me, but . . .'

'You need to sort this! If Alice finds out, we're both toast. You hear me?'

There was movement beyond the door and Alice bolted back to Isabella, grabbing her hand and running from the property towards the pool enclosure.

50

'Make sure you keep to the shallow end, sweetie,' Alice cautioned Isabella as the young girl splashed about in the pool.

An inflatable swan floated past Alice's feet as she dangled them in the cool, refreshing water. It was probably warmer than it felt between her toes, but the climate inside the enclosure was stifling, with the sun beating in through the large glass windows that faced the main house. She would have got in and engaged more with Isabella but she couldn't concentrate on anything except what she'd heard from behind the living room door.

Another secret, but what was it this time, and what did it have to do with Abdul, a man she barely knew?

Isabella climbed up the side of the pool and plonked herself down next to Alice. The anxiety and fear from earlier had been washed clear by the excitement of a private pool. Alice couldn't blame her, as the pool had been the first thing she'd fallen in love with at the address.

'Are you going to come in?' Isabella chirped as water dripped down her long black hair, landing as droplets on her light brown skin.

Alice looked at her and in that moment could see Johnny's face: the nose and dark eyes were definitely his, yet the skin tone, smile and mass of hair were Faye's. It made Alice wonder what hers and Ben's child might look like.

'Maybe in a minute,' she smiled. 'You have fun. Don't worry about me.'

It was all the reassurance the little girl needed. Pushing herself up, she tottered on the edge of the pool before jumping in, sending waves of water crashing against Alice's legs, and splashes against her one-piece bathing costume.

Her ringing phone broke through the echo of the water, and she pulled it out of her waterproof bag. She didn't recognize the number but knew the '+41' dialling code was Switzerland, and that could mean only one thing.

'Scott?' she stammered into the phone.

'Alice? Oh thank God,' her stepbrother replied, sounding tired and frustrated. 'I take it you've heard what's happened?'

'It's been on the news. They said you were caught smuggling cocaine into the country. What the hell, Scott?' She wanted to say something far sterner, but was conscious that Isabella would be able to overhear every word.

'It's not what you think.'

'Not what I think? How is it then? They didn't find drugs in your hand luggage?'

He was silent for a moment. 'I can't get into any of that right now; I don't have long.'

'What do you need?' she asked after a moment.

'Does Mum know yet? About what happened to me, I mean.'

'She was the one who told me, Scott.'

'Shit!' he sighed, crestfallen.

'What did you expect? You're international news: a professional cyclist – someone tipped to make a splash at next year's Tour de France – is arrested at the airport when his bag sets off a sniffer dog. I know you always longed for fame, but I doubt this is what you were hoping for.'

'It wasn't my fault. Okay? You need to tell her that.'

273

'How is it not your fault?'

Another pause. 'I can't get into that on the phone. I don't know who might be listening in.'

'Well you'd better tell me something. She's probably trying to remortgage the house as we speak to stump up money to post bail for you.'

'Tell her that I'm sorry, and that I'll explain everything when I get things sorted.'

'What things? What are they going to do with you?'

'I don't know yet. I've kept my mouth shut so far.'

An inflatable beach ball splashed in the water near to Alice's left leg, and Isabella sheepishly cut through the water and scooped it up with a shy smile. Alice forced a smile back.

'Mum wants me to fly out and help you. She's worried that you won't be able to communicate because they'll be speaking to you in French or German.'

'There's a translator here – she's English but lives in Geneva. She's been supporting me, translating their questions and responding on my behalf. I don't need you to come out here.'

It was Alice's turn to sigh. 'What do you need me to do then?'

'I was phoning to warn you: you'll probably hear a lot about me over the coming days, but I want you to know that half of what you hear isn't true. Okay?'

Alice frowned, confused. 'Hear a lot about what, Scott? What have you done?'

'I told you, I can't go into that, but someone put those drugs in my bag.'

She scoffed. 'You seriously expect me to believe that you didn't know they were in there?'

'No, that's not what I'm saying. I knew, but . . . it wasn't my idea.'

'Scott, you're not making any sense. If it wasn't your idea, then whose idea . . .' Her words trailed off as her mind connected the dots.

You need to sort this! If Alice finds out, we're both toast.

It was like someone had turned on a light, and suddenly Dave's nervousness became clear; the reason he'd been waiting for their return, and the reason he would only speak to Ben.

She scrunched her eyes tight, not wanting to know the answer, but compelled to ask anyway. 'Oh God, tell me this has nothing to do with Ben.'

'Ben? No, nothing. He doesn't know, at least I don't think he does. Whatever you do though, keep an eye on him, and keep him away from his mates.'

'Dave is here now,' she said quietly.

'Now? What does he want? Did he mention me?'

'I don't know,' she sighed. 'He wanted to speak to Ben alone. What's going on, Scott? Does this have anything to do with Bournemouth?'

Another pause. 'What do you know about what happened in Bournemouth?' He sounded so cold when he uttered the words that the hairs on the back of Alice's neck rose.

'The Kerry Valentine thing. Does this have anything to do with Kerry Valentine?'

'No, nothing. Well, not exactly. I can't go into that over the phone, but I will explain everything to you when I get back – *if* I get back.'

'I overheard them talking about Abdul; does it have anything to do with Abdul?'

'You and Ben should just get away, okay? Let everything blow over, and when it's sorted I'll reach out to you. Listen, they're telling me I need to hang up. Apologize to Mum for me and tell her everything will be okay. Will you do that? I'm sorry, Alice. I'm so sor—' the line disconnected before he could finish.

Alice returned the phone to the waterproof bag, nausea slowly bubbling in the pit of her stomach.

'Are you going to come in and swim now?' Isabella asked.

Alice looked down at those innocent eyes, yet to be scarred

275

by the secrets adults tell to their friends, family and themselves. 'Just give me a minute, sweetie,' she said, pulling her legs out of the water and reaching for her towel.

It was a relief that Scott had said Ben had nothing to do with the cocaine, but that didn't mean Dave wouldn't convince him to become an accessory after the fact. She'd vowed to stand by Ben for better for worse, and if that meant kicking Dave out of their house, then she was ready to do it.

Straightening, she saw Ben and Dave emerge from the house. Both dressed head-to-toe in black, they moved swiftly to Dave's car and climbed in, before pulling away with a screech of tyres and brake dust.

51

Racing from the pool enclosure towards her small sports car, clutching Isabella's hand, Alice's sole focus was on keeping Dave's car in sight. She had to know where he and Ben were going and why. Too many secrets had been kept from her recently, and it was time to stop burying her head in the sand and hoping everything would turn out for the best.

In hindsight, dragging Isabella along for what was essentially a hare-brained chase wasn't such a great idea, but she had no option but to bring her along for the ride.

'Where are we going?' Isabella was asking. 'I don't have any clothes on.'

Isabella paused for just a moment as she reached the passenger side door. Staring down at the skinny child, who had instinctively pulled her arms around her middle, Alice had to think fast. Wrapping the large beach towel around Isabella, Alice belted her into the back seat and hurried around to the driver's side.

'We're going on an adventure,' Alice said as she started the engine and pulled away. 'Do you like adventures?'

Isabella's anxiety immediately lifted, replaced by giddy excitement. 'You mean like the Famous Five?'

Alice had never read the Enid Blyton books herself, but had

heard of them. 'Exactly like that,' she said, beaming. 'Okay? We need to find the car Uncle Ben is in. Did you see the car parked here when we got home?'

'You mean Uncle Dave's car?'

'That's right. Ben and Dave have gone off to hide and it's up to us to find them. Like hide-and-seek but in cars. Does that sound good?'

Isabella put on her most serious face. 'Do we get a prize if we find them?'

'Absolutely!' Alice declared as they neared the gates. 'How does a burger and chips sound? We'll stop at the drive-thru on the way home.'

'Can I have a milkshake, too?'

'Of course you can, sweetie.'

Alice had seen Dave's car dart to the right and she copied the move, though there was no sign of him on the road immediately ahead of them. Accelerating forwards, knowing that they could have been going anywhere and that the chances of her finding them were virtually non-existent, Alice persevered.

The other properties soon disappeared into the distance as they hit a road with a 50 mph speed limit, but that ended too abruptly as they reached red traffic lights. Four cars separated her from the front of the queue, but she spotted the taillights of Dave's Land Rover as it continued straight – the last car through before the lights had changed. At least it meant they were going the right way. The road would eventually lead to Romsey and beyond that the options were the M27 west to Portsmouth or the A31 east to Bournemouth. Her gut told her they'd head east, as that's where Abdul lived, but it was all conjecture at this point.

The car's stereo cut out as the Bluetooth system interrupted, announcing an incoming call. Hoping it was Ben, she flicked a switch on the steering wheel to answer it.

'Ben?'

'Um, no, it's DC Hazelton,' came the reply. 'Is now a bad time?'

Alice looked at Isabella in the rear-view mirror. If Hazelton was phoning to give bad news about Faye, the last thing she needed was for Isabella to hear it from a stranger.

'I'm driving,' Alice said quickly. 'I have Faye's daughter, Isabella, in the car with me.'

'Is Ben with you too?'

'Ben? No, why?'

'Can I come over? It would be better to tell you in person than over the phone. Are you near home?'

Alice couldn't inform her of her present location or the reason why. The lights turned to green and the cars ploughed forwards.

'No, won't be home for a while yet. What do you need to speak to Ben about?'

Hazelton sighed, blowing loud air into the car's speakers. 'We've identified a second source of DNA on Kerry. Is Ben at home? Perhaps I could speak to him directly instead—'

'No, he's not home,' Alice interrupted.

'Ah, do you know when he'll be back? I need to ask him some questions about that night.'

Alice pulled around the car in front, which had been barely hitting thirty, despite the national speed limit sign they'd passed a moment earlier. She cut back in before a lorry trundled past on the opposite side of the carriageway.

'I'm not sure, sorry.'

In the circumstances it was better not to lie. The truth was she didn't know when Ben would be back. All she was omitting was that she believed he was going to get himself into trouble and that she was hotfooting it after him.

'I tried phoning him, but the answerphone cuts in every time. Do you know *where* he is?'

'No, sorry.' Alice thought again. 'Um, what I mean is, I'm not sure what he's up to. He said something about work, but I wasn't really listening to be honest.'

'Not to worry. I'll keep trying his phone. If you see him before

I've managed to make contact, can you ask him to give me a call urgently?'

'Will do,' Alice said, ending the call.

'Who's Kerry?' Isabella asked, looking up at Alice's reflection in the mirror.

Alice met her stare but didn't know how to answer. Did the second DNA profile belong to Johnny? Is that why Hazelton hadn't named the suspect, because she didn't want Isabella to hear? Or was it because it belonged to someone Alice hadn't considered? And whatever the answer, why did she want to speak to Ben about it?

Alice was tempted to pull over and phone Hazelton back to demand answers, even taking the call outside of the car so Isabella wouldn't overhear, but as they reached the roundabout leading to the motorway, she spotted Dave's Land Rover. It was heading clockwise around the roundabout, exiting at the slip road for the A31. They had to be heading towards Bournemouth or Poole, and she felt slightly relieved that it would be easier to keep track of them on the dual carriageway.

'I'm hungry,' Isabella whined. 'When are we going to get food?'

'Soon, sweetie,' Alice replied absently as she pulled onto the roundabout, indicated and followed it around to the slip road. 'See if you can spot Dave's car again, and you might earn yourself a pudding as well. How does that sound?'

Alice settled into a spot three cars behind the Land Rover, on an unshakeable course to whatever destiny had in store.

52

The Land Rover suddenly indicated for the off ramp at Ringwood. Alice, four cars behind, had been in the process of overtaking a caravan when the manoeuvre happened, and but for the last-minute glance at the turning she would have been oblivious to the fact that they'd left the road. It was too late for her to replicate their move and now she desperately hunted for somewhere she could come off and retrace her steps.

The whole time she'd been working on the assumption that they were headed to Bournemouth, but unless they were taking a scenic route to the town, they were headed elsewhere. With the Land Rover now out of sight, she had no way of knowing where it was they were going.

Thumping the steering wheel in frustration, Alice bit her tongue to stop herself cursing, conscious of Isabella dozing gently in the seat behind her. To have come so far and now lost them all because of that bloody caravan was hugely frustrating. Now she'd never know for certain why they'd suddenly rushed here or what they were planning.

Spotting the exit for Verwood and Matchams, Alice made the decision to get off the road and end the pursuit. There was no point in continuing driving west, especially when even her own stomach was starting to grumble. Following the exit road around and underneath the A31, they were soon on the eastbound side of the road.

'We'll stop for food in a bit,' Alice said apologetically. 'You still want that milkshake?'

Isabella nodded, half-asleep, but the earlier excitement had waned.

Alice had a vague memory that there was a McDonald's at one of the service stops on the way back. She tried calling Ben's phone via the Bluetooth, but as Hazelton had said, it went straight to voicemail, which meant he'd switched it off. That in itself was an odd thing for him to do. Ben was one of those people who had his phone at his side at all times, never far from social media and calls from the office. She could only think of one reason why he might have switched it off: because he didn't want to be traced. Trying Dave's phone as well, that too went straight to voicemail.

She tried to ignore the rising dread in the pit of her stomach.

Pulling off the road as the services loomed, she drove past the petrol station, alarmed to see half a dozen sets of blue flashing lights blocking the entrance to the restaurant. An officer was stationed by the line of cars, speaking to the long line of drivers ahead of them. Each time the officer would ask the driver to lower their window, talk for a few seconds and then the car would pull away and rejoin the main road.

As Alice lowered her window, the officer in a bright yellow, high-vis vest offered an empathetic nod. 'I'm sorry, we've had to close the services due to a major incident. If you continue along the road, the next services is in about fifteen miles.' He straightened to indicate the conversation was over.

'I'm sorry,' Alice called out through the window. 'Can you tell me what's happened?'

He bent forward again, clearly conscious of the queue building behind her, with other hungry drivers waiting to be delivered the bad news.

'Just a local incident, madam, nothing for you to be alarmed about. We anticipate reopening the services in the next few hours.'

He straightened again, leaving Alice with no option but to do as instructed.

'What's going on?' Isabella asked in a disappointed tone. 'Does this mean we're not getting food?'

'No, sweetie, it just means we can't eat here. I'm sorry, but it won't be long until we get to the next one, and then we can eat.'

Releasing the handbrake, Alice couldn't help but glance through the line of police cars, to try and see what could have possibly caused such activity. That's when she spotted Dave's Land Rover parked in one of the bays towards the rear of the small car park.

If Dave was there, she had no doubt that the police presence had something to do with him, and her heart dropped as she realized that Ben would also then be in trouble. She wanted to stop, to know for certain, but it wouldn't be fair on Isabella – she would just have to wait for the inevitable phone call. If only she'd seen them pulling off at Ringwood sooner, maybe she could have prevented whatever had occurred.

With that thought still in her mind, she pulled onto the slip road down to the A31, but was alarmed to see a dark figure suddenly emerge from the trees, waving frantically. Drawing closer, she was even more alarmed when she realized the figure in black was Ben.

53

'I don't believe it,' Ben said as he dived into the front of the car. 'I guess God really does answer prayers.'

Alice hadn't taken her eyes from the rear-view mirror, urging the police officer in the high-vis vest not to notice that she'd pulled over on the slip road to allow Ben to leap in.

'What are the two of you doing here?' Ben asked, as he struggled to wrap the seatbelt around him.

Alice didn't respond, allowing the next car to pass before pulling back onto the slip road. Her eyes didn't leave the high-vis jacket until they'd rejoined the carriageway.

'Babe?' Ben said, remaining low in the seat. 'I've never been so relieved to see anyone in my life. You're a lifesaver, you truly are.'

Alice allowed herself to breathe again as the slip road and police officer disappeared from view. 'What the bloody hell is going on, Ben? Don't give me any of your usual bullsh—' but she stopped herself from swearing just in time. 'Don't lie to me. I know you were with Dave and I saw his car back at those services. You'd better give me a bloody good explanation, or I'm turning around and driving you back there myself!'

Checking the services were now out of sight, Ben pulled out

his mobile phone and a set of headphones and passed them back to Isabella. 'You like Disney films?'

The little girl nodded nervously.

Ben smiled to put her at ease. 'Me too! My favourite is *The Jungle Book*, and I've got a copy on my phone. You want to watch it?'

Isabella's eyes widened with excitement and she pushed the buds into her ears as Ben started the video. He waited until bright colours filled the screen before facing Alice. 'I had no idea the police would be there. Did you see Dave? Do you know if he managed to get away?'

She glared harder. 'Away from *what*?'

Ben lifted his hands in surrender. 'Okay, okay, I'll tell you everything, but just bear in mind, I didn't know about any of this until Dave rocked up at the house this afternoon. If I'd known, I'd have done something to stop it. I swear on my life I had no idea what Dave and Scott had been up to.'

She shuddered at the mention of her stepbrother's name. 'What exactly have Scott and Dave been up to?'

'Obviously, you know why Scott was arrested at the airport,' he said, studying a bloody gash in his hand, presumably from when he'd been climbing through the trees to reach the slip road. 'It has something to do with a bit of business he and Dave were conducting behind our backs.'

'My brother isn't a druggie,' she fired back dismissively. 'Whatever your best mate has got him mixed up in is not his fault.'

'That's precisely where you're wrong, babe – it's all Scott's fault.' He paused, clearly searching for a way to soften the blow. 'Scott has been taking performance-enhancing drugs since his last accident. I knew nothing about it, but apparently he's become quite the addict – according to Dave anyway. With this big race coming up, Scott approached Dave and asked him to help find a new supplier. Apparently the regular guy he'd dealt with was arrested last month, and Scott couldn't handle going cold turkey with such a vital race on the horizon.

'Dave is the sort of person who knows people, and after some discussion, Dave agreed to set up a meeting between Scott and someone based near Ringwood. Scott was planning to meet with him the night of the stag do. According to Dave, Scott leaving the party had little to do with him wanting to get home and rest. I never realized it at the time, but looking back on it, he was quite jumpy, and knocking back energy drinks like they were going out of fashion.'

Alice watched Ben's eyes, allowing him to speak without interruption, all the time searching his face for any sign of deceit, but there was nothing. He was staring at her eyes, and didn't once look away or make any unnatural movements. He couldn't be telling the truth, but she had no doubt that he meant every word he said.

'So apparently, Dave had set up the meeting, and Scott left in order to meet the guy and hand over the cash for whatever it was he was after. Because the new supplier didn't know Scott's face, he got a bit jumpy, questioning whether Scott was an undercover narc. Turns out, Scott was pretty jumpy too, and pulled out a gun. Now God only knows where he laid his hands on the weapon – Dave swears it was nothing to do with him – but a melee broke out between Scott and this dealer and ended with the gun going off. The bullet grazed the dealer and in blind panic, Scott raced away from the scene and phoned Dave to help him. While the others chained me to that lamppost, Dave snuck away to meet with Scott and told him to go home and let him sort out the mess.'

Alice glanced at Isabella's reflection, relieved that her attention was focused on the talking animals on screen.

'Anyway,' Ben continued, 'Dave returned with the others and a fresh supply of booze, and they eventually untied me. I was fast asleep by this point, absolutely wasted, and I had no idea what

286

had gone on between Scott and Dave. The following morning Dave went and met with the dealer to try and smooth things over. Scott was really struggling at this point, barely able to walk straight apparently, and Dave tried to do what he could to sort out a supply for him. The dealer was angry about what had happened and the only way he would help out Scott was if he did something in return to prove he wasn't police. Which is how the block of coke wound up in Scott's bag. The trade-off was for Scott to take the package to one of the dealer's contacts in Zurich. When that all went tits up this morning, Dave came over in a panic, convinced Scott would break his silence and tell the Swiss police everything. If he did that, it would then implicate Dave and the rest of the stag party who never told the local cops that Dave's whereabouts were unknown for the best part of an hour that night.'

Alice knew how badly Scott had taken his last injury layoff, and had been so proud to see how well he'd managed to recover, but now she felt sick to know that he'd cheated his way back into contention. Why hadn't he reached out to her?

'Why did Dave drag you to Ringwood, and why were you running from the police?'

'As far as that dealer was concerned – the one Scott grazed – he'd now lost his bag of coke and wouldn't get his money, which meant he would seek any means of getting the money back, including threatening your life. Dave was heading to meet him to settle the payment, and everything seemed fine. We initially drove way past the services, looking for any sign of police, and then we headed back, pulling in and parking up. We must have been there for five minutes when the dealer arrived. Dave got out of the car to meet him, while I stayed put. I saw them head away from the restaurant towards the petrol station, but as Dave handed over the bag of money, the whole place erupted with cops. Blue lights raced in from all directions, and officers armed with weapons swarmed the car park. I panicked, and after what happened the other day, I jumped out of the car and ran anywhere I could to get away from them. Given my recent run-in with the law I knew they'd hold me and accuse me of collaborating and I couldn't stand the thought of phoning you to say I'd been arrested again. Especially when it had nothing to do with me. I was hidden in those trees for what felt like a lifetime, half-expecting one of them to find me. Then when I spotted your car I thought I was hallucinating or something. I mean, if you hadn't come along I'd probably be in the back of one of their vans now.'

He broke off, and thick lines penetrated his brow. 'Speaking of which, you still haven't told me what the two of you were doing at Burley services. When I left, you were both in the pool.'

She wasn't prepared to give him the satisfaction of the truth. 'Just be grateful that I was passing.'

He knew better than to challenge her when she was in this kind of mood, and she was glad of the silence as they continued the journey home. Was that what Scott had wanted to tell her over the phone? Nearing the exit, she couldn't ignore the growing list of questions.

'How did the police know Dave would be at Burley services?'

Ben shrugged. 'I can only assume they were following the dealer. I think we were unfortunate to get caught in the crossfire.'

'Did anyone see you in Dave's car before you made it to the trees?'

'I don't think so, but I guess time will tell. Hopefully not.'

'If Dave is arrested, will he drop you in it?'

'Dave's not a grass. He has my back, I have no doubt.'

Alice could only hope Ben's faith in his best friend wasn't misplaced. As the next services loomed, Alice pulled off the road, heading for the drive-thru.

54

With bellies full, faces wiped with paper napkins, and Isabella holding the remains of her milkshake in the back of the car, Alice's mood had softened. Still annoyed that Ben had managed to entangle himself in another criminal activity, she couldn't help but feel that the sooner he was separated from Dave the better. After all, it was Dave's idea to sneak Ben off to Bournemouth, it was Dave who had booked Kerry Valentine for the night, and it was Dave who was now responsible for this latest debacle.

She hated herself for secretly hoping the police had arrested Dave and would keep him locked up for a few years. If she and Ben wanted to start a family, she didn't need Dave's bad influence leading Ben astray when he had children to protect.

Starting the engine, they headed for home, and after ten minutes of silence the gates of the property came into view, as did the safety of their home. They were surprised to see a car parked near the garage, the figure of DC Hazelton behind the wheel. The feeling of dread swiftly returned to Alice's stomach.

'You two had better go inside,' Ben said calmly. 'I'll handle her.'

'What if she's been sent to bring you in following what happened at Burley services? What if Dave did give you up or someone saw you?'

'Watch from the window, and if you see her put me in the back of the car, call my solicitor. I've done nothing wrong; I was an unwitting passenger.'

'What if she arrests me for aiding your escape?'

He considered her. 'Babe, I'll just tell her you didn't know why you were picking me up. I'll say I phoned you, but didn't explain why I was there. I wouldn't drop you in it.'

A wave of nausea swept through her as she opened the car door before heading around to open Isabella's door. She'd barely got the four-year-old out of the car when she realized Hazelton was behind her.

'I see you managed to catch up with him then?' Hazelton said warmly, nodding in Ben's direction as he struggled to get out of the small space from the back seat.

'Yeah, I was going to get him to call you when we got back. Sorry.'

'It's no bother, I'm here now anyway.'

Alice eyed her suspiciously. Hazelton was far too calm for someone who'd been commanded to apprehend a fleeing suspect. Either she had no idea about the operation at the services or she was playing her cards very close to her chest.

'You must be Isabella,' Hazelton said, smiling at the youngster. 'You look just like your mother. I'm Vanessa,' she added, extending her hand, but Isabella pushed herself back and behind the safety of Alice's legs.

'Sorry, she's a little shy around strangers,' Alice said.

Hazelton was looking curiously at Alice's outfit. 'You been to the beach?'

'Not exactly,' Alice said, quickly turning so Hazelton wouldn't see her reddening cheeks. 'I'd better get this one inside before she catches a cold.'

'Before you do that,' Hazelton said, leaning round Alice to look at Isabella again, 'I have a surprise for Isabella in the back of my car. Would you like to see it?'

Isabella looked from Hazelton to Alice and back again.

Hazelton held out her hand, gesturing for Isabella to take it and go with her. 'It's okay, I won't bite, I promise.'

Alice nodded that it would be okay, gently manoeuvred the child towards Hazelton and watched as the two of them made their way to the back of the detective's car. Isabella squealed with excitement as they drew closer. The rear door of the car opened, and a swollen face emerged. Tears streamed down Faye's face as her little girl rushed over to her.

Alice's eyes instantly filled as she watched Faye tentatively drop to her knees so she could look at her daughter and tell her how much she loved her.

'She's been released for now,' Hazelton said quietly, returning to Alice's side. 'Her account of what happened matches the conclusions drawn by the forensic team. Unless anything is found to contradict the story then it will be ruled as an accidental death. I hope it was okay to bring Faye here? I didn't think she would want to go home yet.'

Alice wiped her eyes with her fingers. 'It's absolutely fine. Thank you. Thank you for getting her back to us.'

Hazelton fixed her with a look. 'I told you before, Mrs Goodman, my job is about finding the truth, not just about locking people up. An innocent person deserves the same level of respect as a hardened criminal. It's about truth and justice.'

Ben had made his way to the front door and opened it, when Hazelton noticed him disappearing inside.

'Mr Goodman? I wonder if I can have a word with you before I go. I know it's getting late but I just have a few questions. We can do it at the station if you prefer, but it would be less hassle for us both just to go through it now.'

Ben looked nervously at Alice before nodding and going inside.

Alice showed Faye and Isabella up to the guest room and told Faye they could stay with them for as long as was needed.

Hazelton and Ben were deep in conversation when Alice rejoined them in the living room.

'He was arrested earlier this evening,' Hazelton was explaining. 'DNA recovered from a scratch on the victim's neck was a match to the sample we took from him on Sunday morning.'

Ben was perched on the sofa, his face buried in his hands. Hazelton was on her feet in front of the television.

'So, Mr Goodman, what I want to know from you is whether you wish to change your statement about what happened during your stag do in Bournemouth?'

Alice quietly sat down, waiting to see whether Ben would turn in Dave, or whether he would obstinately support his best friend.

It couldn't be easy for him, knowing that he was all that stood between his friend and a life behind bars, but he had to understand that a young mother had been needlessly killed and that the person responsible for that deserved to be punished.

'My statement stands,' Ben said after a moment, his face still buried. 'After the dance the boys said we needed to get more booze and supplies, and as we went outside they jumped me and cuffed me to the lamppost. I remember watching them go, thinking they would come back and free me, but after a few minutes I realized this was part of their plan all along. I must have fallen asleep, because the next thing I remember is them splashing water on my face and untying me. We headed back inside and drank until about three before we all passed out. He was with the group the whole time.'

'Then how do you explain the scratch on Kerry's neck? Did you see them interact inside the venue? According to your and everyone else's statements, you were the only one she danced for, and the rest just watched. So either *that's* a lie, or your account of your friend's actions after you left the venue is a lie.'

Alice couldn't take the deceit any longer. 'Just tell her, Ben. Tell her the truth. Please? That poor girl is dead and her young son will never experience her love and kisses again. I know he's your friend, but you need to do the right thing. Dave doesn't deserve your loyalty.'

Both Hazelton and Ben looked over at her.

'Mrs Goodman, the man we arrested tonight was Abdul Farrar. His DNA was recovered from the body. He's in a cell in Bournemouth as we speak.'

55

Ben didn't react to the mention of Abdul's name. Either he was already over the shock of hearing it first from Hazelton, or he'd been expecting this news for some time. Whichever it was, he was now giving Alice a confused look.

'You thought Dave killed her?' Ben said incredulously. 'He's been our greatest ally for so many years; how could you . . .?'

She wanted to list a dozen reasons why she didn't trust Dave, particularly given this evening's events, but she bit her tongue with Hazelton in the room.

'I don't know,' she lied, before making eye contact with Hazelton. 'How come it's taken so long to connect the murder to Abdul?'

Hazelton rolled her eyes. 'Unfortunately it's the nature of these things. Real police work isn't quite as slick as they make it seem in TV dramas and books. The pathologist discovered the scratch and extracted a possible DNA profile, but it didn't match anyone in the system. Then on Sunday we took samples of everyone's DNA from the stag party, but with other competing priorities, it took until today for Mr Farrar's sample to be processed and compared. As soon as we saw it was a match, we put word out to local uniform, and he was brought in for questioning less than an hour ago.'

'Has he admitted to anything yet?' Alice asked, eager to see closure for Kerry and her son Finn.

Hazelton shrugged. 'I don't have any more information at this time.'

The room was stifling. What should have sounded like good news was making Alice feel claustrophobic again. Even though she barely knew Abdul, it still angered her that the real culprit had been there because of Ben and his friends. It would have been slightly more palatable had an unrelated stranger been responsible.

Hazelton moved closer to Ben. 'So I ask you again, Mr Goodman, is there anything you can recall from that night that would lead you to suspect Mr Farrar of wrongdoing?'

He looked up at her and shook his head. 'Nothing.'

Alice had seen him twitch. It was barely noticeable to the naked eye, but it was something he did when he was trying his hardest to convince someone he wasn't lying. If Hazelton had spotted it, she certainly wasn't letting on.

'I should warn you, Mr Goodman, if we find evidence that you have misled this inquiry, there will be repercussions.'

Ben stood suddenly, towering several inches above Hazelton, trying to project a dominant force. 'I understand that.'

Hazelton took an instinctive step backwards, not retreating but regaining her control of the situation. She reached into her inside jacket pocket before removing her hand and offering it out to Ben. 'I thought I should drop this by too. I meant to bring it over last night, but with what happened with Faye and her husband, it slipped my mind. I know you were keen to book a trip away.'

Ben accepted the passport, turning it over in his hands before dropping it into his back pocket. 'What about my clothes from that night? When do I get those back?'

'You'll be contacted about those in due course, but as I warned you before, there's a chance they'll hold on to them, at least until the case goes to trial.'

'You said nothing was found.'

'There are procedures for these kinds of situations. I'll ask the forensics team for an update and let you know in due course. Now, I should leave the two of you alone. Enjoy the rest of your night.'

Alice showed her to the door, but the detective didn't say anything else as she exited and headed to her car.

'Why did you lie to her?' Alice barked, bursting into the living room where Ben was now pouring himself a large glass of whiskey from the liquor cabinet. He didn't answer, instead necking the entire drink and refilling the glass.

'I didn't lie.'

'Bullshit, Ben! You were holding something back.'

He sneered at her. 'You're out of your mind.'

'I overheard you and Dave arguing earlier on today. I was behind this very door when you said: *is everything still in place with Abdul.* You remember that?'

Ben narrowed his eyes and took another large gulp of his drink. 'That was nothing to do with this! What do you take me for? You think if I knew Abdul was guilty of murder I would cover for him?'

He sounded hurt, and she didn't want him to think she didn't trust him. 'It's not that, it's—'

'And why were you eavesdropping on my conversation with Dave? What have you got against him?'

'Nothing, but you must admit he brings out the worst in you. I know he's your best friend, but trouble follows him around like a shadow. If it wasn't for me picking you up tonight, you'd probably be in a cell yourself right now; that's because of *him.*'

Ben looked like he wanted to shout something back, but he reached for the bottle of whiskey instead and stomped out of the room, heading into the kitchen and placing the glass and bottle on the side while he opened the freezer for ice cubes.

He sighed loudly. 'I don't want to fight with you, Alice. I swear

296

to you I didn't know about Abdul, and I know you're right about Dave being dangerous, but he's like my brother and I can't turn my back on family; my dad raised me to leave no man behind. Let's not fall out because of other people's fucked-up ways.'

He was right and it pained her to admit as much.

'I'm going to go and check on Faye and Isabella,' Alice said, turning on her heel, needing to get away from the toxic atmosphere. She hoped to find Isabella asleep and Faye available to chat, but as she reached the landing and looked into the guestroom, she found Isabella fast asleep, tucked up in bed, and Faye lying next to her, gently snoring. Alice didn't want to disturb the two of them. Instead, she found a blanket and rested it over Faye, then switched off the light and closed the door.

Slumping onto the top step, she couldn't help imagining what she'd be doing now had they made their flight on Sunday night. None of this nightmare would have unfolded and it would just be the two of them alone, enjoying the well-deserved break. Still, at least they had their lives, and each other. What did Finn Valentine have left? No father, no mother and a life full of uncertainty. It was time to start counting blessings, not cursing them.

Taking a deep breath, Alice was determined to put the mess behind her and to be the bigger person – she would apologize for shouting at Ben. He needed her support as much as she needed his.

As she neared the bottom of the staircase, there was an awful banging at the front door. The guards hadn't radioed to announce a guest, at least not that she knew of. Opening the door, she immediately wished she hadn't, as Dave's muddy and scratched face swung into view. Before she could close the door and stop him entering, Ben appeared and pulled the door open, supporting Dave's body weight as he slumped inside.

'Jesus, man, what happened?' Ben asked.

Dave could barely put weight on his left foot, his left wrist looked twice its normal size, and deep crimson scratch marks raked both arms.

'I managed to get away, but I tumbled down a ravine. It stung like a bitch, but it probably saved my bacon. You got any pain-killers? My foot and arm are in agony.'

They'd already made it into the kitchen before Alice's voice of reason engaged.

'He can't stay here, Ben. He's a fugitive now. Even if they didn't identify him at the bust at the services, they'll have his car and they'll find out it's registered to him. Then they'll find the two of you are friends, and it won't be long before the police come knocking at our door again. I'm sorry, Dave, but you need to go.'

'I know, I know,' he grimaced, reaching for Ben's bottle of whiskey and putting it to his lips. 'Just help me get sorted and I'll be on my way. I swear.'

Ben glared at Alice. 'It's fine, mate, whatever you need. I'm here for you. How the hell did you get back here anyway?'

'I hitched a lift with a truck driver who was headed this way. I think my wrist is broken. Have you got anything I can use to strap it? Maybe a sling too?'

Alice could contain her frustration no more. 'Goddamn it, Ben! Either he goes, or I do. I'm not prepared to watch you get dragged in by the police again. You hear me?'

56

Alice wasn't one for ultimatums. She didn't enjoy confrontation at the best of times, and she'd never dared give Ben an ultimatum before, but enough was enough! If she'd learned one thing from the last week it was that secrets – no matter how innocent – could have devastating consequences. It was time to stop allowing Ben to mess things up; if someone needed to step in and take control of their lives, then she was prepared to do whatever was necessary to achieve that.

The fact that she was now virtually home alone told her a lot about where Ben's loyalties lay. Isabella and Faye were still sound asleep upstairs and thankfully hadn't been woken by the argument that had ensued after she'd dropped the ultimatum.

'Babe, you know I'd pick you a thousand times over,' Ben had declared. 'It's you and me first *every* time. But . . .'

That was the moment she'd dreaded. There hadn't needed to be a 'but'. He could just as easily have left things as they were, shown Dave the door and allowed them to move on with their lives.

'I can't just feed Dave to the wolves. He's my brother and I owe him more than you'll ever know.'

He'd quickly backtracked, maybe sensing her rising anger, or maybe seeing her glowering cheeks.

'I'm not siding with him, but look at the state of him; he'll get barely a hundred yards before he can't go on, and then how would that look? Him being anywhere near our place is as bad as him being physically found here. The police will see that we were involved in his absconding.'

She hadn't thought that far ahead, and it had troubled her slightly that he'd been weighing up such angles.

'Let me drive him somewhere safe. Yeah? Somewhere far away from here, to give him half a chance to sort shit out. Don't forget that the only reason we were at Burley services was to fix the mess *your* stepbrother caused. If Scott wasn't a junkie, he'd never have asked Dave for help, he wouldn't have fucked up and shot at the dealer last Saturday, and he wouldn't have been busted at the airport. None of this is Dave's fault, not really.'

She hadn't been prepared to let Dave off that easily. 'He could have told Scott to get himself cleaned up, or to get some help. Nobody made Dave set him up with a new dealer.'

'Give me an hour,' Ben had continued. 'I'll take him somewhere he can sort out his injuries, and we won't speak again of this night.'

That had been forty minutes earlier, and there was still no sign of Ben returning. He'd left his mobile at home so that if anyone later tried to trace his GPS they'd find he was here the whole time.

As Alice snuggled on the sofa, the television on mute in the background, she wrapped her arms around her knees, pulling her legs closer. She had no idea what time it was, but it was pitch-black outside the French doors, with only a shard of moonlight to show that there was a garden somewhere in the abyss.

After some time to cool down, she'd decided she wasn't angry that Ben had agreed to drive Dave away from the house – it showed loyalty to his friend and it showed consideration of her feelings. At the same time, she'd rather he was here with her now instead of risking his neck. For all she knew, the police could have picked the two of them up by now. Without his mobile, she had no way of knowing what was happening.

She was tempted to head up to bed – she was certainly tired enough to sleep – but she wanted to be awake when Ben got back, as it was important that they talk before either turned in for the night. Her father had taught her not to go to bed on an argument, and she also wanted reassurance that there would be no further run-ins with the law. Her life in the past week had become a real-life soap opera, and she didn't want that additional stress. She deserved her own *happily ever after*.

Trying to picture a future with Ben and a young family, her thoughts returned to the lost life of Kerry Valentine – where was her happily ever after? Snatched away by a man Alice barely knew. Dave had said Abdul was the one who'd sourced the vacated bar for them, and she was sure he'd said he was an estate agent, so obviously he was someone relatively familiar with the town and surrounding area. Did that possibly mean he'd have known some-where to hide Kerry's body after what he'd done? Hazelton had said the body hadn't been dumped in the river immediately, which meant Kerry's body had to have been stored somewhere. Somewhere the smell of a rotting corpse wouldn't be noticed. Alice couldn't begin to imagine what kind of place that was, but if anyone would have an idea, an estate agent probably would. And, hadn't Abdul also supplied the rope they'd tied up Ben with? She hadn't thought anything of it at the time, but it seemed a little convenient that he'd just happened to find rope lying around – surely it was more likely that he'd taken it with him.

She pictured their meeting at the wedding – his dark skin, goatee beard, and shaved head, how warm his hand had felt when he'd shaken hers, how he avoided eye contact with her as he'd said he would go to the police station with Dave to offer the police a witness statement. She should have known something suspicious was going on then.

At least he would get his comeuppance now. Even though he

and Ben had been close at university, the fact that she hadn't met him until the wedding suggested the two of them weren't as close as they once were.

Another memory flashed in her mind. Ben and Dave's argument earlier: *have you spoken to Abdul yet? Is everything still in place?*

Did that conversation have anything to do with Abdul being arrested? What was it that was still in place?

Standing, she moved across to the French windows and rested her back against the glass. This was getting her nowhere. She didn't know enough about Abdul to be certain of his motives for killing Kerry. Had he gone after her and tried to have sex? Had they somehow become embroiled in a fight? Did he know her before that night? Was it possible he was one of her regular clients? She desperately wanted answers, but she knew that in all likelihood she would never really know what had happened, and that made her feel like she was letting down Kerry and Finn.

The living room carpet was suddenly bathed in white light as the security cameras in the garden were tripped. Spinning and pressing her face against the window, Alice searched for any sign of an animal that could have triggered the sensor, but what she saw was a figure in a wide-brimmed hat emerge from the trees at the far side of the garden and race forward across the dry lawn.

Alice froze. She knew she should get away from the imminent danger, but the signal from her brain to her legs was blocked by sheer terror. The only way this man could have emerged from those trees was if he'd scaled the tall fence, or . . . if he had been there all along. He was clutching something in his hand and was making a beeline straight towards her – he must have seen her backlit by the lamps in the living room. Only the French doors and twenty feet separated them, and Alice could now see there was definitely something familiar about the figure beneath the hat. With only ten feet to go, though, two of the guards in black emerged and rugby tackled the figure to the ground.

They'd underestimated just how strong the man was, and how determined he was to get the letter in his hand to the intended recipient. He rolled over onto one of the guards, using his elbows to fight off the guard immediately on top of him, and as the two men in black loosened their grip, the figure was suddenly back on his feet, stumbling across the patio towards her. As he drew closer, Alice desperately wanted to peel herself away, but her feet wouldn't budge.

Suddenly he was pressed against the outside frame of glass, but the two guards caught up with him again and slammed him into the window. In doing so, they knocked the hat from the man's head. Alice's eyes widened as her colleague Andrew's large eyes met hers.

57

'Please, Alice,' Andrew's muffled voice called through the window, 'I need to speak to you. Please?'

Alice blinked several times, certain her eyes were playing tricks on her. How could such a friendly and shy colleague be the same person who'd been leaving her letters, making unproven allegations against Ben? She would never have believed it if she wasn't seeing it with her own eyes.

'Please,' he called again, as the two guards gripped his upper arms and peeled his face from the window.

Alice managed several steps backwards, but her eyes never left Andrew's rapidly shrinking image. Finally, she allowed herself to breathe, and the sudden gasp of air was enough to charge her brain with a reaction. Rushing into the kitchen, she unlocked the back door and marched out into the decidedly cooler air.

'Wait,' she shouted towards the guards who were manhandling Andrew around the side of the property, where they were presumably planning on holding him until the police arrived. 'I want to know why. I want to know why he's here and what he thought he'd achieve.'

The guards stopped still, and exchanged a curious look.

'Our orders are to call the police,' one of the men shouted back.

'I know him,' Alice challenged. 'Bring him inside until the police arrive.'

She headed back into the kitchen and pulled out one of the kitchen chairs so they could sit him down. He looked far less intimidating without his hat, and as Alice sat on the remaining unoccupied chair, she watched as the two guards pulled Andrew's coat down over his arms to keep him restrained, before frisking him for weapons. All they located was a set of keys to a motorcycle, and a wallet.

There was panic in Andrew's eyes as the men's hands moved over his body, as if he feared for his life, but once they were satisfied there was nothing hidden on his person, one of the guards excused himself. The other remained halfway behind Andrew and the now-locked back door.

The creased letter lay on the table between them, this time without sticky tape. Had he planned to hand deliver it? Or maybe just leave it on the doormat for her to find the following morning? He must have seen the guards patrolling the front gate and decided to take his chances with the fence, though Alice had no idea how he could have scaled it given his rotund physique and age.

He looked different without his large spectacles, and she couldn't be certain whether he had come without them, or if they'd been knocked off during the struggle. Either way, their absence was clearly causing him difficulty as he squinted awkwardly, his face a mess of sweat and dirt where he'd been tackled to the ground.

'Well?' Alice growled when she could take the silence no more. 'Are you going to tell me what you're doing trespassing on my property? How did you even know where I live?'

His face crumpled into a look of shameful regret. 'I'm sorry if I scared you,' he said quietly. 'The last thing I wanted to do was cause you unnecessary stress, but I had to see you; I had to tell you the truth about your husband. I found your address on the staff directory.'

Alice snatched up the envelope before he had even finished, tearing it open and pulling out the single sheet of typed paper, with the same font and size as the others.

Dear Alice,
You're not safe with Ben, and now I have proof.
    I'll share what I know if you'll give me the chance.
    I know that you love him, but that's blinding you from the truth.
    He's killed before and he'll kill again.

She felt the nausea growing before she could stop it and only just made it to the sink before throwing up the undigested remains of her fast-food dinner. What was it with all the men in her life and the lies they told? All these years she'd seen Andrew as a lonely but ultimately sweet acquaintance. Now she discovered he'd been plotting against her – for what reason?

Running the tap, she ducked her mouth beneath it and spat out the hideous taste, before washing the contents of the sink down the plughole. Returning to the table, she couldn't control the shaking of her hands and legs, and it was all she could do to sit on the chair without knocking it over. The security guard stepped forward to help her, but she batted his hand away.

'Do you hate me, Andrew? Is that why you're trying to destroy my marriage?'

The look of shame remained as he gently shook his head. 'Quite the opposite in fact.' He closed his eyes and took a deep breath. 'I've been in love with you, Alice, since the first time I set eyes on you. You probably don't remember, but I was the first person you met at school on the morning you came for your first interview. I was chatting to Tina on reception when you entered and asked where the head teacher's office was. I offered to escort you there. I was so shy, and I knew you could never be attracted to a bumbling old fool like me, but that didn't stop me dreaming that a friendship could one day blossom between us. When I heard you'd got the job and would be joining us at the start of the new school term I thought it was fate's way of confirming that we would become good friends.

'I instantly knew Ben was trouble when you first brought him to the teachers' Christmas meal. He had this look, like he thought he was better than us because he owned his own business, and he refused to talk to any of the rest of us. I remember the two of you left the meal before dessert, and I could see he'd been badgering you to go. Call me old-fashioned, but partners shouldn't behave that way. It was your night, your chance to enjoy yourself, and he should have been supportive.

'I was devastated when you announced the two of you would be getting married, but I made a promise to myself that I would be civil to him if we met at your wedding. Then you didn't invite me to come along. That was hard to stomach, but it didn't stop me coming to the church on Saturday and watching from the choir balcony. You really did look sensational in your dress. Like an angel sent from heaven – and Ben the devil with his grubby hooves all over you.'

'You think you're in love with me?' Alice asked as her brain tried to process his declaration. 'And you thought the best way to show that was to leave sinister letters accusing Ben of crimes he didn't commit?'

'I really wish for your sake he is as innocent as you blindly believe, but he isn't. He's a killer, Alice. He got away with it once, and now he's going to get away with it again, unless you stop him. I'm terrified that you'll be the next victim they discover, and if that happened, I don't think I'd be able to carry on – knowing that I could have saved you and failed.'

The comment stirred something inside her – she knew the guilt he was feeling as it was the same she'd been feeling about both Kerry and Faye for the last week.

'Ben hasn't killed anybody, Andrew. The police have arrested the person responsible for Kerry Valentine's death. It had nothing to do with Ben.'

Andrew's eyes stared tearfully at her. 'Even if he didn't kill that dancer, he has definitely killed before. It was eighteen or so years ago, but he pushed an innocent woman to her death so he could claim on her insurance policy.'

Alice narrowed her eyes. 'How could you know about that?'

'Mary,' he said plainly.

'How do you . . . how could you . . .?'

'We were at school together,' he shrugged. 'She was one of the few girls who would talk to me, and I was even at her wedding to Ben all those years ago. We lost touch, but recently we reconnected at the birdwatching club. Remember, I told you I'd bumped into someone I hadn't seen for a number of years?

'Fate brought us back together so we could save you from making the same mistake she made. When she told me what Ben did to her and her mother, I knew it was my calling in life to do something.'

Andrew blinked several times as sweat ran from his brow to his eyes. 'I never meant to hurt you. I knew if I came and spoke to you in person I'd get flustered and you wouldn't want to listen to me. This was the only way I could see to get through to you. But even after my first two letters you still didn't leave him, which is why I had to come and see you in person – so that you would know I was telling the truth.'

'Don't pretend you care,' Alice said. 'She's used you, that Mary, you know that, don't you? She's a spiteful and vindictive woman.'

'She freely admits that her relationship with Ben wasn't good, but her motivation for reaching out now is to stop him hurting you as he has others. I know you don't want to believe it, but we think he killed that girl in Bournemouth, too.'

'You're wrong! It couldn't have been Ben; he was tied to a lamppost when she died. Plus, the police examined his clothes and found no trace of Kerry's DNA.'

'Maybe he bought replacement clothes which he gave to the police. And the photographs of Ben tied to that lamppost could have been staged at any time.'

Alice pulled out her phone and opened the images app, determined to shut Andrew up with cold, hard fact. 'Here you go. Just look. Here's Ben, securely tied up with his mates looking on.' She swiped right, 'and here's Ben again, an hour or so later when they came to let him go. See!'

Andrew squinted at the phone. 'That isn't evidence! The shirt doesn't even look the same. In this one his shirt sleeves are rolled up, but in the other one they're down.'

She pulled the phone back and stared at the image. How hadn't she noticed that detail before? Sure enough, in the later image the cuffs of both sleeves were rolled up, revealing a line of embroidered material inside. The pattern was hard to determine, even with the image zoomed in, but there was definitely a pattern of some sort. She couldn't recall Ben's white shirt having any such material inside the cuffs, but then maybe he'd bought a new shirt for that night. Returning to the first image – the one with the cuffs rolled down – she saw something else she hadn't noticed before. She zoomed in, moving the screen closer to her eyes, before skipping back to the later shot.

Andrew had noticed her sudden urgency. 'What is it? What have you seen?'

She wasn't prepared to utter the words aloud.

It was impossible, but according to the images, if Ben's version of events was to be believed, not only had he managed to roll up the cuffs on both sleeves despite having his hands bound at the wrist, but somehow a breast pocket had miraculously appeared on his shirt.

58

Alice's eyes remained firmly fixed to the image on the screen.

'I didn't want to be the one to break your heart, but you see it now, don't you?' Andrew sighed.

It was impossible, wasn't it? Since he'd been released on bail on Sunday morning, Ben had sworn blindly that he'd spent at least an hour tied to that lamppost while Kerry Valentine was being murdered; a story echoed by Dave and the others, even under police interrogation. How many in the group knew that Ben hadn't been tied to that lamppost? In fact, had the whole thing been staged for her and the police's benefit?

If he wasn't tied up where they'd said, where had he been and why had it resulted in the need to change his shirt?

'I can stay with you,' Andrew offered. 'If you want, that is.'

Before she could even consider the offer, the front door burst open and Ben strode in. 'The police are on their way. I explained that this creep was trespassing on our property and is the same man responsible for the criminal damage to our security cameras.'

Andrew ignored the jibe and focused his attention on Alice. 'I don't have to go.'

Ben clearly didn't like the implication and shoved Andrew up and out of the chair. 'I feel sick just breathing the same air as scum like you,' he said, dragging Andrew away from the table.

'Alice? Alice?' Andrew called out.

'Don't hurt him,' Alice called out, as Ben pushed Andrew towards the front door.

Suddenly alone in the kitchen, Alice was finally able to suck in a deep breath. None of the conclusions her mind was racing to made any sense, yet for the first time it felt like her eyes were truly open.

Still, she tried to find an innocent explanation. The two images she'd taken from Dave's phone – the before and after shots – didn't prove that Ben had been involved in what had happened to Kerry. Wasn't it possible that the angle of the image could have made it appear like Ben's shirt hadn't had the pocket, when actually it had been there all along? Was she now seeing things because it fit a predetermined outcome?

There was only one way to know for certain. Moving to the counter, she typed the PIN into Ben's phone and unlocked the screen. She wouldn't have long – the moment he opened the front door, he'd see her with his phone.

Opening the images app, she scrolled through to the folder of received images, and looked for what Dave had sent over to him on Sunday, the 'evidence' they planned to share with the police.

Working backwards, she found the two images she'd been looking at on her own phone, and zoomed in on both shirts. The second shirt definitely had a breast pocket, but the angle of Ben's arm in the first made it difficult to tell. So she continued to scroll backwards, through the images of a naked Ben tied to the chair, covered in cream. Kerry gyrated around him, yet Alice felt no animosity towards her; she'd been doing her job.

Finally she came to the group shots, but in most Ben was either turned to the side, or had somebody standing in front of him. All the group had been wearing white shirts and dark trousers, looking like gangsters from the twenties.

Then she found it: a selfie snapped by Dave of him and Ben, presumably just before they reached Bournemouth, taken in the back of the taxi. Dave's shirt had a breast pocket, Ben's didn't. She shuddered as the evidence stared back at her. Yet despite what she could see, something continued to niggle somewhere at the back of her mind, something she still couldn't quite glimpse. Forwarding the images to her own phone, she froze as she heard keys jangling in the front door. Locking the phone, Alice darted back to the table, desperately hoping Ben hadn't seen what she was doing. He walked into the kitchen and leaned in to kiss her cheek. Her skin crawled as he did.

'Are there any more crazy stalkers at your school I should know about?' he asked, searching the fridge for a snack.

She didn't respond, still disappointed that even Andrew had been keeping things from her.

He closed the fridge door, having failed to find anything to eat. 'Are you okay? You look pale as a sheet.'

'Mum phoned,' she quickly lied. 'She's had a fall – not a major one – but I said I'd go round there.'

'Oh no, not again, is she okay?'

'She'll be fine, she's just a bit shaken up I think. I guess with everything that's going on with Scott, and her rattling about the place alone . . . I shouldn't be too long.'

'You're going now? My parents are due any minute. Dad phoned and said Mum's feeling guilty about keeping the divorce from you. I think she wants to explain why she agreed not to say anything, and to tell you what Mary was really like. Mum was never keen on her, and neither was Dad. They could see her for what she was, and I blindly ignored them to my detriment.'

The last thing Alice wanted was to hear whatever excuses Ben had enticed his parents to come and share. 'I'm sorry, but Mum needs me.'

'How about I drive you over there, and we bring her back to

stay with us? We've got the room, and it would give our mums the chance to get to know each other better.'

'No,' Alice practically shouted, before softening her tone. 'There's really no need. It's not that I don't appreciate the offer, but it doesn't need two of us to go across there. Besides, if I go on my own, I can use you as an excuse to get away and back here. I'll be fine.'

He gave her a cursory glance before nodding. 'Okay, well if you're sure.'

She forced a thin smile. 'I'll try not to be too long.'

Grabbing her keys from the dish on the side, Alice headed for the front door, jumping as her eyes fell on a figure in the doorway.

'That's good timing,' Ray said, smiling, his jacket draped over his arm.

Hermione's face poked out from behind her husband. 'You two off out?'

'Alice's mum's had a fall,' Ben explained, pulling the door wider, allowing them to enter. 'She just needs to go and visit her.'

Hermione's face crumpled in concern. 'Oh I'm so sorry to hear that. Will you send her our best?'

A wave of nausea swept through Alice as her own lie wreaked havoc with her moral compass.

'Oh, I think I've blocked you in,' Ray said, turning and pointing at the Range Rover he'd abandoned in front of their cars. 'Why don't I drive you to your mum's? It'll give us a chance to talk.'

'That's kind of you,' Alice said, 'but I could be a while.'

'I won't take no for an answer,' Ray said warmly, heading towards the vehicle, fishing in his pocket for the keys.

'Hey wait,' Ben said, reaching for her arm. 'Don't I even get a kiss goodbye?'

As Ben pulled her into him, his lips felt so foreign on hers.

'I'll see you later,' she said, breaking free of the embrace.

The air felt cooler as she stepped outside into the darkness. Three figures still huddled near the gate with Andrew while they waited for the police to arrive.

'You really don't need to drive me,' Alice tried again as Ray reached the passenger door and opened it for her. 'If you just pull back, I should be able to get my car out.'

Ray didn't respond, nodding instead to the open door.

Alice reluctantly climbed in, deciding that she could phone DC Hazelton from her mum's house, and send her the images of the changed shirt. Confronting Ben about it would only lead to more lies, of that she had no doubt.

'He's a good lad, our Ben,' Ray said, starting the engine and pulling to the end of the drive. 'He's made mistakes, it's true, but you shouldn't ever doubt how he feels about you. I see it in his eyes and hear it in his voice whenever he speaks about you. I've known him all his life, and he's never been as smitten with anyone as much as he is with you. I know I'm biased, but you really could have done a lot worse than Ben.'

The gate slid open, and Alice avoided looking at Andrew's nervous eyes as they moved through it.

'This mess with the police,' Ray continued, 'really wasn't his fault. He had no idea that Dave and Scott had arranged for that girl to come and dance for them. He was just in the wrong place at the wrong time, and in case you have any lingering doubts, I know that my son isn't capable of killing anyone. He doesn't have that kind of hate in his veins.'

Staying silent, Alice removed her phone from her handbag and flicked to the photos she'd sent from Ben's phone. How had she not noticed the changed shirt sooner? How had the police missed it too? Unless Dave and Ben hadn't actually provided the police with those images after all. Had Hazelton mentioned seeing them? Alice couldn't recall. Hazelton had said they hadn't found any of Kerry's DNA on the shirt they'd taken from Ben, but he owned several white shirts and could have just as easily given them a different one he knew wouldn't contain Kerry's DNA.

Looking back to the initial group shot of the ten men, she tried to piece together the fragments of the timeline she'd been given. Scott had left early to meet the dealer, and had then phoned Dave when things went wrong. By that stage, Ben would have already been tied to the lamppost. Flicking to the picture of Ben at the lamppost, the group were fewer. There was no longer any sign of Gary, Duke, or Michael, but Abdul, James and Pete remained, along with Johnny, Dave and Ben.

Alice shuddered as she saw Johnny's face. What was she missing? She'd become so convinced that Johnny had to be responsible for killing Kerry because he'd been violent towards Faye, but his shirt in all the images remained consistent. Unlike the others, Johnny's white shirt had a black collar, making him stand out from the crowd. Did that mean he couldn't have killed Kerry? Surely there would have been blood spatter on his shirt. If not Johnny, then who did that leave? The police had arrested Abdul; but if he was guilty, had he acted alone, or had the group bound together to help their friend cover up the crime?

Alice skipped back through the images and then forwards again, holding the phone out, allowing her eyes to glaze over, looking for any minute detail she'd missed. Blinking, her brain suddenly shifted into focus, and she realized what had been niggling at the back of her mind.

59

'What you looking at?' Ray asked.

Alice quickly locked the screen, her mind racing with one question. 'Nothing really.'

'Are you able to direct me to your mum's house? You can punch the postcode into the satnav if that's easier.'

The road before them was dark and narrow, with only the Range Rover's headlights to keep them from drifting into a ditch. Surrounded by shadowy fields, there were no street lights in the vicinity.

Alice typed the postcode into the small screen on the dashboard, and was relieved when it confirmed they were less than ten minutes away.

Holding the phone tightly in her lap, she couldn't believe she hadn't seen it sooner. In an age when everybody was taking selfies and updating social media with filtered pictures of themselves, she hadn't realized that with the exception of the photo in the taxi, each of the pictures Dave had sent to Ben had been taken by someone missing from the images. While it was possible the group had taken it in turns to be photographer, in the large group shot, all ten men were in the image. That meant they'd either asked a stranger to take it, or there was another guest at the party she'd failed to account for.

'Ben tells me the two of you are planning to start a family soon,' Ray said warmly.

Alice's head snapped around, her cheeks flushing. 'Did he?'

'Oh, I'm sorry,' Ray said quickly, sensing her discomfort, 'I didn't mean to embarrass you. I think he's just so excited by the idea of becoming a dad. He deserves to be happy – you both do – and you are going to be an amazing mother. The way you are with Ben, and how you looked after Isabella when Faye was . . . well, you know, it just shows how kind a person you are.'

Alice frowned. 'How did you know about Faye?'

'Ben phoned last night. You know what he's like, we talk all the time. Don't be offended, we don't talk about things between you and him, he just likes to use me as a sounding board from time to time.'

Something stirred in Alice's head. 'So what else do the two of you talk about? Did he tell you what happened in Bournemouth? What *really* happened, I mean.'

The road ahead widened, and a street light appeared, casting Ray in an orange glow. He gave her a curious look. 'I know about what happened with your stepbrother and Dave if that's what you mean?'

'No,' she said firmly, 'I mean what happened after that – when Ben was tied to the lamppost. Did he tell you who attacked Kerry Valentine?'

Ray's focus returned to the road. 'I know what you know: he was tied up when she was killed.'

Alice heard the uncertainty in his tone, and decided to press home her advantage. If Ben wouldn't give her the truth, she was sure Ray would break with gentle pushing. Unlocking the phone again, she flicked back to the large group shot of the ten men.

'Did Ben show you these?' she asked, raising the phone above the satnav.

Ray glanced at the group shot. 'Are these from that night? No, he didn't show me, but he did mention some pictures he was going to show the police to prove he couldn't have murdered Kerry.'

The images of Kerry dancing flashed across the screen as Alice flicked to the image of Ben at the lamppost. 'I didn't spot it at first, but in this first image, Ben's sleeves are down and his shirt doesn't have a breast pocket . . .' she flicked to the final shot, 'in this one his sleeves are rolled up and his shirt suddenly has a pocket.'

The car jerked as Ray's hands slipped on the wheel, but he quickly regained control. 'Are you sure? It's probably just the way he's sitting in the first shot that means you can't see the pocket.'

'No, I've checked and in the earlier images his shirt doesn't have a pocket either. It's the most incredible thing – despite him being tied to that post, he manages to change his shirt and roll up the sleeves. How do you explain that?'

There was a brief pause. 'Have you asked Ben about this? Perhaps we should turn around and ask him directly.'

'No, I don't want him to lie to me again. I'm sick of everyone lying to me all the time. Please, Ray, don't be like your son. Tell me the truth.'

Ray slowed and brought the car to a stop, removing a handkerchief from his trouser pocket and wiping his forehead.

The next street light was a good thirty yards away, so they were in virtual darkness, save for the glow from the phone's screen.

'Can I have a look at the pictures?' Ray asked, his voice shaking.

Alice couldn't ignore the pang of guilt as she handed the phone over to him; it wasn't fair to force Ray to confront the possibility that his son wasn't the man he believed. But it was too late to turn back now. 'Can you see what I mean?' she said, pointing at the pocket. 'Here it is, but in this one,' she swiped back, 'there is no pocket. If you swipe back through the others,' the images of Kerry flashed across the screen, 'there's no pocket there either. Ben changed his shirt in Bournemouth, and what I want to know is when, and why.'

Alice froze as something in one of the images caught her attention. It showed Kerry straddling Ben, his shirt unbuttoned, and Ben looking away as she liberally squirted cream onto his chest. To the far right of the image was a coat stand, cloaked in darkness, but with an unmistakeable jacket hanging from one of the hooks. She had to have seen the image a dozen times, and had never noticed the coat stand, but now she couldn't pull her eyes from it. The white jacket embossed with military awards couldn't belong to anyone but the man sweating next to her.

Alice's hand shot up to her mouth in shock. 'You were there. In Bournemouth. You saw Kerry dancing in the Merry Berry bar.'

Ray pocketed the phone, wiping his forehead again, and slowly rolled up the sleeves of his shirt. Alice immediately recognized the pattern inside the shirt, and fear flooded her body.

'Serving in the military,' he began, his voice now steadier, as if a weight had been lifted from his chest, 'the one thing they drilled into us was never to leave a man behind. No matter the danger or risk to one's own life, you never left a fallen comrade. I've tried to instil that ethos in Ben since the day he was born.'

He paused and looked over at her. There was no anger or fear in his eyes, nothing but a determination to prove that he hadn't done anything wrong. 'I don't expect you to understand. Until you've put your life on the line for your country, you'll never understand what it means to do what is necessary.'

Saliva pooled in Alice's throat as she realized what Ray was about to say. 'It was you. You killed Kerry Valentine.'

Ray's eyes narrowed. 'She had a phone, and I saw her discreetly take a picture of Ben while he was still tied up to the chair. I knew what she planned to do with the picture – she was going to use it to blackmail him. Just like Mary, she was going to use him for her own nefarious ends. I went after her and offered to pay her off, but she came at me with a knife, and . . . I never meant for her to get stabbed, but I was protecting myself, and I was protecting my son.'

Alice choked down the vomit and desperately tried to steady her breathing. Her vision started to blur as tears formed. 'Ben swapped shirts with you.'

'After it had happened, I came back to where he was tied up and explained the situation. I untied him and he came with me to where Kerry's body was, and he said I should go and get Dave to help. I raced to the off-licence where the boys were, but Dave wasn't around, so I collared Ben's mate Abdul. I knew he was local to the area and would know where we could stash the body until we were sober enough to work out what to do. That was a bad decision on my part; if I'd known how spineless Abdul was I wouldn't have taken him back. He nearly threw up on her – can you believe that? I told him to help us move her somewhere or he'd be joining her.

'We carried her down to the cellar of the Merry Berry, and hurried back to the lamppost so none of the others would realize what had happened. Ben suggested we change shirts as some of her blood had splashed up on his when we'd moved her. With my jacket buttoned up, none of the others would see that I wasn't wearing a shirt. We got back just before the others returned, and then we went back inside and kept drinking.

'Abdul scarpered at dawn, before we'd had chance to settle him down. Ben was worried Abdul would go to the police and tell them what had happened, so I paid him a visit at work. For a man with such dark skin, he went so pale when he saw me. I told him we needed to dump the body, and forced him to take me back to the cellar. I took a picture of him with the body, and told him that if he admitted to anyone what he'd seen, I'd tell the police he was the one who'd killed her. I have no idea how his DNA wound up in the scratch on her cheek, but it didn't surprise me.'

Alice could feel the door's handle between her fingertips, and quickly yanked on it as Ray once again wiped his forehead. The handle moved but the door remained firm. Turning to study the door, she found it locked.

'The truth is more difficult to hear than you'd anticipated, isn't it?' Ray said, looking over at her, unconcerned by her attempts to escape the car. 'The question is – what are you going to do now that you know?'

60

There was a cold disconnect to Ray's voice. 'If the police learn the truth, it won't just be me they bring in. Ben helped cover up the crime, and the sentence will be equally as punishing to him. I can't allow that to happen.'

The hairs on the back of Alice's neck tingled at the implication of Ray's words. She looked out through the windscreen, but there was no sign of passing traffic. There were no houses on the road they'd stopped on either, so the chance of a resident passing by was slim. Even if another car drove past them, the driver would be unlikely to see the two of them or realize how much danger she was in.

Ray was watching her again. She was his prisoner and he would determine how soon she could escape, or if she even would. She'd never seen such an ice cold stare before and her bones chilled instantly. 'You're not going to cause trouble, are you, Alice?'

'Ray, a crime has been committed, you need to talk to the police.'

'No,' he said, more calmly than she'd expected. 'That isn't best for any of us.'

'Kerry's family deserve to know what happened to her. She has a son.' Alice tried the door handle again, but it still didn't budge. 'Let me go, Ray. Ben wouldn't be happy if he knew you were holding me against my will.'

Ray removed his glasses, resting them on the dashboard, and pinched the bridge of his nose between thumb and forefinger. 'I'm not holding you. You're free to go, but first . . . I just need you to promise you'll keep what I've told you to yourself.'

Alice's instinct was to just agree, to tell him whatever he wanted to hear that would get her out of the car and allow her to call Hazelton and relay the news. Something told her it wouldn't be that easy.

'Ben tells me you're different to Mary,' Ray continued. 'Is that true, Alice? Do you love my son for the man he is?'

She would reserve judgement on her feelings towards Ben until she'd had a chance to ask him whether he really had helped Ray cover up his crime.

'I knew Mary was trouble the first time we met her,' Ray continued quietly. 'She spent the best part of an hour telling us how she and Ben would marry and start a family and buy a new house. She was painting this picture-perfect vision of the future, making all the decisions without Ben's input. He was only eighteen for heaven's sake! He'd never lived alone, and he was nowhere near ready to get married and start a family. I wanted to intervene there and then, but Hermione convinced me not to. I should have trusted my instinct.'

Alice tilted her head a fraction, trying to assess whether she could smash the window and escape that way, but since she was dressed only in a T-shirt, the glass would cut her arm to shreds. If only she hadn't allowed Ray to pocket her phone. Her only chance of survival was to keep him talking and pray that some stranger would pass by and intervene.

'You still let them get married though,' she challenged. 'If you thought it was such a bad idea, why not talk to Ben then?'

'I tried, believe me, I tried. Ben thought he was in love, and was blinded by it, but she soon proved I'd been right all along. Three months in and the cracks were already showing. Then when she seduced poor Dave, the writing was on the wall. Ben tried hard to make it work, but he realized he'd made a huge mistake. He told me he wanted to wipe the slate clean and be rid of her, but didn't know where to start. I told him I would speak to Mary's mum, see if she could convince her daughter to do the right thing . . .'

Alice's breath caught in her chest.

'Ben had always got on well with Mary's mum. I think she liked the idea of having a man around who could do little jobs for her: changing light bulbs, unblocking the toilet, that kind of thing. When I told her Ben wanted a divorce she wasn't happy. She begged me to convince him to give things another try.'

Alice gasped. 'You killed her?'

His brow furrowed in anger. 'No! What do you take me for? Her fall had nothing to do with me, and more importantly it had nothing to do with Ben. He wasn't there.'

'You were there though,' she said through gritted teeth. 'Why didn't you call for an ambulance?'

'It was too late for that. She'd had a good life, and she looked at peace. Even if a paramedic had managed to resuscitate her, her quality of life wouldn't have been great. It gave Ben the out he needed. Free from Mary's clutches and with a handsome pot of money to go with it.'

'He was charged with murder – he went on trial!'

'They never would have found him guilty,' Ray roared back, losing control for the first time. 'I paid for the best barrister money could buy. I made sure he was safe.'

There was no point in trying to reason with him, nothing Alice could say would convince Ray that his actions were unreasonable – he was too set in his ways. 'So what happens now?' she asked, her voice straining. 'Are you going to kill me too?'

'You misunderstand me, Alice. I'm not a monster. What happened to that girl was self-defence; I didn't mean her harm, and I don't mean you any harm.'

'Let me out of the car then. Let me go and then we can talk about it.'

She flinched as he raised his hand suddenly, but rather than slap her, he pressed his palm gently against her cheek. 'You don't need to be scared of me, Alice. My God, you're shaking. What is it you think is going to happen? We're just talking.'

Alice couldn't breathe, she wanted to, but her mouth refused to open. 'I want to get out, Ray. Please? I promise I won't say anything.'

His expression softened, and there was a hint of a smile, as the lines in his brow disappeared. 'I know you won't. I know you love Ben, and that's all I need to remember.'

Alice started as the lock clicked up. All she needed to do now was open the door and she'd be free. She would have to figure out where to go once she was out.

Ray returned his hand to the steering wheel, looking straight ahead. 'You're right, of course. Our relationship needs to be built on trust. Why don't you let me drive you to your mum's?'

'No,' she said quickly. 'It's not far from here and I could do with the fresh air. It might put things into perspective.'

He fixed her with a smile and nodded. 'As you wish.'

Alice pulled on the handle and was hit with a wave of relief as the door opened. She practically fell out of the car, her legs barely able to hold her weight as her feet reached the concrete.

'Are you sure you'll be all right from here?' Ray said, leaning across the passenger seat. 'It's the middle of nowhere and it must be another half a mile to your mum's house.'

'I'll be fine,' Alice said, still unable to breathe normally.

'I can trust you, can't I, Alice?'

She nodded, willing him to drive away.

Ray suddenly straightened, reaching for his glasses and pushing them back up his nose. 'I'll let Ben know what we've discussed. Take care.'

Alice pushed the door closed, finally exhaling and sucking in a long, deep breath. The Range Rover's engine started and Ray pulled away, leaving Alice alone in the dark, wishing she would wake from the nightmare.

Her legs still felt weak, but staying where she was wasn't an option. In the darkness, she wouldn't be seen by any passing traffic until the last minute, and she didn't want to risk getting knocked down. Forcing one foot in front of the other, she stumbled towards the safety of the street light. Knowing her mum's house – and the opportunity to phone DC Hazelton – was not far, she ploughed onwards.

Up ahead, she could still just about make out the rear lights of the Range Rover through the darkness, and then suddenly they were gone, presumably around the bend at the end of the road. Alice allowed herself a momentary sigh of relief, knowing she'd done well to talk herself out of danger, but horrified that her father-in-law could have wreaked such havoc on so many lives.

Rubbing her hands against the goosebumps on her arms, Alice kept her head bent low, willing her feet to keep moving, to take her closer to safety. Somewhere in the distance she could hear an engine nearing, but with no lights on the road ahead of her she paused, looking back over her shoulder. No immediate sign of lights there either.

Turning back to check ahead again, she was bathed in a sudden bright light as the Range Rover's full beam hit her.

61

'How's the head?' a familiar voice asked, splitting through Alice's dream.

Trying to open her eyes and focus on the voice, Alice momentarily saw a thin figure standing between two doors shrouded by light. She blinked again and the figure was gone. As her mind tried to process the noises and lights around her, she became aware of the feeling of motion. A series of ceiling tiles and bright bulbs whizzed above her head. Blinking again, she saw two figures in light blue staring over her, their face masks moving as if they were speaking, but no sound came out.

Darkness returned, and it took all her strength to fight against the grip of the painkillers flooding her system to concentrate enough to force her eyes open. The thin figure was back, no longer shrouded by light, but sitting in a low chair near the edge of the bed.

DC Hazelton sat forward in the chair and smiled empathetically. 'Try not to speak. You've been through a lot, but all you need to know is you're safe now.'

The sky through the window told her it was day, but she had no idea if it was early or late. A series of beeps sounded somewhere behind Alice, but it felt like her spirit was floating just above the mangled body in the bed.

'Where am I?' Alice asked, unable to recall anything immediate.

'You were brought here anonymously,' Hazelton said. 'You had no identification or phone, it was only when an eagle-eyed nurse recognized your face that I was called. One of the nurses who was tending to Faye's injuries was just about to finish her shift when you were brought in on the stretcher.'

A hospital room certainly explained the array of strange noises, but that didn't account for the dull ache in her leg or the heat around her neck. The smell of disinfectant assaulted her nostrils.

'Try not to move,' Hazelton cautioned, coming closer as Alice struggled to sit up. 'The plaster on your leg is temporary.'

Alice tried to wiggle her toes and felt the constriction around her right ankle.

'What happened?' she croaked, her throat dry and hoarse.

'Looks like a hit-and-run,' Hazelton said. 'What's the last thing you can remember?'

Alice allowed her eyes to temporarily close, focusing on any memories, seeing Hazelton bringing Faye to the house, the excitement on Isabella's face as she was reunited with her mother, Dave appearing at the front door, a flash of Andrew Hook slamming into the patio door.

'You were found in a ditch on the track near your mum's house,' Hazelton continued, 'but there was no sign of your car. I spoke to your mum but she said she hadn't seen you, and wasn't expecting to. I woke her up in fact. I tried to speak to your husband, but there was no answer at your house.'

Ben's smiling face appeared in her mind, and she felt her own lips curling up, but then an image of Ray in his embossed jacket, arm around Ben, flashed up, and her joy turned to anger.

'Ray,' Alice coughed. 'Ray . . . Ben's dad, he . . . he . . .'

The beeping behind Alice's head grew louder and faster.

'Calm down, Alice, you need to relax,' Hazelton soothed. 'Okay? Are you in pain? Do you want me to call the nurse in?'

Alice was suddenly back in the Range Rover, watching Ray's

lips confess to killing Kerry and watching Mary's mother die. The words wouldn't come out in a logical order. 'Murder . . . cover-up . . . Ben . . . Kerry dead . . . he did it.'

Hazelton pressed a cool hand against Alice's forehead. 'It's okay, Alice, we've arrested the man responsible for Kerry's murder. Remember? Abdul Farrar is in custody. Stay calm.'

'No, no,' Alice said, her eyes filling as she shook her head.

The door at the far side of the room flew open, and a woman dressed in blue came over to the bed, firing questions at Hazelton and reading the output from the machine.

'He did it,' Alice tried again, taking shallow breaths, trying to compose herself.

The nurse moved around to the opposite side of the bed and adjusted the dial on the intravenous tube in Alice's arm, and suddenly the pain and the angst evaporated.

The light behind the blinds was fading when Alice next came around. The effect of the painkillers had now vastly reduced and the dull throb in her leg was suddenly more apparent. Propping herself up on her elbows, she surveyed the room. It looked almost identical to the room they'd kept Faye in after her attack, but Alice doubted it was the same one. That was the problem with hospitals, they all tended to look the same. Though this time she noticed the small bunch of flowers in a glass vase on the cabinet to the right of her bed.

Her leg, covered in an enormous plaster cast, was being held in the air by some kind of harness, and as she attempted to wiggle her toes, she was relieved to see them jiggle slightly.

Everything after the moment she'd climbed into the Range Rover was a blur in her memory. Pressing her hand against her temple, she could feel the raising of the skin where a large bump remained, presumably caused when the car had collided with her.

She froze at this fresh memory. Ray had tried to kill her. He'd driven straight at her, and it was blind luck that she'd survived.

A knock at the door was followed by a much more alert DC Hazelton entering. Now dressed in jeans and a thin sweater, she no longer carried the air of a crime fighter. To an untrained observer, she could have been Alice's sister.

'Ah good, you're awake,' Hazelton said, placing a small brown paper bag on the cabinet next to the flowers. 'Grapes,' she clarified, pulling one from the stalk and popping it in her mouth. 'I know it's a cliché, but it felt weird turning up empty-handed. How are you feeling?'

'Like I was run over,' Alice replied, her throat feeling as if it hadn't been lubricated in weeks.

'Here,' Hazelton offered, moving a plastic beaker from the cabinet and placing the straw between Alice's dry and cracked lips.

Alice sipped, grimacing at the pain as she swallowed. 'Thank you.'

Hazelton returned the beaker to its place on the cabinet, before pulling the seat over and perching on the edge. 'Has the doctor spoken to you yet?'

Alice shook her head, feeling an ache in her neck.

'I'll let them explain why they've had to put pins in your leg. The short version is you'll live, and were lucky to escape with a few bumps and bruises. They did X-rays of your neck and back as soon as the bleeding in your leg was sorted. It was touch and go for a bit – it was lucky you were brought in when you were.'

Back on the road in Ray's Range Rover, she'd hoped for the kindness of a stranger to save her from Ray, and now it sounded as though the prayers had been answered.

Events felt clearer in her mind, even though the blur of memories of Ray's confession felt more like the fragments of a dream. Taking a deep breath, Alice said, 'I know who killed Kerry Valentine. It wasn't Abdul.'

Hazleton pressed her fingertips together, like she was summoning the courage to speak. 'I know. A lot has happened since you were brought in last night, Alice. I checked the hospital's security cameras, and it was Ben's friend Dave who brought you in. He was wanted in connection with an incident in Ringwood yesterday: a drugs bust. He was caught trying to board a ferry from Portsmouth early this morning, and admitted to finding you in the ditch. He wanted me to let you know that he's sorry for any pain his actions have caused. He didn't say any more than that, but I could see in his eyes how fond of you he is.'

'Ben's dad killed Kerry,' Alice sighed, unsure why she felt guilty uttering the words.

Hazelton nodded. 'We know.'

Alice frowned in confusion. 'You do? How?'

'Ben called me and asked if I would come out to the house this morning. He told me his dad attacked Kerry and then forced Ben and Abdul to help cover his crime. He also wanted me to know that you knew nothing about his involvement, and that only the three of them were in on it.'

Alice's hand shot up to her mouth. 'He told you that?'

Hazelton raised her eyebrows. 'It came as a surprise to me too. Ben is at the station now making a formal statement of his actions following events in Bournemouth.'

'What about Ray?'

'We haven't located him yet, but it'll only be a matter of time until we catch up with him. We've spoken to his wife, but she claims not to know where he is.'

Alice's frown deepened. 'I don't understand. Ray is Ben's hero. He would never betray his dad.'

'It seems there's someone Ben loves more than his father. Ray must have told Ben what he'd done to you, and that was all the motivation Ben needed to decide who meant more to him.'

The ache in Alice's heart grew. 'So you know that Ray stabbed Kerry and that the shirt Ben gave to your forensics team wasn't the one he was wearing that night?'

'Ben's account was very detailed. Only time will tell, but my instinct is he's telling the truth. If only he'd done so when we first spoke to him on Saturday, all of this mess could have been avoided.'

'Will Ben be charged?'

'I don't know,' Hazelton said, though her expression suggested she was trying to spare Alice's feelings.

Alice felt fresh tears splash against her cheek, but didn't bother to wipe them away. 'Will Kerry's son be told? That his mum's killer will be brought to justice?'

The expression on Hazelton's face changed – not quite a smirk, but somewhere between incredulity and indifference. 'What is it with you and that kid?'

Alice couldn't answer.

'I don't know whether he'll be told,' the detective finally sighed. 'It's up to social services now. The important thing is that a killer is off the streets.'

62

Wincing, Alice lifted the large plaster cast into the foot well of Tara's Mini. Even with the passenger seat cranked back as far as it would go, she still needed to lean onto the driver's seat and pull and shuffle the cast until it was in place. By this point, she could no longer reach the door handle to pull the door closed, but thankfully Tara was on hand to slam it for her.

'Are you sure you want to do this?' Tara asked, once she was seated in the driver's side and had helped Alice secure her seatbelt.

Alice placed a protective hand across her middle. 'I have to do it. Please don't ask me why, it's just . . . I just need to. Okay?'

Tara started the engine and pulled out of the driveway of Alice's mum's house, where Alice had been recuperating since leaving the hospital. Three weeks had passed since then, and although she was getting steadier on the crutches, moving about still required a lot of effort, and she was ashamed to admit she'd spent most of her time lying on the sofa.

Tara glanced over several times without speaking, but the silence between them was comfortable. They'd practically lived inside each other's pockets since Alice had been released from hospital, with Tara fawning over her friend.

The radio was playing cheesy pop music, but at least it was upbeat, and it was important for Alice to keep her spirits up, especially today. The sun was shining overhead and the traffic on the M3 crawled along the route to Winchester. It didn't matter though – they had plenty of time to reach their destination.

Despite Alice's efforts to get a message to Kerry's son Finn, all Hazelton had said was that she would try. Alice wished there was some way – any way – she could make amends for what her family had done to his. Her attempts to contact social services had been in vain too. For now she would need to carry the burden.

Ray was discovered hidden beneath a pile of coats in the back of an old military friend's car as he attempted to board the Eurostar three days after Ben's confession. The arrests of Ray, Ben, Abdul and Dave had made the national news. The story had been broken by Liam O'Neill who constantly seemed to be on the television sharing his inside knowledge. Alice had done her best to avoid reading or watching any of it. Their day in court would come soon enough, but she had yet to decide whether she would attend the trial or not. Part of her wanted to see the look in Ray's eyes when the jury passed their verdict, but the other part didn't want to step foot in the same room as him ever again.

The new school term was due to start on Monday, but with Alice's leg likely to remain in the cast for a few more weeks, she had been granted extended leave with a substitute teacher scheduled to watch over her class until at least half-term. Alice was determined to get back sooner, but she would follow the doctors' and physio's advice.

Spending every day at her mum's had taken its own toll. Scott was still in Switzerland, as the two nations debated where he should stand trial for drug smuggling. Whatever the decision, his professional cycling career was over, and that would take him a long time to come to terms with. Cycling was his only real passion, and their mum seemed to be feeling the strain as much as he was.

They would find a way to get through it. If Alice had learned anything over the last month, it was that her will to fight and succeed was stronger than she'd ever realized. If she could survive the events since the wedding, she could survive anything.

'We're nearly there,' Tara said as she left the main road and turned into a residential estate. 'Are you ready for this?'

Alice bit her lip and nodded. She'd deliberately avoided thinking about what she was about to do so that she couldn't convince herself not to go through with it, and as the satnav flashed up to say they were only yards from the address, she was suddenly keen to turn around.

'Do you want me to come in with you?' Tara asked, pulling past the building and parking at the side of the road.

'It's something I need to do alone,' Alice replied.

Exiting the car, Alice used the crutches to lift herself from the seat, looping the strap of her handbag over her head and shoulder and allowing her eyes to follow the enormous redbrick building to the sky.

Once inside, the transition through security was awkward. She had to show her identification several times, continually repeating the prison number Ben had been assigned upon his arrival at HMP Winchester, where he would remain on remand until trial.

Placing her handbag in the locker she was directed to, Alice held tightly to the envelope she'd brought with her. She was finally led into the large canteen, where she located Ben – equipped with beard – sitting at a table.

He stood to kiss her as she approached, but she shook her head gently. She was proud that he'd taken responsibility for his actions, but it would be some time before she felt able to trust him again.

Lowering herself into the chair across from him, the crutches clattered to the floor as she attempted to stand them against the table.

'How are you?' Ben asked, his features tight with concern. 'If I'd known why he wanted to drive you to your mum's, I'd never—'

Alice reached for his outstretched hand and squeezed it. 'I know. You don't have to explain again.'

His attempt to smile made his eyes shine more. 'He's in here too, but on a different wing. I haven't asked the guards how he's coping.'

The thin envelope felt heavy in her hands, and she knew the sooner she shared the news the sooner she could come to terms with it. Slipping her finger beneath the envelope's edge, she gently prised open the flap and pulled out the contents, lying them flat on the table before him.

Ben stared at the three black and white images with confusion, until his mind processed what he was seeing. 'Is this . . .?'

Alice nodded as she strained to keep the tears breaking free.

'You're pregnant?'

She nodded again.

Ben's mouth opened and closed, and when his eyes made contact with hers, she saw the deep remorse that cloaked him. A hand shot up to his eyes and wiped at them without success. 'Oh my God, that's incredible. I mean, wow! Um, I . . . I can't believe it.'

'Due in early February,' Alice said, her lips curling up for the first time since she'd seen the blue line on the pregnancy test. 'I knew the dress felt tighter on our wedding day.'

'I don't know what to say,' Ben said, his eyes back on the images of the round blob. 'Are you okay? Are you happy?'

Alice couldn't answer, instead looking up at the clear sky streaming through the glass in the roof. Her dream of raising a family with a loving husband in a beautiful home no longer felt achievable, and that saddened her just as much as the prospect of Ben spending years behind bars for his part in Kerry's death. It was impossible to know what the future held for any of them, but what she was certain of was the bond already blossoming with the being growing inside her. Whether she allowed Ben back into her life, or chose to continue her journey without him, their child would know love every day, and she would strive to make he or she her priority, as Kerry had with Finn.

A Message from Stephen

Thank you for taking the time to read *Till Death Do Us Part*. If you enjoyed it, please post a review on Amazon or Goodreads and share the story with your friends. If a book is written to entertain, then the reader is the target audience, and I feel honoured that you chose one of my books to read.

Please don't be afraid to contact me via Facebook or Twitter to let me know what you thought of the story. There's nothing more joyful for an author than hearing from a reader who loved one of their books (believe me!). I really do respond to *every* message.

If you'd like to keep up-to-date with all my latest releases, you can join my mailing list (www.stephenedger.com). Your email address will never be shared and you can unsubscribe at any time.

Thank you again for reading my book. I hope to hear from you soon.

Stephen Edger

Website: www.stephenedger.com
🅕: /AuthorStephenEdger
🅣: @StephenEdger

Acknowledgements

Thank you to my editor Kathryn Cheshire for pushing me to make *Till Death Do Us Part* as strong as it can be, and for getting the cover spot on. Also thanks to Janette Currie for her swift responses to copyedits, and for picking up those moments where a stray character name appeared. This book is so much better because of your input and questions.

Thank you to the wonderful Carol E. Wyer who took time out of her own busy writing schedule to read an early draft of the book, and for providing such positive feedback.

Thank you to all those who requested, read and reviewed an ARC of the book ahead of publication day. I don't think I understood what a difference reviews of books made until I started writing (they really are so important!)

Special mention as always to my friend Parashar Ramanuj who is always on the end of the phone when I have any weird medical / psychology questions that Google won't answer.

Of course I have to acknowledge my wife and soul-mate Hannah who has the patience of a saint when I drone on about the latest exciting twist I've devised, and she smiles even though she has no idea what I'm on about. I used our own wedding ceremony to help shape the day that Alice and Ben experience (thankfully I wasn't arrested).

Final mention goes to the fabulous followers of my Facebook and Twitter accounts. Your comments, posts, and messages of support make such a difference, particularly when I'm feeling low of confidence about my writing. Please don't stop messaging me, as it always brightens the day.

KILLER READS

DISCOVER THE BEST
IN CRIME AND THRILLER

Follow us on social media to get to know the team behind the books, enter exclusive giveaways, learn about the latest competitions, hear from our authors, and lots more:

/KillerReads  /KillerReads